HARRY SINCLAIR LEWIS, the son of a country doctor, was born in Sauk Centre, Minnesota, in 1885. His childhood and early youth were spent in the Middle West and later he attended Yale University, where he was editor of the literary magazine. After being graduated in 1907, he went to New York, tried free-lance work for a time and then worked in a variety of editorial positions in various places from the East Coast to California. He was able to give this work up after a few of his stories had appeared in magazines and his first novel, *Our Mr. Wrenn* (1914), had been published. However, *Main Street* (1920) was his first really successful novel and his reputation was enhanced by the publication of *Babbitt* (1922). Lewis was awarded a Pulitzer Prize for *Arrowsmith* (1925) in 1926 but refused to accept this honor. However, he accepted the Nobel Prize which was awarded to him in 1930 and went to Stockholm to receive it formally. During the last part of his life he spent a great deal of time in Europe and continued to write both novels and plays. In 1950, after completing his last novel, *World So Wide* (1951), he intended to take an extended tour. He became ill, however, and was forced to settle in Rome, where he spent some months working on his poems. He died there in 1951.

Drawing based on photograph by MAN RAY

MAIN STREET

Sinclair Lewis

Buccaneer Books
Cutchogue New York

To
James Branch Cabell
and
Joseph Hergesheimer

This is America—a town of a few thousand, in a region of wheat and corn and dairies and little groves.

The town is, in our tale, called "Gopher Prairie, Minnesota." But its Main Street is the continuation of Main Streets everywhere. The story would be the same in Ohio or Montana, in Kansas or Kentucky or Illinois, and not very differently would it be told Up York State or in the Carolina hills.

Main Street is the climax of civilization. That this Ford car might stand in front of the Bon Ton Store, Hannibal invaded Rome and Erasmus wrote in Oxford cloisters. What Ole Jenson the grocer says to Ezra Stowbody the banker is the new law for London, Prague, and the unprofitable isles of the sea; whatsoever Ezra does not know and sanction, that thing is heresy, worthless for knowing and wicked to consider.

Our railway station is the final aspiration of architecture. Sam Clark's annual hardware turnover is the envy of the four counties which constitute God's Country. In the sensitive art of the Rosebud Movie Palace there is a Message, and humor strictly moral.

Such is our comfortable tradition and sure faith. Would he not betray himself an alien cynic who should otherwise portray Main Street, or distress the citizens by speculating whether there may not be other faiths?

chapter 1

ON a hill by the Mississippi where Chippewas camped two generations ago, a girl stood in relief against the cornflower blue of Northern sky. She saw no Indians now; she saw flour-mills and the blinking windows of skyscrapers in Minneapolis and St. Paul. Nor was she thinking of squaws and portages, and the Yankee fur-traders whose shadows were all about her. She was meditating upon walnut fudge, the plays of Brieux, the reasons why heels run over, and the fact that the chemistry instructor had stared at the new coiffure which concealed her ears.

A breeze which had crossed a thousand miles of wheat-lands bellied her taffeta skirt in a line so graceful, so full of animation and moving beauty, that the heart of a chance watcher on the lower road tightened to wistfulness over her quality of suspended freedom. She lifted her arms, she leaned back against the wind, her skirt dipped and flared, a lock blew wild. A girl on a hilltop; credulous, plastic, young; drinking the air as she longed to drink life. The eternal aching comedy of expectant youth.

It is Carol Milford, fleeing for an hour from Blodgett College.

The days of pioneering, of lassies in sunbonnets, and bears killed with axes in piney clearings, are deader now than Came-

7

lot; and a rebellious girl is the spirit of that bewildered empire called the American Middlewest.

II

Blodgett College is on the edge of Minneapolis. It is a bulwark of sound religion. It is still combating the recent heresies of Voltaire, Darwin, and Robert Ingersoll. Pious families in Minnesota, Iowa, Wisconsin, the Dakotas send their children thither, and Blodgett protects them from the wickedness of the universities. But it secretes friendly girls, young men who sing, and one lady instructress who really likes Milton and Carlyle. So the four years which Carol spent at Blodgett were not altogether wasted. The smallness of the school, the fewness of rivals, permitted her to experiment with her perilous versatility. She played tennis, gave chafing-dish parties, took a graduate seminar in the drama, went "twosing," and joined half a dozen societies for the practise of the arts or the tense stalking of a thing called General Culture.

In her class there were two or three prettier girls but none more eager. She was noticeable equally in the classroom grind and at dances, though out of the three hundred students of Blodgett, scores recited more accurately and dozens Bostoned more smoothly. Every cell of her body was alive—thin wrists, quince-blossom skin, ingénue eyes, black hair.

The other girls in her dormitory marveled at the slightness of her body when they saw her in sheer negligée, or darting out wet from a shower-bath. She seemed then but half as large as they had supposed; a fragile child who must be cloaked with understanding kindness. "Psychic," the girls whispered, and "spiritual." Yet so radioactive were her nerves, so adventurous her trust in rather vaguely conceived sweetness and light, that she was more energetic than any of the hulking young women who, with calves bulging in heavy-ribbed woolen stockings beneath decorous blue serge bloomers, thuddingly galloped across the floor of the "gym" in practice for the Blodgett Ladies' Basket-Ball Team.

Even when she was tired her dark eyes were observant. She did not yet know the immense ability of the world to be casually cruel and proudly dull, but if she should ever learn those dismaying powers, her eyes would never become sullen or heavy or rheumily amorous.

For all her enthusiasms, for all the fondness and the

"crushes" which she inspired, Carol's acquaintances were shy of her. When she was most ardently singing hymns or planning deviltry she yet seemed gently aloof and critical. She was credulous, perhaps; a born hero-worshipper; yet she did question and examine unceasingly. Whatever she might become she would never be static.

Her versatility ensnared her. By turns she hoped to discover that she had an unusual voice, a talent for the piano, the ability to act, to write, to manage organizations. Always she was disappointed, but always she effervesced anew—over the Student Volunteers, who intended to become missionaries, over painting scenery for the dramatic club, over soliciting advertisements for the college magazine.

She was on the peak that Sunday afternoon when she played in chapel. Out of the dusk her violin took up the organ theme, and the candle-light revealed her in a straight golden frock, her arm arched to the bow, her lips serious. Every man fell in love then with religion and Carol.

Throughout Senior year she anxiously related all her experiments and partial successes to a career. Daily, on the library steps or in the hall of the Main Building, the co-eds talked of "What shall we do when we finish college?" Even the girls who knew that they were going to be married pretended to be considering important business positions; even they who knew that they would have to work hinted about fabulous suitors. As for Carol, she was an orphan; her only near relative was a vanilla-flavored sister married to an optician in St. Paul. She had used most of the money from her father's estate. She was not in love—that is, not often, nor ever long at a time. She would earn her living.

But how she was to earn it, how she was to conquer the world—almost entirely for the world's own good—she did not see. Most of the girls who were not betrothed meant to be teachers. Of these there were two sorts: careless young women who admitted that they intented to leave the "beastly classroom and grubby children" the minute they had a chance to marry; and studious, sometimes bulbous-browed and pop-eyed maidens who at class prayer-meetings requested God to "guide their feet along the paths of greatest usefulness." Neither sort tempted Carol. The former seemed insincere (a favorite word of hers at this era). The earnest virgins were, she fancied, as likely to do harm as to do good by their faith in the value of parsing Cæsar.

At various times during Senior year Carol finally decided

upon studying law, writing motion-pictures scenarios, professional nursing, and marrying an unidentified hero.

Then she found a hobby in sociology.

The sociology instructor was new. He was married, and therefore taboo, but he had come from Boston, he had lived among poets and socialists and Jews and millionaire uplifters at the University Settlement in New York, and he had a beautiful white strong neck. He led a giggling class through the prisons, the charity bureaus, the employment agencies of Minneapolis and St. Paul. Trailing at the end of the line Carol was indignant at the prodding curiosity of the others, their manner of staring at the poor as at a Zoo. She felt herself a great liberator. She put her hand to her mouth, her forefinger and thumb quite painfully pinching her lower lip, and frowned, and enjoyed being aloof.

A classmate named Stewart Snyder, a competent bulky young man in a gray flannel shirt, a rusty black bow tie, and the green-and-purple class cap, grumbled to her as they walked behind the others in the muck of the South St. Paul stockyards, "These college chumps make me tired. They're so top-lofty. They ought to of worked on the farm, the way I have. These workmen put it all over them."

"I just love common workmen," glowed Carol.

"Only you don't want to forget that common workmen don't think they're common!"

"You're right! I apologize!" Carol's brows lifted in the astonishment of emotion, in a glory of abasement. Her eyes mothered the world. Stewart Snyder peered at her. He rammed his large red fists into his pockets, he jerked them out, he resolutely got rid of them by clenching his hands behind him, and he stammered:

"I know. You *get* people. Most of these darn co-eds—— Say, Carol, you could do a lot for people."

"How?"

"Oh—oh well—you know—sympathy and everything—if you were—say you were a lawyer's wife. You'd understand his clients. I'm going to be a lawyer. I admit I fall down in sympathy sometimes. I get so dog-gone impatient with people that can't stand the gaff. You'd be good for a fellow that was too serious. Make him more—more—*you* know—sympathetic!"

His slightly pouting lips, his mastiff eyes, were begging her to beg him to go on. She fled from the steam-roller of his sentiment. She cried, "Oh, see those poor sheep—millions and millions of them." She darted on.

Stewart was not interesting. He hadn't a shapely white neck, and he had never lived among celebrated reformers. She wanted, just now, to have a cell in a settlement-house, like a nun without the bother of a black robe, and be kind, and read Bernard Shaw, and enormously improve a horde of grateful poor.

The supplementary reading in sociology led her to a book on village-improvement—tree-planting, town pageants, girls' clubs. It had pictures of greens and garden-walls in France, New England, Pennsylvania. She had picked it up carelessly, with a slight yawn which she patted down with her finger-tips as delicately as a cat.

She dipped into the book, lounging on her window-seat, with her slim, lisle-stockinged legs crossed, and her knees up under her chin. She stroked a satin pillow while she read. About her was the clothy exuberance of a Blodgett College room: cretonne-covered window-seat, photographs of girls, a carbon print of the Coliseum, a chafing-dish, and a dozen pillows embroidered or beaded or pyrographed. Shockingly out of place was a miniature of the Dancing Bacchante. It was the only trace of Carol in the room. She had inherited the rest from generations of girl students.

It was as a part of all this commonplaceness that she regarded the treatise on village-improvement. But she suddenly stopped fidgeting. She strode into the book. She had fled half-way through it before the three o'clock bell called her to the class in English history.

She sighed, "That's what I'll do after college! I'll get my hands on one of these prairie towns and make it beautiful. Be an inspiration. I suppose I'd better become a teacher then, but—I won't be that kind of a teacher. I won't drone. Why should they have all the garden suburbs on Long Island? Nobody has done anything with the ugly towns here in the Northwest except hold revivals and build libraries to contain the Elsie books. I'll make 'em put in a village green, and darling cottages, and a quaint Main Street!"

Thus she triumphed through the class, which was a typical Blodgett contest between a dreary teacher and unwilling children of twenty, won by the teacher because his opponents had to answer his questions, while their treacherous queries he could counter by demanding, "Have you looked that up in the library? Well then, suppose you do!"

The history instructor was a retired minister. He was sarcastic today. He begged of sporting young Mr. Charley Holmberg, "Now Charles, would it interrupt your undoubtedly fascinating pursuit of that malevolent fly if I were to ask you to tell us that you do not know anything about King John?" He spent three delightful minutes in assuring himself of the fact that no one exactly remembered the date of Magna Charta.

Carol did not hear him. She was completing the roof of a half-timbered town hall. She had found one man in the prairie village who did not appreciate her picture of winding streets and arcades, but she had assembled the town council and dramatically defeated him.

III

Though she was Minnesota-born Carol was not an intimate of the prairie villages. Her father, the smiling and shabby, the learned and teasingly kind, had come from Massachusetts, and through all her childhood he had been a judge in Mankato, which is not a prairie town, but in its garden-sheltered streets and aisles of elms is white and green New England reborn. Mankato lies between cliffs and the Minnesota River, hard by Traverse des Sioux, where the first settlers made treaties with the Indians, and the cattle-rustlers once came galloping before hell-for-leather posses.

As she climbed along the banks of the dark river Carol listened to its fables about the wide land of yellow waters and bleached buffalo bones to the West; the Southern levees and singing darkies and palm trees toward which it was forever mysteriously gliding; and she heard again the startled bells and thick puffing of high-stacked river steamers wrecked on sand-reefs sixty years ago. Along the decks she saw missionaries, gamblers in tall pot hats, and Dakota chiefs with scarlet blankets. . . . Far off whistles at night, round the river bend, plunking paddlers reechoed by the pines, and a glow on black sliding waters.

Carol's family were self-sufficent in their inventive life, with Christmas a rite full of surprises and tenderness, and "dressing-up parties" spontaneous and joyously absurd. The beasts in the Milford hearth-mythology were not the obscene Night Animals who jump out of closets and eat little girls, but beneficent and bright-eyed creatures—the tam htab, who is woolly and blue and lives in the bathroom, and runs rapidly to warm small feet; the ferruginous oil stove, who purrs and knows stories; and the skitamarigg, who will play with children before breakfast if they spring out of bed and close the window at the very first line of the song about puellas which father sings while shaving.

Judge Milford's pedagogical scheme was to let the children read whatever they pleased, and in his brown library Carol absorbed Balzac and Rabelais and Thoreau and Max Müller. He gravely taught them the letters on the backs of the encyclopedias, and when polite visitors asked about the mental progress of the "little ones," they were horrified to hear the children earnestly repeating A-And, And-Aus, Aus-Bis, Bis-Cal, Cal-Cha.

Carol's mother died when she was nine. Her father retired from the judiciary when she was eleven, and took the family to Minneapolis. There he died, two years after. Her sister, a busy proper advisory soul, older than herself, had become a stranger to her even when they lived in the same house.

From those early brown and silver days and from her independence of relatives Carol retained a willingness to be different from brisk efficient book-ignoring people; an instinct to observe and wonder at their bustle even when she was taking part in it. But, she felt approvingly, as she discovered her career of town-planning, she was now roused to being brisk and efficient herself.

IV

In a month Carol's ambition had clouded. Her hesitancy about becoming a teacher had returned. She was not, she worried, strong enough to endure the routine, and she could not picture herself standing before grinning children and pretending to be wise and decisive. But the desire for the creation of a beautiful town remained. When she encountered an item about small-town women's clubs or a photograph of a straggling Main Street, she was homesick for it, she felt robbed of her work.

It was the advice of the professor of English which led her to study professional library-work in a Chicago school. Her imagination carved and colored the new plan. She saw herself persuading children to read charming fairy tales, helping young men to find books on mechanics, being ever so courteous to old men who were hunting for newspapers—the light of the library, an authority on books, invited to dinners with poets and explorers, reading a paper to an association of distinguished scholars.

V

The last faculty reception before commencement. In five days they would be in the cyclone of final examinations.

The house of the president had been massed with palms suggestive of polite undertaking parlors, and in the library, a ten-foot room with a globe and the portraits of Whittier and Martha Washington, the student orchestra was playing "Carmen" and "Madame Butterfly." Carol was dizzy with music and the emotions of parting. She saw the palms as a jungle, the pink-shaded electric globes as an opaline haze, and the eye-glassed faculty as Olympians. She was melancholy at sight of the mousey girls with whom she had "always intended to get acquainted," and the half dozen young men who were ready to fall in love with her.

But it was Stewart Snyder whom she encouraged. He was so much manlier than the others; he was an even warm brown, like his new ready-made suit with its padded shoulders. She sat with him, and with two cups of coffee and a chicken patty, upon a pile of presidential overshoes in the coat-closet under the stairs, and as the thin music seeped in, Stewart whispered:

"I can't stand it, this breaking up after four years! The happiest years of life."

She believed it. "Oh, I know! To think that in just a few days we'll be parting, and we'll never see some of the bunch again!"

"Carol, you got to listen to me! You always duck when I try to talk seriously to you, but you got to listen to me. I'm going to be a big lawyer, maybe a judge, and I need you, and I'd protect you——"

His arm slid behind her shoulders. The insinuating music drained her independence. She said mournfully, "Would you take care of me?" She touched his hand. It was warm, solid.

"You bet I would! We'd have, Lord, we'd have bully times in Yankton, where I'm going to settle——"

"But I want to do something with life."

"What's better than making a comfy home and bringing up some cute kids and knowing nice homey people?"

It was the immemorial male reply to the restless woman.

Thus to the young Sappho spake the melon-venders; thus the captains to Zenobia; and in the damp cave over gnawed bones the hairy suitor thus protested to the woman advocate of matriarchy. In the dialect of Blodgett College but with the voice of Sappho was Carol's answer:

"Of course. I know. I suppose that's so. Honestly, I do love children. But there's lots of women that can do housework, but I—well, if you *have* got a college education, you ought to use it for the world."

"I know, but you can use it just as well in the home. And gee, Carol, just think of a bunch of us going out on an auto picnic some nice spring evening."

"Yes."

"And sleigh-riding in winter, and going fishing——"

Blarrrrrrr! The orchestra had crashed into the "Soldiers' Chorus"; and she was protesting, "No! No! You're a dear, but I want to do things. I don't understand myself but I want —everything in the world! Maybe I can't sing or write, but I know I can be an influence in library work. Just suppose I encouraged some boy and he became a great artist! I will! I will do it! Stewart dear, I can't settle down to nothing but dish-washing!"

Two minutes later—two hectic minutes—they were disturbed by an embarrassed couple also seeking the idyllic seclusion of the overshoe-closet.

After graduation she never saw Stewart Snyder again. She wrote to him once a week—for one month.

VI

A year Carol spent in Chicago. Her study of library-cataloguing, recording, books of reference, was easy and not too somniferous. She reveled in the Art Institute, in symphonies and violin recitals and chamber music, in the theater and classic dancing. She almost gave up library work to become one of the young women who dance in cheese-cloth in the moonlight. She was taken to a certified Studio Party, with beer, cigarettes, bobbed hair, and a Russian Jewess who sang the Internationale. It cannot be reported that Carol had anything significant to say to the Bohemians. She was awkward with them, and felt ignorant, and she was shocked by the free manners which she had for years desired. But she heard and remembered discussions of Freud, Romain Rolland, syndicalism, the Confédération Générale du Travail, feminism vs. haremism, Chinese lyrics, nationalization of mines, Christian Science, and fishing in Ontario.

She went home, and that was the beginning and end of her Bohemian life.

The second cousin of Carol's sister's husband lived in Winnetka, and once invited her out to Sunday dinner. She walked back through Wilmette and Evanston, discovered new forms of suburban architecture, and remembered her desire to recreate villages. She decided that she would give up library work and, by a miracle whose nature was not very clearly revealed to her, turn a prairie town into Georgian houses and Japanese bungalows.

The next day in library class she had to read a theme on the use of the *Cumulative Index,* and she was taken so seriously in the discussion that she put off her career of town-planning —and in the autumn she was in the public library of St. Paul.

VII

Carol was not unhappy and she was not exhilarated, in the St. Paul Library. She slowly confessed that she was not visibly affecting lives. She did, at first, put into her contact with the patrons a willingness which should have moved worlds. But so few of these stolid worlds wanted to be moved. When she was in charge of the magazine room the readers did not ask for suggestions about elevated essays. They grunted, "Wanta find the *Leather Goods Gazette* for last February." When she was giving out books the principal query was, "Can you tell me of a good, light, exciting love story to read? My husband's going away for a week."

She was fond of the other librarians; proud of their aspirations. And by the chance of propinquity she read scores of books unnatural to her gay white littleness: volumes of anthropology with ditches of foot-notes filled with heaps of small dusty type, Parisian imagistes, Hindu recipes for curry, voyages to the Solomon Isles, theosophy with modern American improvements, treatises upon success in the real-estate business. She took walks, and was sensible about shoes and diet. And never did she feel that she was living.

She went to dances and suppers at the houses of college acquaintances. Sometimes she one-stepped demurely; sometimes, in dread of life's slipping past, she turned into a bacchanal, her tender eyes excited, her throat tense, as she slid down the room.

During her three years of library work several men showed diligent interest in her—the treasurer of a fur-manufacturing firm, a teacher, a newspaper reporter, and a petty railroad official. None of them made her more than pause in thought For months no male emerged from the mass. Then, at the Marburys', she met Dr. Will Kennicott.

chapter 2

IT WAS a frail and blue and lonely Carol who trotted to the flat of the Johnson Marburys for Sunday evening supper. Mrs. Marbury was a neighbor and friend of Carol's sister; Mr. Marbury a traveling representative of an insurance company. They made a specialty of sandwich-salad-coffee lap suppers, and they regarded Carol as their literary and artistic representative. She was the one who could be depended upon to appreciate the Caruso phonograph record, and the Chinese lantern which Mr. Marbury had brought back as his present from San Francisco. Carol found the Marburys admiring and therefore admirable.

This September Sunday evening she wore a net frock with a pale pink lining. A nap had soothed away the faint lines of tiredness beside her eyes. She was young, naive, stimulated by the coolness. She flung her coat at the chair in the hall of the flat, and exploded into the green-plush living-room. The familiar group were trying to be conversational. She saw Mr. Marbury, a woman teacher of gymnastics in a high school, a chief clerk from the Great Northern Railway offices, a young lawyer. But there was also a stranger, a thick tall man of thirty-six or -seven, with stolid brown hair, lips used to giving orders, eyes which followed everything good-naturedly, and clothes which you could never quite remember.

Mr. Marbury boomed, "Carol, come over here and meet Doc Kennicott—Dr. Will Kennicott of Gopher Prairie. He does all our insurance-examining up in that neck of the woods, and they do say he's some doctor!"

As she edged toward the stranger and murmured nothing in particular, Carol remembered that Gopher Prarie was a Minnesota wheat-prairie town of something over three thousand people.

"Pleased to meet you," stated Dr. Kennicott. His hand was strong; the palm soft, but the back weathered, showing golden hairs against firm red skin.

He looked at her as though she was an agreeable discovery. She tugged her hand free and fluttered, "I must go out to the kitchen and help Mrs. Marbury." She did not speak to him again till, after she had heated the rolls and passed the paper napkins, Mr. Marbury captured her with a loud, "Oh, quit fussing now. Come over here and sit down and tell us how's tricks." He herded her to a sofa with Dr. Kennicott, who was rather vague about the eyes, rather drooping of bulky shoulder, as though he was wondering what he was expected to do next. As their host left them, Kennicott awoke:

"Marbury tells me you're a high mogul in the public library. I was surprised. Didn't hardly think you were old enough. I thought you were a girl, still in college maybe."

"Oh, I'm dreadfully old. I expect to take to a lip-stick, and to find a gray hair any morning now."

"Huh! You must be frightfully old—prob'ly too old to be my granddaughter, I guess!"

Thus in the Vale of Arcady nymph and satyr beguiled the hours; precisely thus, and not in honeyed pentameters, discoursed Elaine and the worn Sir Launcelot in the pleached alley.

"How do you like your work?" asked the doctor.

"It's pleasant, but sometimes I feel shut off from things—the steel stacks, and the everlasting cards smeared all over with red rubber stamps."

"Don't you get sick of the city?"

"St. Paul? Why, don't you like it? I don't know of any lovelier view than when you stand on Summit Avenue and look across Lower Town to the Mississippi cliffs and the upland farms beyond."

"I know but—— Of course I've spent nine years around the Twin Cities—took my B.A. and M.D. over at the U., and had my internship in a hospital in Minneapolis, but still oh well, you don't get to know folks here, way you do up home. I feel I've got something to say about running Gopher Prairie, but you take it in a big city of two-three hundred thousand, and I'm just one flea on the dog's back. And then

I like country driving, and the hunting in the fall. Do you know Gopher Prairie at all?"

"No, but I hear it's a very nice town."

"Nice? Say honestly—— Of course I may be prejudiced, but I've seen an awful lot of towns—one time I went to Atlantic City for the American Medical Association meeting, and I spent practically a week in New York! But I never saw a town that had such up-and-coming people as Gopher Prairie. Bresnahan—you know—the famous auto manufacturer—he comes from Gopher Prairie. Born and brought up there! And it's a darn pretty town. Lots of fine maples and box-elders, and there's two of the dandiest lakes you ever saw, right near town! And we've got seven miles of cement walks already, and building more every day! Course a lot of these towns still put up with plank walks, but not for us, you bet!"

"Really?"

(Why was she thinking of Stewart Snyder?)

"Gopher Prairie is going to have a great future. Some of the best dairy and wheat land in the state right near there— some of it selling right now at one-fifty an acre, and I bet it will go up to two and a quarter in ten years!"

"Is—— Do you like your profession?"

"Nothing like it. Keeps you out, and yet you have a chance to loaf in the office for a change."

"I don't mean that way. I mean—it's such an opportunity for sympathy."

Dr. Kennicott launched into a heavy, "Oh, these Dutch farmers don't want sympathy. All they need is a bath and a good dose of salts."

Carol must have flinched, for instantly he was urging, "What I mean is—I don't want you to think I'm one of these old salts-and-quinine peddlers, but I mean: so many of my patients are husky farmers that I suppose I get kind of case-hardened."

"It seems to me that a doctor could transform a whole community, if he wanted to—if he saw it. He's usually the only man in the neighborhood who has any scientific training, isn't he?"

"Yes, that's so, but I guess most of us get rusty. We land in a rut of obstetrics and typhoid and busted legs. What we need is women like you to jump on us. It'd be you that would transform the town."

"No, I couldn't. Too flighty. I did used to think about

doing just that, curiously enough, but I seem to have drifted away from the idea. Oh, I'm a fine one to be lecturing you!"

"No! You're just the one. You have ideas without having lost feminine charm. Say! Don't you think there's a lot of these women that go out for all these movements and so on that sacrifice——"

After his remarks upon suffrage he abruptly questioned her about herself. His kindliness and the firmness of his personality enveloped her and she accepted him as one who had a right to know what she thought and wore and ate and read. He was positive. He had grown from a sketched-in stranger to a friend, whose gossip was important news. She noticed the healthy solidity of his chest. His nose, which had seemed irregular and large, was suddenly virile.

She was jarred out of this serious sweetness when Marbury bounced over to them and with horrible publicity yammered, "Say, what do you two think you're doing? Telling fortunes or making love? Let me warn you that the doc is a frisky bacheldore, Carol. Come on now, folks, shake a leg. Let's have some stunts or a dance or something."

She did not have another word with Dr. Kennicott until their parting:

"Been a great pleasure to meet you, Miss Milford. May I see you some time when I come down again? I'm here quite often—taking patients to hospitals for majors, and so on."

"Why——"

"What's your address?"

"You can ask Mr. Marbury next time you come down —if you really want to know!"

"Want to know? Say, you wait!"

II

Of the love-making of Carol and Will Kennicott there is nothing to be told which may not be heard on every summer evening, on every shadowy block.

They were biology and mystery; their speech was slang phrases and flares of poetry; their silences were contentment, or shaky crises when his arm took her shoulder. All the beauty of youth, first discovered when it is passing—and all the commonplaceness of a well-to-do unmarried man encountering a pretty girl at the time when she is slightly weary of her employment and sees no glory ahead nor any man she is glad to serve.

They liked each other honestly—they were both honest. She was disappointed by his devotion to making money, but she was sure that he did not lie to patients, and that he did keep up with the medical magazines. What aroused her to something more than liking was his boyishness when they went tramping.

They walked from St. Paul down the river to Mendota, Kennicott more elastic-seeming in a cap and a soft crêpe shirt, Carol youthful in a tam-o'-shanter of mole velvet, a blue serge suit with an absurdly and agreeably broad turn-down linen collar, and frivolous ankles above athletic shoes. The High Bridge crosses the Mississippi, mounting from low banks to a palisade of cliffs. Far down beneath it on the St. Paul side, upon mud flats, is a wild settlement of chicken-infested gardens and shanties patched together from discarded sign-boards, sheets of corrugated iron, and planks fished out of the river. Carol leaned over the rail of the bridge to look down at this Yang-tse village; in delicious imaginary fear she shrieked that she was dizzy with the height; and it was an extremely human satisfaction to have a strong male snatch her back to safety, instead of having a logical woman teacher or librarian sniff, "Well, if you're scared, why don't you get away from the rail, then?"

From the cliffs across the river Carol and Kennicott looked back at St. Paul on its hills; an imperial sweep from the dome of the cathedral to the dome of the state capitol.

The river road led past rocky field slopes, deep glens, woods flamboyant now with September, to Mendota, white walls and a spire among trees beneath a hill, old-world in its placid ease. And for this fresh land, the place is ancient. Here is the bold stone house which General Sibley, the king of fur-traders, built in 1835, with plaster of river mud, and ropes of twisted grass for laths. It has an air of centuries. In its solid rooms Carol and Kennicott found prints from other days which the house had seen—tail-coats of robin's-egg blue, clumsy Red River carts laden with luxurious furs, whiskered Union soldiers in slant forage caps and rattling sabers.

It suggested to them a common American past, and it was memorable because they had discovered it together. They talked more trustingly, more personally, as they trudged on. They crossed the Minnesota River in a rowboat ferry. They climbed the hill to the round stone tower of Fort Snelling. They saw the junction of the Mississippi and the Minnesota,

and recalled the men who had come here eighty years ago—
Maine lumbermen, York traders, soldiers from the Maryland
hills.

"It's a good country, and I'm proud of it. Let's make it all
that those old boys dreamed about," the unsentimental Kennicott was moved to vow.

"Let's!"

"Come on. Come to Gopher Prairie. Show us. Make the
town—well—make it artistic. It's mighty pretty, but I'll
admit we aren't any too darn artistic. Probably the lumber-
yard isn't as scrumptious as all these Greek temples. But go
to it! Make us change!"

"I would like to. Some day!"

"Now! You'd love Gopher Prairie. We've been doing a
lot with lawns and gardening the past few years, and it's so
homey—the big trees and—— And the best people on earth.
And keen. I bet Luke Dawson——"

Carol but half listened to the names. She could not fancy
their ever becoming important to her.

"I bet Luke Dawson has got more money than most of the
swells on Summit Avenue; and Miss Sherwin in the high school
is a regular wonder—reads Latin like I do English; and Sam
Clark, the hardware man, he's a corker—not a better man in
the state to go hunting with; and if you want culture, besides
Vida Sherwin there's Reverend Warren, the Congregational
preacher, and Professor Mott, the superintendent of schools,
and Guy Pollock, the lawyer—they say he writes regular poetry
and—and Raymie Wutherspoon, he's not such an awful boob
when you get to *know* him, and he sings swell. And—— And
there's plenty of others. Lym Cass. Only of course none of
them have your finesse, you might call it. But they don't make
'em any more appreciative and so on. Come on! We're ready
for you to boss us!"

They sat on the bank below the parapet of the old fort,
hidden from observation. He circled her shoulder with his
arm. Relaxed after the walk, a chill nipping her throat, conscious of his warmth and power, she leaned gratefully against
him.

"You know I'm in love with you, Carol!"

She did not answer, but she touched the back of his hand
with an exploring finger.

"You say I'm so darn materialistic. How can I help it, unless I have you to stir me up?"

She did not answer. She could not think.

"You say a doctor could cure a town the way he does a person. Well, you cure the town of whatever ails it, if anything does, and I'll be your surgical kit."

She did not follow his words, only the burring resoluteness of them.

She was shocked, thrilled, as he kissed her cheek and cried, "There's no use saying things and saying things and saying things. Don't my arms talk to you—now?"

"Oh, please, please!" She wondered if she ought to be angry, but it was a drifting thought, and she discovered that she was crying.

Then they were sitting six inches apart, pretending that they had never been nearer, while she tried to be impersonal:

"I would like to—would like to see Gopher Prairie."

"Trust me! Here she is! Brought some snapshots down to show you."

Her cheek near his sleeve, she studied a dozen village pictures. They were streaky; she saw only trees, shrubbery, a porch indistinct in leafy shadows. But she exclaimed over the lakes: dark water reflecting wooded bluffs, a flight of ducks, a fisherman in shirt sleeves and a wide straw hat, holding up a string of croppies. One winter picture of the edge of Plover Lake had the air of an etching: lustrous slide of ice, snow in the crevices of a boggy bank, the mound of a muskrat house, reeds in thin black lines, arches of frosty grasses. It was an impression of cool clear vigor.

"How'd it be to skate there for a couple of hours, or go zinging along on a fast ice-boat, and skip back home for coffee and some hot wienies?" he demanded.

"It might be—fun."

"But here's the picture. Here's where you come in."

A photograph of a forest clearing: pathetic new furrows straggling among stumps, a clumsy log cabin chinked with mud and roofed with hay. In front of it a sagging woman with tight-drawn hair, and a baby bedraggled, smeary, glorious-eyed.

"Those are the kind of folks I practise among, good share of the time. Nels Erdstrom, fine clean young Svenska. He'll have a corking farm in ten years, but now—— I operated his wife on a kitchen table, with my driver giving the anesthetic. Look at that scared baby! Needs some woman with hands like yours. Waiting for you! Just look at that baby's eyes, look how he's begging——"

"Don't! They hurt me. Oh, it would be sweet to help him—so sweet."

As his arms moved toward her she answered all her doubts with "Sweet, so sweet."

chapter 3

UNDER the rolling clouds of the prairie a moving mass of steel. An irritable clank and rattle beneath a prolonged roar. The sharp scent of oranges cutting the soggy smell of unbathed people and ancient baggage.

Towns as planless as a scattering of pasteboard boxes on an attic floor. The stretch of faded gold stubble broken only by clumps of willows encircling white houses and red barns.

No. 7, the way train, grumbling through Minnesota, imperceptibly climbing the giant tableland that slopes in a thousand-mile rise from hot Mississippi bottoms to the Rockies.

It is September, hot, very dusty.

There is no smug Pullman attached to the train, and the day coaches of the East are replaced by free chair cars, with each seat cut into two adjustable plush chairs, the head-rests covered with doubtful linen towels. Halfway down the car is a semi-partition of carved oak columns, but the aisle is of bare, splintery, grease-blackened wood. There is no porter, no pillows, no provision for beds, but all today and all tonight they will ride in this long steel box—farmers with perpetually tired wives and children who seem all to be of the same age; workmen going to new jobs; traveling salesmen with derbies and freshly shined shoes.

They are parched and cramped, the lines of their hands filled with grime; they go to sleep curled in distorted attitudes, heads against the window-panes or propped on rolled coats on seat-arms, and legs thrust into the aisle. They do not read; apparently they do not think. They wait. An early-wrinkled, young-old mother, moving as though her joints were dry, opens a suit-case in which are seen creased blouses, a pair of slippers worn through at the toes, a bottle of patent medicine, a tin cup, a paper-covered book about dreams which the news-butcher has coaxed her into buying. She brings out a graham cracker which she feeds to a baby lying flat on a seat and wailing hopelessly. Most of the crumbs drop on the red plush of the seat, and the woman sighs and tries to brush them away, but they leap up impishly and fall back on the plush.

A soiled man and woman munch sandwiches and throw the crusts on the floor. A large brick-colored Norwegian takes off his shoes, grunts in relief, and props his feet in their thick gray socks against the seat in front of him.

An old woman whose toothless mouth shuts like a mud-turtle's, and whose hair is not so much white as yellow like moldy linen, with bands of pink skull apparent between the tresses, anxiously lifts her bag, opens it, peers in, closes it, puts it under the seat, and hastily picks it up and opens it and hides it all over again. The bag is full of treasures and of memories: a leather buckle, an ancient band-concert program, scraps of ribbon, lace, satin. In the aisle beside her is an extremely indignant parrakeet in a cage.

Two facing seats, overflowing with a Slovene iron-miner's family, are littered with shoes, dolls, whisky bottles, bundles wrapped in newspapers, a sewing bag. The oldest boy takes a mouth-organ out of his coat pocket, wipes the tobacco crumbs off, and plays "Marching through Georgia" till every head in the car begins to ache.

The news-butcher comes through selling chocolate bars and lemon drops. A girl-child ceaselessly trots down to the water-cooler and back to her seat. The stiff paper envelope which she uses for cup drips in the aisle as she goes, and on each trip she stumbles over the feet of a carpenter, who grunts, "Ouch! Look out!"

The dust-caked doors are open, and from the smoking-car drifts back a visible blue line of stinging tobacco smoke, and with it a crackle of laughter over the story which the young man in the bright blue suit and lavender tie and light yellow shoes has just told to the squat man in garage overalls.

The smell grows constantly thicker, more stale.

II

To each of the passengers his seat was his temporary home, and most of the passengers were slatternly house-keepers. But one seat looked clean and deceptively cool. In it were an obviously prosperous man and a black-haired, fine-skinned girl whose pumps rested on an immaculate horsehide bag.

They were Dr. Will Kennicott and his bride, Carol.

They had been married at the end of a year of conversational courtship, and they were on their way to Gopher Prairie after a wedding journey in the Colorado mountains.

The hordes of the way-train were not altogether new to Carol. She had seen them on trips from St. Paul to Chicago. But now that they had become her own people, to bathe and encourage and adorn, she had an acute and uncomfortable interest in them. They distressed her. They were so stolid. She had always maintained that there is no American peasantry, and she sought now to defend her faith by seeing imagination and enterprise in the young Swedish farmers, and in a traveling man working over his order-blanks. But the older people, Yankees as well as Norwegians, Germans, Finns, Canucks, had settled into submission to poverty. They were peasants, she groaned.

"Isn't there any way of waking them up? What would happen if they understood scientific agriculture?" she begged of Kennicott, her hand groping for his.

It had been a transforming honeymoon. She had been frightened to discover how tumultuous a feeling could be roused in her. Will had been lordly—stalwart, jolly, impressively competent in making camp, tender and understanding through the hours when they had lain side by side in a tent pitched among pines high up a lonely mountain spur.

His hand swallowed hers as he started from thoughts of the practise to which he was returning. "These people? Wake 'em up? What for? They're happy."

"But they're so provincial. No, that isn't what I mean. They're—oh, so sunk in the mud."

"Look here, Carrie. You want to get over your city idea that because a man's pants aren't pressed, he's a fool. These farmers are mighty keen and up-and-coming."

"I know! That's what hurts. Life seems so hard for them —these lonely farms and this gritty train."

"Oh, they don't mind it. Besides, things are changing. The auto, the telephone, rural free delivery; they're bringing the farmers in closer touch with the town. Takes time, you know, to change a wilderness like this was fifty years ago. But already, why, they can hop into the Ford or the Overland and get in to the movies on Saturday evening quicker than you could get down to 'em by trolley in St. Paul."

"But if it's these towns we've been passing that the farmers run to for relief from their bleakness—— Can't you understand? Just *look* at them!"

Kennicott was amazed. Ever since childhood he had seen these towns from trains on this same line. He grumbled, "Why, what's the matter with ·'em? Good hustling burgs. It would astonish you to know how much wheat and rye and corn and potatoes they ship in a year."

"But they're so ugly."

"I'll admit they aren't comfy like Gopher Prairie. But give 'em time."

"What's the use of giving them time unless some one has desire and training enough to plan them? Hundreds of factories trying to make attractive motor cars, but these towns— left to chance. No! That can't be true. It must have taken genius to make them so scrawny!"

"Oh, they're not so bad," was all he answered. He pretended that his hand was the cat and hers the mouse. For the first time she tolerated him rather than encouraged him. She was staring out at Schoenstrom, a hamlet of perhaps a hundred and fifty inhabitants, at which the train was stopping.

A bearded German and his pucker-mouthed wife tugged their enormous imitation-leather satchel from under a seat and waddled out. The station agent hoisted a dead calf aboard the baggage-car. There were no other visible activities in Schoenstrom. In the quiet of the halt, Carol could hear a horse kicking his stall, a carpenter shingling a roof.

The business-center of Schoenstrom took up one side of one block, facing the railroad. It was a row of one-story shops covered with galvanized iron, or with clapboards painted red and bilious yellow. The buildings were as ill-assorted, as temporary-looking, as a mining-camp street in the motion-pictures. The railroad station was a one-room frame box, a mirey cattle-pen on one side and a crimson wheat-elevator on the other. The elevator, with its cupola on the ridge of a shingled roof, resembled a broad-shouldered man with a small, vicious, pointed head. The only habitable structures to be seen were the florid red-brick Catholic church and rectory at the end of Main Street.

Carol picked at Kennicott's sleeve. "You wouldn't call this a not-so-bad town, would you?"

"These Dutch burgs *are* kind of slow. Still, at that—— See that fellow coming out of the general store there, getting into the big car? I met him once. He owns about half the town, besides the store. Rauskukle, his name is. He owns a lot of mortgages, and he gambles in farm-lands. Good nut on him, that fellow. Why, they say he's worth three or four hundred thousand dollars! Got a dandy great big yellow brick house with tiled walks and a garden and everything, other end of town—can't see it from here—I've gone past it when I've driven through here. Yes sir!"

"Then, if he has all that, there's no excuse whatever for this place! If his three hundred thousand went back into the town, where it belongs, they could burn up these shacks, and build a dream-village, a jewel! Why do the farmers and the town-people let the Baron keep it?"

"I must say I don't quite get you sometimes, Carrie. Let him? They can't help themselves! He's a dumm old Dutchman, and probably the priest can twist him around his finger, but when it comes to picking good farming land, he's a regular wiz!"

"I see. He's their symbol of beauty. The town erects him, instead of erecting buildings."

"Honestly, don't know what you're driving at. You're kind of played out, after this long trip. You'll feel better when you get home and have a good bath, and put on the blue negligée. That's some vampire costume, you witch!"

He squeezed her arm, looked at her knowingly.

They moved on from the desert stillness of the Schoenstrom station. The train creaked, banged, swayed. The air was nauseatingly thick. Kennicott turned her face from the window, rested her head on his shoulder. She was coaxed from her unhappy mood. But she came out of it unwillingly and when Kennicott was satisfied that he had corrected all her worries and had opened a magazine of saffron detective stories, she sat upright.

Here—she meditated—is the newest empire of the world; the Northern Middlewest; a land of dairy herds and exquisite lakes, of new automobiles and tar-paper shanties and silos like red towers, of clumsy speech and a hope that is boundless. An empire which feeds a quarter of the world—yet its work is merely begun. They are pioneers, these sweaty wayfarers, for all their telephones and bank-accounts and automatic pianos and co-operative leagues. And for all its fat richness, theirs is a pioneer land. What is its future? she wondered. A future of cities and factory smut where now are loping empty fields? Homes universal and secure? Or placid châteaux ringed with sullen huts? Youth free to find knowledge and laughter? Willingness to sift the sanctified lies? Or creamy-skinned fat women, smeared with grease and chalk, gorgeous in the skins of beasts and the bloody feathers of slain birds, playing bridge with puffy pink-nailed jeweled fingers, women who after much expenditure of labor and bad temper still grotesquely resemble their own flatulent lap-dogs? The ancient stale inequalities, or something different in history, unlike the tedious maturity of other empires? What future and what hope?

Carol's head ached with the riddle.

She saw the prairie, flat in giant patches or rolling in long hummocks. The width and bigness of it, which had expanded her spirit an hour ago, began to frighten her. It spread out so; it went on so uncontrollably; she could never know it. Kennicott was closeted in his detective story. With the loneliness which comes most depressingly in the midst of many people she tried to forget problems, to look at the prairie objectively.

The grass beside the railroad had been burnt over; it was a smudge prickly with charred stalks of weeds. Beyond the undeviating barbed-wire fences were clumps of golden rod. Only this thin hedge shut them off from the plains—shorn wheat-lands of autumn, a hundred acres to a field, prickly and gray near-by but in the blurred distance like tawny velvet stretched over dipping hillocks. The long rows of wheat-shocks marched like soldiers in worn yellow tabards. The newly plowed fields were black banners fallen on the distant slope. It was a martial immensity, vigorous, a little harsh, unsoftened by kindly gardens.

The expanse was relieved by clumps of oaks with patches of short wild grass; and every mile or two was a chain of cobalt slews, with the flicker of blackbirds' wings across them.

All this working land was turned into exuberance by the light. The sunshine was dizzy on open stubble; shadows from immense cumulus clouds were forever sliding across low mounds; and the sky was wider and loftier and more resolutely blue than the sky of cities . . . she declared.

"It's a glorious country; a land to be big in," she crooned.

Then Kennicott startled her by chuckling, "D' you realize the town after the next is Gopher Prairie? Home!"

III

That one word—home—it terrified her. Had she really bound herself to live, inescapably, in this town called Gopher Prairie? And this thick man beside her, who dared to define her future, he was a stranger! She turned in her seat, stared at him. Who was he? Why was he sitting with her? He wasn't of her kind! His neck was heavy; his speech was heavy; he was twelve or thirteen years older than she; and about him was none of the magic of shared adventures and eagerness. She could not believe that she had ever slept in his arms. That was one of the dreams which you had but did not officially admit.

She told herself how good he was, how dependable and understanding. She touched his ear, smoothed the plane of his solid jaw, and, turning away again, concentrated upon liking his town. It wouldn't be like these barren settlements. It couldn't be! Why, it had three thousand population. That was a great many people. There would be six hundred houses or more. And—— The lakes near it would be so lovely. She'd seen them in the photographs. They had looked charming . . . hadn't they?

As the train left Wahkeenyan she began nervously to watch for the lakes—the entrance to all her future life. But when she discovered them, to the left of the track, her only impression of them was that they resembled the photographs.

A mile from Gopher Prairie the track mounts a curving low ridge, and she could see the town as a whole. With a passionate jerk she pushed up the window, looked out, the arched fingers of her left hand trembling on the sill, her right hand at her breast.

And she saw that Gopher Prairie was merely an enlargement of all the hamlets which they had been passing. Only to the eyes of a Kennicott was it exceptional. The huddled low wooden houses broke the plains scarcely more than would a hazel thicket. The fields swept up to it, past it. It was unprotected and unprotecting; there was no dignity in it nor any hope of greatness. Only the tall red grain-elevator and a few tinny church-steeples rose from the mass. It was a frontier camp. It was not a place to live in, not possibly, not conceivably.

The people—they'd be as drab as their houses, as flat as

their fields. She couldn't stay here. She would have to wrench loose from this man, and flee.

She peeped at him. She was at once helpless before his mature fixity, and touched by his excitement as he sent his magazine skittering along the aisle, stooped for their bags, came up with flushed face, and gloated, "Here we are!"

She smiled loyally, and looked away. The train was entering town. The houses on the outskirts were dusky old red mansions with wooden frills, or gaunt frame shelters like grocery boxes, or new bungalows with concrete foundations imitating stone.

Now the train was passing the elevator, the grim storage-tanks for oil, a creamery, a lumber-yard, a stock-yard muddy and trampled and stinking. Now they were stopping at a squat red frame station, the platform crowded with unshaven farmers and with loafers—unadventurous people with dead eyes. She was here. She could not go on. It was the end— the end of the world. She sat with closed eyes, longing to push past Kennicott, hide somewhere in the train, flee on toward the Pacific.

Something large arose in her soul and commanded, "Stop it! Stop being a whining baby!" She stood up quickly; she said, "Isn't it wonderful to be here at last!"

He trusted her so. She would make herself like the place. And she was going to do tremendous things——

She followed Kennicott and the bobbing ends of the two bags which he carried. They were held back by the slow line of disembarking passengers. She reminded herself that she was actually at the dramatic moment of the bride's home-coming. She ought to feel exalted. She felt nothing at all except irritation at their slow progress toward the door.

Kennicott stooped to peer through the windows. He shyly exulted:

"Look! Look! There's a bunch come down to welcome us! Sam Clark and the missus and Dave Dyer and Jack Elder, and, yes sir, Harry Haydock and Juanita, and a whole crowd! I guess they see us now. Yuh, yuh sure, they see us! See 'em waving!"

She obediently bent her head to look out at them. She had hold of herself. She was ready to love them. But she was embarrassed by the heartiness of the cheering group. From the vestibule she waved to them, but she clung a second to the sleeve of the brakeman who helped her down before she had the courage to dive into the cataract of hand-shaking people,

people whom she could not tell apart. She had the impression
that all the men had coarse voices, large damp hands, tooth-
brush mustaches, bald spots, and Masonic watch-charms.

She knew that they were welcoming her. Their hands, their
smiles, their shouts, their affectionate eyes overcame her. She
stammered, "Thank you, oh, thank you!"

One of the men was clamoring at Kennicott, "I brought
my machine down to take you home, doc."

"Fine business, Sam!" cried Kennicott; and, to Carol,
"Let's jump in. That big Paige over there. Some boat, too,
believe me! Sam can show speed to any of these Marmons
from Minneapolis!"

Only when she was in the motor car did she distinguish
the three people who were to accompany them. The owner,
now at the wheel, was the essence of decent self-satisfaction;
a baldish, largish, level-eyed man, rugged of neck but sleek
and round of face—face like the back of a spoon bowl. He
was chuckling at her, "Have you got us all straight yet?"

"Course she has! Trust Carrie to get things straight and get
'em darn quick! I bet she could tell you every date in history!" boasted her husband.

But the man looked at her reassuringly and with a certainty that he was a person whom she could trust she confessed,
"As a matter of fact I haven't got anybody straight."

"Course you haven't, child. Well, I'm Sam Clark, dealer in
hardware, sporting goods, cream separators, and almost any
kind of heavy junk you can think of. You can call me Sam
—anyway, I'm going to call you Carrie, seein' 's you've been
and gone and married this poor fish of a bum medic that we
keep round here." Carol smiled lavishly, and wished that she
called people by their given names more easily. "The fat
cranky lady back there beside you, who is pretending that
she can't hear me giving her away, is Mrs. Sam'l Clark; and
this hungry-looking squirt up here beside me is Dave Dyer,
who keeps his drug store running by not filling your hubby's
prescriptions right—fact you might say he's the guy that put
the 'shun' in 'prescription.' So! Well, leave us take the bonny
bride home. Say, doc, I'll sell you the Candersen place for
three thousand plunks. Better be thinking about building a
new home for Carrie. Prettiest *Frau* in G. P., if you asks me!"

Contentedly Sam Clark drove off, in the heavy traffic of
three Fords and the Minniemashie House Free 'Bus.

"I shall like Mr. Clark . . . I *can't* call him 'Sam'! They're
all so friendly." She glanced at the houses; tried not to see

what she saw; gave way in: "Why do these stories lie so? They always make the bride's home-coming a bower of roses. Complete trust in noble spouse. Lies about marriage. I'm *not* changed. And this town—O my God! I can't go through with it. This junk-heap!"

Her husband bent over her. "You look like you were in a brown study. Scared? I don't expect you to think Gopher Prairie is a paradise, after St. Paul. I don't expect you to be crazy about it, at first. But you'll come to like it so much—life's so free here and best people on earth."

She whispered to him (while Mrs. Clark considerately turned away), "I love you for understanding. I'm just—I'm beastly over-sensitive. Too many books. It's my lack of shoulder-muscles and sense. Give me time, dear."

"You bet! All the time you want!"

She laid the back of his hand against her cheek, snuggled near him. She was ready for her new home.

Kennicott had told her that, with his widowed mother as housekeeper, he had occupied an old house, "but nice and roomy, and well-heated, best furnace I could find on the market." His mother had left Carol her love, and gone back to Lac-qui-Meurt.

It would be wonderful, she exulted, not to have to live in Other People's Houses, but to make her own shrine. She held his hand tightly and stared ahead as the car swung round a corner and stopped in the street before a prosaic frame house in a small parched lawn.

IV

A concrete sidewalk with a "parking" of grass and mud. A square smug brown house, rather damp. A narrow concrete walk up to it. Sickly yellow leaves in a window with dried wings of box-elder seeds and snags of wool from the cottonwoods. A screened porch with pillars of thin painted pine surmounted by scrolls and brackets and bumps of jig-sawed wood. No shrubbery to shut off the public gaze. A lugubrious bay-window to the right of the porch. Window curtains of starched cheap lace revealing a pink marble table with a conch shell and a Family Bible.

"You'll find it old-fashioned—what do you call it?—Mid-Victorian. I left it as is, so you could make any changes you felt were necessary." Kennicott sounded doubtful for the first time since he had come back to his town.

"It's a real home!" She was moved by his humility. She gaily motioned good-by to the Clarks. He unlocked the door —he was leaving the choice of a maid to her, and there was no one in the house. She jiggled while he turned the key, and scampered in. . . . It was next day before either of them remembered that in their honeymoon camp they had planned that he should carry her over the sill.

In hallway and front parlor she was conscious of dinginess and lugubriousness and airlessness, but she insisted, "I'll make it all jolly." As she followed Kennicott and the bags up to their bedroom she quavered to herself the song of the fat little gods of the hearth:

> I have my own home,
> To do what I please with,
> To do what I please with,
> My den for me and my mate and my cubs,
> My own!

She was close in her husband's arms; she clung to him; whatever of strangeness and slowness and insularity she might find in him, none of that mattered so long as she could slip her hands beneath his coat, run her fingers over the warm smoothness of the satin back of his waistcoat, seem almost to creep into his body, find in him strength, find in the courage and kindness of her man a shelter from the perplexing world.

"Sweet, so sweet," she whispered.

chapter 4

THE Clarks have invited some folks to their house to meet us, tonight," said Kennicott, as he unpacked his suit-case.

"Oh, that is nice of them!"

"You bet. I told you you'd like 'em. Squarest people on earth. Uh, Carrie—— Would you mind if I sneaked down to the office for an hour, just to see how things are?"

"Why, no. Of course not. I know you're keen to get back to work."

"Sure you don't mind?"

"Not a bit. Out of my way. Let me unpack."

But the advocate of freedom in marriage was as much disappointed as a drooping bride at the alacrity with which he took that freedom and escaped to the world of men's affairs. She gazed about their bedroom, and its full dismalness crawled over her: the awkward knuckly L-shape of it; the black walnut bed with apples and spotty pears carved on the headboard; the imitation maple bureau, with pink-daubed scent-bottles and a petticoated pin-cushion on a marble slab uncomfortably like a gravestone; the plain pine washstand and the garlanded water-pitcher and bowl. The scent was of horsehair and plush and Florida Water.

"How could people ever live with things like this?" she shuddered. She saw the furniture as a circle of elderly judges, condemning her to death by smothering. The tottering brocade chair squeaked, "Choke her—choke her—smother her." The old linen smelled of the tomb. She was alone in this house, this strange still house, among the shadows of dead thoughts and haunting repressions. "I hate it! I hate it!" she panted. "Why did I ever——"

She remembered that Kennicott's mother had brought these family relics from the old home in Lac-qui-Meurt. "Stop it! They're perfectly comfortable things. They're—comfortable. Besides—— Oh, they're horrible! We'll change them, right away."

Then, "But of course he *has* to see how things are at the office——"

She made a pretense of busying herself with unpacking. The chintz-lined, silver-fitted bag which had seemed so desirable a luxury in St. Paul was an extravagant vanity here. The daring black chemise of frail chiffon and lace was a hussy at which the deep-bosomed bed stiffened in disgust, and she hurled it into a bureau drawer, hid it beneath a sensible linen blouse.

She gave up unpacking. She went to the window, with a purely literary thought of village charm—hollyhocks and lanes and apple-cheeked cottagers. What she saw was the side of the Seventh-Day Adventist Church—a plain clapboard wall of a sour liver color; the ash-pile back of the church; an unpainted stable; and an alley in which a Ford delivery-wagon had been stranded. This was the terraced garden below her boudoir; this was to be her scenery for——

"I mustn't! I mustn't! I'm nervous this afternoon. Am I

sick? . . . Good Lord, I hope it isn't that! Now now! How
people lie! How these stories lie! They say the bride is always so blushing and proud and happy when she finds that
out, but—I'd hate it! I'd be scared to death! Some day
but——— Please, dear nebulous Lord, not now! Bearded sniffy
old men sitting and demanding that we bear children. If
they had to bear them———! I wish they did have to! Not
now! Not till I've got hold of this job of liking the ash-pile
out there! . . . I must shut up. I'm mildly insane. I'm going
out for a walk. I'll see the town by myself. My first view of
the empire I'm going to conquer!"

She fled from the house.

She stared with seriousness at every concrete crossing,
every hitching-post, every rake for leaves; and to each house
she devoted all her speculation. What would they come to
mean? How would they look six months from now? In which
of them would she be dining? Which of these people whom
she passed, now mere arrangements of hair and clothes,
would turn into intimates, loved or dreaded, different from
all the other people in the world?

As she came into the small business-section she inspected
a broad-beamed grocer in an alpaca coat who was bending
over the apples and celery on a slanted platform in front of
his store. Would she ever talk to him? What would he say if
she stopped and stated, "I am Mrs. Dr. Kennicott. Some day
I hope to confide that a heap of extremely dubious pumpkins
as a window-display doesn't exhilarate me much."

(The grocer was Mr. Frederick F. Ludelmeyer, whose
market is at the corner of Main Street and Lincoln Avenue.
In supposing that only she was observant Carol was ignorant,
misled by the indifference of cities. She fancied that she
was slipping through the streets invisible; but when she had
passed, Mr. Ludelmeyer puffed into the store and coughed at
his clerk, "I seen a young woman, she come along the side
street. I bet she iss Doc Kennicott's new bride, good-looker,
nice legs, but she wore a hell of a plain suit, no style, I wonder will she pay cash, I bet she goes to Howland & Gould's
more as she does here, what you done with the poster for
Fluffed Oats?")

II

When Carol had walked for thirty-two minutes she had
completely covered the town, east and west, north and south;

and she stood at the corner of Main Street and Washington Avenue and despaired.

Main Street with its two-story brick shops, its story-and-a-half wooden residences, its muddy expanse from concrete walk to walk, its huddle of Fords and lumber-wagons, was too small to absorb her. The broad, straight, unenticing gashes of the streets let in the grasping prairie on every side. She realized the vastness and the emptiness of the land. The skeleton iron windmill on the farm a few blocks away, at the north end of Main Street, was like the ribs of a dead cow. She thought of the coming of the Northern winter, when the unprotected houses would crouch together in terror of storms galloping out of that wild waste. They were so small and weak, the little brown houses. They were shelters for sparrows, not homes for warm laughing people.

She told herself that down the street the leaves were a splendor. The maples were orange; the oaks a solid tint of raspberry. And the lawns had been nursed with love. But the thought would not hold. At best the trees resembled a thinned woodlot. There was no park to rest the eyes. And since not Gopher Prairie but Wakamin was the county-seat, there was no court-house with its grounds.

She glanced through the fly-specked windows of the most pretentious building in sight, the one place which welcomed strangers and determined their opinion of the charm and luxury of Gopher Prairie—the Minniemashie House. It was a tall lean shabby structure, three stories of yellow-streaked wood, the corners covered with sanded pine slabs purporting to symbolize stone. In the hotel office she could see a stretch of bare unclean floor, a line of rickety chairs with brass cuspidors between, a writing-desk with advertisements in mother-of-pearl letters upon the glass-covered back. The dining-room beyond was a jungle of stained table-cloths and catsup bottles.

She looked no more at the Minniemashie House.

A man in cuffless shirt-sleeves with pink arm-garters, wearing a linen collar but no tie, yawned his way from Dyer's Drug Store across to the hotel. He leaned against the wall, scratched a while, sighed, and in a bored way gossiped with a man tilted back in a chair. A lumber-wagon, its long green box filled with large spools of barbed-wire fencing, creaked down the block. A Ford, in reverse, sounded as though it were shaking to pieces, then recovered and rattled away. In the Greek candy-store was the whine of a peanut-roaster, and the oily smell of nuts.

There was no other sound nor sign of life.

She wanted to run, fleeing from the encroaching prairie, demanding the security of a great city. Her dreams of creating a beautiful town were ludicrous. Oozing out from every drab wall, she felt a forbidding spirit which she could never conquer.

She trailed down the street on one side, back on the other, glancing into the cross streets. It was a private Seeing Main Street tour. She was within ten minutes beholding not only the heart of a place called Gopher Prairie, but ten thousand towns from Albany to San Diego:

Dyer's Drug Store, a corner building of regular and unreal blocks of artificial stone. Inside the store, a greasy marble soda-fountain with an electric lamp of red and green and curdled-yellow mosaic shade. Pawed-over heaps of toothbrushes and combs and packages of shaving-soap. Shelves of soap-cartons, teething-rings, garden-seeds, and patent medicines in yellow packages—nostrums for consumption, for "women's diseases"—notorious mixtures of opium and alcohol, in the very shop to which her husband sent patients for the filling of prescriptions.

From a second-story window the sign "W. P. Kennicott, Phys. & Surgeon," gilt on black sand.

A small wooden motion-picture theater called "The Rosebud Movie Palace." Lithographs announcing a film called "Fatty in Love."

Howland & Gould's Grocery. In the display window, black, overripe bananas and lettuce on which a cat was sleeping. Shelves lined with red crêpe paper which was now faded and torn and concentrically spotted. Flat against the wall of the second story the signs of lodges—the Knights of Pythias, the Maccabees, the Woodmen, the Masons.

Dahl & Oleson's Meat Market—a reek of blood.

A jewelry shop with tinny-looking wrist-watches for women. In front of it, at the curb, a huge wooden clock which did not go.

A fly-buzzing saloon with a brilliant gold and enamel whisky sign across the front. Other saloons down the block. From them a stink of stale beer, and thick voices bellowing pidgin German or trolling out dirty songs—vice gone feeble and unenterprising and dull—the delicacy of a mining-camp minus its vigor. In front of the saloons, farmwives sitting on the seats of wagons, waiting for their husbands to become drunk and ready to start home.

A tobacco shop called "The Smoke House," filled with young men shaking dice for cigarettes. Racks of magazines, and pictures of coy fat prostitutes in striped bathing-suits.

A clothing store with a display of "ox-blood-shade Oxfords with bull-dog toes." Suits which looked worn and glossless while they were still new, flabbily draped on dummies like corpses with painted cheeks.

The Bon Ton Store—Haydock & Simons'—the largest shop in town. The first-story front of clear glass, the plates cleverly bound at the edges with brass. The second story of pleasant tapestry brick. One window of excellent clothes for men, interspersed with collars of floral piqué which showed mauve daisies on a saffron ground. Newness and an obvious notion of neatness and service. Haydock & Simons. Haydock. She had met a Haydock at the station; Harry Haydock; an active person of thirty-five. He seemed great to her, now, and very like a saint. His shop was clean!

Axel Egge's General Store, frequented by Scandinavian farmers. In the shallow dark window-space heaps of sleazy sateens, badly woven galateas, canvas shoes designed for women with bulging ankles, steel and red glass buttons upon cards with broken edges, a cottony blanket, a granite-ware frying-pan reposing on a sun-faded crêpe blouse.

Sam Clark's Hardware Store. An air of frankly metallic enterprise. Guns and churns and barrels of nails and beautiful shiny butcher knives.

Chester Dashaway's House Furnishing Emporium. A vista of heavy oak rockers with leather seats, asleep in a dismal row.

Billy's Lunch. Thick handleless cups on the wet oilcloth-covered counter. An odor of onions and the smoke of hot lard. In the doorway a young man audibly sucking a toothpick.

The warehouse of the buyer of cream and potatoes. The sour smell of a dairy.

The Ford Garage and the Buick Garage, competent one-story brick and cement buildings opposite each other. Old and new cars on grease-blackened concrete floors. Tire advertisements. The roaring of a tested motor; a racket which beat at the nerves. Surly young men in khaki union-overalls. The most energetic and vital places in town.

A large warehouse for agricultural implements. An impres-

sive barricade of green and gold wheels, of shafts and sulky
seats, belonging to machinery of which Carol knew nothing—
potato-planters, manure-spreaders, silage-cutters, disk-har-
rows, breaking-plows.

A feed store, its windows opaque with the dust of bran, a
patent medicine advertisement painted on its roof.

Ye Art Shoppe, Prop. Mrs. Mary Ellen Wilks, Christian
Science Library open daily free. A touching fumble at beauty.
A one-room shanty of boards recently covered with rough
stucco. A show-window delicately rich in error: vases starting
out to imitate tree-trunks but running off- into blobs of gilt
—an aluminum ash-tray labeled "Greetings from Gopher
Prairie"—a Christian Science magazine—a stamped sofa-
cushion portraying a large ribbon tied to a small poppy, the
correct skeins of embroidery-silk lying on the pillow. Inside
the shop, a glimpse of bad carbon prints of bad and famous
pictures, shelves of phonograph records and camera films,
wooden toys, and in the midst an anxious small woman sitting in a padded rocking chair.

A barber shop and pool room. A man in shirt sleeves,
presumably Del Snafflin the proprietor, shaving a man who
had a large Adam's apple.

Nat Hicks's Tailor Shop, on a side street off Main. A one-
story building. A fashion-plate showing human pitchforks in
garments which looked as hard as steel plate.

On another side street a raw red-brick Catholic Church
with a varnished yellow door.

The post-office—merely a partition of glass and brass shut-
ting off the rear of a mildewed room which must once have
been a shop. A tilted writing-shelf against a wall rubbed
black and scattered with official notices and army recruiting-
posters.

The damp, yellow-brick schoolbuilding in its cindery
grounds.

The State Bank, stucco masking wood.

The Farmers' National Bank. An Ionic temple of marble.
Pure, exquisite, solitary. A brass plate with "Ezra Stowbody,
Pres't."

A score of similar shops and establishments.

Behind them and mixed with them, the houses, meek cottages or large, comfortable, soundly uninteresting symbols.
of prosperity.

In all the town not one building save the Ionic bank which
gave pleasure to Carol's eyes; not a dozen buildings which

suggested that, in the fifty years of Gopher Prairie's existence, the citizens had realized that it was either desirable or
possible to make this, their common home, amusing or attractive.

It was not only the unsparing unapologetic ugliness and
the rigid straightness which overwhelmed her. It was the
planlessness, the flimsy temporariness of the buildings, their
faded unpleasant colors. The street was cluttered with
electric-light poles, telephone poles, gasoline pumps for motor
cars, boxes of goods. Each man had built with the most
valiant disregard of all the others. Between a large new
"block" of two-story brick shops on one side, and the fire-
brick Overland garage on the other side, was a one-story
cottage turned into a millinery shop. The white temple of
the Farmers' Bank was elbowed back by a grocery of glaring
yellow brick. One store-building had a patchy galvanized
iron cornice; the building beside it was crowned with battlements and pyramids of brick capped with blocks of red
sandstone.

She escaped from Main Street, fled home.

She wouldn't have cared, she insisted, if the people had
been comely. She had noted a young man loafing before a
shop, one unwashed hand holding the cord of an awning; a
middle-aged man who had a way of staring at women as
though he had been married too long and too prosaically; an
old farmer, solid, wholesome, but not clean—his face like a
potato fresh from the earth. None of them had shaved for
three days.

"If they can't build shrines, out here on the prairie, surely
there's nothing to prevent their buying safety-razors!" she
raged.

She fought herself: "I must be wrong. People do live here.
It *can't* be as ugly as—as I know it is! I must be wrong.
But I can't do it. I can't go through with it."

She came home too seriously worried for hysteria; and
when she found Kennicott waiting for her, and exulting,
"Have a walk? Well, like the town? Great lawns and trees,
eh?" she was able to say, with a self-protective maturity new
to her, "It's very interesting."

III

The train which brought Carol to Gopher Prairie also
brought Miss Bea Sorenson.

Miss Bea was a stalwart, corn-colored, laughing young woman, and she was bored by farm-work. She desired the excitements of city-life, and the way to enjoy city-life was, she had decided, to "go get a yob as hired girl in Gopher Prairie." She contentedly lugged her pasteboard telescope from the station to her cousin, Tina Malmquist, maid of all work in the residence of Mrs. Luke Dawson.

"Vell, so you come to town," said Tina.

"Ya. Ay get a yob," said Bea.

"Vell. . . . You got a fella now?"

"Ya. Yim Yacobson."

"Vell. I'm glat to see you. How much you vant a veek?"

"Sex dollar."

"There ain't nobody pay dat. Vait! Dr. Kennicott, I t'ink he marry a girl from de Cities. Maybe she pay dat. Vell. You go take a valk."

"Ya," said Bea.

So it chanced that Carol Kennicott and Bea Sorenson were viewing Main Street at the same time.

Bea had never before been in a town larger than Scandia Crossing, which has sixty-seven inhabitants.

As she marched up the street she was meditating that it didn't hardly seem like it was possible there could be so many folks all in one place at the same time. My! It would take years to get acquainted with them all. And swell people, too! A fine big gentleman in a new pink shirt with a diamond, and not no washed-out blue denim working-shirt. A lovely lady in a longery dress (but it must be an awful hard dress to wash). And the stores!

Not just three of them, like there were at Scandia Crossing, but more than four whole blocks!

The Bon Ton Store—big as four barns—my! it would simply scare a person to go in there, with seven or eight clerks all looking at you. And the men's suits, on figures just like human. And Axel Egge's, like home, lots of Swedes and Norskes in there, and a card of dandy buttons, like rubies.

A drug store with a soda fountain that was just huge, awful long, and all lovely marble; and on it there was a great big lamp with the biggest shade you ever saw—all different kinds colored glass stuck together; and the soda spouts, they were silver, and they came right out of the bottom of the lamp-stand! Behind the fountain there were glass shelves, and bottles of new kinds of soft drinks, that nobody ever heard of. Suppose a fella took you *there!*

A hotel, awful high, higher than Oscar Tollefson's new red barn; three stories, one right on top of another; you had to stick your head back to look clear up to the top. There was a swell traveling man in there—probably been to Chicago, lots of times.

Oh, the dandiest people to know here! There was a lady going by, you wouldn't hardly say she was any older than Bea herself; she wore a dandy new gray suit and black pumps. She almost looked like she was looking over the town, too. But you couldn't tell what she thought. Bea would like to be that way—kind of quiet, so nobody would get fresh. Kind of —oh, elegant.

A Lutheran Church. Here in the city there'd be lovely sermons, and church twice on Sunday, *every* Sunday!

And a movie show!

A regular theater, just for movies. With the sign "Change of bill every evening." Pictures every evening!

There were movies in Scandia Crossing, but only once every two weeks, and it took the Sorensons an hour to drive in—papa was such a tightwad he wouldn't get a Ford. But here she could put on her hat any evening, and in three minutes' walk be to the movies, and see lovely fellows in dress-suits and Bill Hart and everything!

How could they have so many stores? Why! There was one just for tobacco alone, and one (a lovely one—the Art Shoppy it was) for pictures and vases and stuff, with oh, the dandiest vase made so it looked just like a tree trunk!

Bea stood on the corner of Main Street and Washington Avenue. The roar of the city began to frighten her. There were five automobuls on the street all at the same time—and one of 'em was a great big car that must of cost two thou- sand dollars—and the 'bus was starting for a train with five elegant-dressed fellows, and a man was pasting up red bills with lovely pictures of washing-machines on them, and the jeweler was laying out bracelets and wrist-watches and *everything* on real velvet.

What did she care if she got six dollars a week? Or two! It was worth while working for nothing, to be allowed to stay here. And think how it would be in the evening, all lighted up—and not with no lamps, but with electrics! And maybe a gentleman friend taking you to the movies and buying you a strawberry ice cream soda!

Bea trudged back.

"Vell? You lak it?" said Tina.
"Ya. Ay lak it. Ay t'ink maybe Ay stay here," said Bea.

IV

The recently built house of Sam Clark, in which was given the party to welcome Carol, was one of the largest in Gopher Prairie. It had a clean sweep of clapboards, a solid squareness, a small tower, and a large screened porch. Inside, it was as shiny, as hard, and as cheerful as a new oak upright piano.

Carol looked imploringly at Sam Clark as he rolled to the door and shouted, "Welcome, little lady! The keys of the city are yourn!"

Beyond him, in the hallway and the living-room, sitting in a vast prim circle as though they were attending a funeral, she saw the guests. They were *waiting* so! They were waiting for her! The determination to be all one pretty flowerlet of appreciation leaked away. She begged of Sam, "I don't dare face them! They expect so much. They'll swallow me in one mouthful—glump!—like that!"

"Why, sister, they're going to love you—same as I would if I didn't think the doc here would beat me up!"

"B-but—— I don't dare! Faces to the right of me, faces in front of me, volley and wonder!"

She sounded hysterical to herself; she fancied that to Sam Clark she sounded insane. But he chuckled, "Now you just cuddle under Sam's wing, and if anybody rubbers at you too long, I'll shoo 'em off. Here we go! Watch my smoke—Sam'l, the ladies' delight and the bridegrooms' terror!"

His arm about her, he led her in and bawled, "Ladies and worser halves, the bride! We won't introduce her round yet, because she'll never get your bum names straight anyway. Now bust up this star-chamber!"

They tittered politely, but they did not move from the social security of their circle, and they did not cease staring.

Carol had given creative energy to dressing for the event. Her hair was demure, low on her forehead with a parting and a coiled braid. Now she wished that she had piled it high. Her frock was an ingénue slip of lawn, with a wide gold sash and a low square neck, which gave a suggestion of throat and molded shoulders. But as they looked her over she was certain that it was all wrong. She wished alternately that she had worn a spinsterish high-necked dress, and that she had dared to shock them with a violent brick-red scarf which she had bought in Chicago.

She was led about the circle. Her voice mechanically produced safe remarks:

"Oh, I'm sure I'm going to like it here ever so much," and "Yes, we did have the best time in Colorado—mountains," and "Yes, I lived in St. Paul several years. Euclid P. Tinker? No, I don't *remember* meeting him, but I'm pretty sure I've heard of him."

Kennicott took her aside and whispered, "Now I'll introduce you to them, one at a time."

"Tell me about them first."

"Well, the nice-looking couple over there are Harry Haydock and his wife, Juanita. Harry's dad owns most of the Bon Ton, but it's Harry who runs it and gives it the pep. He's a hustler. Next to him is Dave Dyer the druggist—you met him this afternoon—mighty good duck-shot. The tall husk beyond him is Jack Elder—Jackson Elder—owns the planing-mill, and the Minniemashie House, and quite a share in the Farmers' National Bank. Him and his wife are good sports—him and Sam and I go hunting together a lot. The old cheese there is Luke Dawson, the richest man in town. Next to him is Nat Hicks, the tailor."

"Really? A tailor?"

"Sure. Why not? Maybe we're slow, but we are democratic. I go hunting with Nat same as I do with Jack Elder."

"I'm glad. I've never met a tailor socially. It must be charming to meet one and not have to think about what you owe him. And do you—— Would you go hunting with your barber, too?"

"No but—— No use running this democracy thing into the ground. Besides, I've known Nat for years, and besides, he's a mighty good shot and—— That's the way it is, see? Next to Nat is Chet Dashaway. Great fellow for chinning. He'll talk your arm off, about religion or politics or books or anything."

Carol gazed with a polite approximation to interest at Mr. Dashaway, a tan person with a wide mouth. "Oh, I know! He's the furniture-store man!" She was much pleased with herself.

"Yump, and he's the undertaker. You'll like him. Come shake hands with him."

"Oh no, no! He doesn't—he doesn't do the embalming and all that—himself? I couldn't shake hands with an undertaker!"

"Why not? You'd be proud to shake hands with a great surgeon, just after he'd been carving up people's bellies."

She sought to regain her afternoon's calm of maturity. "Yes. You're right. I want—oh, my dear, do you know how much I want to like the people you like? I want to see people as they are."

"Well, don't forget to see people as other folks see them as they are! They have the stuff. Did you know that Percy Bresnahan came from here? Born and brought up here!"

"Bresnahan?"

"Yes—you know—president of the Velvet Motor Company of Boston, Mass.—make the Velvet Twelve—biggest automobile factory in New England."

"I think I've heard of him."

"Sure you have. Why, he's a millionaire several times over! Well, Perce comes back here for the black-bass fishing almost every summer, and he says if he could get away from business, he'd rather live here than in Boston or New York or any of those places. *He* doesn't mind Chet's undertaking."

"Please! I'll—I'll like everybody! I'll be the community sunbeam!"

He led her to the Dawsons.

Luke Dawson, lender of money on mortgages, owner of Northern cut-over land, was a hesitant man in unpressed soft gray clothes, with bulging eyes in a milky face. His wife had bleached cheeks, bleached hair, bleached voice, and a bleached manner. She wore her expensive green frock, with its passementeried bosom, bead tassels, and gaps between the buttons down the back, as though she had bought it second-hand and was afraid of meeting the former owner. They were shy. It was "Professor" George Edwin Mott, superintendent of schools, a Chinese mandarin turned brown, who held Carol's hand and made her welcome.

When the Dawsons and Mr. Mott had stated that they were "pleased to meet her," there seemed to be nothing else to say, but the conversation went on automatically.

"Do you like Gopher Prairie?" whimpered Mrs. Dawson.

"Oh, I'm sure I'm going to be ever so happy."

"There's so many nice people." Mrs. Dawson looked to Mr. Mott for social and intellectual aid. He lectured:

"There's a fine class of people. I don't like some of these retired farmers who come here to spend their last days—especially the Germans. They hate to pay school-taxes. They hate to spend a cent. But the rest are a fine class of people. Did you know that Percy Bresnahan came from here? Used to go to school right at the old building!"

"I heard he did."

"Yes. He's a prince. He and I went fishing together, last time he was here."

The Dawsons and Mr. Mott teetered upon weary feet, and smiled at Carol with crystallized expressions. She went on:

"Tell me, Mr. Mott: Have you ever tried any experiments with any of the new educational systems? The modern kindergarten methods or the Gary system?"

"Oh. Those. Most of these would-be reformers are simply notoriety-seekers. I believe in manual training, but Latin and mathematics always will be the backbone of sound Americanism, no matter what these faddists advocate—heaven knows what they do want—knitting, I suppose, and classes in wiggling the ears!"

The Dawsons smiled their appreciation of listening to a savant. Carol waited till Kennicott should rescue her. The rest of the party waited for the miracle of being amused.

Harry and Juanita Haydock, Rita Simons and Dr. Terry Gould—the young smart set of Gopher Prairie. She was led to them. Juanita Haydock flung at her in a high, cackling, friendly voice:

"Well, this is *so* nice to have you here. We'll have some good parties—dances and everything. You'll have to join the Jolly Seventeen. We play bridge and we have a supper once a month. You play, of course?"

"N-no, I don't."

"Really? In St. Paul?"

"I've always been such a book-worm."

"We'll have to teach you. Bridge is half the fun of life." Juanita had become patronizing, and she glanced disrespectfully at Carol's golden sash, which she had previously admired.

Harry Haydock said politely, "How do you think you're going to like the old burg?"

"I'm sure I shall like it tremendously."

"Best people on earth here. Great hustlers, too. Course I've had lots of chances to go live in Minneapolis, but we like it here. Real he-town. Did you know that Percy Bresnahan came from here?"

Carol perceived that she had been weakened in the biological struggle by disclosing her lack of bridge. Roused to nervous desire to regain her position she turned on Dr. Terry

Gould, the young and pool-playing competitor of her husband. Her eyes coquetted with him while she gushed:

"I'll learn bridge. But what I really love most is the outdoors. Can't we all get up a boating party, and fish, or whatever you do, and have a picnic supper afterwards?"

"Now you're talking!" Dr. Gould affirmed. He looked rather too obviously at the cream-smoothed slope of her shoulder. "Like fishing? Fishing is my middle name. I'll teach you bridge. Like cards at all?"

"I used to be rather good at bezique."

She knew that bezique was a game of cards—or a game of something else. Roulette, possibly. But her lie was a triumph. Juanita's handsome, high-colored, horsey face showed doubt. Harry stroked his nose and said humbly, "Bezique? Used to be great gambling game, wasn't it?"

While others drifted to her group, Carol snatched up the conversation. She laughed and was frivolous and rather brittle. She could not distinguish their eyes. They were a blurry theater-audience before which she self-consciously enacted the comedy of being the Clever Little Bride of Doc Kennicott:

"These-here celebrated Open Spaces, that's what I'm going out for. I'll never read anything but the sporting-page again. Will converted me on our Colorado trip. There were so many mousey tourists who were afraid to get out of the motor 'bus that I decided to be Annie Oakley, the Wild Western Wampire, and I bought oh! a vociferous skirt which revealed my perfectly nice ankles to the Presbyterian glare of all the Ioway schoolma'ams, and I leaped from peak to peak like the nimble chamoys, and—— You may think that Herr Doctor Kennicott is a Nimrod, but you ought to have seen me daring him to strip to his B. V. D.'s and go swimming in an icy mountain brook."

She knew that they were thinking of becoming shocked, but Juanita Haydock was admiring, at least. She swaggered on:

"I'm sure I'm going to ruin Will as a respectable practitioner—— Is he a good doctor, Dr. Gould?"

Kennicott's rival gasped at this insult to professional ethics, and he took an appreciable second before he recovered his social manner. "I'll tell you, Mrs. Kennicott." He smiled at Kennicott, to imply that whatever he might say in the stress of being witty was not to count against him in the commercio-medical warfare. "There's some people in town that say the doc is a fair to middlin' diagnostician and prescription-writer, but let me whisper this to you—but for heaven's sake don't tell him I said so—don't you ever go to him for anything more serious than a pendectomy of the left ear or a strabismus of the cardiograph."

No one save Kennicott knew exactly what this meant, but they laughed, and Sam Clark's party assumed a glittering lemon-yellow color of brocade panels and champagne and tulle and crystal chandeliers and sporting duchesses. Carol saw that George Edwin Mott and the blanched Mr. and Mrs. Dawson were not yet hypnotized. They looked as though they wondered whether they ought to look as though they disapproved. She concentrated on them:

"But I know whom I wouldn't have dared to go to Colorado with! Mr. Dawson there! I'm sure he's a regular heart-breaker. When we were introduced he held my hand and squeezed it frightfully."

"Haw! Haw! Haw!" The entire company applauded. Mr. Dawson was beatified. He had been called many things— loan-shark, skinflint, tightwad, pussyfoot—but he had never before been called a flirt.

"He is wicked, isn't he, Mrs. Dawson? Don't you have to lock him up?"

"Oh no, but maybe I better," attempted Mrs. Dawson, a tint on her pallid face.

For fifteen minutes Carol kept it up. She asserted that she was going to stage a musical comedy, that she preferred café parfait to beefsteak, that she hoped Dr. Kennicott would never lose his ability to make love to charming women, and that she had a pair of gold stockings. They gaped for more. But she could not keep it up. She retired to a chair behind Sam Clark's bulk. The smile-wrinkles solemnly flattened out in the faces of all the other collaborators in having a party, and again they stood about hoping but not expecting to be amused.

Carol listened. She discovered that conversation did not exist in Gopher Prairie. Even at this affair, which brought out the young smart set, the hunting squire set, the respectable intellectual set, and the solid financial set, they sat up with gaiety as with a corpse.

Juanita Haydock talked a good deal in her rattling voice but it was invariably of personalities: the rumor that Raymie Wutherspoon was going to send for a pair of patent leather shoes with gray buttoned tops; the rheumatism of Champ

Perry; the state of Guy Pollock's grippe; and the dementia
of Jim Howland in painting his fence salmon-pink.

Sam Clark had been talking to Carol about motor cars, but
he felt his duties as host. While he droned, his brows popped
up and down. He interrupted himself, "Must stir 'em up." He
worried at his wife, "Don't you think I better stir 'em up?"
He shouldered into the center of the room, and cried:

"Let's have some stunts, folks."

"Yes, let's!" shrieked Juanita Haydock.

"Say, Dave, give us that stunt about the Norwegian catching a hen."

"You bet; that's a slick stunt; do that, Dave!" cheered Chet
Dashaway.

Mr. Dave Dyer obliged.

All the guests moved their lips in anticipation of being
called on for their own stunts.

"Ella, come on and recite 'Old Sweetheart of Mine,' for us,"
demanded Sam.

Miss Ella Stowbody, the spinster daughter of the Ionic
bank, scratched her dry palms and blushed. "Oh, you don't
want to hear that old thing again."

"Sure we do! You bet!" asserted Sam.

"My voice is in terrible shape tonight."

"Tut! Come on!"

Sam loudly explained to Carol, "Ella is our shark at elocuting. She's had professional training. She studied singing and
oratory and dramatic art and shorthand for a year, in Milwaukee."

Miss Stowbody was reciting. As encore to "An Old Sweetheart of Mine," she gave a peculiarly optimistic poem regarding the value of smiles.

There were four other stunts: one Jewish, one Irish, one
juvenile, and Nat Hicks's parody of Mark Antony's funeral
oration.

During the winter Carol was to hear Dave Dyer's hen-
catching impersonation seven times, "An Old Sweetheart of
Mine" nine times, the Jewish story and the funeral oration
twice; but now she was ardent and, because she did so want
to be happy and simple-hearted, she was as disappointed as
the others when the stunts were finished, and the party instantly sank back into coma.

They gave up trying to be festive; they began to talk
naturally, as they did at their shops and homes.

The men and women divided, as they had been tending to do all evening. Carol was deserted by the men, left to a group of matrons who steadily pattered of children, sickness, and cooks—their own shop-talk. She was piqued. She remembered visions of herself as a smart married woman in a drawing-room, fencing with clever men. Her dejection was relieved by speculation as to what the men were discussing, in the corner between the piano and the phonograph. Did they rise from these housewifely personalities to a larger world of abstractions and affairs?

She made her best curtsy to Mrs. Dawson; she twittered, "I won't have my husband leaving me so soon! I'm going over and pull the wretch's ears." She rose with a *jeune fille* bow. She was self-absorbed and self-approving because she had attained that quality of sentimentality. She proudly dipped across the room and, to the interest and commendation of all beholders, sat on the arm of Kennicott's chair.

He was gossiping with Sam Clark, Luke Dawson, Jackson Elder of the planing-mill, Chet Dashaway, Dave Dyer, Harry Haydock, and Ezra Stowbody, president of the Ionic bank.

Ezra Stowbody was a troglodyte. He had come to Gopher Prairie in 1865. He was a distinguished bird of prey—swooping thin nose, turtle mouth, thick brows, port-wine cheeks, floss of white hair, contemptuous eyes. He was not happy in the social changes of thirty years. Three decades ago, Dr. Westlake, Julius Flickerbaugh the lawyer, Merriman Peedy the Congregational pastor and himself had been the arbiters. That was as it should be; the fine arts—medicine, law, religion, and finance—recognized as aristocratic; four Yankees democratically chatting with but ruling the Ohioans and Illini and Swedes and Germans who had ventured to follow them. But Westlake was old, almost retired; Julius Flickerbaugh had lost much of his practice to livelier attorneys; Reverend (not The Reverend) Peedy was dead; and nobody was impressed in this rotten age of automobiles by the "spanking grays" which Ezra still drove. The town was as heterogeneous as Chicago. Norwegians and Germans owned stores. The social leaders were common merchants. Selling nails was considered as sacred as banking. These upstarts—the Clarks, the Haydocks—had no dignity. They were sound and conservative in politics, but they talked about motor cars and pump-guns and heaven only knew what new-fangled fads. Mr. Stowbody felt out of place with them. But his brick house with the mansard roof was still the largest

residence in town, and he held his position as squire by occasionally appearing among the younger men and reminding
them by a wintry eye that without the banker none of them
could carry on their vulgar businesses.

As Carol defied decency by sitting down with the men, Mr.
Stowbody was piping to Mr. Dawson, "Say, Luke, when was't
Biggins first settled in Winnebago Township? Wa'n't it in
1879?"

"Why no 'twa'n't!" Mr. Dawson was indignant. "He come
out from Vermont in 1867—no, wait, in 1868, it must have
been—and took a claim on the Rum River, quite a ways above
Anoka."

"He did not!" roared Mr. Stowbody. "He settled first in
Blue Earth County, him and his father!"

("What's the point at issue?" Carol whispered to Kennicott.

("Whether this old duck Biggins had an English setter or
a Llewellyn. They've been arguing it all evening!")

Dave Dyer interrupted to give tidings, "D' tell you that
Clara Biggins was in town couple days ago? She bought a
hot-water bottle—expensive one, too—two dollars and thirty
cents!"

"Yaaaaaah!" snarled Mr. Stowbody. "Course. She's just like
her grandad was. Never save a cent. Two dollars and twenty
—thirty, was it?—two dollars and thirty cents for a hot-
water bottle! Brick wrapped up in a flannel petticoat just as
good, anyway!"

"How's Ella's tonsils, Mr. Stowbody?" yawned Chet Dashaway.

While Mr. Stowbody gave a somatic and psychic study of
them, Carol reflected, "Are they really so terribly interested
in Ella's tonsils, or even in Ella's esophagus? I wonder if I
could get them away from personalities? Let's risk damnation and try."

"There hasn't been much labor trouble around here, has
there, Mr. Stowbody?" she asked innocently.

"No, ma'am, thank God, we've been free from that, except
maybe with hired girls and farm-hands. Trouble enough with
these foreign farmers; if you don't watch these Swedes they
turn socialist or populist or some fool thing on you in a minute. Of course, if they have loans you can make 'em listen
to reason. I just have 'em come into the bank for a talk,
and tell 'em a few things. I don't mind their being democrats,
so much, but I won't stand having socialists around. But
thank God, we ain't got the labor trouble they have in these

cities. Even Jack Elder here gets along pretty well, in the planing-mill, don't you, Jack?"

"Yep. Sure. Don't need so many skilled workmen in my place, and it's a lot of these cranky, wage-hogging, half-baked skilled mechanics that start trouble—reading a lot of this anarchist literature and union papers and all."

"Do you approve of union labor?" Carol inquired of Mr. Elder.

"Me? I should say not! It's like this: I don't mind dealing with my men if they think they've got any grievances—though Lord knows what's come over workmen, nowadays—don't appreciate a good job. But still, if they come to me honestly, as man to man, I'll talk things over with them. But I'm not going to have any outsider, any of these walking delegates, or whatever fancy names they call themselves now —bunch of rich grafters, living on the ignorant workmen! Not going to have any of those fellows butting in and telling *me* how to run *my* business!"

Mr. Elder was growing more excited, more belligerent and patriotic. "I stand for freedom and constitutional rights. If any man don't like my shop, he can get up and git. Same way, if I don't like him, he gits. And that's all there is to it. I simply can't understand all these complications and hoop-te-doodles and government reports and wage-scales and God knows what all that these fellows are balling up the labor situation with, when it's all perfectly simple. They like what I pay 'em, or they get out. That's all there is to it!"

"What do you think of profit-sharing?" Carol ventured.

Mr. Elder thundered his answer, while the others nodded, solemnly and in tune, like a shop-window of flexible toys, comic mandarins and judges and ducks and clowns, set quivering by a breeze from the open door:

"All this profit-sharing and welfare work and insurance and old-age pension is simply poppycock. Enfeebles a workman's independence—and wastes a lot of honest profit. The half-baked thinker that isn't dry behind the ears yet, and these suffragettes and God knows what all buttinskis there are that are trying to tell a business man how to run his business, and some of these college professors are just about as bad, the whole kit and bilin' of 'em are nothing in God's world but socialism in disguise! And it's my bounden duty as a producer to resist every attack on the integrity of American industry to the last ditch. Yes—SIR!"

Mr. Elder wiped his brow.

Dave Dyer added, "Sure! You bet! What they ought to
do is simply to hang every one of these agitatprs, and that
would settle the whole thing right off. Don't you think so,
doc?"

"You bet," agreed Kennicott.

The conversation was at last relieved of the plague of
Carol's intrusions and they settled down to the question of
whether the justice of the peace had sent that hobo drunk to
jail for ten days or twelve. It was a matter not readily determined. Then Dave Dyer communicated his carefree adventures on the gipsy trail:

"Yep. I get good time out of the flivver. 'Bout a week ago
I motored down to New Wurttemberg. That's forty-three——
No, let's see: It's seventeen miles to Belldale, and 'bout six
and three-quarters, call it seven, to Torgenquist, and it's a
good nineteen miles from there to New Wurttemberg—seventeen and seven and nineteen, that makes, uh, let me see:
seventeen and seven 's twenty-four, plus nineteen, well say
plus twenty, that makes forty-four, well anyway, say about
forty-three or -four miles from here to New Wurttemberg.
We got started about seven-fifteen, prob'ly seven-twenty,
because I had to stop and fill the radiator, and we ran along,
just keeping up a good steady gait——"

Mr. Dyer did finally, for reasons and purposes admitted
and justified, attain to New Wurttemberg.

Once—only once—the presence of the alien Carol was
recognized. Chet Dashaway leaned over and said asthmatically,
"Say, uh, have you been reading this serial 'Two Out' in
Tingling Tales? Corking yarn! Gosh, the fellow that wrote it
certainly can sling baseball slang!"

The others tried to look literary. Harry Haydock offered,
"Juanita is a great hand for reading high-class stuff, like
'Mid the Magnolias' by this Sara Hetwiggin Butts, and
'Riders of Ranch Reckless.' Books. But me," he glanced
about importantly, as one convinced that no other hero had
ever been in so strange a plight, "I'm so darn busy I don't
have much time to read."

"I never read anything I can't check against," said Sam
Clark.

Thus ended the literary portion of the conversation, and
for seven minutes Jackson Elder outlined reasons for believing that the pike-fishing was better on the west shore
of Lake Minniemashie than on the east—though it was

indeed quite true that on the east shore Nat Hicks had caught a pike altogether admirable.

The talk went on. It did go on! Their voices were monotonous, thick, emphatic. They were harshly pompous, like men in the smoking-compartments of Pullman cars. They did not bore Carol. They frightened her. She panted, "They will be cordial to me, because my man belongs to their tribe. God help me if I were an outsider!"

Smiling as changelessly as an ivory figurine she sat quiescent, avoiding thought, glancing about the living-room and hall, noting their betrayal of unimaginative commercial prosperity. Kennicott said, "Dandy interior, eh? My idea of how a place ought to be furnished. Modern." She looked polite, and observed the oiled floors, hard-wood staircase, unused fireplace with tiles which resembled brown linoleum, cut-glass vases standing upon doilies, and the barred, shut, forbidding unit bookcases that were half filled with swashbuckler novels and unread-looking sets of Dickens, Kipling, O. Henry, and Elbert Hubbard.

She perceived that even personalities were failing to hold the party. The room filled with hesitancy as with a fog. People cleared their throats, tried to choke down yawns. The men shot their cuffs and the women stuck their combs more firmly into their back hair.

Then a rattle, a daring hope in every eye, the swinging of a door, the smell of strong coffee, Dave Dyer's mewing voice in a triumphant, "The eats!" They began to chatter. They had something to do. They could escape from themselves. They fell upon the food—chicken sandwiches, maple cake, drug-store ice cream. Even when the food was gone they remained cheerful. They could go home, any time now, and go to bed!

They went, with a flutter of coats, chiffon scarfs, and goodbys.

Carol and Kennicott walked home.

"Did you like them?" he asked.

"They were terribly sweet to me."

"Uh, Carrie—— You ought to be more careful about shocking folks. Talking about gold stockings, and about showing your ankles to schoolteachers and all!" More mildly: "You gave 'em a good time, but I'd watch out for that, 'f I were you. Juanita Haydock is such a damn cat. I wouldn't give her a chance to criticize me."

"My poor effort to lift up the party! Was I wrong to try to amuse them?"

"No! No! Honey, I didn't mean—— You were the only up-and-coming person in the bunch. I just mean—— Don't get onto legs and all that immoral stuff. Pretty conservative. crowd."

She was silent, raw with the shameful thought that the attentive circle might have been criticizing her, laughing at her.

"Don't, please don't worry!" he pleaded.

Silence.

"Gosh, I'm sorry I spoke about it. I just meant—— But they were crazy about you. Sam said to me, 'That little lady of yours is the slickest thing that ever came to this town,' he said; and Ma Dawson—I didn't hardly know whether she'd like you or not, she's such a dried-up old bird, but she said, 'Your bride is so quick and bright, I declare, she just wakes me up.'"

Carol liked praise, the flavor and fatness of it, but she was so energetically being sorry for herself that she could not taste this commendation.

"Please! Come on! Cheer up!" His lips said it, his anxious shoulder said it, his arm about her said it, as they halted on the obscure porch of their house.

"Do you care if they think I'm flighty, Will?"

"Me? Why, I wouldn't care if the whole world thought you were this or that or anything else. You're my—well, you're my soul!"

He was an undefined mass, as solid-seeming as rock. She found his sleeve, pinched it, cried, "I'm glad! It's sweet to be wanted! You must tolerate my frivolousness. You're all I have!"

He lifted her, carried her into the house, and with her arms about his neck she forgot Main Street.

chapter 5

WE'LL steal the whole day, and go hunting. I want you to see the country round here," Kennicott announced at breakfast. "I'd take the car—want you to see how swell she runs since I put in a new piston. But we'll take a team, so we can get right out into the fields. Not many prairie chickens left now, but we might just happen to run onto a small covey."

He fussed over his hunting-kit. He pulled his hip boots out to full length and examined them for holes. He feverishly counted his shotgun shells, lecturing her on the qualities of smokeless powder. He drew the new hammerless shotgun out of its heavy tan leather case and made her peep through the barrels to see how dazzlingly free they were from rust.

The world of hunting and camping-outfits and fishing-tackle was unfamiliar to her, and in Kennicott's interest she found something creative and joyous. She examined the smooth stock, the carved hard rubber butt of the gun. The shells, with their brass caps and sleek green bodies and hieroglyphics on the wads, were cool and comfortably heavy in her hands.

Kennicott wore a brown canvas hunting-coat with vast pockets lining the inside, corduroy trousers which bulged at the wrinkles, peeled and scarred shoes, a scarecrow felt hat. In this uniform he felt virile. They clumped out to the livery buggy, they packed the kit and the box of lunch into the back, crying to each other that it was a magnificent day.

Kennicott had borrowed Jackson Elder's red and white English setter, a complacent dog with a waving tail of silver hair which flickered in the sunshine. As they started, the dog yelped, and leaped at the horses' heads, till Kennicott took him into the buggy, where he nuzzled Carol's knees and leaned out to sneer at farm mongrels.

The grays clattered out on the hard dirt road with a pleasant song of hoofs: "Ta ta ta rat! Ta ta ta rat!" It was early and fresh, the air whistling, frost bright on the golden rod. As the sun warmed the world of stubble into a

57

welter of yellow they turned from the highroad, through the
bars of a farmer's gate, into a field, slowly bumping over
the uneven earth. In a hollow of the rolling prairie they lost
sight even of the country road. It was warm and placid.
Locusts trilled among the dry wheat-stalks, and brilliant little
flies hurtled across the buggy. A buzz of content filled the
air. Crows loitered and gossiped in the sky.

The dog had been let out and after a dance of excitement
he settled down to a steady quartering of the field, forth
and back, forth and back, his nose down.

"Pete Rustad owns this farm, and he told me he saw a
small covey of chickens in the west forty, last week. Maybe
we'll get some sport after all," Kennicott chuckled blissfully.

She watched the dog in suspense, breathing quickly
every time he seemed to halt. She had no desire to slaughter
birds, but she did desire to belong to Kennicott's world.

The dog stopped, on the point, a forepaw held up.

"By golly! He's hit a scent! Come on!" squealed Kennicott.
He leaped from the buggy, twisted the reins about the whip-
socket, swung her out, caught up his gun, slipped in two
shells, stalked toward the rigid dog, Carol pattering after
him. The setter crawled ahead, his tail quivering, his belly
close to the stubble. Carol was nervous. She expected clouds
of large birds to fly up instantly. Her eyes were strained with
staring. But they followed the dog for a quarter of a mile,
turning, doubling, crossing two low hills, kicking through
a swale of weeds, crawling between the strands of a barbed-
wire fence. The walking was hard on her pavement-trained
feet. The earth was lumpy, the stubble prickly and lined with
grass, thistles, abortive stumps of clover. She dragged and
floundered.

She heard Kennicott gasp, "Look!" Three gray birds were
starting up from the stubble. They were round, dumpy, like
enormous bumble bees. Kennicott was sighting, moving the
barrel. She was agitated. Why didn't he fire? The birds would
be gone! Then a crash, another, and two birds turned somer-
saults in the air, plumped down.

When he showed her the birds she had no sensation of
blood. These heaps of feathers were so soft and unbruised—
there was about them no hint of death. She watched her conquering man tuck them into his inside pocket, and trudged
with him back to the buggy.

They found no more prairie chickens that morning.

At noon they drove into her first farmyard, a private village, a white house with no porches save a low and quite dirty stoop at the back, a crimson barn with white trimmings, a glazed brick silo, an ex-carriage-shed, now the garage of a Ford, an unpainted cow-stable, a chicken-house, a pig-pen, a corn-crib, a granary, the galvanized-iron skeleton tower of a windmill. The dooryard was of packed yellow clay, treeless, barren of grass, littered with rusty plowshares and wheels of discarded cultivators. Hardened trampled mud, like lava, filled the pig-pen. The doors of the house were grime-rubbed, the corners and eaves were rusted with rain, and the child who stared at them from the kitchen window was smeary-faced. But beyond the barn was a clump of scarlet geraniums; the prairie breeze was sunshine in motion; the flashing metal blades of the windmill revolved with a lively hum; a horse neighed, a rooster crowed, martins flew in and out of the cow-stable.

A small spare woman with flaxen hair trotted from the house. She was twanging a Swedish patois—not in mono-tone, like English, but singing it, with a lyrical whine:

"Pete he say you kom pretty soon hunting, doctor. My, dot's fine you kom. Is dis de bride? Ohhhh! Ve yoost say las' night, ve hope maybe ve see her som day. My, soch a pretty lady!" Mrs. Rustad was shining with welcome. "Vell, vell! Ay hope you lak dis country! Von't you stay for dinner, doctor?"

"No, but I wonder if you wouldn't like to give us a glass of milk?" condescended Kennicott.

"Vell Ay should say Ay vill! You vait har a second and Ay run on de milk-house!" She nervously hastened to a tiny red building beside the windmill; she came back with a pitcher of milk from which Carol filled the thermos bottle.

As they drove off Carol admired, "She's the dearest thing I ever saw. And she adores you. You are the Lord of the Manor."

"Oh no," much pleased, "but still they do ask my advice about things. Bully people, these Scandinavian farmers. And prosperous, too. Helga Rustad, she's still scared of America, but her kids will be doctors and lawyers and governors of the state and any darn thing they want to."

"I wonder——" Carol was plunged back into last night's *Weltschmerz.* "I wonder if these farmers aren't bigger than we are? So simple and hard-working. The town lives on them. We townies are parasites, and yet we feel superior to them. Last night I heard Mr. Haydock talking about 'hicks.'

Apparently he despises the farmers because they haven't reached the social heights of selling thread and buttons."

"Parasites? Us? Where'd the farmers be without the town? Who lends them money? Who—why, we supply them with everything!"

"Don't you find that some of the farmers think they pay too much for the services of the towns?"

"Oh, of course there's a lot of cranks among the farmers same as there are among any class. Listen to some of these kickers, a fellow'd think that the farmers ought to run the state and the whole shooting-match—probably if they had their way they'd fill up the legislature with a lot of farmers in manure-covered boots—yes, and they'd come tell me I was hired on a salary now, and couldn't fix my fees! That'd be fine for you, wouldn't it!"

"But why shouldn't they?"

"Why? That bunch of—— Telling *me*—— Oh, for heaven's sake, let's quit arguing. All this discussing may be all right at a party but—— Let's forget it while we're hunting."

"I know. The Wonderlust—probably it's a worse affliction than the Wanderlust. I just wonder——"

She told herself that she had everything in the world. And after each self-rebuke she stumbled again on "I just wonder——"

They ate their sandwiches by a prairie slew: long grass reaching up out of clear water, mossy bogs, red-winged blackbirds, the scum a splash of gold-green. Kennicott smoked a pipe while she leaned back in the buggy and let her tired spirit be absorbed in the Nirvana of the incomparable sky.

They lurched to the highroad and awoke from their sunsoaked drowse at the sound of the clopping hoofs. They paused to look for partridges in a rim of woods, little woods, very clean and shiny and gay, silver birches and poplars with immaculate green trunks, encircling a lake of sandy bottom, a splashing seclusion demure in the welter of hot prairie.

Kennicott brought down a fat red squirrel and at dusk he had a dramatic shot at a flight of ducks whirling down from the upper air, skimming the lake, instantly vanishing.

They drove home under the sunset. Mounds of straw, and wheat-stacks like bee-hives, stood out in startling rose and gold, and the green-tufted stubble glistened. As the vast girdle of crimson darkened, the fulfilled land became autumnal in deep reds and browns. The black road before the buggy turned to a faint lavender, then was blotted to uncertain grayness. Cattle came in a long line up to the barred gates of the farmyards, and over the resting land was a dark glow.

Carol had found the dignity and greatness which had failed her in Main Street.

II

Till they had a maid they took noon dinner and six o'clock supper at Mrs. Gurrey's boarding-house.

Mrs. Elisha Gurrey, relict of Deacon Gurrey the dealer in hay and grain, was a pointed-nosed, simpering woman with iron-gray hair drawn so tight that it resembled a soiled hand-kerchief covering her head. But she was unexpectedly cheer-ful, and her dining-room, with its thin tablecloth on a long pine table, had the decency of clean bareness.

In the line of unsmiling, methodically chewing guests, like horses at a manger, Carol came to distinguish one counte-nance: the pale, long, spectacled face and sandy pompadour hair of Mr. Raymnd P. Wutherspoon, known as "Raymie," professional bachelor, manager and one half the sales-force in the shoe-department of the Bon Ton Store.

"You will enjoy Gopher Prairie very much, Mrs. Kenni-cott," petitioned Raymie. His eyes were like those of a dog waiting to be let in out of the cold. He passed the stewed apricots effusively. "There are a great many bright cultured people here. Mrs. Wilks, the Christian Science reader, is a very bright woman—though I am not a Scientist myself, in fact I sing in the Episcopal choir. And Miss Sherwin of the high school—she is such a pleasing, bright girl—I was fit-ting her to a pair of tan gaiters yesterday, I declare, it really was a pleasure."

"Gimme the butter, Carrie," was Kennicott's comment. She defied him by encouraging Raymie:

"Do you have amateur dramatics and so on here?"

"Oh yes! The town's just full of talent. The Knights of Pythias put on a dandy minstrel show last year."

"It's nice you're so enthusiastic."

"Oh, do you really think so? Lots of folks jolly me for trying to get up shows and so on. I tell them they have more artistic gifts than they know. Just yesterday I was saying to Harry Haydock: if he would read poetry, like Longfellow, or if he would join the band—I get so much pleasure out of playing the cornet, and our band-leader, Del Snafflin, is such a good musician, I often say he ought to give up his barbering and become a professional musician, he could play the clarinet in Minneapolis or New York or anywhere, but—but I couldn't get Harry to see it at all and—I hear you and the doctor went out hunting yesterday. Lovely country, isn't it. And did you make some calls? The mercantile life isn't inspiring like medicine. It must be wonderful to see how patients trust you, doctor."

"Huh. It's me that's got to do all the trusting. Be damn sight more wonderful 'f they'd pay their bills," grumbled Kennicott and, to Carol, he whispered something which sounded like "gentleman hen."

But Raymie's pale eyes were watering at her. She helped him with, "So you like to read poetry?"

"Oh yes, so much—though to tell the truth, I don't get much time for reading, we're always so busy at the store and —— But we had the dandiest professional reciter at the Pythian Sisters sociable last winter."

Carol thought she heard a grunt from the traveling salesman at the end of the table, and Kennicott's jerking elbow was a grunt embodied. She persisted:

"Do you get to see many plays, Mr. Wutherspoon?"

He shone at her like a dim blue March moon, and sighed, "No, but I do love the movies. I'm a real fan. One trouble with books is that they're not so thoroughly safeguarded by intelligent censors as the movies are, and when you drop into the library and take out a book you never know what you're wasting your time on. What I like in books is a wholesome, really improving story, and sometimes—— Why, once I started a novel by this fellow Balzac that you read about, and it told how a lady wasn't living with her husband, I mean she wasn't his wife. It went into details, disgustingly! And the English was real poor. I spoke to the library about it, and they took it off the shelves. I'm not narrow, but I must say I don't see any use in this deliberately dragging in immorality! Life itself is so full of temptations that in literature one wants only that which is pure and uplifting."

"What's the name of that Balzac yarn. Where can I get hold of it?" giggled the traveling salesman.

Raymie ignored him. "But the movies, they are mostly clean, and their humor—— Don't you think that the most essential quality for a person to have is a sense of humor?"

"I don't know. I really haven't much," said Carol.

He shook his finger at her. "Now, now, you're too modest. I'm sure we can all see that you have a perfectly corking sense of humor. Besides, Dr. Kennicott wouldn't marry a lady that didn't have. We all know how he loves his fun!"

"You bet. I'm a jokey old bird. Come on, Carrie; let's beat it," remarked Kennicott.

Raymie implored, "And what is your chief artistic interest, Mrs. Kennicott?"

"Oh——" Aware that the traveling salesman had murmured, "Dentistry," she desperately hazarded, "Architecture."

"That's a real nice art. I've always said—when Haydock & Simons were finishing the new front on the Bon Ton building, the old man came to me, you know, Harry's father, 'D. H.,' I always call him, and he asked me how I liked it, and I said to him, 'Look here, D. H.,' I said—you see, he was going to leave the front plain, and I said to him, 'It's all very well to have modern lighting and a big display-space,' I said, 'but when you get that in, you want to have some architecture, too,' I said, and he laughed and said he guessed maybe I was right, and so he had 'em put on a cornice."

"Tin!" observed the traveling salesman.

Raymie bared his teeth like a belligerent mouse. "Well, what if it is tin? That's not my fault. I told D. H. to make it polished granite. You make me tired!"

"Leave us go! Come on, Carrie, leave us go!" from Kennicott.

Raymie waylaid them in the hall and secretly informed Carol that she mustn't mind the traveling salesman's coarseness—he belonged to the hwa pollwa.

Kennicott chuckled. "Well, child, how about it? Do you prefer an artistic guy like Raymie to stupid boobs like Sam Clark and me?"

"My dear! Let's go home, and play pinochle, and laugh, and be foolish, and slip up to bed, and sleep without dreaming. It's beautiful to be just a solid citizeness!"

III

From the *Gopher Prairie Weekly Dauntless:*

One of the most charming affairs of the season was held Tuesday evening at the handsome new residence of Sam and Mrs. Clark, when many of our most prominent citizens gathered to greet the lovely new bride of our popular local physician, Dr. Will Kennicott. All present spoke of the many

charms of the bride, formerly Miss Carol Milford of St.
Paul. Games and stunts were the order of the day, with
merry talk and conversation. At a late hour dainty refreshments were served, and the party broke up with many expressions of pleasure at the pleasant affair. Among those
present were Mesdames Kennicott, Elder——

*   *   *

Dr. Will Kennicott, for the past several years one of our
most popular and skilful physicians and surgeons, gave the
town a delightful surprise when he returned from an extended honeymoon tour in Colorado this week with his
charming bride, née Miss Carol Milford of St. Paul, whose
family are socially prominent in Minneapolis and Mankato.
Mrs. Kennicott is a lady of manifold charms, not only of
striking charm of appearance but is also a distinguished
graduate of a school in the East and has for the past year
been prominently connected in an important position of responsibility with the St. Paul Public Library, in which city
Dr. "Will" had the good fortune to meet her. The city of
Gopher Prairie welcomes her to our midst and prophesies
for her many happy years in the energetic city of the twin
lakes and the future. The Dr. and Mrs. Kennicott will re-
side for the present at the Doctor's home on Poplar Street
which his charming mother has been keeping for him who
has now returned to her own home at Lac-qui-Meurt leaving
a host of friends who regret her absence and hope to see
her soon with us again.

IV

She knew that if she was ever to effect any of the "reforms"
which she had pictured, she must have a starting-place.
What confused her during the three or four months after her
marriage was not lack of perception that she must be definite,
but sheer careless happiness of her first home.

In the pride of being a houewife she loved every detail—
the brocade armchair with the weak back, even the brass
water-cock on the hot-water reservoir, when she had become
familiar with it by trying to scour it to brilliance.

She found a maid—plump radiant Bea Sorenson from
Scandia Crossing. Bea was droll in her attempt to be at once
a respectful servant and a bosom friend. They laughed together over the fact that the stove did not draw, over the
slipperiness of fish in the pan.

Like a child playing Grandma in a trailing skirt, Carol
paraded uptown for her marketing, crying greetings to housewives along the way. Everybody bowed to her, strangers
and all, and made her feel that they wanted her, that she

belonged here. In city shops she was merely A Customer—a hat, a voice to bore a harassed clerk. Here she was Mrs. Doc Kennicott, and her preferences in grape-fruit and manners were known and remembered and worth discussing . . . even if they weren't worth fulfilling.

Shopping was a delight of brisk conferences. The very merchants whose droning she found the dullest at the two or three parties which were given to welcome her were the pleasantest confidants of all when they had something to talk about—lemons or cotton voile or floor-oil. With that skipjack Dave Dyer, the druggist, she conducted a long mock-quarrel. She pretended that he cheated her in the price of magazines and candy; he pretended she was a detective from the Twin Cities. He hid behind the prescription-counter, and when she stamped her foot he came out wailing, "Honest, I haven't done nothing crooked today—not yet."

She never recalled her first impression of Main Street; never had precisely the same despair at its ugliness. By the end of two shopping-tours everything had changed proportions. As she never entered it, the Minniemashie House ceased to exist for her. Clark's Hardware Store, Dyers Drug Store, the groceries of Ole Jenson and Frederick Ludelmeyer and Howland & Gould, the meat markets, the notions shop—they expanded, and hid all other structures. When she entered Mr. Ludelmeyer's store and he wheezed, "Goot mornin', Mrs. Kennicott. Vell, dis iss a fine day," she did not notice the dustiness of the shelves nor the stupidity of the girl clerk; and she did not remember the mute colloquy with him on her first view of Main Street.

She could not find half the kinds of food she wanted, but that made shopping more of an adventure. When she did contrive to get sweetbreads at Dahl & Oleson's Meat Market the triumph was so vast that she buzzed with excitement and admired the strong wise butcher, Mr. Dahl.

She appreciated the homely ease of village life. She liked the old men, farmers, G.A.R. veterans, who when they gossiped sometimes squatted on their heels on the sidewalk, like resting Indians, and reflectively spat over the curb.

She found beauty in the children.

She had suspected that her married friends exaggerated their passion for children. But in her work in the library, children had become individuals to her, citizens of the State with their own rights and their own senses of humor. In the library she had not had much time to give them, but now she knew the luxury of stopping, gravely asking Bessie Clark whether her doll had yet recovered from its rheumatism, and agreeing with Oscar Martinsen that it would be Good Fun to go trapping "mushrats."

She touched the thought, "It would be sweet to have a baby of my own. I do want one. Tiny—— No! Not yet! There's so much to do. And I'm still tired from the job. It's in my bones."

She rested at home. She listened to the village noises common to all the world, jungle or prairie; sounds simple and charged with magic—dogs barking, chickens making a gurgling sound of content, children at play, a man beating a rug, wind in the cottonwood trees, a locust fiddling, a footstep on the walk, jaunty voices of Bea and a grocer's boy in the kitchen, a clinking anvil, a piano—not too near.

Twice a week, at least, she drove into the country with Kennicott, to hunt ducks in lakes enameled with sunset, or to call on patients who looked up to her as the squire's lady and thanked her for toys and magazines. Evenings she went with her husband to the motion pictures and was boisterously greeted by every other couple; or, till it became too cold, they sat on the porch, bawling to passers-by in motors, or to neighbors who were raking the leaves. The dust became golden in the low sun; the street was filled with the fragrance of burning leaves.

v

But she hazily wanted some one to whom she could say what she thought.

On a slow afternoon when she fidgeted over sewing and wished that the telephone would ring, Bea announced Miss Vida Sherwin.

Despite Vida Sherwin's lively blue eyes, if you had looked at her in detail you would have found her face slightly lined, and not so much sallow as with the bloom rubbed off; you would have found her chest flat, and her fingers rough from needle and chalk and penholder; her blouses and plain cloth skirts undistinguished; and her hat worn too far back, betraying a dry forehead. But you never did look at Vida Sherwin in detail. You couldn't. Her electric activity veiled her. She was as energetic as a chipmunk. Her fingers fluttered; her sympathy came out in spurts; she sat on the edge of a chair in eagerness to be near her auditor, to send her enthusiasms and optimism across.

She rushed into the room pouring out: "I'm afraid you'll think the teachers have been shabby in not coming near you, but we wanted to give you a chance to get settled. I am Vida Sherwin, and I try to teach French and English and a few other things in the high school."

"I've been hoping to know the teachers. You see, I was a librarian——"

"Oh, you needn't tell me. I know all about you! Awful how much I know—this gossipy village. We need you so much here. It's a dear loyal town (and isn't loyalty the finest thing in the world!) but it's a rough diamond, and we need you for the polishing, and we're ever so humble——" She stopped for breath and finished her compliment with a smile.

"If I *could* help you in any way—— Would I be committing the unpardonable sin if I whispered that I think Gopher Prairie is a tiny bit ugly?"

"Of course it's ugly. Dreadfully! Though I'm probably the only person in town to whom you could safely say that. (Except perhaps Guy Pollock the lawyer—have you met him? —oh, you *must!*—he's simply a darling—intelligence and culture and so gentle.) But I don't care so much about the ugliness. That will change. It's the spirit that gives me hope. It's sound. Wholesome. But afraid. It needs live creatures like you to awaken it. I shall slave-drive you!"

"Splendid. What shall I do? I've been wondering if it would be possible to have a good architect come here to lecture."

"Ye-es, but don't you think it would be better to work with existing agencies? Perhaps it will sound slow to you, but I was thinking—— It would be lovely if we could get you to teach Sunday School."

Carol had the empty expression of one who finds that she has been affectionately bowing to a complete stranger. "Oh yes. But I'm afraid I wouldn't be much good at that. My religion is so foggy."

"I know. So is mine. I don't care a bit for dogma. Though I do stick firmly to the belief in the fatherhood of God and the brotherhood of man and the leadership of Jesus. As you do, of course."

Carol looked respectable and thought about having tea.

"And that's all you need teach in Sunday School. It's the personal influence. Then there's the library-board. You'd be

so useful on that. And of course there's our women's study
club—the Thanatopsis Club."

"Are they doing anything? Or do they read papers made
out of the Encyclopedia?"

Miss Sherwin shrugged. "Perhaps. But still, they are so
earnest. They will respond to your fresher interest. And the
Thanatopsis does do a good social work—they've made the
city plant ever so many trees, and they run the rest-room for
farmers' wives. And they do take such an interest in refinement and culture. So—in fact, so very unique."

Carol was disappointed—by nothing very tangible. She
said politely, "I'll think them all over. I must have a while
to look around first."

Miss Sherwin darted to her, smoothed her hair, peered at
her. "Oh, my dear, don't you suppose I know? These first
tender days of marriage—they're sacred to me. Home, and
children that need you, and depend on you to keep them
alive, and turn to you with their wrinkly little smiles. And the
hearth and——" She hid her face from Carol as she made an
activity of patting the cushion of her chair, but she went on
with her former briskness:

"I mean, you must help us when you're ready. . . . I'm
afraid you'll think I'm conservative. I am! So much to con-
serve. All this treasure of American ideals. Sturdiness and
democracy and opportunity. Maybe not at Palm Beach.
But, thank heaven, we're free from such social distinctions
in Gopher Prairie. I have only one good quality—overwhelming belief in the brains and hearts of our nation, our
state, our town. It's so strong that sometimes I do have a
tiny effect on the haughty ten-thousandaires. I shake 'em up
and make 'em believe in ideals—yes, in themselves. But I get
into a rut of teaching. I need young critical things like you
to punch me up. Tell me, what are you reading?"

"I've been re-reading 'The Damnation of Theron Ware.'
Do you know it?"

"Yes. It was clever. But hard. Man wanted to tear down,
not build up. Cynical. Oh, I do hope I'm not a sentimentalist.
But I can't see any use in this high-art stuff that doesn't encourage us day-laborers to plod on."

Ensued a fifteen-minute argument about the oldest topic
in the world: It's art but is it pretty? Carol tried to be eloquent
regarding honesty of observation. Miss Sherwin stood out
for sweetness and a cautious use of the uncomfortable prop-
erties of light. At the end Carol cried:

"I don't care how much we disagree. It's a relief to have somebody talk something besides crops. Let's make Gopher Prairie rock to its foundations: let's have afternoon tea instead of afternoon coffee."

The delighted Bea helped her bring out the ancestral folding sewing-table, whose yellow and black top was scarred with dotted lines from a dressmaker's tracing-wheel, and to set it with an embroidered lunch-cloth, and the mauve-glazed Japanese tea-set which she had brought from St. Paul. Miss Sherwin confided her latest scheme—moral motion pictures for country districts, with light from a portable dynamo hitched to a Ford engine. Bea was twice called to fill the hot-water pitcher and to make cinnamon toast.

When Kennicott came home at five he tried to be courtly, as befits the husband of one who has afternoon tea. Carol suggested that Miss Sherwin stay for supper, and that Kennicott invite Guy Pollock, the much-praised lawyer, the poetic bachelor.

Yes, Pollock could come. Yes, he was over the grippe which had prevented his going to Sam Clark's party.

Carol regretted her impulse. The man would be an opinionated politician, heavily jocular about The Bride. But at the entrance of Guy Pollock she discovered a personality. Pollock was a man of perhaps thirty-eight, slender, still, deferential. His voice was low. "It was very good of you to want me," he said, and he offered no humorous remarks, and did not ask her if she didn't think Gopher Prairie was "the livest little burg in the state."

She fancied that his even grayness might reveal a thousand tints of lavender and blue and silver.

At supper he hinted his love for Sir Thomas Browne, Thoreau, Agnes Repplier, Arthur Symons, Claude Washburn, Charles Flandrau. He presented his idols diffidently, but he expanded in Carol's bookishness, in Miss Sherwin's voluminous praise, in Kennicott's tolerance of any one who amused his wife.

Carol wondered why Guy Pollock went on digging at routine law-cases; why he remained in Gopher Prairie. She had no one whom she could ask. Neither Kennicott nor Vida Sherwin would understand that there might be reasons why a Pollock should not remain in Gopher Prairie. She enjoyed the faint mystery. She felt triumphant and rather literary. She already had a Group. It would be only a while now before she provided the town with fanlights and a knowledge of

Galsworthy. She was doing things! As she served the emergency dessert of cocoanut and sliced oranges, she cried to Pollock, "Don't you think we ought to get up a dramatic club?"

chapter 6

WHEN the first dubious November snow had filtered down, shading with white the bare clods in the plowed fields, when the first small fire had been started in the furnace, which is the shrine of a Gopher Prairie home, Carol began to make the house her own. She dismissed the parlor furniture—the golden oak table with brass knobs, the moldy brocade chairs, the picture of "The Doctor." She went to Minneapolis, to scamper through department stores and small Tenth Street shops devoted to ceramics and high thought. She had to ship her treasures, but she wanted to bring them back in her arms.

Carpenters had torn out the partition between front parlor and back parlor, thrown it into a long room on which she lavished yellow and deep blue; a Japanese obi with an intricacy of gold thread on stiff ultramarine tissue, which she hung as a panel against the maize wall; a couch with pillows of sapphire velvet and gold bands; chairs which, in Gopher Prairie, seemed flippant. She hid the sacred family phonograph in the dining-room, and replaced its stand with a square cabinet on which was a squat blue jar between yellow candles.

Kennicott decided against a fireplace. "We'll have a new house in a couple of years, anyway."

She decorated only one room. The rest, Kennicott hinted, she'd better leave till he "made a ten-strike."

The brown cube of a house stirred and awakened; it seemed to be in motion; it welcomed her back from shopping; it lost its mildewed repression.

The supreme verdict was Kennicott's "Well, by golly, I was afraid the new junk wouldn't be so comfortable, but I must say this divan, or whatever you call it, is a lot better than that bumpy old sofa we had, and when I look around—— Well, it's worth all it cost, I guess."

Every one in town took an interest in the refurnishing. The carpenters and painters who did not actually assist crossed the lawn to peer through the windows and exclaim, "Fine! Looks swell!" Dave Dyer at the drug store, Harry Haydock and Raymie Wutherspoon at the Bon Ton, repeated daily, "How's the good work coming? I hear the house is getting to be real classy."

Even Mrs. Bogart.

Mrs. Bogart lived across the alley from the rear of Carol's house. She was a widow, and a Prominent Baptist, and a Good Influence. She had so painfully reared three sons to be Christian gentlemen that one of them had become an Omaha bartender, one a professor of Greek, and one, Cyrus N. Bogart, a boy of fourteen who was still at home, the most brazen member of the toughest gang in Boytown.

Mrs. Bogart was not the acid type of Good Influence. She was the soft, damp, fat, sighing, indigestive, clinging, melancholy, depressingly hopeful kind. There are in every large chicken-yard a number of old and indignant hens who resemble Mrs. Bogart, and when they are served at Sunday noon dinner, as fricasseed chicken with thick dumplings, they keep up the resemblance.

Carol had noted that Mrs. Bogart from her side window kept an eye upon the house. The Kennicotts and Mrs. Bogart did not move in the same sets—which meant precisely the same in Gopher Prairie as it did on Fifth Avenue or in Mayfair. But the good widow came calling.

She wheezed in, sighed, gave Carol a pulpy hand, sighed, glanced sharply at the revelation of ankles as Carol crossed her legs, sighed, inspected the new blue chairs, smiled with a coy sighing sound, and gave voice:

"I've wanted to call on you so long, dearie, you know we're neighbors, but I thought I'd wait till you got settled, you must run in and see me, how much did that big chair cost?"

"Seventy-seven dollars!"

"Sev—— Sakes alive! Well, I suppose it's all right for them that can afford it, though I do sometimes think—— Of course as our pastor said once, at Baptist Church—— By the way, we haven't seen you there yet, and of course your husband was raised up a Baptist, and I do hope he won't drift away from the fold, of course we all know there isn't anything, not cleverness or gifts of gold or anything, that can make up for humility and the inward grace and they can say what they want to about the P. E. church, but of course there's no church that has more history or has stayed by the true principles of Christianity better than the Baptist Church and—— In what church were you raised, Mrs. Kennicott?"

"W-why, I went to Congregational, as a girl in Mankato, but my college was Universalist."

"Well—— But of course as the Bible says, is it the Bible, at least I know I have heard it in church and everybody admits it, it's proper for the little bride to take her husband's vessel of faith, so we all hope we shall see you at the Baptist Church and—— As I was saying, of course I agree with Reverend Zitterel in thinking that the great trouble with this nation today is lack of spiritual faith—so few going to church, and people automobiling on Sunday and heaven knows what all. But still I do think that one trouble is this terrible waste of money, people feeling that they've got to have bath-tubs and telephones in their houses—— I heard you were selling the old furniture cheap."

"Yes!"

"Well—of course you know your own mind, but I can't help thinking, when Will's ma was down here keeping house for him—*she* used to run in to *see* me, real *often!*—it was good enough furniture for her. But there, there, I mustn't croak, I just wanted to let you know that when you find you can't depend on a lot of these gadding young folks like the Haydocks and the Dyers—and heaven only knows how much money Juanita Haydock blows in in a year—why then you may be glad to know that slow old Aunty Bogart is always right there, and heaven knows——" A portentous sigh. "—I *hope* you and your husband won't have any of the troubles, with sickness and quarreling and wasting money and all that so many of these young couples do have and—— But I must be running along now, dearie. It's been such a pleasure and—— Just run in and see me any time. I hope Will is well? I thought he looked a wee mite peaked."

It was twenty minutes later when Mrs. Bogart finally oozed out of the front door. Carol ran back into the living-room and jerked open the windows. "That woman has left damp finger-prints in the air," she said.

II

Carol was extravagant, but at least she did not try to clear herself of blame by going about whimpering, "I know I'm terribly extravagant but I don't seem to be able to help it."

Kennicott had never thought of giving her an allowance. His mother had never had one! As a wage-earning spinster Carol had asserted to her fellow librarians that when she was married, she was going to have an allowance and be business-like and modern. But it was too much trouble to explain to Kennicott's kindly stubbornness that she was a practical housekeeper as well as a flighty playmate. She bought a budget-plan account book and made her budgets as exact as budgets are likely to be when they lack budgets.

For the first month it was a honeymoon jest to beg prettily, to confess, "I haven't a cent in the house, dear," and to be told, "You're an extravagant little rabbit." But the budget book made her realize how inexact were her finances. She became self-conscious; occasionally she was indignant that she should always have to petition him for the money with which to buy his food. She caught herself criticizing his belief that, since his joke about trying to keep her out of the poor-house had once been accepted as admirable humor, it should continue to be his daily *bon mot*. It was a nuisance to have to run down the street after him because she had forgotten to ask him for money at breakfast.

But she couldn't "hurt his feelings," she reflected. He liked the lordliness of giving largess.

She tried to reduce the frequency of begging by opening accounts and having the bills sent to him. She had found that staple groceries, sugar, flour, could be most cheaply purchased at Axel Egge's rustic general store. She said sweetly to Axel:

"I think I'd better open a charge account here."

"I don't do no business except for cash," grunted Axel. She flared, "Do you know who I am?"

"Yuh, sure, I know. The doc is good for it. But that's yoost a rule I made. I make low prices. I do business for cash."

She stared at his red impassive face, and her fingers had the undignified desire to slap him, but her reason agreed with him. "You're quite right. You shouldn't break your rule for me."

Her rage had not been lost. It had been transferred to her

husband. She wanted ten pounds of sugar in a hurry, but she had no money. She ran up the stairs to Kennicott's office. On the door was a sign advertising a headache cure and stating, "The doctor is out, back at——" Naturally, the blank space was not filled out. She stamped her foot. She ran down to the drug store—the doctor's club.

As she entered she heard Mrs. Dyer demanding, "Dave, I've got to have some money."

Carol saw that her husband was there, and two other men, all listening in amusement.

Dave Dyer snapped, "How much do you want? Dollar be enough?"

"No, it won't! I've got to get some underclothes for the kids."

"Why, good Lord, they got enough now to fill the closet so I couldn't find my hunting boots, last time I wanted them."

"I don't care. They're all in rags. You got to give me ten dollars——"

Carol perceived that Mrs. Dyer was accustomed to this indignity. She perceived that the men, particularly Dave, regarded it as an excellent jest. She waited—she knew what would come—it did. Dave yelped, "Where's that ten dollars I gave you last year?" and he looked to the other men to laugh. They laughed.

Cold and still, Carol walked up to Kennicott and commanded, "I want to see you upstairs."

"Why—something the matter?"

"Yes!"

He clumped after her, up the stairs, into his barren office. Before he could get out a query she stated:

"Yesterday, in front of a saloon, I heard a German farmwife beg her husband for a quarter, to get a toy for the baby—and he refused. Just now I've heard Mrs. Dyer going through the same humiliation. And I—I'm in the same position! I have to beg you for money. Daily! I have just been informed that I couldn't have any sugar because I hadn't the money to pay for it!"

"Who said that? By God, I'll kill any——"

"Tut. It wasn't his fault. It was yours. And mine. I now humbly beg you to give me the money with which to buy meals for you to eat. And hereafter to remember it. The next time, I shan't beg. I shall simply starve. Do you understand? I can't go on being a slave——"

Her defiance, her enjoyment of the rôle, ran out. She was

sobbing against his overcoat, "How can you shame me so?"
and he was blubbering, "Dog-gone it, I meant to give you
some, and I forgot it. I swear I won't again. By golly I
won't!"

He pressed fifty dollars upon her, and after that he remembered to give her money regularly. . . . sometimes.

Daily she determined, "But I must have a stated amount—
be business-like. System. I must do something about it." And
daily she didn't do anything about it.

III

Mrs. Bogart had, by the simpering viciousness of her
comments on the new furniture, stirred Carol to economy.
She spoke judiciously to Bea about left-overs. She read the
cookbook again and, like a child with a picture-book, she
studied the diagram of the beef which gallantly continues
to browse though it is divided into cuts.

But she was a deliberate and joyous spendthrift in her
preparations for her first party, the housewarming. She made
lists on every envelope and laundry-slip in her desk. She sent
orders to Minneapolis "fancy grocers." She pinned patterns
and sewed. She was irritated when Kennicott was jocular
about "these frightful big doings that are going on." She
regarded the affair as an attack on Gopher Prairie's timidity
in pleasure. "I'll make 'em lively, if nothing else. I'll make
'em stop regarding parties as committee-meetings."

Kennicott usually considered himself the master of the
house. At his desire, she went hunting, which was his symbol
of happiness, and she ordered porridge for breakfast, which
was his symbol of morality. But when he came home on the
afternoon before the housewarming he found himself a slave,
an intruder, a blunderer. Carol wailed, "Fix the furnace so
you won't have to touch it after supper. And for heaven's
sake take that horrible old door-mat off the porch. And put on
your nice brown and white shirt. Why did you come home
so late? Would you mind hurrying? Here it is almost supper-
time, and those fiends are just as likely as not to come at
seven instead of eight. *Please* hurry!"

She was as unreasonable as an amateur leading woman
on a first night, and he was reduced to humility. When she
came down to supper, when she stood in the doorway, he
gasped. She was in a silver sheath, the calyx of a lily, her
piled hair like black glass; she had the fragility and costli-

ness of a Viennese goblet; and her eyes were intense. He was stirred to rise from the table and to hold the chair for her; and all through supper he ate his bread dry because he felt that she would think him common if he said "Will you hand me the butter?"

IV

She had reached the calmness of not caring whether her guests liked the party or not, and a state of satisfied suspense in regard to Bea's technique in serving, before Kennicott cried from the bay-window in the living-room, "Here comes somebody!" and Mr. and Mrs. Luke Dawson faltered in, at a quarter to eight. Then in a shy avalanche arrived the entire aristocracy of Gopher Prairie: all persons engaged in a profession, or earning more than twenty-five hundred dollars a year, or possessed of grandparents born in America.

Even while they were removing their overshoes they were peeping at the new decorations. Carol saw Dave Dyer secretively turn over the gold pillows to find a price-tag, and heard Mr. Julius Flickerbaugh, the attorney, gasp, "Well, I'll be switched," as he viewed the vermilion print hanging against the Japanese obi. She was amused. But her high spirits slackened as she beheld them form in dress parade, in a long, silent, uneasy circle clear round the living-room. She felt that she had been magically whisked back to her first party, at Sam Clark's.

"Have I got to lift them, like so many pigs of iron? I don't know that I can make them happy, but I'll make them hectic."

A silver flame in the darkling circle, she whirled around, drew them with her smile, and sang, "I want my party to be noisy and undignified! This is the christening of my house, and I want you to help me have a bad influence on it, so that it will be a giddy house. For me, won't you all join in an old-fashioned square dance? And Mr. Dyer will call."

She had a record on the phonograph; Dave Dyer was capering in the center of the floor, loose-jointed, lean, small, rusty-headed, pointed of nose, clapping his hands and shouting, "Swing y' pardners—alamun lef!"

Even the millionaire Dawsons and Ezra Stowbody and "Professor" George Edwin Mott danced, looking only slightly foolish; and by rushing about the room and being coy and coaxing to all persons over forty-five, Carol got them into a waltz and a Virginia Reel. But when she left them to disenjoy themselves in their own way Harry Haydock put a one-step record on the phonograph, the younger people took the floor, and all the elders sneaked back to their chairs, with crystallized smiles which meant, "Don't believe I'll try this one myself, but I do enjoy watching the youngsters dance."

Half of them were silent; half resumed the discussions of that afternoon in the store. Ezra Stowbody hunted for something to say, hid a yawn, and offered to Lyman Cass, the owner of the flour-mill, "How d' you folks like the new furnace, Lym? Huh? So."

"Oh, let them alone. Don't pester them. They must like it, or they wouldn't do it." Carol warned herself. But they gazed at her so expectantly when she flickered past that she was reconvinced that in their debauches of respectability they had lost the power of play as well as the power of impersonal thought. Even the dancers were gradually crushed by the invisible force of fifty perfectly pure and well-behaved and negative minds; and they sat down, two by two. In twenty minutes the party was again elevated to the decorum of a prayer-meeting.

"We're going to do something exciting," Carol exclaimed to her new confidante, Vida Sherwin. She saw that in the growing quiet her voice had carried across the room. Nat Hicks, Ella Stowbody, and Dave Dyer were abstracted, fingers and lips slightly moving. She knew with a cold certainty that Dave was rehearsing his "stunt" about the Norwegian catching the hen, Ella running over the first lines of "An Old Sweetheart of Mine," and Nat thinking of his popular parody on Mark Antony's oration.

"But I will not have anybody use the word 'stunt' in my house," she whispered to Miss Sherwin.

"That's good. I tell you: why not have Raymond Wutherspoon sing?"

"Raymie? Why, my dear, he's the most sentimental yearner in town!"

"See here, child! Your opinions on house-decorating are sound, but your opinions of people are rotten! Raymie does wag his tail. But the poor dear—— Longing for what he calls 'self-expression' and no training in anything except selling shoes. But he can sing. And some day when he gets away from Harry Haydock's patronage and ridicule, he'll do something fine."

Carol apologized for her superciliousness. She urged

Raymie, and warned the planners of "stunts," "We all want you to sing, Mr. Wutherspoon. You're the only famous actor I'm going to let appear on the stage tonight."

While Raymie blushed and admitted, "Oh, they don't want to hear me," he was clearing his throat, pulling his clean handkerchief farther out of his breast pocket, and thrusting his fingers between the buttons of his vest.

In her affection for Raymie's defender, in her desire to "discover artistic talent," Carol prepared to be delighted by the recital.

Raymie sang "Fly as a Bird," "Thou Art My Dove," and "When the Little Swallow Leaves Its Tiny Nest," all in a reasonably bad offertory tenor.

Carol was shuddering with the vicarious shame which sensitive people feel when they listen to an "elocutionist" being humorous, or to a precocious child publicly doing badly what no child should do at all. She wanted to laugh at the gratified importance in Raymie's half-shut eyes; she wanted to weep over the meek ambitiousness which clouded like an aura his pale face, flap ears, and sandy pompadour. She tried to look admiring, for the benefit of Miss Sherwin, that trusting admirer of all that was or conceivably could be the good, the true, and the beautiful.

At the end of the third ornithological lyric Miss Sherwin roused from her attitude of inspired vision and breathed to Carol, "My! That was sweet! Of course Raymond hasn't an unusually good voice, but don't you think he puts such a lot of feeling into it?"

Carol lied blackly and magnificently, but without originality: "Oh yes, I do think he has so much *feeling!*"

She saw that after the strain of listening in a cultured manner the audience had collapsed; had given up their last hope of being amused. She cried, "Now we're going to play an idiotic game which I learned in Chicago. You will have to take off your shoes, for a starter! After that you will probably break your knees and shoulder-blades."

Much attention and incredulity. A few eyebrows indicating a verdict that Doc Kennicott's bride was noisy and improper.

"I shall choose the most vicious, like Juanita Haydock and myself, as the shepherds. The rest of you are wolves. Your shoes are the sheep. The wolves go out into the hall. The shepherds scatter the sheep through this room, then turn off all the lights, and the wolves crawl in from the hall and in the darkness they try to get the shoes away from the shepherds—who are permitted to do anything except bite and use blackjacks. The wolves chuck the captured shoes out into the hall. No one excused! Come on! Shoes off!"

Every one looked at every one else and waited for every one else to begin.

Carol kicked off her silver slippers, and ignored the universal glance at her arches. The embarrassed but loyal Vida Sherwin unbuttoned her high black shoes. Ezra Stowbody cackled, "Well, you're a terror to old folks. You're like the gals I used to go horseback-riding with, back in the sixties. Ain't much accustomed to attending parties barefoot, but here goes!" With a whoop and a gallant jerk Ezra snatched off his elastic-sided Congress shoes.

The others giggled and followed.

When the sheep had been penned up, in the darkness the timorous wolves crept into the living-room, squealing, halting, thrown out of their habit of stolidity by the strangeness of advancing through nothingness toward a waiting foe, a mysterious foe which expanded and grew more menacing. The wolves peered to make out landmarks, they touched gliding arms which did not seem to be attached to a body, they quivered with a rapture of fear. Reality had vanished. A yelping squabble suddenly rose, then Juanita Haydock's high titter, and Guy Pollock's astonished, "Ouch! Quit! You're scalping me!"

Mrs. Luke Dawson galloped backward on stiff hands and knees into the safety of the lighted hallway, moaning, "I declare, I nev' was so upset in my life!" But the propriety was shaken out of her, and she delightedly continued to ejaculate "Nev' in my *life*" as she saw the living-room door opened by invisible hands and shoes hurling through it, as she heard from the darkness beyond the door a squawling, a bumping, a resolute "Here's a lot of shoes. Come on, you wolves. Ow! Y' would, would you!"

When Carol abruptly turned on the lights in the embattled living-room, half of the company were sitting back against the walls, where they had craftily remained throughout the engagement, but in the middle of the floor Kennicott was wrestling with Harry Haydock—their collars torn off, their hair in their eyes; and the owlish Mr. Julius Flickerbaugh was retreating from Juanita Haydock, and gulping with unaccustomed laughter. Guy Pollock's discreet brown scarf hung down his back. Young Rita Simons's net blouse had lost two buttons, and betrayed more of her delicious plump shoulder than was regarded as pure in Gopher Prairie. Whether by shock, disgust, joy of combat, or physical activity, all the party were freed from their years of social decorum. George Edwin Mott giggled; Luke Dawson twisted his beard; Mrs. Clark insisted, "I did too, Sam—I got a shoe —I never knew I could fight so terrible!"

Carol was certain that she was a great reformer.

She mercifully had combs, mirrors, brushes, needle and thread ready. She permitted them to restore the divine decency of buttons.

The grinning Bea brought down-stairs a pile of soft thick sheets of paper with designs of lotos blossoms, dragons, apes, in cobalt and crimson and gray, and patterns of purple birds flying among sea-green trees in the valleys of Nowhere.

"These," Carol announced, "are real Chinese masquerade costumes. I got them from an importing shop in Minneapolis. You are to put them on over your clothes, and please forget that you are Minnesotans, and turn into mandarins and coolies and—and samurai (isn't it?), and anything else you can think of."

While they were shyly rustling the paper costumes she disappeared. Ten minutes after she gazed down from the stairs upon grotesquely ruddy Yankee heads above Oriental robes, and cried to them, "The Princess Winky Poo salutes her court!"

As they looked up she caught their suspense of admiration. They saw an airy figure in trousers and coat of green brocade edged with gold; a high gold collar under a proud chin; black hair pierced with jade pins; a languid peacock fan in an out-stretched hand; eyes uplifted to a vision of pagoda towers. When she dropped her pose and smiled down she discovered Kennicott apoplectic with domestic pride—and gray Guy Pollock staring beseechingly. For a second she saw nothing in all the pink and brown mass of their faces save the hunger of the two men.

She shook off the spell and ran down. "We're going to have a real Chinese concert. Messrs. Pollock, Kennicott, and, well, Stowbody are drummers; the rest of us sing and play the fife."

The fifes were combs with tissue paper; the drums were tabourets and the sewing-table. Loren Wheeler, editor of the *Dauntless,* led the orchestra, with a ruler and a totally inaccurate sense of rhythm. The music was a reminiscence of tom-toms heard at circus fortune-telling tents or at the Minnesota State Fair, but the whole company pounded and puffed and whined in a sing-song, and looked rapturous.

Before they were quite tired of the concert Carol led them in a dancing procession to the dining-room, to blue bowls of chow mein, with Lichee nuts and ginger preserved in syrup.

None of them save that city-rounder Harry Haydock had heard of any Chinese dish except chop sooey. With agreeable doubt they ventured through the bamboo shoots into the golden fried noodles of the chow mein; and Dave Dyer did a not very humorous Chinese dance with Nat Hicks; and there was hubbub and contentment.

Carol relaxed, and found that she was shockingly tired. She had carried them on her thin shoulders. She could not keep it up. She longed for her father, that artist at creating hysterical parties. She thought of smoking a cigarette, to shock them, and dismissed the obscene thought before it was quite formed. She wondered whether they could for five minutes be coaxed to talk about something besides the winter top of Knute Stamquist's Ford, and what Al Tingley had said about his mother-in-law. She sighed, "Oh, let 'em alone. I've done enough." She crossed her trousered legs, and snuggled luxuriously above her saucer of ginger; she caught Pollock's congratulatory still smile, and thought well of herself for having thrown a rose light on the pallid lawyer; repented the heretical supposition that any male save her husband existed; jumped up to find Kennicott and whisper, "Happy, my lord? . . . No, it didn't cost much!"

"Best party this town ever saw. Only—— Don't cross your legs in that costume. Shows your knees too plain."

She was vexed. She resented his clumsiness. She returned to Guy Pollock and talked of Chinese religions—not that she knew anything whatever about Chinese religions, but he had read a book on the subject as, on lonely evenings in his office, he had read at least one book on every subject in the world. Guy's thin maturity was changing in her vision to flushed youth and they were roaming an island in the yellow sea of chatter when she realized that the guests were beginning that cough which indicated, in the universal instinctive language, that they desired to go home and go to bed.

While they asserted that it had been "the nicest party they'd ever seen—my! so clever and original," she smiled tremendously, shook hands, and cried many suitable things

regarding children, and being sure to wrap up warmly, and
Raymie's singing and Juanita Haydock's prowess at games.
Then she turned wearily to Kennicott in a house filled with
quiet and crumbs and shreds of Chinese costumes.

He was gurgling, "I tell you, Carrie, you certainly are a
wonder, and guess you're right about waking folks up. Now
you've showed 'em how, they won't go on having the same old
kind of parties and stunts and everything. Here! Don't touch
a thing! Done enough. Pop up to bed, and I'll clear up."

His wise surgeon's-hands stroked her shoulder, and her
irritation at his clumsiness was lost in his strength.

v

From the *Weekly Dauntless*:

> One of the most delightful social events of recent months
> was held Wednesday evening in the housewarming of Dr.
> and Mrs. Kennicott, who have completely redecorated their
> charming home on Poplar Street, and is now extremely nifty
> in modern color scheme. The doctor and his bride were at
> home to their numerous friends and a number of novelties
> in diversions were held, including a Chinese orchestra in
> original and genuine Oriental costumes, of which Ye Edi-
> tor was leader. Dainty refreshments were served in true Orien-
> tal style, and one and all voted a delightful time.

vi

The week after, the Chet Dashaways gave a party. The
circle of mourners kept its place all evening, and Dave Dyer
did the "stunt" of the Norwegian and the hen.

chapter 7

GOPHER PRAIRIE was digging in for the winter. Through
late November and all December it snowed daily; the
thermometer was at zero and might drop to twenty below, or
thirty. Winter is not a season in the North Middlewest; it is
an industry. Storm sheds were erected at every door. In

every block the householders, Sam Clark, the wealthy Mr. Dawson, all save asthmatic Ezra Stowbody who extravagantly hired a boy, were seen perilously staggering up ladders, carrying storm windows and screwing them to second-story jambs. While Kennicott put up his windows Carol danced inside the bedrooms and begged him not to swallow the screws, which he held in his mouth like an extraordinary set of external false teeth.

The universal sign of winter was the town handyman— Miles Bjornstam, a tall, thick, red-mustached bachelor, opinionated atheist, general-store arguer, cynical Santa Claus. Children loved him, and he sneaked away from work to tell them improbable stories of sea-faring and horse-trading and bears. The children's parents either laughed at him or hated him. He was the one democrat in town. He called both Lyman Cass the miller and the Finn homesteader from Lost Lake by their first names. He was known as "The Red Swede," and considered slightly insane.

Bjornstam could do anything with his hands—solder a pan, weld an automobile spring, soothe a frightened filly, tinker a clock, carve a Gloucester schooner which magically went into a bottle. Now, for a week, he was commissioner general of Gopher Prairie. He was the only person besides the repairman at Sam Clark's who understood plumbing. Everybody begged him to look over the furnace and the water-pipes. He rushed from house to house till after bedtime—ten o'clock. Icicles from burst water-pipes hung along the skirt of his brown dog-skin overcoat; his plush cap, which he never took off in the house, was a pulp of ice and coal-dust; his red hands were cracked to rawness; he chewed the stub of a cigar.

But he was courtly to Carol. He stooped to examine the furnace flues; he straightened, glanced down at her, and hemmed, "Got to fix your furnace, no matter what else I do."

The poorer houses of Gopher Prairie, where the services of Miles Bjornstam were a luxury—which included the shanty of Miles Bjornstam—were banked to the lower windows with earth and manure. Along the railroad the sections of snow fence, which had been stacked all summer in romantic wooden tents occupied by roving small boys, were set up to prevent drifts from covering the track.

The farmers came into town in home-made sleighs, with bed-quilts and hay piled in the rough boxes.

Fur coats, fur caps, fur mittens, overshoes buckling almost to the knees, gray knitted scarfs ten feet long, thick woolen

socks, canvas jackets lined with fluffy yellow wool like the
plumage of ducklings, moccasins, red flannel wristlets for the
blazing chapped wrists of boys—these protections against
winter were busily dug out of moth-ball-sprinkled drawers
and tar-bags in closets, and all over town small boys were
squealing, "Oh, there's my mittens!" or "Look at my shoe-
packs!" There is so sharp a division between the panting
summer and the stinging winter of the Northern plains that
they rediscovered with surprise and a feeling of heroism this
armor of an Arctic explorer.

Winter garments surpassed even personal gossip as the
topic at parties. It was good form to ask, "Put on your
heavies yet?" There were as many distinctions in wraps as in
motor cars. The lesser sort appeared in yellow and black
dogskin coats, but Kennicott was lordly in a long raccoon
ulster and a new seal cap. When the snow was too deep for
his motor he went off on country calls in a shiny, floral, steel-
tipped cutter, only his ruddy nose and his cigar emerging
from the fur.

Carol herself stirred Main Street by a loose coat of nutria.
Her finger-tips loved the silken fur.

Her liveliest activity now was organizing outdoor sports
in the motor-paralyzed town.

The automobile and bridge-whist had not only made more
evident the social divisions in Gopher Prairie but they had
also enfeebled the love of activity. It was so rich-looking to
sit and drive—and so easy. Skiing and sliding were "stupid"
and "old-fashioned." In fact, the village longed for the elegance of city recreations almost as much as the cities longed
for village sports; and Gopher Prairie took as much pride in
neglecting coasting as St. Paul—or New York—in going
coasting. Carol did inspire a successful skating-party in mid-
November. Plover Lake glistened in clear sweeps of gray-
green ice, ringing to the skates. On shore the ice-tipped reeds
clattered in the wind, and oak twigs with stubborn last
leaves hung against a milky sky. Harry Haydock did figure-
eights and Carol was certain that she had found the perfect
life. But when snow had ended the skating and she tried to
get up a moonlight sliding party, the matrons hesitated to
stir away from their radiators and their daily bridge-whist
imitations of the city. She had to nag them. They scooted
down a long hill on a bob-sled, they upset and got snow
down their necks, they shrieked that they would do it again
immediately—and they did not do it again at all.

She badgered another group into going skiing. They shouted and threw snowballs, and informed her that it was *such* fun, and they'd have another skiing expedition right away, and they jollily returned home and never thereafter left their manuals of bridge.

Carol was discouraged. She was grateful when Kennicott invited her to go rabbit-hunting in the woods. She waded down stilly cloisters between burnt stump and icy oak, through drifts marked with a million hieroglyphics of rabbit and mouse and bird. She squealed as he leaped on a pile of brush and fired at the rabbit which ran out. He belonged there, masculine in reefer and sweater and high-laced boots. That night she ate prodigiously of steak and fried potatoes; she produced electric sparks by touching his ear with her finger-tip; she slept twelve hours; and awoke to think how glorious was this brave land.

She rose to a radiance of sun on snow. Snug in her furs she trotted up-town. Frosted shingles smoked against a sky colored like flax-blossoms, sleigh-bells clinked, shouts of greeting were loud in the thin bright air, and everywhere was a rhythmic sound of wood-sawing. It was Saturday, and the neighbors' sons were getting up the winter fuel. Behind walls of corded wood in back yards their sawbucks stood in depressions scattered with canary-yellow flakes of sawdust. The frames of their buck-saws were cherry-red, the blades blued steel, and the fresh cut ends of the sticks—poplar, maple, iron-wood, birch—were marked with engraved rings of growth. The boys wore shoe-packs, blue flannel shirts with enormous pearl buttons, and mackinaws of crimson, lemon yellow, and foxy brown.

Carol cried "Fine day!" to the boys; she came in a glow to Howland & Gould's grocery, her collar white with frost from her breath; she bought a can of tomatoes as though it were Orient fruit; and returned home planning to surprise Kennicott with an omelet creole for dinner.

So brilliant was the snow-glare that when she entered the house she saw the door-knobs, the newspaper on the table, every white surface as dazzling mauve, and her head was dizzy in the pyrotechnic dimness. When her eyes had recovered she felt expanded, drunk with health, mistress of life. The world was so luminous that she sat down at her rickety little desk in the living-room to make a poem. (She got no farther than "The sky is bright, the sun is warm, there ne'er will be another storm.")

In the mid-afternoon of this same day Kennicott was called into the country. It was Bea's evening out—her evening for the Lutheran Dance. Carol was alone from three till midnight. She wearied of reading pure love stories in the magazines and sat by a radiator, beginning to brood.

Thus she chanced to discover that she had nothing to do.

II

She had, she meditated, passed through the novelty of seeing the town and meeting people, of skating and sliding and hunting. Bea was competent; there was no household labor except sewing and darning and gossipy assistance to Bea in bed-making. She couldn't satisfy her ingenuity in planning meals. At Dahl & Oleson's Meat Market you didn't give orders—you woefully inquired whether there was anything today besides steak and pork and ham. The cuts of beef were not cuts. They were hacks. Lamb chops were as exotic as sharks' fins. The meat-dealers shipped their best to the city, with its higher prices.

In all the shops there was the same lack of choice. She could not find a glass-headed picture-nail in town; she did not hunt for the sort of veiling she wanted—she took what she could get; and only at Howland & Gould's was there such a luxury as canned asparagus. Routine care was all she could devote to the house. Only by such fussing as the Widow Bogart's could she make it fill her time.

She could not have outside employment. To the village doctor's wife it was taboo.

She was a woman with a working brain and no work.

There were only three things which she could do: Have children; start her career of reforming; or become so definitely a part of the town that she would be fulfilled by the activities of church and study-club and bridge-parties.

Children, yes, she wanted them, but—— She was not quite ready. She had been embarrassed by Kennicott's frankness, but she agreed with him that in the insane condition of civilization, which made the rearing of citizens more costly and perilous than any other crime, it was inadvisable to have children till he had made more money. She was sorry—— Perhaps he had made all the mystery of love a mechanical cautiousness but—— She fled from the thought with a dubious, "Some day."

Her "reforms," her impulses toward beauty in raw Main

Street, they had become indistinct. But she would set them going now. She would! She swore it with soft fist beating the edges of the radiator. And at the end of all her vows she had no notion as to when and where the crusade was to begin.

Become an authentic part of the town? She began to think with unpleasant lucidity. She reflected that she did not know whether the people liked her. She had gone to the women at afternoon-coffees, to the merchants in their stores, with so many outpouring comments and whimsies that she hadn't given them a chance to betray their opinions of her. The men smiled—but did they like her? She was lively among the women—but was she one of them? She could not recall many times when she had been admitted to the whispering of scandal which is the secret chamber of Gopher Prairie conversation.

She was poisoned with doubt, as she drooped up to bed.

Next day, through her shopping, her mind sat back and observed. Dave Dyer and Sam Clark were as cordial as she had been fancying; but wasn't there an impersonal abruptness in the "H' are yuh?" of Chet Dashaway? Howland the grocer was curt. Was that merely his usual manner?

"It's infuriating to have to pay attention to what people think. In St. Paul I didn't care. But here I'm spied on. They're watching me. I mustn't let it make me self-conscious," she coaxed herself—overstimulated by the drug of thought, and offensively on the defensive.

III

A thaw which stripped the snow from the sidewalks; a ringing iron night when the lakes could be heard booming; a clear roistering morning. In tam o'shanter and tweed skirt Carol felt herself a college junior going out to play hockey. She wanted to whoop, her legs ached to run. On the way home from shopping she yielded, as a pup would have yielded. She galloped down a block and as she jumped from a curb across a welter of slush, she gave a student "Yippee!"

She saw that in a window three old women were gasping. Their triple glare was paralyzing. Across the street, at another window, the curtain had secretively moved. She stopped, walked on sedately, changed from the girl Carol into Mrs. Dr. Kennicott.

She never again felt quite young enough and defiant enough

and free enough to run and halloo in the public streets; and
it was as a Nice Married Woman that she attended the next
weekly bridge of the Jolly Seventeen.

IV

The Jolly Seventeen (the membership of which ranged
from fourteen to twenty-six) was the social cornice of
Gopher Prairie. It was the country club, the diplomatic set,
the St. Cecilia, the Ritz oval room, the Club de Vingt. To belong to it was to be "in." Though its membership partly coin-
cided with that of the Thanatopsis study club, the Jolly
Seventeen as a separate entity guffawed at the Thanatopsis,
and considered it middle-class and even "highbrow."

Most of the Jolly Seventeen were young married women,
with their husbands as associate members. Once a week they
had a women's afternoon-bridge; once a month the husbands joined them for supper and evening-bridge; twice a year
they had dances at I. O. O. F. Hall. Then the town exploded.
Only at the annual balls of the Firemen and of the Eastern
Star was there such prodigality of chiffon scarfs and tan-
going and heart-burnings, and these rival institutions were
not select—hired girls attended the Firemen's Ball, with sec-
tion-hands and laborers. Ella Stowbody had once gone to a
Jolly Seventeen Soirée in the village hack, hitherto confined to chief mourners at funerals; and Harry Haydock and
Dr. Terry Gould always appeared in the town's only speci-
mens of evening clothes.

The afternoon-bridge of the Jolly Seventeen which followed
Carol's lonely doubting was held at Juanita Haydock's new
concrete bungalow, with its door of polished oak and beveled
plate-glass, jar of ferns in the plastered hall, and in the
living-room, a fumed oak Morris chair, sixteen color-prints,
and a square varnished table with a mat made of cigar-ribbons
on which was one Illustrated Gift Edition and one pack of
cards in a burnt-leather case.

Carol stepped into a sirocco of furnace heat. They were
already playing. Despite her flabby resolves she had not yet
learned bridge. She was winningly apologetic about it to
Juanita, and ashamed that she should have to go on being
apologetic.

Mrs. Dave Dyer, a sallow woman with a thin prettiness,
devoted to experiments in religious cults, illnesses, and scan-
dal-bearing, shook her finger at Carol and trilled, "You're a

naughty one! I don't believe you appreciate the honor, when you got into the Jolly Seventeen so easy!"

Mrs. Chet Dashaway nudged her neighbor at the second table. But Carol kept up the appealing bridal manner so far as possible. She twittered, "You're perfectly right. I'm a lazy thing. I'll make Will start teaching me this very evening." Her supplication had all the sound of birdies in the nest, and Easter church-bells, and frosted Christmas cards. Internally she snarled, "That ought to be saccharine enough." She sat in the smallest rocking-chair, a model of Victorian modesty. But she saw or she imagined that the women who had gurgled at her so welcomingly when she had first come to Gopher Prairie were nodding at her brusquely.

During the pause after the first game she petitioned Mrs. Jackson Elder, "Don't you think we ought to get up another bob-sled party soon?"

"It's so cold when you get dumped in the snow," said Mrs. Elder, indifferently.

"I hate snow down my neck," volunteered Mrs. Dave Dyer, with an unpleasant look at Carol and, turning her back, she bubbled at Rita Simons, "Dearie, won't you run in this evening? I've got the loveliest new Butterick pattern I want to show you."

Carol crept back to her chair. In the fervor of discussing the game they ignored her. She was not used to being a wallflower. She struggled to keep from oversensitiveness, from becoming unpopular by the sure method of believing that she was unpopular; but she hadn't much reserve of patience, and at the end of the second game, when Ella Stowbody sniffily asked her, "Are you going to send to Minneapolis for your dress for the next soirée—heard you were," Carol said "Don't know yet" with unnecessary sharpness.

She was relieved by the admiration with which the *jeune fille* Rita Simons looked at the steel buckles on her pumps; but she resented Mrs. Howland's tart demand, "Don't you find that new couch of yours is too broad to be practical?" She nodded, then shook her head, and touchily left Mrs. Howland to get out of it any meaning she desired. Immediately she wanted to make peace. She was close to simpering in the sweetness with which she addressed Mrs. Howland: "I think that is the prettiest display of beef-tea your husband has in his store."

"Oh yes, Gopher Prairie isn't so much behind the times," gibed Mrs. Howard. Some one giggled.

Their rebuffs made her haughty; her haughtiness irritated them to franker rebuffs; they were working up to a state of painfully righteous war when they were saved by the coming of food.

Though Juanita Haydock was highly advanced in the matters of finger-bowls, doilies, and bath-mats, her "refreshments" were typical of all the afternoon-coffees. Juanita's best friends, Mrs. Dyer and Mrs. Dashaway, passed large dinner plates, each with a spoon, a fork, and a coffee cup without saucer. They apologized and discussed the afternoon's game as they passed through the thicket of women's feet. Then they distributed hot buttered rolls, coffee poured from an enamelware pot, stuffed olives, potato salad, and angel's-food cake. There was, even in the most strictly conforming Gopher Prairie circles, a certain option as to collations. The olives need not be stuffed. Doughnuts were in some houses well thought of as a substitute for the hot buttered rolls. But there was in all the town no heretic save Carol who omitted angel's-food.

They ate enormously. Carol had a suspicion that the thriftier housewives made the afternoon treat do for evening supper.

She tried to get back into the current. She edged over to Mrs. McGanum. Chunky, amiable, young Mrs. McGanum, with her breast and arms of a milkmaid, and her loud delayed laugh which burst startlingly from a sober face, was the daughter of old Dr. Westlake, and the wife of Westlake's partner, Dr. McGanum. Kennicott asserted that Westlake and McGanum and their contaminated families were tricky, but Carol had found them gracious. She asked for friendliness by crying to Mrs. McGanum, "How is the baby's throat now?" and she was attentive while Mrs. McGanum rocked and knitted and placidly described symptoms.

Vida Sherwin came in after school, with Miss Ethel Villets, the town librarian. Miss Sherwin's optimistic presence gave Carol more confidence. She talked. She informed the circle, "I drove almost down to Wahkeenyan with Will, a few days ago. Isn't the country lovely! And I do admire the Scandinavian farmers down there so: their big red barns and silos and milking-machines and everything. Do you all know that lonely Lutheran church, with the tin-covered spire, that stands out alone on a hill? It's so bleak; somehow it seems so brave. I do think the Scandinavians are the hardiest and best people——"

"Oh, do you *think* so?" protested Mrs. Jackson Elder. "My husband says the Svenskas that work in the planing-mill are perfectly terrible—so silent and cranky, and so selfish, the way they keep demanding raises. If they had their way they'd simply ruin the business."

"Yes, and they're simply *ghastly* hired girls!" wailed Mrs. Dave Dyer. "I swear, I work myself to skin and bone trying to please my hired girls—when I can get them! I do everything in the world for them. They can have their gentleman friends call on them in the kitchen any time, and they get just the same to eat as we do, if there's any left over, and I practically never jump on them."

Juanita Haydock rattled, "They're ungrateful, all that class of people. I do think the domestic problem is simply becoming awful. I don't know what the country's coming to, with these Scandahoofian clodhoppers demanding every cent you can save, and so ignorant and impertinent, and on my word, demanding bath-tubs and everything—as if they weren't mighty good and lucky at home if they got a bath in the wash-tub."

They were off, riding hard. Carol thought of Bea and way-laid them:

"But isn't it possibly the fault of the mistresses if the maids are ungrateful? For generations we've given them the leavings of food, and holes to live in. I don't want to boast, but I must say I don't have much trouble with Bea. She's so friendly. The Scandinavians are sturdy and honest——"

Mrs. Dave Dyer snapped, "Honest? Do you call it honest to hold us up for every cent of pay they can get? I can't say that I've had any of them steal anything (though you might call it stealing to eat so much that a roast of beef hardly lasts three days), but just the same I don't intend to let them think they can put anything over on *me!* I always make them pack and unpack their trunks down-stairs, right under my eyes, and then I know they aren't being tempted to dishonesty by any slackness on *my* part!"

"How much do the maids get here?" Carol ventured.

Mrs. B. J. Gougerling, wife of the banker, stated in a shocked manner, "Any place from three-fifty to five-fifty a week! I know positively that Mrs. Clark, after swearing that she wouldn't weaken and encourage them in their outrageous demands, went and paid five-fifty—think of it! practically a dollar a day for unskilled work and, of course, her food and room and a chance to do her own washing right in with the rest of the wash. *How much do you pay, Mrs. Kennicott?*"

"Yes! How much do you pay?" insisted half a dozen.

"W-why, I pay six a week," she feebly confessed.

They gasped. Juanita protested, "Don't you think it's hard on the rest of us when you pay so much?" Juanita's demand was re-inforced by the universal glower.

Carol was angry. "I don't care! A maid has one of the hardest jobs on earth. She works from ten to eighteen hours a day. She has to wash slimy dishes and dirty clothes. She tends the children and runs to the door with wet chapped hands and——"

Mrs. Dave Dyer broke into Carol's peroration with a furious, "That's all very well, but believe me, I do those things myself when I'm without a maid—and that's a good share of the time for a person that isn't willing to yield and pay exorbitant wages!"

Carol was retorting, "But a maid does it for strangers, and all she gets out of it is the pay——"

Their eyes were hostile. Four of them were talking at once. Vida Sherwin's dictatorial voice cut through, took control of the revolution:

"Tut, tut, tut, tut! What angry passions—and what an idiotic discussion! All of you getting too serious. Stop it! Carol Kennicott, you're probably right, but you're too much ahead of the times. Juanita, quit looking so belligerent. What is this, a card party or a hen fight? Carol, you stop admiring yourself as the Joan of Arc of the hired girls, or I'll spank you. You come over here and talk libraries with Ethel Villets. Boooooo! If there's any more pecking, I'll take charge of the hen roost myself!"

They all laughed artificially, and Carol obediently "talked libraries."

A small-town bungalow, the wives of a village doctor and a village dry-goods merchant, a provincial teacher, a colloquial brawl over paying a servant a dollar more a week. Yet this insignificance echoed cellar-plots and cabinet meetings and labor conferences in Persia and Prussia, Rome and Boston, and the orators who deemed themselves international leaders were but the raised voices of a billion Juanitas denouncing a million Carols, with a hundred thousand Vida Sherwins trying to shoo away the storm.

Carol felt guilty. She devoted herself to admiring the spinsterish Miss Villets—and immediately committed another offense against the laws of decency.

"We haven't seen you at the library yet," Miss Villets reproved.

"I've wanted to run in so much but I've been getting settled and—— I'll probably come in so often you'll get tired of me! I hear you have such a nice library."

"There are many who like it. We have two thousand more books than Wakamin."

"Isn't that fine. I'm sure you are largely responsible. I've had some experience, in St. Paul."

"So I have been informed. Not that I entirely approve of library methods in these large cities. So careless, letting tramps and all sorts of dirty persons practically sleep in the reading-rooms."

"I know, but the poor souls—— Well, I'm sure you will agree with me in one thing: The chief task of a librarian is to get people to read."

"You feel so? My feeling, Mrs. Kennicott, and I am merely quoting the librarian of a very large college, is that the first duty of the *conscientious* librarian is to preserve the books."

"Oh!" Carol repented her "Oh." Miss Villets stiffened, and attacked:

"It may be all very well in cities, where they have unlimited funds, to let nasty children ruin books and just deliberately tear them up, and fresh young men take more books out than they are entitled to by the regulations, but I'm never going to permit it in this library!"

"What if some children are destructive? They learn to read. Books are cheaper than minds."

"Nothing is cheaper than the minds of some of these children that come in and bother me simply because their mothers don't keep them home where they belong. Some librarians may choose to be so wishy-washy and turn their libraries into nursing-homes and kindergartens, but as long as I'm in charge, the Gopher Prairie library is going to be quiet and decent, and the books well kept!"

Carol saw that the others were listening, waiting for her to be objectionable. She flinched before their dislike. She hastened to smile in agreement with Miss Villets, to glance publicly at her wrist-watch, to warble that it was "so late— have to hurry home—husband—such nice party—maybe you were right about maids, prejudiced because Bea so nice—such perfectly divine angel's-food, Mrs. Haydock must give me the recipe—good-by, such happy party——"

She walked home. She reflected, "It was my fault. I was touchy. And I opposed them so much. Only—— I can't! I can't be one of them if I must damn all the maids toiling in filthy kitchens, all the ragged hungry children. And these women are to be my arbiters, the rest of my life!"

She ignored Bea's call from the kitchen; she ran up-stairs to the unfrequented guest-room; she wept in terror, her body a pale arc as she knelt beside a cumbrous black-walnut bed, beside a puffy mattress covered with a red quilt, in a shuttered and airless room.

chapter 8

DON'T I, in looking for things to do, show that I'm not attentive enough to Will? Am I impressed enough by his work? I will be. Oh, I will be. If I can't be one of the town, if I must be an outcast——"

When Kennicott came home she bustled, "Dear, you must tell me a lot more about your cases. I want to know. I want to understand."

"Sure. You bet." And he went down to fix the furnace.

At supper she asked, "For instance, what did you do today?"

"Do today? How do you mean?"

"Medically. I want to understand——"

"Today? Oh, there wasn't much of anything: couple chumps with bellyaches, and a sprained wrist, and a fool woman that thinks she wants to kill herself because her husband doesn't like her and—— Just routine work."

"But the unhappy woman doesn't sound routine!"

"Her? Just case of nerves. You can't do much with these marriage mix-ups."

"But dear, *please,* will you tell me about the next case that you do think is interesting?"

"Sure. You bet. Tell you about anything that—— Say, that's pretty good salmon. Get it at Howland's?"

II

Four days after the Jolly Seventeen débâcle Vida Sherwin called and casually blew Carol's world to pieces.

"May I come in and gossip a while?" she said, with such excess of bright innocence that Carol was uneasy. Vida took off her furs with a bounce, she sat down as though it was a gymnasium exercise, she flung out:

"Feel disgracefully good, this weather! Raymond Wutherspoon says if he had my energy he'd be a grand opera singer. I always think this climate is the finest in the world, and my friends are the dearest people in the world, and my work is the most essential thing in the world. Probably I fool myself. But I know one thing for certain: You're the pluckiest little idiot in the world."

"And so you are about to flay me alive." Carol was cheerful about it.

"Am I? Perhaps. I've been wondering—I know that the third party to a squabble is often the most to blame: the one who runs between A and B having a beautiful time telling each of them what the other has said. But I want you to take a big part in vitalizing Gopher Prairie and so—— Such a very unique opportunity and—— Am I silly?"

"I know what you mean. I was too abrupt at the Jolly Seventeen."

"It isn't that. Matter of fact, I'm glad you told them some wholesome truths about servants. (Though perhaps you were just a bit tactless.) It's bigger than that. I wonder if you understand that in a secluded community like this every newcomer is on test? People cordial to her but watching her all the time. I remember when a Latin teacher came here from Wellesley, they resented her broad A. Were sure it was affected. Of course they have discussed you——"

"Have they talked about me much?"

"My dear!"

"I always feel as though I walked around in a cloud, looking out at others but not being seen. I feel so inconspicuous and so normal—so normal that there's nothing about me to discuss. I can't realize that Mr. and Mrs. Haydock must gossip about me." Carol was working up a small passion of distaste. "And I don't like it. It makes me crawly to think of their daring to talk over all I do and say. Pawing me over! I resent it. I hate——"

"Wait, child! Perhaps they resent some things in you. I want you to try and be impersonal. They'd paw over anybody who came in new. Didn't you, with newcomers in College?"

"Yes."

"Well then! Will you be impersonal? I'm paying you the compliment of supposing that you can be. I want you to be big enough to help me make this town worth while."

"I'll be as impersonal as cold boiled potatoes. (Not that I shall ever be able to help you 'make the town worth while.') What do they say about me? Really. I want to know."

"Of course the illiterate ones resent your references to anything farther away than Minneapolis. They're so suspicious—that's it, suspicious. And some think you dress too well."

"Oh, they do, do they! Shall I dress in gunny-sacking to suit them?"

"Please! Are you going to be a baby?"

"I'll be good," sulkily.

"You certainly will, or I won't tell you one single thing. You must understand this: I'm not asking you to change yourself. Just want you to know what they think. You must do that, no matter how absurd their prejudices are, if you're going to handle them. Is it your ambition to make this a better town, or isn't it?"

"I don't know whether it is or not!"

"Why-why—— Tut, tut, now, of course it is! Why, I depend on you. You're a born reformer."

"I am not—not any more!"

"Of course you are."

"Oh, if I really could help—— So they think I'm affected?"

"My lamb, they do! Now don't say they're nervy. After all, Gopher Prairie standards are as reasonable to Gopher Prairie as Lake Shore Drive standards are to Chicago. And there's more Gopher Prairies than there are Chicagos. Or Londons. And—— I'll tell you the whole story: They think you're showing off when you say 'American' instead of 'Ammurrican.' They think you're too frivolous. Life's so serious to them that they can't imagine any kind of laughter except Juanita's snortling. Ethel Villets was sure you were patronizing her when——"

"Oh, I was not!"

"——you talked about encouraging reading; and Mrs. Elder thought you were patronizing when you said she had 'such a pretty little car.' She thinks it's an enormous car! And some of the merchants say you're too flip when you talk to them in the store and——"

"Poor me, when I was trying to be friendly!"

"——every housewife in town is doubtful about your being so chummy with your Bea. All right to be kind, but they say you act as though she were your cousin. (Wait now! There's plenty more.) And they think you were eccentric in furnishing this room—they think the broad couch and that Japanese dingus are absurd. (Wait! I know they're silly.) And I guess I've heard a dozen criticize you because you don't go to church oftener and——"

"I can't stand it—I can't bear to realize that they've been saying all these things while I've been going about so happily and liking them. I wonder if you ought to have told me? It will make me self-conscious."

"I wonder the same thing. Only answer I can get is the old saw about knowledge being power. And some day you'll see how absorbing it is to have power, even here; to control the town—— Oh, I'm a crank. But I do like to see things moving."

"It hurts. It makes these people seem so beastly and treacherous, when I've been perfectly natural with them. But let's have it all. What did they say about my Chinese housewarming party?"

"Why, uh——"

"Go on. Or I'll make up worse things than anything you can tell me."

"They did enjoy it. But I guess some of them felt you were showing off—pretending that your husband is richer than he is."

"I can't—— Their meanness of mind is beyond any horrors I could imagine. They really thought that I—— And you want to 'reform' people like that when dynamite is so cheap? Who dared to say that? The rich or the poor?"

"Fairly well assorted."

"Can't they at least understand me well enough to see that though I might be affected and culturine, at least I simply couldn't commit that other kind of vulgarity? If they must know, you may tell them, with my compliments, that Will makes about four thousand a year, and the party cost half of what they probably thought it did. Chinese things are not very expensive, and I made my own costume——"

"Stop it! Stop beating me! I know all that. What they

meant was: they felt you were starting dangerous competition
by giving a party such as most people here can't afford. Four
thousand is a pretty big income for this town."

"I never thought of starting competition. Will you believe
that it was in all love and friendliness that I tried to give
them the gayest party I could? It was foolish; it was childish
and noisy. But I did mean it so well."

"I know, of course. And it certainly is unfair of them to
make fun of your having that Chinese food—chow men, was
it?—and to laugh about your wearing those pretty trousers——"

Carol sprang up, whimpering, "Oh, they didn't do that!
They didn't poke fun at my feast, that I ordered so carefully
for them! And my little Chinese costume that I was so happy
making—I made it secretly, to surprise them. And they've
been ridiculing it, all this while!"

She was huddled on the couch.

Vida was stroking her hair, muttering, "I shouldn't——"

Shrouded in shame, Carol did not know when Vida slipped
away. The clock's bell, at half past five, aroused her. "I must
get hold of myself before Will comes. I hope he never knows
what a fool his wife is. . . . Frozen, sneering, horrible hearts."

Like a very small, very lonely girl she trudged up-stairs,
slow step by step, her feet dragging, her hand on the rail.
It was not her husband to whom she wanted to run for protection—it was her father, her smiling understanding father,
dead these twelve years.

III

Kennicott was yawning, stretched in the largest chair, between the radiator and a small kerosene stove.

Cautiously, "Will dear, I wonder if the people here don't
criticize me sometimes? They must. I mean: if they ever do,
you mustn't let it bother you."

"Criticize you? Lord, I should say not. They all keep telling me you're the swellest girl they ever saw."

"Well, I've just fancied—— The merchants probably think
I'm too fussy about shopping. I'm afraid I bore Mr. Dashaway and Mr. Howland and Mr. Ludelmeyer."

"I can tell you how that is. I didn't want to speak of it,
but since you've brought it up: Chet Dashaway probably
resents the fact that you got this new furniture down in the
Cities instead of here. I didn't want to raise any objection at

the time but——— After all, I make my money here and they naturally expect me to spend it here."

"If Mr. Dashaway will kindly tell me how any civilized person can furnish a room out of the mortuary pieces that he calls———" She remembered. She said meekly, "But I understand."

"And Howland and Ludelmeyer——— Oh, you've probably handed 'em a few roasts for the bum stocks they carry, when you just meant to jolly 'em. But rats, what do we care! This is an independent town, not like these Eastern holes where you have to watch your step all the time, and live up to fool demands and social customs, and a lot of old tabbies always busy criticizing. Everybody's free here to do what he wants to." He said it with a flourish, and Carol perceived that he believed it. She turned her breath of fury into a yawn.

"By the way, Carrie, while we're talking of this: Of course I like to keep independent, and I don't believe in this business of binding yourself to trade with the man that trades with you unless you really want to, but same time: I'd be just as glad if you dealt with Jenson or Ludelmeyer as much as you can, instead of Howland & Gould, who go to Dr. Gould every last time, and the whole tribe of 'em the same way. I don't see why I sould be paying out my good money for groceries and having them pass it on to Terry Gould!"

"I've gone to Howland & Gould because they're better, and cleaner."

"I know. I don't mean cut them out entirely. Course Jenson is tricky—give you short weight—and Ludelmeyer is a shiftless old Dutch hog. But same time, I mean let's keep the trade in the family whenever it is convenient, see how I mean?"

"I see."

"Well, guess it's about time to turn in."

He yawned, went out to look at the thermometer, slammed the door, patted her head, unbuttoned his waistcoat, yawned, wound the clock, went down to look at the furnace, yawned, and clumped up-stairs to bed, casually scratching his thick woolen undershirt.

Till he bawled, "Aren't you ever coming up to bed?" she sat unmoving.

chapter 9

S HE had tripped into the meadow to teach the lambs a
pretty educational dance and found that the lambs were
wolves. There was no way out between their pressing gray
shoulders. She was surrounded by fangs and sneering eyes.

She could not go on enduring the hidden derision. She
wanted to flee. She wanted to hide in the generous indifference
of cities. She practised saying to Kennicott, "Think perhaps
I'll run down to St. Paul for a few days." But she could not
trust herself to say it carelessly; could not abide his certain
questioning.

Reform the town? All she wanted was to be tolerated!

She could not look directly at people. She flushed and
winced before citizens who a week ago had been amusing
objects of study, and in their good-mornings she heard a
cruel sniggering.

She encountered Juanita Haydock at Ole Jenson's grocery.
She besought, "Oh, how do you do! Heavens, what beautiful
celery that is!"

"Yes, doesn't it look fresh. Harry simply has to have his
celery on Sunday, drat the man!"

Carol hastened out of the shop exulting, "She didn't make
fun of me. . . . Did she?"

In a week she had recovered from consciousness of in-
security, of shame and whispering notoriety, but she kept her
habit of avoiding people. She walked the streets with her
head down. When she spied Mrs. McGanum or Mrs. Dyer
ahead she crossed over with an elaborate pretense of looking
at a billboard. Always she was acting, for the benefit of
every one she saw—and for the benefit of the ambushed
leering eyes which she did not see.

She perceived that Vida Sherwin had told the truth. Whether
she entered a store, or swept the back porch, or stood at the
bay-window in the living-room, the village peeped at her.
Once she had swung along the street triumphant in making
a home. Now she glanced at each house, and felt, when she

100

was safely home, that she had won past a thousand enemies armed with ridicule. She told herself that her sensitiveness was preposterous, but daily she was thrown into panic. She saw curtains slide back into innocent smoothness. Old women who had been entering their houses slipped out again to stare at her—in the wintry quiet she could hear them tiptoeing on their porches. When she had for a blessed hour forgotten the searchlight, when she was scampering through a chill dusk, happy in yellow windows against gray night, her heart checked as she realized that a head covered with a shawl was thrust up over a snow-tipped bush to watch her.

She admitted that she was taking herself too seriously; that villagers gape at every one. She became placid, and thought well of her philosophy. But next morning she had a shock of shame as she entered Ludelmeyér's. The grocer, his clerk, and neurotic Mrs. Dave Dyer had been giggling about something. They halted, looked embarrassed, babbled about onions. Carol felt guilty. That evening when Kennicott took her to call on the crochety Lyman Casses, their hosts seemed flustered at their arrival. Kennicott jovially hooted, "What makes you so hang-dog, Lym?" The Casses tittered feebly.

Except Dave Dyer, Sam Clark, and Raymie Wutherspoon, there were no merchants of whose welcome Carol was certain. She knew that she read mockery into greetings but she could not control her suspicion, could not rise from her psychic collapse. She alternately raged and flinched at the superiority of the merchants. They did not know that they were being rude, but they meant to have it understood that they were prosperous and "not scared of no doctor's wife." They often said, "One man's good as another—and a darn sight better." This motto, however, they did not commend to farmer customers who had had crop failures. The Yankee merchants were crabbed; and Ole Jenson, Ludelmeyer, and Gus Dahl, from the "Old Country," wished to be taken for Yankees. James Madison Howland, born in New Hampshire, and Ole Jenson, born in Sweden, both proved that they were free American citizens by grunting, "I don't know whether I got any or not," or "Well, you can't expect me to get it delivered by noon."

It was good form for the customers to fight back. Juanita Haydock cheerfully jabbered, "You have it there by twelve or I'll snatch that fresh delivery-boy bald-headed." But Carol had never been able to play the game of friendly rudeness;

and now she was certain that she never would learn it. She formed the cowardly habit of going to Axel Egge's.

Axel was not respectable and rude. He was still a foreigner, and he expected to remain one. His manner was heavy and uninterrogative. His establishment was more fantastic than any cross-roads store. No one save Axel himself could find anything. A part of the assortment of children's stockings was under a blanket on a shelf, a part in a tin ginger-snap box, the rest heaped like a nest of black-cotton snakes upon a flour-barrel which was surrounded by brooms, Norwegian Bibles, dried cod for *ludfisk*, boxes of apricots, and a pair and a half of lumbermen's rubber-footed boots. The place was crowded with Scandinavian farmwives, standing aloof in shawls and ancient fawn-colored leg o' mutton jackets, awaiting the return of their lords. They spoke Norwegian or Swedish, and looked at Carol uncomprehendingly. They were a relief to her—they were not whispering that she was a poseur.

But what she told herself was that Axel Egge's was "so picturesque and romantic."

It was in the matter of clothes that she was most self-conscious.

When she dared to go shopping in her new checked suit with the black-embroidered sulphur collar, she had as good as invited all of Gopher Prairie (which interested itself in nothing so intimately as in new clothes and the cost thereof) to investigate her. It was a smart suit with lines unfamiliar to the dragging yellow and pink frocks of the town. The Widow Bogart's stare, from her porch, indicated, "Well I never saw anything like that before!" Mrs. McGanum stopped Carol at the notions shop to hint, "My, that's a nice suit—wasn't it terribly expensive?" The gang of boys in front of the drug store commented, "Hey, Pudgie, play you a game of checkers on that dress." Carol could not endure it. She drew her fur coat over the suit and hastily fastened the buttons, while the boys snickered.

II

No group angered her quite so much as these staring young roués.

She had tried to convince herself that the village, with its fresh air, its lakes for fishing and swimming, was healthier than the artificial city. But she was sickened by glimpses of the gang of boys from fourteen to twenty who loafed before Dyer's Drug Store, smoking cigarettes, displaying "fancy" shoes and purple ties and coats of diamond-shaped buttons, whistling the Hoochi-Koochi and catcalling, "Oh, you baby-doll" at every passing girl.

She saw them playing pool in the stinking room behind Del Snafflin's barber shop, and shaking dice in "The Smoke House," and gathered in a snickering knot to listen to the "juicy stories" of Bert Tybee, the bartender of the Minniemashie House. She heard them smacking moist lips over every love-scene at the Rosebud Movie Palace. At the counter of the Greek Confectionery Parlor, while they ate dreadful messes of decayed bananas, acid cherries, whipped cream, and gelat-inous ice-cream, they screamed to one another, "Hey, lemme 'lone," "Quit dog-gone you, looka what you went and done, you almost spilled my glass swater," "Like hell I did," "Hey, gol darn your hide, don't you go sticking your coffin nail in my i-scream," "Oh you Batty, how juh like dancing with Tillie McGuire, last night? Some squeezing, heh, kid?"

By diligent consultation of American fiction she discovered that this was the only virile and amusing manner in which boys could function; that boys who were not compounded of the gutter and the mining-camp were mollycoddles and un-happy. She had taken this for granted. She had studied the boys pityingly, but impersonally. It had not occurred to her that they might touch her.

Now she was aware that they knew all about her; that they were waiting for some affectation over which they could guffaw. No schoolgirl passed their observation-posts more flushingly than did Mrs. Dr. Kennicott. In shame she knew that they glanced appraisingly at her snowy overshoes, spec-ulating about her legs. Theirs were not young eyes—there was no youth in all the town, she agonized. They were born old, grim and old and spying and censorious.

She cried again that their youth was senile and cruel on the day when she overheard Cy Bogart and Earl Haydock.

Cyrus N. Bogart, son of the righteous widow who lived across the alley, was at this time a boy of fourteen or fifteen. Carol had already seen quite enough of Cy Bogart. On her first evening in Gopher Prairie Cy had appeared at the head of a "charivari," banging immensely upon a dis-carded automobile fender. His companions were yelping in imitation of coyotes. Kennicott had felt rather complimented; had gone out and distributed a dollar. But Cy was a capitalist in charivaris. He returned with an entirely new group, and this time there were three automobile fenders and a carnival rattle. When Kennicott again interrupted his shaving, Cy piped, "Naw, you got to give us two dollars," and he got it. A week later Cy rigged a tic-tac to a window of the living-room, and the tattoo out of the darkness frightened Carol into screaming. Since then, in four months, she had beheld Cy hanging a cat, stealing melons, throwing tomatoes at the Kennicott house, and making ski-tracks across the lawn, and had heard him explaining the mysteries of generation, with great audibility and dismaying knowledge. He was, in fact, a museum specimen of what a small town, a well-disciplined public school, a tradition of hearty humor, and a pious mother could produce from the material of a courageous and ingenious mind.

Carol was afraid of him. Far from protesting when he set his mongrel on a kitten, she worked hard at not seeing him.

The Kennicott garage was a shed littered with paint-cans, tools, a lawn-mower, and ancient wisps of hay. Above it was a loft which Cy Bogart and Earl Haydock, young brother of Harry, used as a den, for smoking, hiding from whippings, and planning secret societies. They climbed to it by a ladder on the alley side of the shed.

This morning of late January, two or three weeks after Vida's revelations, Carol had gone into the stable-garage to find a hammer. Snow softened her step. She heard voices in the loft above her:

"Ah gee, lez—oh, lez go down the lake and swipe some mushrats out of somebody's traps," Cy was yawning.

"And get our ears beat off!" grumbled Earl Haydock.

"Gosh, these cigarettes are dandy. 'Member when we were just kids, and used to smoke corn-silk and hayseed?"

"Yup. Gosh!"

Spit. Silence.

"Say Earl, ma says if you chew tobacco you get consumption."

"Aw rats, your old lady is a crank."

"Yuh, that's so." Pause. "But she says she knows a fella that did."

"Aw, gee whiz, didn't Doc Kennicott used to chew tobacco all the time before he married this-here girl from the Cities? He used to spit—— Gee! Some shot! He could hit a tree ten feet off."

This was news to the girl from the Cities.

"Say, how is she?" continued Earl.

"Huh? How's who?"

"You know who I mean, smarty."

A tussle, a thumping of loose boards, silence, weary narration from Cy:

"Mrs. Kennicott? Oh, she's all right, I guess." Relief to Carol, below. "She gimme a hunk o' cake, one time. But Ma says she's stuck-up as hell. Ma's always talking about her. Ma says if Mrs. Kennicott thought as much about the doc as she does about her clothes, the doc wouldn't look so peaked."

Spit. Silence.

"Yuh. Juanita's always talking about her, too," from Earl. "She says Mrs. Kennicott thinks she knows it all. Juanita says she has to laugh till she almost bursts every time she sees Mr. Kennicott peerading along the street with that 'take a look—I'm a swell skirt' way she's got. But gosh, I don't pay no attention to Juanita. She's meaner 'n a crab."

"Ma was telling somebody that she heard that Mrs. Kennicott claimed she made forty dollars a week when she was on some job in the Cities, and Ma says she knows posolutely that she never made but eighteen a week—Ma says that when she's lived here a while she won't go round making a fool of herself, pulling that bighead stuff on folks that know a whole lot more than she does. They're all laughing up their sleeves at her."

"Say, jever notice how Mrs. Kennicott fusses around the house? Other evening when I was coming over here, she'd forgot to pull down the curtain, and I watched her for ten minutes. Jeeze, you'd 'a' died laughing. She was there all alone, and she must 'a' spent five minutes getting a picture straight. It was funny as hell the way she'd stick out her finger to straighten the picture—deedle-dee, see my tunnin' 'ittle finger, oh my, ain't I cute, what a fine long tail my cat's got!"

"But say, Earl, she's some good-looker, just the same, and O Ignatz! the glad rags she must of bought for her wedding. Jever notice these low-cut dresses and these thin shimmy-shirts she wears? I had a good squint at 'em when they were out on the line with the wash. And some ankles she's got, heh?"

Then Carol fled.

In her innocence she had not known that the whole town could discuss even her garments, her body. She felt that she was being dragged naked down Main Street.

The moment it was dusk she pulled down the window-shades, all the shades, flush with the sill, but beyond them she felt moist fleering eyes.

III

She remembered, and tried to forget, and remembered more sharply the vulgar detail of her husband's having observed the ancient customs of the land by chewing tobacco. She would have preferred a prettier vice—gambling or a mistress. For these she might have found a luxury of forgiveness. She could not remember any fascinatingly wicked hero of fiction who chewed tobacco. She asserted that it proved him to be a man of the bold free West. She tried to align him with the hairy-chested heroes of the motion-pictures. She curled on the couch, a pallid softness in the twilight, and fought herself, and lost the battle. Spitting did not identify him with rangers riding the buttes; it merely bound him to Gopher Prairie—to Nat Hicks the tailor and Bert Tybee the bartender.

"But he gave it up for me. Oh, what does it matter! We're all filthy in some things. I think of myself as so superior, but I do eat and digest, I do wash my dirty paws and scratch. I'm not a cool slim goddess on a column. There aren't any! He gave it up for me. He stands by me, believing that every one loves me. He's the Rock of Ages—in a storm of meanness that's driving me mad. . . . it will drive me mad."

All evening she sang Scotch ballads to Kennicott, and when she noticed that he was chewing an unlighted cigar she smiled maternally at his secret.

She could not escape asking (in the exact words and mental intonations which a thousand million women, dairy wenches and mischief-making queens, had used before her, and which a million million women will know hereafter), "Was it all a horrible mistake, my marrying him?" She quieted the doubt—without answering it.

IV

Kennicott had taken her north to Lac-qui-Meurt, in the Big Woods. It was the entrance to a Chippewa Indian reservation, a sandy settlement among Norway pines on the shore of a huge snow-glaring lake. She had her first sight of his mother, except the glimpse at the wedding. Mrs. Kennicott had a hushed and delicate breeding which dignified her woodeny over-scrubbed cottage with its worn hard cushions in heavy rockers. She had never lost the child's miraculous power of wonder. She asked questions about books and cities. She murmured:

"Will is a dear hard-working boy but he's inclined to be too serious, and you've taught him how to play. Last night I heard you both laughing about the old Indian basket-seller, and I just lay in bed and enjoyed your happiness."

Carol forgot her misery-hunting in this solidarity of family life. She could depend upon them; she was not battling alone. Watching Mrs. Kennicott flit about the kitchen she was better able to translate Kennicott himself. He was matter-of-fact, yes, and incurably mature. He didn't really play; he let Carol play with him. But he had his mother's genius for trusting, her disdain for prying, her sure integrity.

From the two days at Lac-qui-Meurt Carol drew confidence in herself, and she returned to Gopher Prairie in a throbbing calm like those golden drugged seconds when, because he is for an instant free from pain, a sick man revels in living.

A bright hard winter day, the wind shrill, black and silver clouds booming across the sky, everything in panicky motion during the brief light. They struggled against the surf of wind, through deep snow. Kennicott was cheerful. He hailed Loren Wheeler, "Behave yourself while I been away?" The editor bellowed, "B' gosh you stayed so long that all your patients have got well!" and importantly took notes for the *Dauntless* about their journey. Jackson Elder cried, "Hey, folks! How's tricks up North?" Mrs. McGanum waved to them from her porch.

"They're glad to see us. We mean something here. These people are satisfied. Why can't I be? But can I sit back all my life and be satisfied with 'Hey, folks'? They want shouts on Main Street, and I want violins in a paneled room. Why——?"

v

Vida Sherwin ran in after school a dozen times. She was tactful, torrentially anecdotal. She had scuttled about town and plucked compliments: Mrs. Dr. Westlake had pronounced Carol a "very sweet, bright, cultured young woman," and Brad Bemis, the tinsmith at Clark's Hardware Store, had declared that she was "easy to work for and awful easy to look at."

But Carol could not yet take her in. She resented this outsider's knowledge of her shame. Vida was not too long tolerant. She hinted, "You're a great brooder, child. Buck up now. The town's quit criticizing you, almost entirely. Come with me to the Thanatopsis Club. They have some of the *best* papers, and current-events discussions—*so* interesting."

In Vida's demands Carol felt a compulsion, but she was too listless to obey.

It was Bea Sorenson who was really her confidante.

However charitable toward the Lower Classes she may have thought herself, Carol had been reared to assume that servants belong to a distinct and inferior species. But she discovered that Bea was extraordinarily like girls she had loved in college, and as a companion altogether superior to the young matrons of the Jolly Seventeen. Daily they became more frankly two girls playing at housework. Bea artlessly considered Carol the most beautiful and accomplished lady in the country; she was always shrieking, "My, dot's a swell hat!" or, "Ay t'ink all dese ladies yoost die when dey see how elegant you do your hair!" But it was not the humbleness of a servant, nor the hypocrisy of a slave; it was the admiration of Freshman for Junior.

They made out the day's menus together. Though they began with propriety, Carol sitting by the kitchen table and Bea at the sink or blacking the stove, the conference was likely to end with both of them by the table, while Bea gurgled over the ice-man's attempt to kiss her, or Carol admitted, "Everybody knows that the doctor is lots more clever than Dr. McGanum." When Carol came in from marketing, Bea plunged into the hall to take off her coat, rub her frosted hands, and ask, "Vos dere lots of folks up-town today?" This was the welcome upon which Carol depended.

VI

Through her weeks of cowering there was no change in her surface life. No one save Vida was aware of her agonizing. On her most despairing days she chatted to women on the street, in stores. But without the protection of Kennicott's presence she did not go to the Jolly Seventeen; she delivered herself to the judgment of the town only when she went shopping and on the ritualistic occasions of formal afternoon calls, when Mrs. Lyman Cass or Mrs. George Edwin Mott, with clean gloves and minute handkerchiefs and sealskin card-cases and countenances of frozen approbation, sat on the edges of chairs and inquired, "Do you find Gopher Prairie pleasing?" When they spent evenings of social profit-and-loss at the Haydocks' or the Dyers' she hid behind Kennicott, playing the simple bride.

Now she was unprotected. Kennicott had taken a patient to Rochester for an operation. He would be away for two or three days. She had not minded; she would loosen the matrimonial tension and be a fanciful girl for a time. But now that he was gone the house was listeningly empty. Bea was out this afternoon—presumably drinking coffee and talking about "fellows" with her cousin Tina. It was the day for the monthly supper and evening-bridge of the Jolly Seventeen, but Carol dared not go.

She sat alone.

chapter 10

THE house was haunted, long before evening. Shadows slipped down the walls and waited behind every chair.

Did that door move?

No. She wouldn't go to the Jolly Seventeen. She hadn't energy enough to caper before them, to smile blandly at Juanita's rudeness. Not today. But she did want a party. Now! If some one would come in this afternoon, some one who liked her—Vida or Mrs. Sam Clark or old Mrs. Champ Perry or gentle Mrs. Dr. Westlake. Or Guy Pollock! She'd telephone——

No. That wouldn't be it. They must come of themselves.

Perhaps they would.

Why not?

She'd have tea ready, anyway. If they came—splendid. If not—what did she care? She wasn't going to yield to the village and let down; she was going to keep up a belief in the rite of tea, to which she had always looked forward as the symbol of a leisurely fine existence. And it would be just as much fun, even if it was so babyish, to have tea by herself and pretend that she was entertaining clever men. It would!

She turned the shining thought into action. She bustled to the kitchen, stoked the wood-range, sang Schumann while she boiled the kettle, warmed up raisin cookies on a newspaper spread on the rack in the oven. She scampered up-stairs to bring down her filmiest tea-cloth. She arranged a silver tray. She proudly carried it into the living-room and set it on the long cherrywood table, pushing aside a hoop of embroidery, a volume of Conrad from the library, copies of the *Saturday Evening Post*, the *Literary Digest*, and Kennicott's *National Geographic Magazine*.

She moved the tray back and forth and regarded the effect. She shook her head. She busily unfolded the sewing-table, set it in the bay-window, patted the tea-cloth to smoothness, moved the tray. "Some time I'll have a mahogany tea-table," she said happily.

She had brought in two cups, two plates. For herself, a straight chair, but for the guest the big wing-chair, which she pantingly tugged to the table.

She had finished all the preparations she could think of. She sat and waited. She listened for the door-bell, the telephone. Her eagerness was stilled. Her hands drooped.

Surely Vida Sherwin would hear the summons.

She glanced through the bay-window. Snow was sifting over the ridge of the Howland house like sprays of water from a hose. The wide yards across the street were gray with moving eddies. The black trees shivered. The roadway was gashed with ruts of ice.

She looked at the extra cup and plate. She looked at the wing-chair. It was so empty.

The tea was cold in the pot. With wearily dipping finger-tip she tested it. Yes. Quite cold. She couldn't wait any longer.

The cup across from her was icily clean, glisteningly empty.

Simply absurd to wait. She poured her own cup of tea. She sat and stared at it. What was it she was going to do now? Oh yes; how idiotic; take a lump of sugar.

She didn't want the beastly tea.

She was springing up. She was on the couch, sobbing.

II

She was thinking more sharply than she had for weeks.

She reverted to her resolution to change the town—awaken

it, prod it, "reform" it. What if they were wolves instead of lambs? They'd eat her all the sooner if she was meek to them. Fight or be eaten. It was easier to change the town completely than to conciliate it! She could not take their point of view; it was a negative thing; an intellectual squalor; a swamp of prejudices and fears. She would have to make them take hers. She was not a Vincent de Paul, to govern and mold a people. What of that? The tiniest change in their distrust of beauty would be the beginning of the end; a seed to sprout and some day with thickening roots to crack their wall of mediocrity. If she could not, as she desired, do a great thing nobly and with laughter, yet she need not be content with village nothingness. She would plant one seed in the blank wall.

Was she just? Was it merely a blank wall, this town which to three thousand and more people was the center of the universe? Hadn't she, returning from Lac-qui-Meurt, felt the heartiness of their greetings? No. The ten thousand Gopher Prairies had no monopoly of greetings and friendly hands. Sam Clark was no more loyal than girl librarians she knew in St. Paul, the people she had met in Chicago. And those others had so much that Gopher Prairie complacently lacked —the world of gaiety and adventure, of music and the integrity of bronze, of remembered mists from tropic isles and Paris nights and the walls of Bagdad, of industrial justice and a God who spake not in doggerel hymns.

One seed. Which seed it was did not matter. All knowledge and freedom were one. But she had delayed so long in finding that seed. Could she do something with this Thanatopsis Club? Or should she make her house so charming that it would be an influence? She'd make Kennicott like poetry. That was it, for a beginning! She conceived so clear a picture of their bending over large fair pages by the fire (in a non-existent fireplace) that the spectral presences slipped away. Doors no longer moved; curtains were not creeping shadows but lovely dark masses in the dusk; and when Bea came home Carol was singing at the piano which she had not touched for many days.

Their supper was the feast of two girls. Carol was in the dining-room, in a frock of black satin edged with gold, and Bea, in blue gingham and an apron, dined in the kitchen; but the door was open between, and Carol was inquiring, "Did you see any ducks in Dahl's window?" and Bea chanting, "No, ma'am. Say, ve have a svell time, dis afternoon. Tina she have coffee and *knäckebröd,* and her fella vos dere, and ve yoost laughed and laughed, and her fella say he vos president and he going to make me queen of Finland, and Ay stick a fedder in may hair and say Ay bane going to go to var—oh, ve vos so foolish and ve *laugh* so!"

When Carol sat at the piano again she did not think of her husband but of the book-drugged hermit, Guy Pollock. She wished that Pollock would come calling.

"If a girl really kissed him, he'd creep out of his den and be human. If Will were as literate as Guy, or Guy were as executive as Will, I think I could endure even Gopher Prairie.

"It's so hard to mother Will. I could be maternal with Guy. Is that what I want, something to mother, a man or a baby or a town? I *will* have a baby. Some day. But to have him isolated here all his receptive years——

"And so to bed.

"Have I found my real level in Bea and kitchen-gossip?

"Oh, I do miss you, Will. But it will be pleasant to turn over in bed as often as I want to, without worrying about waking you up.

"Am I really this settled thing called a 'married woman'? I feel so unmarried tonight. So free. To think that there was once a Mrs. Kennicott who let herself worry over a town called Gopher Prairie when there was a whole world outside it!

"Of course Will is going to like poetry."

III

A black February day. Clouds hewn of ponderous timber weighing down on the earth; an irresolute dropping of snow specks upon the trampled wastes. Gloom but no veiling of angularity. The lines of roofs and sidewalks sharp and inescapable.

The second day of Kennicott's absence.

She fled from the creepy house for a walk. It was thirty below zero; too cold to exhilarate her. In the spaces between houses the wind caught her. It stung, it gnawed at nose and ears and aching cheeks, and she hastened from shelter to shelter, catching her breath in the lee of a barn, grateful for the protection of a billboard covered with ragged posters showing layer under layer of paste-smeared green and streaky red.

The grove of oaks at the end of the street suggested Indians, hunting, snow-shoes, and she struggled past the earth-banked cottages to the open country, to a farm and a low hill corrugated with hard snow. In her loose nutria coat, seal toque, virginal cheeks unmarked by lines of village jealousies, she was as out of place on this dreary hillside as a scarlet tanager on an ice-floe. She looked down on Gopher Prairie. The snow, stretching without break from streets to devouring prairie beyond, wiped out the town's pretense of being a shelter. The houses were black specks on a white sheet. Her heart shivered with that still loneliness as her body shivered with the wind.

She ran back into the huddle of streets, all the while protesting that she wanted a city's yellow glare of shop-windows and restaurants, or the primitive forest with hooded furs and a rifle, or a barnyard warm and steamy, noisy with hens and cattle, certainly not these dun houses, these yards choked with winter ash-piles, these roads of dirty snow and clotted frozen mud. The zest of winter was gone. Three months more, till May, the cold might drag on, with the snow ever filthier, the weakened body less resistant. She wondered why the good citizens insisted on adding the chill of prejudice, why they did not make the houses of their spirits more warm and frivolous, like the wise chatterers of Stockholm and Moscow.

She circled the outskirts of the town and viewed the slum of "Swede Hollow." Wherever as many as three houses are gathered there will be a slum of at least one house. In Gopher Prairie, the Sam Clarks boasted, "you don't get any of this poverty that you find in cities—always plenty of work—no need of charity—man got to be blame shiftless if he don't get ahead." But now that the summer mask of leaves and grass was gone, Carol discovered misery and dead hope. In a shack of thin boards covered with tar-paper she saw the washerwoman, Mrs. Steinhof, working in gray steam. Outside, her six-year-old boy chopped wood. He had a torn jacket, muffler of a blue like skimmed milk. His hands were covered with red mittens through which protruded his chapped raw knuckles. He halted to blow on them, to cry disinterestedly.

A family of recently arrived Finns were camped in an abandoned stable. A man of eighty was picking up lumps of coal along the railroad.

She did not know what to do about it. She felt that these independent citizens, who had been taught that they belonged to a democracy, would resent her trying to play Lady Bountiful.

She lost her loneliness in the activity of the village industries—the railroad-yards with a freight-train switching, the
wheat-elevator, oil-tanks, a slaughter-house with blood-marks
on the snow, the creamery with the sleds of farmers and piles
of milk-cans, an unexplained stone hut labeled "Danger—
Powder Stored Here." The jolly tombstone-yard, where a
utilitarian sculptor in a red calfskin overcoat whistled as he
hammered the shiniest of granite headstones. Jackson Elder's
small planing-mill, with the smell of fresh pine shavings and
the burr of circular saws. Most important, the Gopher Prairie
Flour and Milling Company, Lyman Cass president. Its windows were blanketed with flour-dust, but it was the most
stirring spot in town. Workmen were wheeling barrels of flour
into a box-car; a farmer sitting on sacks of wheat in a bob-
sled argued with the wheat-buyer; machinery within the mill
boomed and whined; water gurgled in the ice-freed millrace.

The clatter was a relief to Carol after months of smug
houses. She wished that she could work in the mill; that she
did not belong to the caste of professional-man's-wife.

She started for home, through the small slum. Before a
tar-paper shack, at a gateless gate, a man in rough brown
dogskin coat and black plush cap with lappets was watching
her. His square face was confident, his foxy mustache was
picaresque. He stood erect, his hands in his side-pockets, his
pipe puffing slowly. He was forty-five or -six, perhaps.

"How do Mrs. Kennicott," he drawled.

She recalled him—the town handyman, who had repaired
their furnace at the beginning of winter.

"Oh, how do you do," she fluttered.

"My name 's Bjornstam. 'The Red Swede' they call me. Remember? Always thought I'd kind of like to say howdy to
you again."

"Ye—yes—— I've been exploring the outskirts of town."

"Yump. Fine mess. No sewage, no street cleaning, and the
Lutheran minister and the priest represent the arts and sci-
ences. Well, thunder, we submerged tenth down here in Swede
Hollow are no worse off than you folks. Thank God, we
don't have to go and purr at Juanity Haydock at the Jolly
Old Seventeen."

The Carol who regarded herself as completely adaptable
was uncomfortable at being chosen as comrade by a pipe-
reeking odd-job man. Probably he was one of her husband's
patients. But she must keep her dignity.

"Yes, even the Jolly Seventeen isn't always so exciting. It's very cold again today, isn't it. Well——"

Bjornstam was not respectfully valedictory. He showed no signs of pulling a forelock. His eyebrows moved as though they had a life of their own. With a subgrin he went on:

"Maybe I hadn't ought to talk about Mrs. Haydock and her Solemcholy Seventeen in that fresh way. I suppose I'd be tickled to death if I was invited to sit in with that gang. I'm what they call a pariah, I guess. I'm the town badman, Mrs. Kennicott: town atheist, and I suppose I must be an anarchist, too. Everybody who doesn't love the bankers and the Grand Old Republican Party is an anarchist."

Carol had unconsciously slipped from her attitude of departure into an attitude of listening, her face full toward him, her muff lowered. She fumbled:

"Yes, I suppose so." Her own grudges came in a flood. "I don't see why you shouldn't criticize the Jolly Seventeen if you want to. They aren't sacred."

"Oh yes, they are! The dollar-sign has chased the crucifix clean off the map. But then, I've got no kick. I do what I please, and I suppose I ought to let them do the same."

"What do you mean by saying you're a pariah?"

"I'm poor, and yet I don't decently envy the rich. I'm an old bach. I make enough money for a stake, and then I sit around by myself, and shake hands with myself, and have a smoke, and read history, and I don't contribute to the wealth of Brother Elder or Daddy Cass."

"You—— I fancy you read a good deal."

"Yep. In a hit-or-a-miss way. I'll tell you: I'm a lone wolf. I trade horses, and saw wood, and work in lumber-camps —I'm a first-rate swamper. Always wished I could go to college. Though I s'pose I'd find it pretty slow, and they'd probably kick me out."

"You really are a curious person, Mr.——"

"Bjornstam. Miles Bjornstam. Half Yank and half Swede. Usually known as 'that damn lazy big-mouthed calamity-howler that ain't satisfied with the way we run things.' No, I ain't curious—whatever you mean by that! I'm just a book-worm. Probably too much reading for the amount of digestion I've got. Probably half-baked. I'm going to get in 'half-baked' first, and beat you to it, because it's dead sure to be handed to a radical that wears jeans!"

They grinned together. She demanded:

116 *Sinclair Lewis*

"You say that the Jolly Seventeen is stupid. What makes
you think so?"

"Oh, trust us borers into the foundation to know about
your leisure class. Fact, Mrs. Kennicott, I'll say that far as
I can make out, the only people in this man's town that do
have any brains—I don't mean ledger-keeping brains or duck-
hunting brains or baby-spanking brains, but real imaginative
brains—are you and me and Guy Pollock and the foreman
at the flour-mill. He's a socialist, the foreman. (Don't tell
Lym Cass that! Lym would fire a socialist quicker than he
would a horse-thief!)"

"Indeed no, I sha'n't tell him."

"This foreman and I have some great set-to's. He's a regular old-line party-member. Too dogmatic. Expects to reform everything from deforestation to nosebleed by saying
phrases like 'surplus value.' Like reading the prayer-book.
But same time, he's a Plato J. Aristotle compared with people
like Ezry Stowbody or Professor Mott or Julius Flickerbaugh."

"It's interesting to hear about him."

He dug his toe into a drift, like a schoolboy. "Rats. You
mean I talk too much. Well, I do, when I get hold of
somebody like you. You probably want to run along and keep
your nose from freezing."

"Yes, I must go, I suppose. But tell me: Why did you leave
Miss Sherwin, of the high school, out of your list of the
town intelligentsia?"

"I guess maybe she does belong in it. From all I can hear
she's in everything and behind everything that looks like a
reform—lot more than most folks realize. She lets Mrs.
Reverend Warren, the president of this-here Thanatopsis
Club, think she's running the works, but Miss Sherwin is the
secret boss, and nags all the easy-going dames into doing
something. But way I figure it out—— You see, I'm not interested in these dinky reforms. Miss Sherwin's trying to repair
the holes in this barnacle-covered ship of a town by keeping
busy bailing out the water. And Pollock tries to repair it by
reading poetry to the crew! Me, I want to yank it up on the
ways, and fire the poor bum of a shoemaker that built it so
it sails crooked, and have it rebuilt right, from the keel up."

"Yes—that—that would be better. But I must run home.
My poor nose is nearly frozen."

"Say, you better come in and get warm, and see what an old bach's shack is like."

She looked doubtfully at him, at the low shanty, the yard that was littered with cord-wood, moldy planks, a hoopless wash-tub. She was disquieted, but Bjornstam did not give her the opportunity to be delicate. He flung out his hand in a welcoming gesture which assumed that she was her own counselor, that she was not a Respectable Married Woman but fully a human being. With a shaky, "Well, just a moment, to warm my nose," she glanced down the street to make sure that she was not spied on, and bolted toward the shanty.

She remained for one hour, and never had she known a more considerate host than the Red Swede.

He had but one room: bare pine floor, small work-bench, wall bunk with amazingly neat bed, frying-pan and ash-stippled coffee-pot on the shelf behind the pot-bellied cannonball stove, backwoods chairs—one constructed from half a barrel, one from a tilted plank—and a row of books incredibly assorted; Byron and Tennyson and Stevenson, a manual of gas-engines, a book by Thorstein Veblen, and a spotty treatise on "The Care, Feeding, Diseases, and Breeding of Poultry and Cattle."

There was but one picture—a magazine color-plate of a steep-roofed village in the Harz Mountains which suggested kobolds and maidens with golden hair.

Bjornstam did not fuss over her. He suggested, "Might throw open your coat and put your feet up on the box in front of the stove." He tossed his dogskin coat into the bunk, lowered himself into the barrel chair, and droned on:

"Yeh, I'm probably a yahoo, but by gum I do keep my independence by doing odd jobs, and that's more 'n these polite cusses like the clerks in the banks do. When I'm rude to some slob, it may be partly because I don't know better (and God knows I'm not no authority on trick forks and what pants you wear with a Prince Albert), but mostly it's because I mean something. I'm about the only man in Johnson County that remembers the joker in the Declaration of Independence about Americans being supposed to have the right to 'life, liberty, and the pursuit of happiness.'

"I meet old Ezra Stowbody on the street. He looks at me like he wants me to remember he's a highmuckamuck and worth two hundred thousand dollars, and he says, 'Uh, Bjornquist—'

118 *Sinclair Lewis*

" 'Bjornstam's my name, Ezra,' I says. *He* knows my name, all rightee.

" 'Well, whatever your name is,' he says, 'I understand you have a gasoline saw. I want you to come around and saw up four cords of maple for me,' he says.

" 'So you like my looks, eh?' I says, kind of innocent.

" 'What difference does that make? Want you to saw that wood before Saturday,' he says, real sharp. Common workman going and getting fresh with a fifth of a million dollars all walking around in a hand-me-down fur coat!

" 'Here's the difference it makes,' I says, just to devil him. 'How do you know I like *your* looks?' Maybe he didn't look sore! 'Nope,' I says, 'thinking it all over, I don't like your application for a loan. Take it to another bank, only there ain't any,' I says, and I walks off on him.

"Sure. Probably I was surly—and foolish. But I figured there had to be *one* man in town independent enough to sass the banker!"

He hitched out of his chair, made coffee, gave Carol a cup, and talked on, half defiant and half apologetic, half wistful for friendliness and half amused by her surprise at the discovery that there was a proletarian philosophy.

At the door, she hinted:

"Mr. Bjornstam, if you were I, would you worry when people thought you were affected?"

"Huh? Kick 'em in the face! Say, if I were a sea-gull, and all over silver, think I'd care what a pack of dirty seals thought about my flying?"

It was not the wind at her back, it was the thrust of Bjornstam's scorn which carried her through town. She faced Juanita Haydock, cocked her head at Maud Dyer's brief nod, and came home to Bea radiant. She telephoned Vida Sherwin to "run over this evening." She lustily played Tschaikowsky —the virile chords an echo of the red laughing philosopher of the tar-paper shack.

(When she hinted to Vida, "Isn't there a man here who amuses himself by being irreverent to the village gods— Bjornstam, some such a name?" the reform-leader said "Bjornstam? Oh yes. Fixes things. He's awfully impertinent.")

IV

Kennicott had returned at midnight. At breakfast he said several times that he had missed her every moment.

On her way to market Sam Clark hailed her, "The top o' the mornin' to yez! Going to stop and pass the time of day mit Sam'l? Warmer, eh? What'd the doc's thermometer say it was? Say, you folks better come round and visit with us, one of these evenings. Don't be so dog-gone proud, staying by yourselves."

Champ Perry the pioneer, wheat-buyer at the elevator, stopped her in the post-office, held her hand in his withered paws, peered at her with faded eyes, and chuckled, "You are so fresh and blooming, my dear. Mother was saying t'other day that a sight of you was better 'n a dose of medicine."

In the Bon Ton Store she found Guy Pollock tentatively buying a modest gray scarf. "We haven't seen you for so long," she said. "Wouldn't you like to come in and play cribbage, some evening?" As though he meant it, Pollock begged, "May I, really?"

While she was purchasing two yards of malines the vocal Raymie Wutherspoon tiptoed up to her, his long sallow face bobbing, and he besought, "You've just got to come back to my department and see a pair of patent leather slippers I set aside for you."

In a manner of more than sacerdotal reverence he unlaced her boots, tucked her skirt about her ankles, slid on the slippers. She took them.

"You're a good salesman," she said.

"I'm not a salesman at all! I just like elegant things. All this is so inartistic." He indicated with a forlornly waving hand the shelves of shoe-boxes, the seat of thin wood perforated in rosettes, the display of shoe-trees and tin boxes of blacking, the lithograph of a smirking young woman with cherry cheeks who proclaimed in the exalted poetry of advertising, "My tootsies never got hep to what pedal perfection was till I got a pair of clever classy Cleopatra Shoes."

"But sometimes," Raymie sighed, "there is a pair of dainty little shoes like these, and I set them aside for some one who will appreciate. When I saw these I said right away, 'Wouldn't it be nice if they fitted Mrs. Kennicott,' and I meant to speak to you first chance I had. I haven't forgotten our jolly talks at Mrs. Gurrey's!"

That evening Guy Pollock came in and, though Kennicott instantly impressed him into a cribbage game, Carol was happy again.

V

She did not, in recovering something of her buoyancy, forget her determination to begin the liberalizing of Gopher Prairie by the easy and agreeable propaganda of teaching Kennicott to enjoy reading poetry in the lamplight. The campaign was delayed. Twice he suggested that they call on neighbors; once he was in the country. The fourth evening he yawned pleasantly, stretched, and inquired, "Well, what'll we do tonight? Shall we go to the movies?"

"I know exactly what we're going to do. Now don't ask questions! Come and sit down by the table. There, are you comfy? Lean back and forget you're a practical man, and listen to me."

It may be that she had been influenced by the managerial Vida Sherwin; certainly she sounded as though she was selling culture. But she dropped it when she sat on the couch, her chin in her hands, a volume of Yeats on her knees, and read aloud.

Instantly she was released from the homely comfort of a prairie town. She was in the world of lonely things—the flutter of twilight linnets, the aching call of gulls along a shore to which the netted foam crept out of darkness, the island of Aengus and the elder gods and the eternal glories that never were, tall kings and women girdled with crusted gold, the woful incessant chanting and the——

"Heh-cha-cha!" coughed Dr. Kennicott. She stopped. She remembered that he was the sort of person who chewed tobacco. She glared, while he uneasily petitioned, "That's great stuff. Study it in college? I like poetry fine—James Whitcomb Riley and some of Longfellow—this 'Hiawatha.' Gosh, I wish I could appreciate that highbrow art stuff. But I guess I'm too old a dog to learn new tricks."

With pity for his bewilderment, and a certain desire to giggle, she consoled him, "Then let's try some Tennyson. You've read him?"

"Tennyson? You bet. Read him in school. There's that:

And let there be no (what is it?) of farewell
When I put out to sea,
But let the——

Well, I don't remember all of it but—— Oh, sure! And

there's that 'I met a little country boy who———' I don't remember exactly how it does, but the chorus ends up, 'We are seven.' "

"Yes. Well—— Shall we try 'The Idylls of the King?' They're so full of color."

"Go to it. Shoot." But he hastened to shelter himself behind a cigar.

She was not transported to Camelot. She read with an eye cocked on him, and when she saw how much he was suffering she ran to him, kissed his forehead, cried, "You poor forced tube-rose that wants to be a decent turnip!"

"Look here now, that ain't———"

"Anyway, I sha'n't torture you any longer."

She could not quite give up. She read Kipling, with a great deal of emphasis:

There's a REGIMENT a-COMING down the
  GRAND Trunk ROAD.

He tapped his foot to the rhythm; he looked normal, and reassured. But when he complimented her, "That was fine. I don't know but what you can elocute just as good as Ella Stowbody," she banged the book and suggested that they were not too late for the nine o'clock show at the movies.

That was her last effort to harvest the April wind, to teach divine unhappiness by a correspondence course, to buy the lilies of Avalon and the sunsets of Cockaigne in tin cans at Ole Jenson's Grocery.

But the fact is that at the motion-pictures she discovered herself laughing as heartily as Kennicott at the humor of an actor who stuffed spaghetti down a woman's evening frock. For a second she loathed her laughter; mourned for the day when on her hill by the Mississippi she had walked the battlements with queens. But the celebrated cinema jester's conceit of dropping toads into a soup-plate flung her into unwilling tittering, and the afterglow faded, the dead queens fled through darkness.

VI

She went to the Jolly Seventeen's afternoon bridge. She had learned the elements of the game from the Sam Clarks. She played quietly and reasonably badly. She had no opinions on anything more polemic than woolen union-suits, a topic on which Mrs. Howland discoursed for five minutes. She smiled frequently, and was the complete canary-bird in her manner of thanking the hostess, Mrs. Dave Dyer.

Her only anxious period was during the conference on husbands.

The young matrons discussed the intimacies of domesticity with a frankness and a minuteness which dismayed Carol. Juanita Haydock communicated Harry's method of shaving, and his interest in deer-shooting. Mrs. Gougerling reported fully, and with some irritation, her husband's inappreciation of liver and bacon. Maud Dyer chronicled Dave's digestive disorders; quoted a recent bedtime controversy with him in regard to Christian Science, socks and the sewing of buttons upon vests; announced that she "simply wasn't going to stand his always pawing girls when he went and got crazy-jealous if a man just danced with her"; and rather more than sketched Dave's varieties of kisses.

So meekly did Carol give attention, so obviously was she at last desirous of being one of them, that they looked on her fondly, and encouraged her to give such details of her honeymoon as might be of interest. She was embarrassed rather than resentful. She deliberately misunderstood. She talked of Kennicott's overshoes and medical ideals till they were thoroughly bored. They regarded her as agreeable but green.

Till the end she labored to satisfy the inquisition. She bubbled at Juanita, the president of the club, that she wanted to entertain them. "Only," she said, "I don't know that I can give you any refreshments as nice as Mrs. Dyer's salad, or that simply delicious angel's-food we had at your house, dear."

"Fine! We need a hostess for the seventeenth of March. Wouldn't it be awfully original if you made it a St. Patrick's Day bridge! I'll be tickled to death to help you with it. I'm glad you've learned to play bridge. At first I didn't hardly know if you were going to like Gopher Prairie. Isn't it dandy that you've settled down to being homey with us! Maybe we aren't as highbrow as the Cities, but we do have the daisiest times and—oh, we go swimming in summer, and dances and—oh, lots of good times. If folks will just take us as we are, *I* think we're a pretty good bunch!"

"I'm sure of it. Thank you so much for the idea about having a St. Patrick's Day bridge."

"Oh, that's nothing. I always think the Jolly Seventeen are so good at original ideas. If you knew these other towns, Wakamin and Joralemon and all, you'd find out and realize that G. P. is the liveliest, smartest town in the state. Did you know that Percy Bresnahan, the famous auto manufacturer, came from here and—— Yes, I think that a St. Patrick's Day party would be awfully cunning and original, and yet not too queer or freaky or anything."

chapter 11

SHE had often been invited to the weekly meetings of the Thanatopsis, the women's study club, but she had put it off. The Thanatopsis was, Vida Sherwin promised, "such a cozy group, and yet it puts you in touch with all the intellectual thoughts that are going on everywhere."

Early in March Mrs. Westlake, wife of the veteran physician, marched into Carol's living-room like an amiable old pussy and suggested, "My dear, you really must come to the Thanatopsis this afternoon. Mrs. Dawson is going to be leader and the poor soul is frightened to death. She wanted me to get you to come. She says she's sure you will brighten up the meeting with your knowledge of books and writings. (English poetry is our topic today.) So shoo! Put on your coat!"

"English poetry? Really? I'd love to go. I didn't realize you were reading poetry."

"Oh, we're not so slow!"

Mrs. Luke Dawson, wife of the richest man in town, gaped at them piteously when they appeared. Her expensive frock of beaver-colored satin with rows, plasters, and pendants of solemn brown beads was intended for a woman twice her size. She stood wringing her hands in front of nineteen folding chairs, in her front parlor with its faded photograph of Minnehaha Falls in 1890, its "colored enlargement" of Mr. Dawson, its bulbous lamp painted with sepia cows and mountains and standing on a mortuary marble column.

She creaked, "O Mrs. Kennicott, I'm in such a fix. I'm supposed to lead the discussion, and I wondered would you come and help?"

"What poet do you take up today?" demanded Carol, in

her library tone of "What book do you wish to take out?"

"Why, the English ones."

"Not all of them?"

"W-why yes. We're learning all of European Literature this year. The club gets such a nice magazine, *Culture Hints,* and we follow its programs. Last year our subject was Men and Women of the Bible, and next year we'll probably take up Furnishings and China. My, it does make a body hustle to keep up with all these new culture subjects, but it is improving. So will you help us with the discussion today?"

On her way over Carol had decided to use the Thanatopsis as the tool with which to liberalize the town. She had immediately conceived enormous enthusiasm; she had chanted, "These are the real people. When the housewives, who bear the burdens, are interested in poetry, it means something. I'll work with them—for them—anything!"

Her enthusiasm had become watery even before thirteen women resolutely removed their overshoes, sat down meatily, ate peppermints, dusted their fingers, folded their hands, composed their lower thoughts, and invited the naked muse of poetry to deliver her most improving message. They had greeted Carol affectionately, and she tried to be a daughter to them. But she felt insecure. Her chair was out in the open, exposed to their gaze, and it was a hard-slatted, quivery, slippery church-parlor chair, likely to collapse publicly and without warning. It was impossible to sit on it without folding the hands and listening piously.

She wanted to kick the chair and run. It would make a magnificent clatter.

She saw that Vida Sherwin was watching her. She pinched her wrist, as though she were a noisy child in church, and when she was decent and cramped again, she listened.

Mrs. Dawson opened the meeting by sighing, "I'm sure I'm glad to see you all here today, and I understand that the ladies have prepared a number of very interesting papers, this is such an interesting subject, the poets, they have been an inspiration for higher thought, in fact wasn't it Reverend Benlick who said that some of the poets have been as much an inspiration as a good many of the ministers, and so we shall be glad to hear——"

The poor lady smiled neuralgically, panted with fright, scrabbled about the small oak table to find her eye-glasses, and continued, "We will first have the pleasure of hearing Mrs. Jenson on the subject 'Shakespeare and Milton.' "

Mrs. Ole Jenson said that Shakespeare was born in 1564 and died 1616. He lived in London, England, and in Stratford-on-Avon, which many American tourists loved to visit, a lovely town with many curios and old houses well worth examination. Many people believed that Shakespeare was the greatest playwright who ever lived, also a fine poet. Not much was known about his life, but after all that did not really make so much difference, because they loved to read his numerous plays, several of the best known of which she would now criticize.

Perhaps the best known of his plays was "The Merchant of Venice," having a beautiful love story and a fine appreciation of a woman's brains, which a woman's club, even those who did not care to commit themselves on the question of suffrage, ought to appreciate. (Laughter.) Mrs. Jenson was sure that she, for one, would love to be like Portia. The play was about a Jew named Shylock, and he didn't want his daughter to marry a Venice gentleman named Antonio——

Mrs. Leonard Warren, a slender, gray, nervous woman, president of the Thanatopsis and wife of the Congregational pastor, reported the birth and death dates of Byron, Scott, Moore, Burns; and wound up:

"Burns was quite a poor boy and he did not enjoy the advantages we enjoy today, except for the advantages of the fine old Scotch kirk where he heard the Word of God preached more fearlessly than even in the finest big brick churches in the big and so-called advanced cities of today, but he did not have our educational advantages and Latin and the other treasures of the mind so richly strewn before the, alas, too ofttimes inattentive feet of our youth who do not always sufficiently appreciate the privileges freely granted to every American boy rich or poor. Burns had to work hard and was sometimes led by evil companionship into low habits. But it is morally instructive to know that he was a good student and educated himself, in striking contrast to the loose ways and so-called aristocratic society-life of Lord Byron, on which I have just spoken. And certainly though the lords and earls of his day may have looked down upon Burns as a humble person, many of us have greatly enjoyed his pieces about the mouse and other rustic subjects, with their message of humble beauty—I am so sorry I have not got the time to quote some of them."

Mrs. George Edwin Mott gave ten minutes to Tennyson and Browning.

Mrs. Nat Hicks, a wry-faced, curiously sweet woman, so awed by her betters that Carol wanted to kiss her, completed the day's grim task by a paper on "Other Poets." The other poets worthy of consideration were Coleridge, Wordsworth, Shelley, Gray, Mrs. Hemans, and Kipling.

Miss Ella Stowbody obliged with a recital of "The Recessional" and extracts from "Lalla Rookh." By request, she gave "An Old Sweetheart of Mine" as encore.

Gopher Prairie had finished the poets. It was ready for the next week's labor: English Fiction and Essays.

Mrs. Dawson besought, "Now we will have a discussion of the papers, and I am sure we shall all enjoy hearing from one who we hope to have as a new member, Mrs. Kennicott, who with her spendid literary training and all should be able to give us many pointers and—many helpful pointers."

Carol had warned herself not to be so "beastly supercilious." She had insisted that in the belated quest of these work-stained women was an aspiration which ought to stir her tears. "But they're so self-satisfied. They think they're doing Burns a favor. They don't believe they have a 'belated quest.' They're sure that they have culture salted and hung up." It was out of this stupor of doubt that Mrs. Dawson's summons roused her. She was in a panic. How could she speak without hurting them?

Mrs. Champ Perry leaned over to stroke her hand and whisper, "You look tired, dearie. Don't you talk unless you want to."

Affection flooded Carol; she was on her feet, searching for words and courtesies:

"The only thing in the way of suggestion—— I know you are following a definite program, but I do wish that now you've had such a splendid introduction, instead of going on with some other subject next year you could return and take up the poets more in detail. Especially actual quotations—even though their lives are so interesting and, as Mrs. Warren said, so morally instructive. And perhaps there are several poets not mentioned today whom it might be worth while considering—Keats, for instance, and Matthew Arnold and Rossetti and Swinburne. Swinburne would be such a— well, that is, such a contrast to life as we all enjoy it in our beautiful Middle-west——"

She saw that Mrs. Leonard Warren was not with her. She captured her by innocently continuing:

"Unless perhaps Swinburne tends to be, uh, more outspoken than you, than we really like. What do you think, Mrs. Warren?"

The pastor's wife decided, "Why, you've caught my very thoughts, Mrs. Kennicott. Of course I have never *read* Swinburne, but years ago, when he was in vogue, I remember Mr. Warren saying that Swinburne (or was it Oscar Wilde? but anyway:) he said that though many so-called intellectual people posed and pretended to find beauty in Swinburne, there can never be genuine beauty without the message from the heart. But at the same time I do think you have an excellent idea, and though we have talked about Furnishings and China as the probable subject for next year, I believe that it would be nice if the program committee would try to work in another day entirely devoted to English poetry! In fact, Madame Chairman, I so move you."

When Mrs. Dawson's coffee and angel's-food had helped them to recover from the depression caused by thoughts of Shakespeare's death they all told Carol that it was a pleasure to have her with them. The membership committee retired to the sitting-room for three minutes and elected her a member.

And she stopped being patronizing.

She wanted to be one of them. They were so loyal and kind. It was they who would carry out her aspiration. Her campaign against village sloth was actually begun! On what specific reform should she first loose her army? During the gossip after the meeting Mrs. George Edwin Mott remarked that the city hall seemed inadequate for the splendid modern Gopher Prairie. Mrs. Nat Hicks timidly wished that the young people could have free dances there—the lodge dances were so exclusive. The city hall. That was it! Carol hurried home.

She had not realized that Gopher Prairie was a city. From Kennicott she discovered that it was legally organized with a mayor and city-council and wards. She was delighted by the simplicity of voting one's self a metropolis. Why not?

She was a proud and patriotic citizen, all evening.

II

She examined the city hall, next morning. She had remembered it only as a bleak inconspicuousness. She found it a liver-colored frame coop half a block from Main Street. The front was an unrelieved wall of clapboards and dirty win-

dows. It had an unobstructed view of a vacant lot and Nat
Hicks's tailor shop. It was larger than the carpenter shop beside it, but not so well built.

No one was about. She walked into the corridor. On one
side was the municipal court, like a country school; on the
other, the room of the volunteer fire company, with a Ford
hose-cart and the ornamental helmets used in parades; at the
end of the hall, a filthy two-cell jail, now empty but smelling of ammonia and ancient sweat. The whole second story
was a large unfinished room littered with piles of folding
chairs, a lime-crusted mortar-mixing box, and the skeletons of
Fourth of July floats covered with decomposing plaster
shields and faded red, white, and blue bunting. At the end
was an abortive stage. The room was large enough for the
community dances which Mrs. Nat Hicks advocated. But Carol
was after something bigger than dances.

In the afternoon she scampered to the public library.

The library was open three afternoons and four evenings
a week. It was housed in an old dwelling, sufficient but unattractive. Carol caught herself picturing pleasanter reading-
rooms, chairs for children, an art collection, a librarian young
enough to experiment.

She berated herself, "Stop this fever of reforming everything! I *will* be satisfied with the library! The city hall is
enough for a beginning. And it's really an excellent library.
It's—it isn't so bad. . . . Is it possible that I am to find
dishonesties and stupidity in every human activity I encounter? In schools and business and government and
everything? Is there never any contentment, never any
rest?"

She shook her head as though she were shaking off water,
and hastened into the library, a young, light, amiable presence, modest in unbuttoned fur coat, blue suit, fresh organdy
collar, and tan boots roughened from scuffling snow. Miss
Villets stared at her, and Carol purred, "I was so sorry not
to see you at the Thanatopsis yesterday. Vida said you
might come."

"Oh. You went to the Thanatopsis. Did you enjoy it?"

"So much. Such good papers on the poets." Carol lied
resolutely. "But I did think they should have had you give
one of the papers on poetry!"

"Well—— Of course I'm not one of the bunch that seem
to have the time to take and run the club, and if they prefer
to have papers on literature by other ladies who have no

literary training—after all, why should I complain? What am
I but a city employee!"

"You're not! You're the one person that does—that does—
oh, you do so much. Tell me, is there, uh—— Who are the
people who control the club?"

Miss Villets emphatically stamped a date in the front of
"Frank on the Lower Mississippi" for a small flaxen boy,
glowered at him as though she were stamping a warning on
his brain, and sighed:

"I wouldn't put myself forward or criticize any one for the
world, and Vida is one of my best friends, and such a
splendid teacher, and there is no one in town more advanced
and interested in all movements, but I must say that no matter who the president or the committees are, Vida Sherwin
seems to be behind them all the time, and though she is
always telling me about what she is pleased to call my 'fine
work in the library,' I notice that I'm not often called
on for papers, though Mrs. Lyman Cass once volunteered and
told me that she thought my paper on 'The Cathedrals of
England' was the most interesting paper we had, the year we
took up English and French travel and architecture. But——
And of course Mrs. Mott and Mrs. Warren are very important
in the club, as you might expect of the wives of the superintendent of schools and the Congregational pastor, and
indeed they are both very cultured, but—— No, you may
regard me as entirely unimportant. I'm sure what I say
doesn't matter a bit!"

"You're much too modest, and I'm going to tell Vida so,
and, uh, I wonder if you can give me just a teeny bit of your
time and show me where the magazine files are kept?"

She had won. She was profusely escorted to a room like a
grandmother's attic, where she discovered periodicals devoted
to house-decoration and town-planning, with a six-year file of
the National Geographic. Miss Villets blessedly left her alone.
Humming, fluttering pages with delighted fingers, Carol sat
cross-legged on the floor, the magazines in heaps about her.

She found pictures of New England streets: the dignity of
Falmouth, the charm of Concord, Stockbridge and Farming-
ton and Hillhouse Avenue. The fairy-book suburb of Forest
Hills on Long Island. Devonshire cottages and Essex manors
and a Yorkshire High Street and Port Sunlight. The Arab
village of Djeddah—an intricately chased jewel-box. A town
in California which had changed itself from the barren brick
fronts and slatternly frame sheds of a Main Street to a way

which led the eye down a vista of arcades and gardens.

Assured that she was not quite mad in her belief that a small American town might be lovely, as well as useful in buying wheat and selling plows, she sat brooding, her thin fingers playing a tattoo on her cheeks. She saw in Gopher Prairie a Georgian city hall: warm brick walls with white shutters, a fanlight, a wide hall and curving stair. She saw it the common home and inspiration not only of the town but of the country about. It should contain the court-room (she couldn't get herself to put in a jail), public library, a collection of excellent prints, rest-room and model kitchen for farmwives, theater, lecture room, free community ballroom, farm-bureau, gymnasium. Forming about it and influenced by it, as mediæval villages gathered about the castle, she saw a new Georgian town as graceful and beloved as Annapolis or that bowery Alexandria to which Washington rode.

All this the Thanatopsis Club was to accomplish with no difficulty whatever, since its several husbands were the controllers of business and politics. She was proud of herself for this practical view.

She had taken only half an hour to change a wire-fenced potato-plot into a walled rose-garden. She hurried out to apprize Mrs. Leonard Warren, as president of the Thanatopsis, of the miracle which had been worked.

III

At a quarter to three Carol had left home; at half-past four she had created the Georgian town; at a quarter to five she was in the dignified poverty of the Congregational parsonage, her enthusiasm pattering upon Mrs. Leonard Warren like summer rain upon an old gray roof; at two minutes to five a town of demure courtyards and welcoming dormer windows had been erected; and at two minutes past five the entire town was as flat as Babylon.

Erect in a black William and Mary chair against gray and speckly-brown volumes of sermons and Biblical commentaries and Palestine geographies upon long pine shelves, her neat, black shoes firm on a rag-rug, herself as correct and low-toned as her background, Mrs. Warren listened without comment till Carol was quite through, then answered delicately:

"Yes, I think you draw a very nice picture of what might easily come to pass—some day. I have no doubt that such villages will be found on the prairie—some day. But if I might make just the least little criticism: it seems to me that you are wrong in supposing either that the city hall would be the proper start, or that the Thanatopsis would be the right instrument. After all, it's the churches, isn't it, that are the real heart of the community. As you may possibly know, my husband is prominent in Congregational circles all through the state for his advocacy of church-union. He hopes to see all the evangelical denominations joined in one strong body, opposing Catholicism and Christian Science, and properly guiding all movements that make for morality and prohibition. Here, the combined churches could afford a splendid club-house, maybe a stucco and half-timber building with gargoyles and all sorts of pleasing decorations on it, which, it seems to me, would be lots better to impress the ordinary class of people than just a plain old-fashioned colonial house, such as you describe. And that would be the proper center for all educational and pleasurable activities, instead of letting them fall into the hands of the politicians."

"I don't suppose it will take more than thirty or forty years for the churches to get together?" Carol said innocently.

"Hardly that long even; things are moving so rapidly. So it would be a mistake to make any other plans."

Carol did not recover her zeal till two days after, when she tried Mrs. George Edwin Mott, wife of the superintendent of schools.

Mrs. Mott commented, "Personally, I am terribly busy with dressmaking and having the seamstress in the house and all, but it would be splendid to have the other members of the Thanatopsis take up the question. Except for one thing: First and foremost, we must have a new schoolbuilding. Mr. Mott says they are terribly cramped."

Carol went to view the old building. The grades and the high school were combined in a damp yellow-brick structure with the narrow windows of an antiquated jail—a hulk which expressed hatred and compulsory training. She conceded Mrs. Mott's demand so violently that for two days she dropped her own campaign. Then she built the school and city hall together, as the center of the reborn town.

She ventured to the lead-colored dwelling of Mrs. Dave Dyer. Behind the mask of winter-stripped vines and a wide porch only a foot above the ground, the cottage was so impersonal that Carol could never visualize it. Nor could she remember anything that was inside it. But Mrs. Dyer was personal enough. With Carol, Mrs. Howland, Mrs. McGanum, and Vida Sherwin she was a link between the Jolly Seventeen and the serious Thanatopsis (in contrast to Juanita Haydock, who unnecessarily boasted of being a "lowbrow" and publicly stated that she would "see herself in jail before she'd write any darned old club papers"). Mrs. Dyer was superfeminine in the kimono in which she received Carol. Her skin was fine, pale, soft, suggesting a weak voluptuousness. At afternoon-coffees she had been rude but now she addressed Carol as "dear," and insisted on being called Maud. Carol did not quite know why she was uncomfortable in this talcumpowder atmosphere, but she hastened to get into the fresh air of her plans.

Maud Dyer granted that the city hall wasn't "so very nice," yet, as Dave said, there was no use doing anything about it till they received an appropriation from the state and combined a new city hall with a national guard armory. Dave had given verdict, "What these mouthy youngsters that hang around the pool-room need is universal military training. Make men of 'em."

Mrs. Dyer removed the new schoolbuilding from the city hall:

"Oh, so Mrs. Mott has got you going on her school craze! She's been dinging at that till everybody's sick and tired. What she really wants is a big office for her dear bald-headed Gawge to sit around and look important in. Of course I admire Mrs. Mott, and I'm very fond of her, she's so brainy, even if she does try to butt in and run the Thanatopsis, but I must say we're sick of her nagging. The old building was good enough for us when we were kids! I hate these would-be women politicians, don't you?"

IV

The first week of March had given promise of spring and stirred Carol with a thousand desires for lakes and fields and roads. The snow was gone except for filthy woolly patches under trees; the thermometer leaped in a day from windbitten chill to itchy warmth. As soon as Carol was convinced that even in this imprisoned North, spring could exist again, the snow came down as abruptly as a paper storm in a theater; the northwest gale flung it up in a half-blizzard; and with her hope of a glorified town went hope of summer meadows.

But a week later, though the snow was everywhere in slushy heaps, the promise was unmistakable. By the invisible hints in air and sky and earth which had aroused her every year through ten thousand generations she knew that spring was coming. It was not a scorching, hard, dusty day like the treacherous intruder of a week before, but soaked with languor, softened with a milky light. Rivulets were hurrying in each alley; a calling robin appeared by magic on the crab-apple tree in the Howlands' yard. Everybody chuckled, "Looks like winter is going," and "This 'll bring the frost out of the roads—have the autos out pretty soon now—wonder what kind of bass-fishing we'll get this summer—ought to be good crops this year."

Each evening Kennicott repeated, "We better not take off our Heavy Underwear or the storm windows too soon—might be 'nother spell of cold—got to be careful 'bout catching cold—wonder if the coal will last through?"

The expanding forces of life within her choked the desire for reforming. She trotted through the house, planning the spring cleaning with Bea. When she attended her second meeting of the Thanatopsis she said nothing about remaking the town. She listened respectably to statistics on Dickens, Thackeray, Jane Austen, George Eliot, Scott, Hardy, Lamb, De Quincey, and Mrs. Humphry Ward, who, it seemed, constituted the writers of English Fiction and Essays.

Not till she inspected the rest-room did she again become a fanatic. She had often glanced at the store-building which had been turned into a refuge in which farmwives could wait while their husbands transacted business. She had heard Vida Sherwin and Mrs. Warren caress the virtue of the Thanatopsis in establishing the rest-room and in sharing with the city council the expense of maintaining it. But she had never entered it till this March day.

She went in impulsively; nodded at the matron, a plump worthy widow named Nodelquist, and at a couple of farm-women who were meekly rocking. The rest-room resembled a second-hand store. It was furnished with discarded patent rockers, lopsided reed chairs, a scratched pine table, a gritty straw mat, old steel engravings of milkmaids being morally amorous under willow-trees, faded chromos of roses and fish, and a kerosene stove for warming lunches. The front window was darkened by torn net curtains and by a mound of geraniums and rubber-plants.

While she was listening to Mrs. Nodelquist's account of how many thousands of farmers' wives used the rest-room every year, and how much they "appreciated the kindness of the ladies in providing them with this lovely place, and all free," she thought, "Kindness nothing! The kind-ladies' husbands get the farmers' trade. This is mere commercial accommodation. And it's horrible. It ought to be the most charming room in town, to comfort women sick of prairie kitchens. Certainly it ought to have a clear window, so that they can see the metropolitan life go by. Some day I'm going to make a better rest-room—a club-room. Why! I've already planned that as part of my Georgian town hall!"

So it chanced that she was plotting against the peace of the Thanatopsis at her third meeting (which covered Scandinavian, Russian, and Polish Literature, with remarks by Mrs. Leonard Warren on the sinful paganism of the Russian so-called church). Even before the entrance of the coffee and hot rolls Carol seized on Mrs. Champ Perry, the kind and ample-bosomed pioneer woman who gave historic dignity to the modern matrons of the Thanatopsis. She poured out her plans. Mrs. Perry nodded and stroked Carol's hand, but at the end she sighed:

"I wish I could agree with you, dearie. I'm sure you're one of the Lord's anointed (even if we don't see you at the Baptist Church as often as we'd like to)! But I'm afraid you're too tender-hearted. When Champ and I came here we teamed-it with an ox-cart from Sauk Centre to Gopher Prairie, and there was nothing here then but a stockade and a few soldiers and some log cabins. When we wanted salt pork and gunpowder, we sent out a man on horseback, and probably he was shot dead by the Injuns before he got back. We ladies—of course we were all farmers at first—we didn't expect any rest-room in those days. My, we'd have thought the one they have now was simply elegant! My house was roofed with hay and it leaked something terrible when it rained—only dry place was under a shelf.

"And when the town grew up we thought the new city hall was real fine. And I don't see any need for dance-halls. Dancing isn't what it was, anyway. We used to dance modest, and we had just as much fun as all these young folks do now with their terrible Turkey Trots and hugging and all. But if they must neglect the Lord's injunction that young girls

ought to be modest, then I guess they manage pretty well
at the K. P. Hall and the Oddfellows', even if some of the
lodges don't always welcome a lot of these foreigners and
hired help to all their dances. And I certainly don't see any
need of a farm-bureau or this domestic science demonstra-
tion you talk about. In my day the boys learned to farm by
honest sweating, and every gal could cook, or her ma learned
her how across her knee! Besides, ain't there a county agent
at Wakamin? He comes here once a fortnight, maybe. That's
enough monkeying with this scientific farming—Champ says
there's nothing to it anyway.

"And as for a lecture hall—haven't we got the churches?
Good deal better to listen to a good old-fashioned sermon than
a lot of geography and books and things that nobody needs
to know—more 'n enough heathen learning right here in the
Thanatopsis. And as for trying to make a whole town in this
Colonial architecture you talk about—— I do love nice
things; to this day I run ribbons into my petticoats, even if
Champ Perry does laugh at me, the old villain! But just
the same I don't believe any of us old-timers would like to
see the town that we worked so hard to build being tore
down to make a place that wouldn't look like nothing but
some Dutch storybook and not a bit like the place we loved.
And don't you think it's sweet now? All the trees and lawns?
And such comfy houses, and hot-water heat and electric
lights and telephones and cement walks and everything? Why,
I thought everybody from the Twin Cities always said it
was such a beautiful town!"

Carol forswore herself; declared that Gopher Prairie had
the color of Algiers and the gaiety of Mardi Gras.

Yet the next afternoon she was pouncing on Mrs. Lyman
Cass, the hook-nosed consort of the owner of the flour-mill.

Mrs. Cass's parlor belonged to the crammed-Victorian
school, as Mrs. Luke Dawson's belonged to the bare-Victo-
rian. It was furnished on two principles: First, everything
must resemble something else. A rocker had a back like a
lyre, a near-leather seat imitating tufted cloth, and arms like
Scotch Presbyterian lions; with knobs, scrolls, shields, and
spear-points on unexpected portions of the chair. The second
principle of the crammed-Victorian school was that every
inch of the interior must be filled with useless objects.

The walls of Mrs. Cass's parlor were plastered with "hand-
painted" pictures, "buckeye" pictures, of birch-trees, news-
boys, puppies, and church-steeples on Christmas Eve; with a

plaque depicting the Exposition Building in Minneapolis, burnt-wood portraits of Indian chiefs of no tribe in particular, a pansy-decked poetic motto, a Yard of Roses, and the banners of the educational institutions attended by the Casses' two sons—Chicopee Falls Business College and McGillicuddy University. One small square table contained a card-receiver of painted china with a rim of wrought and gilded lead, a Family Bible, Grant's Memoirs, the latest novel by Mrs. Gene Stratton Porter, a wooden model of a Swiss chalet which was also a bank for dimes, a polished abalone shell holding one black-headed pin and one empty spool, a velvet pin-cushion in a gilded metal slipper with "Souvenir of Troy, N. Y." stamped on the toe, and an unexplained red glass dish which had warts.

Mrs. Cass's first remark was, "I must show you all my pretty things and art objects."

She piped, after Carol's appeal:

"I see. You think the New England villages and Colonial houses are so much more cunning than these Middlewestern towns. I'm glad you feel that way. You'll be interested to know I was born in Vermont."

"And don't you think we ought to try to make Gopher Prai——"

"My gracious no! We can't afford it. Taxes are much too high as it is. We ought to retrench, and not let the city council spend another cent. Uh—— Don't you think that was a grand paper Mrs. Westlake read about Tolstoy? I was so glad she pointed out how all his silly socialistic ideas failed."

What Mrs. Cass said was what Kennicott said, that evening. Not in twenty years would the council propose or Gopher Prairie vote the funds for a new city hall.

V

Carol had avoided exposing her plans to Vida Sherwin. She was shy of the big-sister manner; Vida would either laugh at her or snatch the idea and change it to suit herself. But there was no other hope. When Vida came in to tea Carol sketched her Utopia.

Vida was soothing but decisive:

"My dear, you're all off. I would like to see it: a real gardeny place to shut out the gales. But it can't be done. What could the clubwomen accomplish?"

"Their husbands are the most important men in town. They *are* the town!"

"But the town as a separate unit is not the husband of the Thanatopsis. If you knew the trouble we had in getting the city council to spend the money and cover the pumping-station with vines! Whatever you may think of Gopher Prairie women, they're twice as progressive as the men."

"But can't the men see the ugliness?"

"They don't think it's ugly. And how can you prove it? Matter of taste. Why should they like what a Boston architect likes?"

"What they like is to sell prunes!"

"Well, why not? Anyway, the point is that you have to work from the inside, with what we have, rather than from the outside, with foreign ideas. The shell ought not to be forced on the spirit. It can't be! The bright shell has to grow out of the spirit, and express it. That means waiting. If we keep after the city council for another ten years they *may* vote the bonds for a new school."

"I refuse to believe that if they saw it the big men would be too tight-fisted to spend a few dollars each for a building—think!—dancing and lectures and plays, all done co-opera-tively!"

"You mention the word 'co-operative' to the merchants and they'll lynch you! The one thing they fear more than mail-order houses is that farmers' co-operative movements may get started."

"The secret trails that lead to scared pocket-books! Always, in everything! And I don't have any of the fine melodrama of fiction: the dictagraphs and speeches by torchlight. I'm merely blocked by stupidity. Oh, I know I'm a fool. I dream of Venice, and I live in Archangel and scold because the Northern seas aren't tender-colored. But at least they sha'n't keep me from loving Venice, and sometime I'll run away —— All right. No more."

She flung out her hands in a gesture of renunciation.

VI

Early May; wheat springing up in blades like grass; corn and potatoes being planted; the land humming. For two days there had been steady rain. Even in town the roads were a furrowed welter of mud, hideous to view and difficult to cross. Main Street was a black swamp from curb to curb;

on residence streets the grass parking beside the walks oozed
gray water. It was prickly hot, yet the town was barren under
the bleak sky. Softened neither by snow nor by waving
boughs the houses squatted and scowled, revealed in their unkempt harshness.

As she dragged homeward Carol looked with distaste at
her clay-loaded rubbers, the smeared hem of her skirt. She
passed Lyman Cass's pinnacled, dark-red, hulking house.
She waded a streaky yellow pool. This morass was not her
home, she insisted. Her home, and her beautiful town, existed
in her mind. They had already been created. The task was
done. What she really had been questing was some one to
share them with her. Vida would not; Kennicott could not.

Some one to share her refuge.

Suddenly she was thinking of Guy Pollock.

She dismissed him. He was too cautious. She needed a spirit
as young and unreasonable as her own. And she would
never find it. Youth would never come singing. She was
beaten.

Yet that same evening she had an idea which solved the
rebuilding of Gopher Prairie.

Within ten minutes she was jerking the old-fashioned bell-
pull of Luke Dawson. Mrs. Dawson opened the door and
peered doubtfully about the edge of it. Carol kissed her
cheek, and frisked into the lugubrious sitting-room.

"Well, well, you're a sight for sore eyes!" chuckled Mr.
Dawson, dropping his newspaper, pushing his spectacles
back on his forehead.

"You seem so excited," sighed Mrs. Dawson.

"I am! Mr. Dawson, aren't you a millionaire?"

He cocked his head, and purred, "Well, I guess if I cashed
in on all my securities and farm-holdings and my interests in
iron on the Mesaba and in Northern timber and cut-over
lands, I could push two million dollars pretty close, and I've
made every cent of it by hard work and having the sense to
not go out and spend every——"

"I think I want most of it from you!"

The Dawsons glanced at each other in appreciation of the
jest; and he chirped, "You're worse than Reverend Benlick!
He don't hardly ever strike me for more than ten dollars—
at a time!"

"I'm not joking. I mean it! Your children in the Cities are
grown-up and well-to-do. You don't want to die and leave
your name unknown. Why not do a big, original thing? Why

49 9 49 9 9 9 9 9 9 4 9 9 9 9 9 9 9 9 9 99 9

not rebuild the whole town? Get a great architect, and have him plan a town that would be suitable to the prairie. Perhaps he'd create some entirely new form of architecture. Then tear down all these shambling buildings——"

Mr. Dawson had decided that she really did mean it. He wailed, "Why, that would cost at least three or four million dollars!"

"But you alone, just one man, have two of those millions!"

"Me? Spend all my hard-earned cash on building houses for a lot of shiftless beggars that never had the sense to save their money? Not that I've ever been mean. Mama could always have a hired girl to do the work—when we could find one. But her and I have worked our fingers to the bone and—spend it on a lot of these rascals——?"

"Please! Don't be angry! I just mean—I mean—— Oh, not spend all of it, of course, but if you led off the list, and the others came in, and if they heard you talk about a more attractive town——"

"Why now, child, you've got a lot of notions. Besides, what's the matter with the town? Looks good to me. I've had people that have traveled all over the world tell me time and again that Gopher Prairie is the prettiest place in the Middlewest. Good enough for anybody. Certainly good enough for Mama and me. Besides! Mama and me are planning to go out to Pasadena and buy a bungalow and live there."

VII

She had met Miles Bjornstam on the street. For the second of welcome encounter this workman with the bandit mustache and the muddy overalls seemed nearer than any one else to the credulous youth which she was seeking to fight beside her, and she told him, as a cheerful anecdote, a little of her story.

He grunted, "I never thought I'd be agreeing with Old Man Dawson, the penny-pinching old land-thief—and a fine briber he is, too. But you got the wrong slant. You aren't one of the people—yet. You want to do something for the town. I don't! I want the town to do something for itself. We don't want old Dawson's money—not if it's a gift, with a string. We'll take it away from him, because it belongs to us. You got to get more iron and cussedness into you. Come join us cheerful bums, and some day—when we educate ourselves and quit being bums—we'll take things and run 'em straight."

He had changed from her friend to a cynical man in overalls. She could not relish the autocracy of "cheerful bums."

She forgot him as she tramped the outskirts of town.

She had replaced the city hall project by an entirely new and highly exhilarating thought of how little was done for these unpicturesque poor.

VIII

The spring of the plains is not a reluctant virgin but brazen and soon away. The mud roads of a few days ago are powdery dust and the puddles beside them have hardened into lozenges of black sleek earth like cracked patent leather.

Carol was panting as she crept to the meeting of the Thanatopsis program committee which was to decide the subject for next fall and winter.

Madam Chairman (Miss Ella Stowbody in an oyster-colored blouse) asked if there was any new business.

Carol rose. She suggested that the Thanatopsis ought to help the poor of the town. She was ever so correct and modern. She did not, she said, want charity for them, but a chance of self-help; an employment bureau, direction in washing babies and making pleasing stews, possibly a municipal fund for home-building. "What do you think of my plans, Mrs. Warren?" she concluded.

Speaking judiciously, as one related to the church by marriage, Mrs. Warren gave verdict:

"I'm sure we're all heartily in accord with Mrs. Kennicott in feeling that wherever genuine poverty is encountered, it is not only *noblesse oblige* but a joy to fulfill our duty to the less fortunate ones. But I must say it seems to me we should lose the whole point of the thing by not regarding it as charity. Why, that's the chief adornment of the true Christian and the church! The Bible has laid it down for our guidance. 'Faith, Hope, and *Charity*,' it says, and, 'The poor ye have with ye always,' which indicates that there never can be anything to these so-called scientific schemes for abolishing charity, never! And isn't it better so? I should hate to think of a world in which we were deprived of all the pleasure of giving. Besides, if these shiftless folks realize they're getting charity, and not something to which they have a right, they're so much more grateful."

"Besides," snorted Miss Ella Stowbody, "they've been fooling you, Mrs. Kennicott. There isn't any real poverty here. Take that Mrs. Steinhof you speak of: I send her our washing whenever there's too much for our hired girl—I must have sent her ten dollars' worth the past year alone! I'm sure Papa would never approve of a city home-building fund. Papa says these folks are fakers. Especially all these tenant farmers that pretend they have so much trouble getting seed and machinery. Papa says they simply won't pay their debts. He says he's sure he hates to foreclose mortgages, but it's the only way to make them respect the law."

"And then think of all the clothes we give these people!" said Mrs. Jackson Elder.

Carol intruded again. "Oh yes. The clothes. I was going to speak of that. Don't you think that when we give clothes to the poor, if we do give them old ones, we ought to mend them first and make them as presentable as we can? Next Christmas when the Thanatopsis makes its distribution, wouldn't it be jolly if we got together and sewed on the clothes, and trimmed hats, and made them——"

"Heavens and earth, they have more time than we have! They ought to be mighty good and grateful to get anything, no matter what shape it's in. I know I'm not going to sit and sew for that lazy Mrs. Vopni, with all I've got to do!" snapped Ella Stowbody.

They were glaring at Carol. She reflected that Mrs. Vopni, whose husband had been killed by a train, had ten children.

But Mrs. Mary Ellen Wilks was smiling. Mrs. Wilks was the proprietor of Ye Art Shoppe and Magazine and Book Store, and the reader of the small Christian Science church. She made it all clear:

"If this class of people had an understanding of Science and that we are the children of God and nothing can harm us, they wouldn't be in error and poverty."

Mrs. Jackson Elder confirmed, "Besides, it strikes me the club is already doing enough, with tree-planting and the anti-fly campaign and the responsibility for the rest-room—to say nothing of the fact that we've talked of trying to get the railroad to put in a park at the station!"

"I think so too!" said Madam Chairman. She glanced uneasily at Miss Sherwin. "But what do you think, Vida?"

Vida smiled tactfully at each of the committee, and announced, "Well, I don't believe we'd better start anything more right now. But it's been a privilege to hear Carol's dear

generous ideas, hasn't it! Oh! There is one thing we must
decide on at once. We must get together and oppose any
move on the part of the Minneapolis clubs to elect another
State Federation president from the Twin Cities. And this
Mrs. Edgar Potbury they're putting forward—I know there
are people who think she's a bright interesting speaker, but I
regard her as very shallow. What do you say to my writing
to the Lake Ojibawasha Club, telling them that if their district will support Mrs. Warren for second vice-president,
we'll support their Mrs. Hagelton (and such a dear, lovely,
cultivated woman, too) for president."

"Yes! We ought to show up those Minneapolis folks!" Ella
Stowbody said acidly. "And oh, by the way, we must
oppose this movement of Mrs. Potbury's to have the state
clubs come out definitely in favor of woman suffrage. Women
haven't any place in politics. They would lose all their dain-
tiness and charm if they became involved in these horrid
plots and log-rolling and all this awful political stuff about
scandal and personalities and so on."

All—save one—nodded. They interrupted the formal
business-meeting to discuss Mrs. Edgar Potbury's husband,
Mrs. Potbury's income, Mrs. Potbury's sedan, Mrs. Potbury's
residence, Mrs. Potbury's oratorical style, Mrs. Potbury's
mandarin evening coat, Mrs. Potbury's coiffure, and Mrs.
Potbury's altogether reprehensible influence on the State
Federation of Women's Clubs.

Before the program committee adjourned they took three
minutes to decide which of the subjects suggested by the
magazine *Culture Hints,* Furnishings and China, or The Bible
as Literature, would be better for the coming year. There
was one annoying incident. Mrs. Dr. Kennicott interfered
and showed off again. She commented, "Don't you think
that we already get enough of the Bible in our churches and
Sunday Schools?"

Mrs. Leonard Warren, somewhat out of order but much
more out of temper, cried, "Well upon my word! I didn't
suppose there was any one who felt that we could get enough
of the Bible! I guess if the Grand Old Book has withstood
the attacks of infidels for these two thousand years it is worth
our *slight* consideration!"

"Oh, I didn't mean——" Carol begged. Inasmuch as she
did mean, it was hard to be extremely lucid. "But I wish,
instead of limiting ourselves either to the Bible, or to anec-
dotes about the Brothers Adam's wigs, which *Culture Hints*

seems to regard as the significant point about furniture, we could study some of the really stirring ideas that are springing up today—whether it's chemistry or anthropology or labor problems—the things that are going to mean so terribly much."

Everybody cleared her polite throat.

Madam Chairman inquired, "Is there any other discussion? Will some one make a motion to adopt the suggestion of Vida Sherwin—to take up Furnishings and China?"

It was adopted, unanimously.

"Checkmate!" murmured Carol, as she held up her hand.

Had she actually believed that she could plant a seed of liberalism in the blank wall of mediocrity? How had she fallen into the folly of trying to plant anything whatever in a wall so smooth and sun-glazed, and so satisfying to the happy sleepers within?

chapter 12

ONE week of authentic spring, one rare sweet week of May, one tranquil moment between the blast of winter and the charge of summer. Daily Carol walked from town into flashing country hysteric with new life.

One enchanted hour when she returned to youth and a belief in the possibility of beauty.

She had walked northward toward the upper shore of Plover Lake, taking to the railroad track, whose directness and dryness make it the natural highway for pedestrians on the plains. She stepped from tie to tie, in long strides. At each road-crossing she had to crawl over a cattle-guard of sharpened timbers. She walked the rails, balancing with arms extended, cautious heel before toe. As she lost balance her body bent over, her arms revolved wildly, and when she toppled she laughed aloud.

The thick grass beside the track, coarse and prickly with many burnings, hid canary-yellow buttercups and the mauve petals and woolly sage-green coats of the pasque flowers. The branches of the kinnikinic brush were red and smooth as lacquer on a saki bowl.

She ran down the gravelly embankment, smiled at children gathering flowers in a little basket, thrust a handful of the soft pasque flowers into the bosom of her white blouse. Fields of springing wheat drew her from the straight propriety of the railroad and she crawled through the rusty barbed-wire fence. She followed a furrow between low wheat blades and a field of rye which showed silver lights as it flowed before the wind. She found a pasture by the lake. So sprinkled was the pasture with rag-baby blossoms and the cottony herb of Indian tobacco that it spread out like a rare old Persian carpet of cream and rose and delicate green. Under her feet the rough grass made a pleasant crunching. Sweet winds blew from the sunny lake beside her, and small waves sputtered on the meadowy shore. She leaped a tiny creek bowered in pussy-willow buds. She was nearing a frivolous grove of birch and poplar and wild plum trees.

The poplar foliage had the downiness of a Corot arbor; the green and silver trunks were as candid as the birches, as slender and lustrous as the limbs of a Pierrot. The cloudy white blossoms of the plum trees filled the grove with a springtime mistiness which gave an illusion of distance.

She ran into the wood, crying out for joy of freedom regained after winter. Choke-cherry blossoms lured her from the outer sun-warmed spaces to depths of green stillness, where a submarine light came through the young leaves. She walked pensively along an abandoned road. She found a moccasin-flower beside a lichen-covered log. At the end of the road she saw the open acres—dipping rolling fields bright with wheat.

"I believe! The woodland gods still live! And out there, the great land. It's beautiful as the mountains. What do I care for Thanatopsises?"

She came out on the prairie, spacious under an arch of boldly cut clouds. Small pools glittered. Above a marsh red-winged blackbirds chased a crow in a swift melodrama of the air. On a hill was silhouetted a man following a drag. His horse bent its neck and plodded, content.

A path took her to the Corinth road, leading back to town. Dandelions glowed in patches amidst the wild grass by the way. A stream galloped through a concrete culvert beneath the road. She trudged in healthy weariness.

A man in a bumping Ford rattled up beside her, hailed, "Give you a lift, Mrs. Kennicott?"

"Thank you. It's awfully good of you, but I'm enjoying the walk."

"Great day, by golly. I seen some wheat that must of been five inches high. Well, so long."

She hadn't the dimmest notion who he was, but his greeting warmed her. This countryman gave her a companionship which she had never (whether by her fault or theirs or neither) been able to find in the matrons and commercial lords of the town.

Half a mile from town, in a hollow between hazelnut bushes and a brook, she discovered a gipsy encampment: a covered wagon, a tent, a bunch of pegged-out horses. A broad-shouldered man was squatted on his heels, holding a frying-pan over a camp-fire. He looked toward her. He was Miles Bjornstam.

"Well, well, what you doing out here?" he roared. "Come have a hunk o' bacon. Pete! Hey, Pete!"

A tousled person came from behind the covered wagon.

"Pete, here's the one honest-to-God lady in my bum town. Come on, crawl in and set a couple minutes, Mrs. Kennicott. I'm hiking off for all summer."

The Red Swede staggered up, rubbed his cramped knees, lumbered to the wire fence, held the strands apart for her. She unconsciously smiled at him as she went through. Her skirt caught on a barb; he carefully freed it.

Beside this man in blue flannel shirt, baggy khaki trousers, uneven suspenders, and vile felt hat, she was small and exquisite.

The surly Pete set out an upturned bucket for her. She lounged on it, her elbows on her knees. "Where are you going?" she asked.

"Just starting off for the summer, horse-trading." Bjornstam chuckled. His red mustache caught the sun. "Regular hoboes and public benefactors we are. Take a hike like this every once in a while. Sharks on horses. Buy 'em from farmers and sell 'em to others. We're honest—frequently. Great time. Camp along the road. I was wishing I had a chance to say good-by to you before I ducked out but—— Say, you better come along with us."

"I'd like to."

"While you're playing mumblety-peg with Mrs. Lym Cass, Pete and me will be rambling across Dakota, through the

Bad Lands, into the butte country, and when fall comes, we'll be crossing over a pass of the Big Horn Mountains, maybe, and camp in a snow-storm, quarter of a mile right straight up above a lake. Then in the morning we'll lie snug in our blankets and look up through the pines at an angle. How'd it strike you? Heh? Eagle soaring and soaring all day —big wide sky——"

"Don't! Or I will go with you, and I'm afraid there might be some slight scandal. Perhaps some day I'll do it. Good-by."

Her hand disappeared in his blackened leather glove. From the turn in the road she waved at him. She walked on more soberly now, and she was lonely.

But the wheat and grass were sleek velvet under the sunset; the prairie clouds were tawny gold; and she swung happily into Main Street.

II

Through the first days of June she drove with Kennicott on his calls. She identified him with the virile land; she admired him as she saw with what respect the farmers obeyed him. She was out in the early chill, after a hasty cup of coffee, reaching open country as the fresh sun came up in that unspoiled world. Meadow larks called from the tops of thin split fence-posts. The wild roses smelled clean.

As they returned in late afternoon the low sun was a solemnity of radial bands, like a heavenly fan of beaten gold; the limitless circle of the grain was a green sea rimmed with fog, and the willow wind-breaks were palmy isles.

Before July the close heat blanketed them. The tortured earth cracked. Farmers panted through corn-fields behind cultivators and the sweating flanks of horses. While she waited for Kennicott in the car, before a farmhouse, the seat burned her fingers and her head ached with the glare on fenders and hood.

A black thunder-shower was followed by a dust storm which turned the sky yellow with the hint of a coming tornado. Impalpable black dust far-borne from Dakota covered the inner sills of the closed windows.

The July heat was ever more stifling. They crawled along Main Street by day; they found it hard to sleep at night. They brought mattresses down to the living-room, and thrashed and turned by the open window. Ten times a night they talked of going out to soak themselves with the hose and wade through the dew, but they were too listless to take the trouble. On cool evenings, when they tried to go walking, the gnats appeared in swarms which peppered their faces and caught in their throats.

She wanted the Northern pines, the Eastern sea, but Kennicott declared that it would be "kind of hard to get away, just *now.*" The Health and Improvement Committee of the Thanatopsis asked her to take part in the anti-fly campaign, and she toiled about town persuading householders to use the flytraps furnished by the club, or giving out money prizes to flyswatting children. She was loyal enough but not ardent, and without ever quite intending to, she began to neglect the task as heat sucked at her strength.

Kennicott and she motored North and spent a week with his mother—that is, Carol spent it with his mother, while he fished for bass.

The great event was their purchase of a summer cottage, down on Lake Minniemashie.

Perhaps the most amiable feature of life in Gopher Prairie was the summer cottages. They were merely two-room shanties, with a seepage of broken-down chairs, peeling veneered tables, chromos pasted on wooden walls, and inefficient kerosene stoves. They were so thin-walled and so close together that you could—and did—hear a baby being spanked in the fifth cottage off. But they were set among elms and lindens on a bluff which looked across the lake to fields of ripened wheat sloping up to green woods.

Here the matrons forgot social jealousies, and sat gossiping in gingham; or, in old bathing-suits, surrounded by hysterical children, they paddled for hours. Carol joined them; she ducked shrieking small boys, and helped babies construct sandbasins for unfortunate minnows. She liked Juanita Haydock and Maud Dyer when she helped them make picnic-supper for the men, who came motoring out from town each evening. She was easier and more natural with them. In the debate as to whether there should be veal loaf or poached egg on hash, she had no chance to be heretical and oversensitive.

They danced sometimes, in the evening; they had a minstrel show, with Kennicott surprisingly good as end-man; always they were encircled by children wise in the lore of woodchucks and gophers and rafts and willow whistles.

If they could have continued this normal barbaric life Carol would have been the most enthusiastic citizen of Gopher Prairie. She was relieved to be assured that she did not want bookish conversation alone; that she did not expect the town to become a Bohemia. She was content now. She did not criticize.

But in September, when the year was at its richest, custom dictated that it was time to return to town; to remove the children from the waste occupation of learning the earth, and send them back to lessons about the number of potatoes which (in a delightful world untroubled by commission-houses or shortages in freight-cars) William sold to John. The women who had cheerfully gone bathing all summer looked doubtful when Carol begged, "Let's keep up an out-door life this winter, let's slide and skate." Their hearts shut again till spring, and the nine months of cliques and radiators and dainty refreshments began all over.

III

Carol had started a salon.

Since Kennicott, Vida Sherwin, and Guy Pollock were her only lions, and since Kennicott would have preferred Sam Clark to all the poets and radicals in the entire world, her private and self-defensive clique did not get beyond one evening dinner for Vida and Guy, on her first wedding anniversary; and that dinner did not get beyond a controversy regarding Raymie Wutherspoon's yearnings.

Guy Pollock was the gentlest person she had found here. He spoke of her new jade and cream frock naturally, not jocosely; he held her chair for her as they sat down to dinner; and he did not, like Kennicott, interrupt her to shout, "Oh say, speaking of that, I heard a good story today." But Guy was incurably hermit. He sat late and talked hard, and did not come again.

Then she met Champ Perry in the post-office—and decided that in the history of the pioneers was the panacea for Gopher Prairie, for all of America. We have lost their sturdi-ness, she told herself. We must restore the last of the veterans to power and follow them on the backward path to the integ-rity of Lincoln, to the gaiety of settlers dancing in a saw-mill.

She read in the records of the Minnesota Territorial Pio-neers that only sixty years ago, not so far back as the birth of her own father, four cabins had composed Gopher Prairie. The log stockade which Mrs. Champ Perry was to find when she trekked in was built afterward by the soldiers as a defense against the Sioux. The four cabins were inhabited by Maine Yankees who had come up the Mississippi to St. Paul and driven north over virgin prairie into virgin woods. They ground their own corn; the men-folks shot ducks and pigeons and prairie chickens; the new breakings yielded the turnip-like rutabagas, which they ate raw and boiled and baked and raw again. For treat they had wild plums and crab-apples and tiny wild strawberries.

Grasshoppers came darkening the sky, and in an hour ate the farmwife's garden and the farmer's coat. Precious horses, painfully brought from Illinois, were drowned in bogs or stampeded by the fear of blizzards. Snow blew through the chinks of new-made cabins, and Eastern children, with flowery muslin dresses, shivered all winter and in summer were red and black with mosquito bites. Indians were everywhere; they camped in dooryards, stalked into kitchens to demand doughnuts, came with rifles across their backs into schoolhouses and begged to see the pictures in the geographies. Packs of timberwolves treed the children; and the settlers found dens of rattlesnakes, killed fifty, a hundred, in a day.

Yet it was a buoyant life. Carol read enviously in the admirable Minnesota chronicles called "Old Rail Fence Corners" the reminiscence of Mrs. Mahlon Black, who settled in Stillwater in 1848:

"There was nothing to parade over in those days. We took it as it came and had happy lives. . . . We would all gather together and in about two minutes would be having a good time—playing cards or dancing. . . . We used to waltz and dance contra dances. None of these new jigs and not wear any clothes to speak of. We covered our hides in those days; no tight skirts like now. You could take three or four steps inside our skirts and then not reach the edge. One of the boys would fiddle a while and then some one would spell him and he could get a dance. Sometimes they would dance and fiddle too."

She reflected that if she could not have ballrooms of gray and rose and crystal, she wanted to be swinging across a puncheon-floor with a dancing fiddler. This smug in-between town, which had exchanged "Money Musk" for phonographs grinding out ragtime, it was neither the heroic old nor the sophisticated new. Couldn't she somehow, some yet unimagined how, turn it back to simplicity?

She herself knew two of the pioneers: the Perrys. Champ Perry was the buyer at the grain-elevator. He weighed wagons of wheat on a rough platform-scale, in the cracks of which the kernels sprouted every spring. Between times he napped in the dusty peace of his office.

She called on the Perrys at their rooms above Howland & Gould's grocery.

When they were already old they had lost the money, which they had invested in an elevator. They had given up their beloved yellow brick house and moved into these rooms over a store, which were the Gopher Prairie equivalent of a flat. A broad stairway led from the street to the upper hall, along which were the doors of a lawyer's office, a dentist's, a photographer's "studio," the lodge-rooms of the Affiliated Order of Spartans and, at the back, the Perrys' apartment.

They received her (their first caller in a month) with aged fluttering tenderness. Mrs. Perry confided, "My, it's a shame we got to entertain you in such a cramped place. And there ain't any water except that ole iron sink outside in the hall, but still, as I say to Champ, beggars can't be choosers. 'Sides, the brick house was too big for me to sweep, and it was way out, and it's nice to be living down here among folks. Yes, we're glad to be here. But—— Some day, maybe we can have a house of our own again. We're saving up—— Oh, dear, if we could have our own home! But these rooms are real nice, ain't they!"

As old people will, the world over, they had moved as much as possible of their familiar furniture into this small space. Carol had none of the superiority she felt toward Mrs. Lyman Cass's plutocratic parlor. She was at home here. She noted with tenderness all the makeshifts: the darned chair-arms, the patent rocker covered with sleazy cretonne, the pasted strips of paper mending the birch-bark napkin-rings labeled "Papa" and "Mama."

She hinted of her new enthusiasm. To find one of the "young folks" who took them seriously heartened the Perrys, and she easily drew from them the principles by which Gopher Prairie should be born again—should again become amusing to live in.

This was their philosophy complete . . . in the era of aeroplanes and syndicalism:

The Baptist Church (and, somewhat less, the Methodist, Congregational, and Presbyterian Churches) is the perfect,

the divinely ordained standard in music, oratory, philan-
thropy, and ethics. "We don't need all this new-fangled
science, or this terrible Higher Criticism that's ruining our
young men in colleges. What we need is to get back to the
true Word of God, and a good sound belief in hell, like we
used to have it preached to us."

The Republican Party, the Grand Old Party of Blaine and
McKinley, is the agent of the Lord and of the Baptist Church
in temporal affairs.

All socialists ought to be hanged.

"Harold Bell Wright is a lovely writer, and he teaches such
good morals in his novels, and folks say he's made prett' near
a million dollars out of 'em."

People who make more than ten thousand a year or less
than eight hundred are wicked.

Europeans are still wickeder.

It doesn't hurt any to drink a glass of beer on a warm day,
but anybody who touches wine is headed straight for hell.

Virgins are not so virginal as they used to be.

Nobody needs drug-store ice cream; pie is good enough for
anybody.

The farmers want too much for their wheat.

The owners of the elevator-company expect too much for
the salaries they pay.

There would be no more trouble or discontent in the world
if everybody worked as hard as Pa did when he cleared our
first farm.

IV

Carol's hero-worship dwindled to polite nodding, and the
nodding dwindled to a desire to escape, and she went home
with a headache.

Next day she saw Miles Bjornstam on the street.

"Just back from Montana. Great summer. Pumped my
lungs chuck-full of Rocky Mountain air. Now for another
whirl at sassing the bosses of Gopher Prairie." She smiled at
him, and the Perrys faded, the pioneers faded, till they were
but daguerreotypes in a black walnut cupboard.

chapter 13

SHE tried, more from loyalty than from desire, to call upon the Perrys on a November evening when Kennicott was away. They were not at home.

Like a child who has no one to play with she loitered through the dark hall. She saw a light under an office door. She knocked. To the person who opened she murmured, "Do you happen to know where the Perrys are?" She realized that it was Guy Pollock.

"I'm awfully sorry, Mrs. Kennicott, but I don't know. Won't you come in and wait for them?"

"W-why——" she observed, as she reflected that in Gopher Prairie it is not decent to call on a man; as she decided that no, really, she wouldn't go in; and as she went in.

"I didn't know your office was up here."

"Yes, office, town-house, and château in Picardy. But you can't see the château and town-house (next to the Duke of Sutherland's). They're beyond that inner door. They are a cot and a wash-stand and my other suit and the blue crêpe tie you said you liked."

"You remember my saying that?"

"Of course. I always shall. Please try this chair."

She glanced about the rusty office—gaunt stove, shelves of tan law-books, desk-chair filled with newspapers so long sat upon that they were in holes and smudged to grayness. There were only two things which suggested Guy Pollock. On the green felt of the table-desk, between legal blanks and a clotted inkwell, was a cloisonné vase. On a swing shelf was a row of books unfamiliar to Gopher Prairie: Mosher editions of the poets, black and red German novels, a Charles Lamb in crushed levant.

Guy did not sit down. He quartered the office, a grayhound on the scent; a grayhound with glasses tilted forward on his thin nose, and a silky indecisive brown mustache. He had a golf jacket of jersey, worn through at the creases in the

152

sleeves. She noted that he did not apologize for it, as Kennicott would have done.

He made conversation: "I didn't know you were a bosom
friend of the Perrys. Champ is the salt of the earth but somehow I can't imagine him joining you in symbolic dancing, or
making improvements on the Diesel engine."

"No. He's a dear soul, bless him, but he belongs in the
National Museum, along with General Grant's sword, and
I'm—— Oh, I suppose I'm seeking for a gospel that will evan-
gelize Gopher Prairie."

"Really? Evangelize it to what?"

"To anything that's definite. Seriousness or frivolousness
or both. I wouldn't care whether it was a laboratory or a
carnival. But it's merely safe. Tell me, Mr. Pollock, what *is*
the matter with Gopher Prairie?"

"Is anything the matter with it? Isn't there perhaps something the matter with you and me? (May I join you in the
honor of having something the matter?)"

"(Yes, thanks.) No, I think it's the town."

"Because they enjoy skating more than biology?"

"But I'm not only more interested in biology than the Jolly
Seventeen, but also in skating! I'll skate with them, or slide, or
throw snowballs, just as gladly as talk with you."

("Oh no!")

("Yes!) But they want to stay home and embroider."

"Perhaps. I'm not defending the town. It's merely——
I'm a confirmed doubter of myself. (Probably I'm conceited
about my lack of conceit!) Anyway, Gopher Prairie isn't
particularly bad. It's like all villages in all countries. Most
places that have lost the smell of earth but not yet acquired the
smell of patchouli—or of factory-smoke—are just as suspicious and righteous. I wonder if the small town isn't, with
some lovely exceptions, a social appendix? Some day these
dull market-towns may be as obsolete as monasteries. I can
imagine the farmer and his local store-manager going by
monorail, at the end of the day, into a city more charming
than any William Morris Utopia—music, a university, clubs
for loafers like me. (Lord, how I'd like to have a real club!)"

She asked impulsively, "You, why do you stay here?"

"I have the Village Virus."

"It sounds dangerous."

"It is. More dangerous than the cancer that will certainly
get me at fifty unless I stop this smoking. The Village Virus
is the germ which—it's extraordinarily like the hook-worm—

it infects ambitious people who stay too long in the provinces. You'll find it epidemic among lawyers and doctors and ministers and college-bred merchants—all these people who have had a glimpse of the world that thinks and laughs, but have returned to their swamp. I'm a perfect example. But I sha'n't pester you with my dolors."

"You won't. And do sit down, so I can see you."

He dropped into the shrieking desk-chair. He looked squarely at her; she was conscious of the pupils of his eyes; of the fact that he was a man, and lonely. They were embarrassed. They elaborately glanced away, and were relieved as he went on:

"The diagnosis of my Village Virus is simple enough. I was born in an Ohio town about the same size as Gopher Prairie, and much less friendly. It'd had more generations in which to form an oligarchy of respectability. Here, a stranger is taken in if he is correct, if he likes hunting and motoring and God and our Senator. There, we didn't take in even our own till we had contemptuously got used to them. It was a red-brick Ohio town, and the trees made it damp, and it smelled of rotten apples. The country wasn't like our lakes and prairie. There were small stuffy corn-fields and brick-yards and greasy oil-wells.

"I went to a denominational college and learned that since dictating the Bible, and hiring a perfect race of ministers to explain it, God has never done much but creep around and try to catch us disobeying it. From college I went to New York, to the Columbia Law School. And for four years I lived. Oh, I won't rhapsodize about New York. It was dirty and noisy and breathless and ghastly expensive. But compared with the moldy academy in which I had been smothered——! I went to symphonies twice a week. I saw Irving and Terry and Duse and Bernhardt, from the top gallery. I walked in Gramercy Park. And I read, oh, everything.

"Through a cousin I learned that Julius Flickerbaugh was sick and needed a partner. I came here. Julius got well. He didn't like my way of loafing five hours and then doing my work (really not so badly) in one. We parted.

"When I first came here I swore I'd 'keep up my interests.' Very lofty! I read Browning, and went to Minneapolis for the theaters. I thought I was 'keeping up.' But I guess the Village Virus had me already. I was reading four copies of cheap fiction-magazines to one poem. I'd put off the Minneapolis trips till I simply had to go there on a lot of legal matters.

"A few years ago I was talking to a patent lawyer from Chicago, and I realized that—— I'd always felt so superior to people like Julius Flickerbaugh, but I saw that I was as provincial and behind-the-times as Julius. (Worse! Julius plows through the *Literary Digest* and the *Outlook* faithfully, while I'm turning over pages of a book by Charles Flandrau that I already know by heart.)

"I decided to leave here. Stern resolution. Grasp the world. Then I found that the Village Virus had me, absolute! I didn't want to face new streets and younger men—real competition. It was too easy to go on making out conveyances and arguing ditching cases. So—— That's all of the biography of a living dead man, except the diverting last chapter, the lies about my having been 'a tower of strength and legal wisdom' which some day a preacher will spin over my lean dry body."

He looked down at his table-desk, fingering the starry enameled vase.

She could not comment. She pictured herself running across the room to pat his hair. She saw that his lips were firm, under his soft faded mustache. She sat still, and maundered, "I know. The Village Virus. Perhaps it will get me. Some day I'm going—— Oh, no matter. At least, I am making you talk! Usually you have to be polite to my garrulousness, but now I'm sitting at your feet."

"It would be rather nice to have you literally sitting at my feet, by a fire."

"Would you have a fireplace for me?"

"Naturally! Please don't snub me now! Let the old man rave. How old are you, Carol?"

"Twenty-six, Guy."

"Twenty-six! I was just leaving New York, at twenty-six. I heard Patti sing, at twenty-six. And now I'm forty-seven. I feel like a child, yet I'm old enough to be your father. So it's decently paternal to imagine you curled at my feet. . . . Of course I hope it isn't, but we'll reflect the morals of Gopher Prairie by officially announcing that it is! . . . These standards that you and I live up to! There's one thing that's the matter with Gopher Prairie, at least with the ruling-class (there is a ruling-class, despite all our professions of democracy). And the penalty we tribal rulers pay is that our subjects watch us every minute. We can't get wholesomely drunk and relax. We have to be so correct about sex morals, and inconspicuous clothes, and doing our commercial trickery only in the traditional ways, that none of us can live up to it, and we become horribly hypocritical. Unavoidably. The widow-robbing deacon of fiction can't help being hypocritical. The widows themselves demand it! They admire his unctuousness. And look at me. Suppose I did dare to make love to—some exquisite married woman. I wouldn't admit it to myself. I giggle with the most revolting salaciousness over *La Vie Parisienne,* when I get hold of one in Chicago, yet I shouldn't even try to hold your hand. I'm broken. It's the historical Anglo-Saxon way of making life miserable. . . . Oh, my dear, I haven't talked to anybody about myself and all our selves for years."

"Guy! Can't we do something with the town? Really?"

"No, we can't!" He disposed of it like a judge ruling out an improper objection; returned to matters less uncomfortably energetic: "Curious. Most troubles are unnecessary. We have Nature beaten; we can make her grow wheat; we can keep warm when she sends blizzards. So we raise the devil just for pleasure—wars, politics, race-hatreds, labor-disputes. Here in Gopher Prairie we've cleared the fields, and become soft, so we make ourselves unhappy artificially, at great expense and exertion: Methodists disliking Episcopalians, the man with the Hudson laughing at the man with the flivver. The worst is the commercial hatred—the grocer feeling that any man who doesn't deal with him is robbing him. What hurts me is that it applies to lawyers and doctors (and decidedly to their wives!) as much as to grocers. The doctors —you know about that—how your husband and Westlake and Gould dislike one another."

"No! I won't admit it!"

He grinned.

"Oh, maybe once or twice, when Will has positively known of a case where Doctor—where one of the others has continued to call on patients longer than necessary, he has laughed about it, but——"

He still grinned.

"No, *really!* And when you say the wives of the doctors share these jealousies—— Mrs. McGanum and I haven't any particular crush on each other; she's so stolid. But her mother, Mrs. Westlake—nobody could be sweeter."

"Yes, I'm sure she's very bland. But I wouldn't tell her my heart's secrets if I were you, my dear. I insist that there's only one professional-man's wife in this town who doesn't plot, and that is you, you blessed, credulous outsider!"

"I won't be cajoled! I won't believe that medicine, the

priesthood of healing, can be turned into a penny-picking business."

"See here: Hasn't Kennicott ever hinted to you that you'd better be nice to some old woman because she tells her friends which doctor to call in? But I oughtn't to——"

She remembered certain remarks which Kennicott had offered regarding the Widow Bogart. She flinched, looked at Guy beseechingly.

He sprang up, strode to her with a nervous step, smoothed her hand. She wondered if she ought to be offended by his caress. Then she wondered if he liked her hat, the new Oriental turban of rose and silver brocade.

He dropped her hand. His elbow brushed her shoulder. He flitted over to the desk-chair, his thin back stooped. He picked up the cloisonné vase. Across it he peered at her with such loneliness that she was startled. But his eyes faded into impersonality as he talked of the jealousies of Gopher Prairie. He stopped himself with a sharp, "Good Lord, Carol, you're not a jury. You are within your legal rights in refusing to be subjected to this summing-up. I'm a tedious old fool analyzing the obvious, while you're the spirit of rebellion. Tell me your side. What is Gopher Prairie to you?"

"A bore!"

"Can I help?"

"How could you?"

"I don't know. Perhaps by listening. I haven't done that tonight. But normally—— Can't I be the confidant of the old French plays, the tiring-maid with the mirror and the loyal ears?"

"Oh, what is there to confide? The people are savorless and proud of it. And even if I liked you tremendously, I couldn't talk to you without twenty old hexes watching, whispering."

"But you will come talk to me, once in a while?"

"I'm not sure that I shall. I'm trying to develop my own large capacity for dullness and contentment. I've failed at every positive thing I've tried. I'd better 'settle down,' as they call it, and be satisfied to be—nothing."

"Don't be cynical. It hurts me, in you. It's like blood on the wing of a humming-bird."

"I'm not a humming-bird. I'm a hawk; a tiny leashed hawk, pecked to death by these large, white, flabby, wormy hens. But I am grateful to you for confirming me in the faith. And I'm going home!"

"Please stay and have some coffee with me."

"I'd like to. But they've succeeded in terrorizing me. I'm afraid of what people might say."

"I'm not afraid of that. I'm only afraid of what you might say!" He stalked to her; took her unresponsive hand. "Carol! You have been happy here tonight? (Yes. I'm begging!)"

She squeezed his hand quickly, then snatched hers away. She had but little of the curiosity of the flirt, and none of the intrigante's joy in furtiveness. If she was the naive girl, Guy Pollock was the clumsy boy. He raced about the office; he rammed his fists into his pockets. He stammered, "I—I—I——— Oh, the devil! Why do I awaken from smooth dustiness to this jagged rawness? I'll make——— I'm going to trot down the hall and bring in the Dillons, and we'll all have coffee or something."

"The Dillons?"

"Yes. Really quite a decent young pair—Harvey Dillon and his wife. He's a dentist, just come to town. They live in a room behind his office, same as I do here. They don't know much of anybody———"

"I've heard of them. And I've never thought to call. I'm horribly ashamed. Do bring them———"

She stopped, for no very clear reason, but his expression said, her faltering admitted, that they wished they had never mentioned the Dillons. With spurious enthusiasm he said, "Splendid! I will." From the door he glanced at her, curled in the peeled leather chair. He slipped out, came back with Dr. and Mrs. Dillon.

The four of them drank rather bad coffee which Pollock made on a kerosene burner. They laughed, and spoke of Minneapolis, and were tremendously tactful; and Carol started for home, through the November wind.

chapter 14

SHE was marching home.

"No. I couldn't fall in love with him. I like him, very much. But he's too much of a recluse. Could I kiss him?

No! No! Guy Pollock at twenty-six—— I could have kissed him then, maybe, even if I were married to some one else, and probably I'd have been glib in persuading myself that 'it wasn't really wrong.'

"The amazing thing is that I'm not more amazed at myself. I, the virtuous young matron. Am I to be trusted? If the Prince Charming came——

"A Gopher Prairie housewife, married a year, and yearning for a 'Prince Charming' like a bachfisch of sixteen! They say that marriage is a magic change. But I'm not changed. But——

"No! I wouldn't want to fall in love, even if the Prince did come. I wouldn't want to hurt Will. I am fond of Will. I am! He doesn't stir me, not any longer. But I depend on him. He is home and children.

"I wonder when we will begin to have children? I do want them.

"I wonder whether I remembered to tell Bea to have hominy tomorrow, instead of oatmeal? She will have gone to bed by now. Perhaps I'll be up early enough——

"Ever so fond of Will. I wouldn't hurt him, even if I had to lose the mad love. If the Prince came I'd look once at him, and run. Darn fast! Oh, Carol, you are not heroic nor fine. You are the immutable vulgar young female.

"But I'm not the faithless wife who enjoys confiding that she's 'misunderstood.' Oh, I'm not, I'm not!

"Am I?

"At least I didn't whisper to Guy about Will's faults and his blindness to my remarkable soul. I didn't! Matter of fact, Will probably understands me perfectly! If only—if he would just back me up in rousing the town.

"How many, how incredibly many wives there must be who tingle over the first Guy Pollock who smiles at them. No! I will not be one of that herd of yearners! The coy virgin brides. Yet probably if the Prince were young and dared to face life——

"I'm not half as well oriented as that Mrs. Dillon. So obviously adoring her dentist! And seeing Guy only as an eccentric fogy.

"They weren't silk, Mrs. Dillon's stockings. They were lisle. Her legs are nice and slim. But no nicer than mine. I hate cotton tops on silk stockings. . . . Are my ankles getting fat? I will *not* have fat ankles!

"No. I am fond of Will. His work—one farmer he pulls

through diphtheria is worth all my yammering for a castle in Spain. A castle with baths.

"This hat is so tight. I must stretch it. Guy liked it.

"There's the house. I'm awfully chilly. Time to get out the fur coat. I wonder if I'll ever have a beaver coat? Nutria is *not* the same thing! Beaver—glossy. Like to run my fingers over it. Guy's mustache like beaver. How utterly absurd!

"I am, I *am* fond of Will, and—— Can't I ever find another word than 'fond'?

"He's home. He'll think I was out late.

"Why can't he ever remember to pull down the shades? Cy Bogart and all the beastly boys peeping in. But the poor dear, he's absent-minded about minute—minush—whatever the word is. He has so much worry and work, while I do nothing but jabber to Bea.

"I *mustn't* forget the hominy——"

She was flying into the hall. Kennicott looked up from the *Journal of the American Medical Society.*

"Hello! What time did you get back?" she cried.

"About nine. You been gadding. Here it is past eleven!" Good-natured yet not quite approving.

"Did it feel neglected?"

"Well, you didn't remember to close the lower draft in the furnace."

"Oh, I'm so sorry. But I don't often forget things like that, do I?"

She dropped into his lap and (after he had jerked back his head to save his eye-glasses, and removed the glasses, and settled her in a position less cramping to his legs, and casually cleared his throat) he kissed her amiably, and remarked:

"Nope, I must say you're fairly good about things like that. I wasn't kicking. I just meant I wouldn't want the fire to go out on us. Leave that draft open and the fire might burn up and go out on us. And the nights are beginning to get pretty cold again. Pretty cold on my drive. I put the side-curtains up, it was so chilly. But the generator is working all right now."

"Yes. It is chilly. But I feel fine after my walk."

"Go walking?"

"I went up to see the Perrys." By a definite act of will she added the truth: "They weren't in. And I saw Guy Pollock. Dropped into his office."

"Why, you haven't been sitting and chinning with him till eleven o'clock?"

"Of course there were some other people there and——
Will! What do you think of Dr. Westlake?"

"Westlake? Why?"

"I noticed him on the street today."

"Was he limping? If the poor fish would have his teeth
X-rayed, I'll bet nine and a half cents he'd find an abscess
there. 'Rheumatism' he calls it. Rheumatism, hell! He's behind the times. Wonder he doesn't bleed himself! Welllllllll
——" A profound and serious yawn. "I hate to break up the
party, but it's getting late, and a doctor never knows when
he'll get routed out before morning." (She remembered that
he had given this explanation, in these words, not less than
thirty times in the year.) "I guess we better be trotting up
to bed. I've wound the clock and looked at the furnace. Did
you lock the front door when you came in?"

They trailed up-stairs, after he had turned out the lights and
twice tested the front door to make sure it was fast. While
they talked they were preparing for bed. Carol still sought to
maintain privacy by undressing behind the screen of the
closet door. Kennicott was not so reticent. Tonight, as every
night, she was irritated by having to push the old plush
chair out of the way before she could open the closet door.
Every time she opened the door she shoved the chair. Ten
times an hour. But Kennicott liked to have the chair in the
room, and there was no place for it except in front of the
closet.

She pushed it, felt angry, hid her anger. Kennicott was
yawning, more portentously. The room smelled stale. She
shrugged and became chatty:

"You were speaking of Dr. Westlake. Tell me—you've
never summed him up: Is he really a good doctor?"

"Oh yes, he's a wise old coot."

("There! You see there is no medical rivalry. Not in my
house!" she said triumphantly to Guy Pollock.)

She hung her silk petticoat on a closet hook, and went on,
"Dr. Westlake is so gentle and scholarly——"

"Well, I don't know as I'd say he was such a whale of a
scholar. I've always had a suspicion he did a good deal of
four-flushing about that. He likes to have people think he
keeps up his French and Greek and Lord knows what all; and
he's always got an old Dago book lying around the sitting-
room, but I've got a hunch he reads detective stories 'bout like
the rest of us. And I don't know where he'd ever learn so
doggone many languages anyway! He kind of lets people as-

sume he went to Harvard or Berlin or Oxford or somewhere, but I looked him up in the medical register, and he graduated from a hick college in Pennsylvania, 'way back in 1861!"

"But this is the important thing: Is he an honest doctor?"

"How do you mean 'honest'? Depends on what you mean."

"Suppose you were sick. Would you call him in? Would you let me call him in?"

"Not if I were well enough to cuss and bite, I wouldn't! No, *sir!* I wouldn't have the old fake in the house. Makes me tired, his everlasting palavering and soft-soaping. He's all right for an ordinary bellyache or holding some fool woman's hand, but I wouldn't call him in for an honest-to-God illness, not much I wouldn't, *no*-sir! You know I don't do much back-biting, but same time—— I'll tell you, Carrie: I've never got over being sore at Westlake for the way he treated Mrs. Jonderquist. Nothing the matter with her, what she really needed was a rest, but Westlake kept calling on her and calling on her for weeks, almost every day, and he sent her a good big fat bill, too, you can bet! I never did forgive him for that. Nice decent hard-working people like the Jonderquists!"

In her batiste nightgown she was standing at the bureau engaged in the invariable rites of wishing that she had a real dressing-table with a triple mirror, of bending toward the streaky glass and raising her chin to inspect a pin-head mole on her throat, and finally of brushing her hair. In rhythm to the strokes she went on:

"But, Will, there isn't any of what you might call financial rivalry between you and the partners—Westlake and Mc-Ganum—is there?"

He flipped into bed with a solemn back-somersault and a ludicrous kick of his heels as he tucked his legs under the blankets. He snorted, "Lord no! I never begrudge any man a nickel he can get away from me—fairly."

"But is Westlake fair? Isn't he sly?"

"Sly is the word. He's a fox, that boy!"

She saw Guy Pollock's grin in the mirror. She flushed.

Kennicott, with his arms behind his head, was yawning:

"Yump. He's smooth, too smooth. But I bet I make prett' near as much as Westlake and McGanum both together, though I've never wanted to grab more than my just share. If anybody wants to go to the partners instead of to me, that's his business. Though I must say it makes me tired when West-lake gets hold of the Dawsons. Here Luke Dawson had been coming to me for every toeache and headache and a lot of little things that just wasted my time, and then when his grandchild was here last summer and had summer-complaint, I suppose, or something like that, probably—you know, the time you and I drove up to Lac-qui-Meurt—why, Westlake got hold of Ma Dawson, and scared her to death, and made her think the kid had appendicitis, and, by golly, if he and McGanum didn't operate, and holler their heads off about the terrible adhesions they found, and what a regular Charley and Will Mayo they were for classy surgery. They let on that if they'd waited two hours more the kid would have developed peritonitis, and God knows what all; and then they collected a nice fat hundred and fifty dollars. And probably they'd have charged three hundred, if they hadn't been afraid of me! I'm no hog, but I certainly do hate to give old Luke ten dollars' worth of advice for a dollar and a half, and then see a hundred and fifty go glimmering. And if I can't do a better 'pendectomy than either Westlake or McGanum, I'll eat my hat!"

As she crept into bed she was dazzled by Guy's blazing grin. She experimented:

"But Westlake is cleverer than his son-in-law, don't you think?"

"Yes, Westlake may be old-fashioned and all that, but he's got a certain amount of intuition, while McGanum goes into everything bull-headed, and butts his way through like a damn yahoo, and tries to argue his patients into having whatever he diagnoses them as having! About the best thing Mac can do is to stick to baby-snatching. He's just about on a par with this bone-pounding chiropractor female, Mrs. Mattie Gooch."

"Mrs. Westlake and Mrs. McGanum, though—they're nice. They've been awfully cordial to me."

"Well, no reason why they shouldn't be, is there? Oh, they're nice enough—though you can bet your bottom dollar they're both plugging for their husbands all the time, trying to get the business. And I don't know as I call it so damn cordial in Mrs. McGanum when I holler at her on the street and she nods back like she had a sore neck. Still, she's all right. It's Ma Westlake that makes the mischief, pussyfooting around all the time. But I wouldn't trust any Westlake out of the whole lot, and while Mrs. McGanum *seems* square enough, you don't never want to forget that she's Westlake's daughter. You bet!"

"What about Dr. Gould? Don't you think he's worse than

either Westlake or McGanum? He's so cheap—drinking, and playing pool, and always smoking cigars in such a cocky way——"

"That's all right now! Terry Gould is a good deal of a tinhorn sport, but he knows a lot about medicine, and don't you forget it for one second!"

She stared down Guy's grin, and asked more cheerfully, "Is he honest, too?"

"Oooooooooooo! Gosh I'm sleepy!" He burrowed beneath the bedclothes in a luxurious stretch, and came up like a diver, shaking his head, as he complained, "How's that? Who? Terry Gould honest? Don't start me laughing—I'm too nice and sleepy! I didn't say he was honest. I said he had savvy enough to find the index in 'Gray's Anatomy,' which is more than McGanum can do! But I didn't say anything about his being honest. He isn't. Terry is crooked as a dog's hind leg. He's done me more than one dirty trick. He told Mrs. Glorbach, seventeen miles out, that I wasn't up-to-date in obstetrics. Fat lot of good it did him! She came right in and told me! And Terry's lazy. He'd let a pneumonia patient choke rather than interrupt a poker game."

"Oh no. I can't believe——"

"Well now, I'm telling you!"

"Does he play much poker? Dr. Dillon told me that Dr. Gould wanted him to play——"

"Dillon told you what? Where'd you meet Dillon? He's just come to town."

"He and his wife were at Mr. Pollock's tonight."

"Say, uh, what'd you think of them? Didn't Dillon strike you as pretty light-waisted?"

"Why no. He seemed intelligent. I'm sure he's much more wide-awake than our dentist."

"Well now, the old man is a good dentist. He knows his business. And Dillon—— I wouldn't cuddle up to the Dillons too close, if I were you. All right for Pollock, and that's none of our business, but we—— I think I'd just give the Dillons the glad hand and pass 'em up."

"But why? He isn't a rival."

"That's—all—right!" Kennicott was aggressively awake now. "He'll work right in with Westlake and McGanum. Matter of fact, I suspect they were largely responsible for his locating here. They'll be sending him patients, and he'll send all that he can get hold of to them. I don't trust anybody that's too much hand-in-glove with Westlake. You give Dillon a shot at some fellow that's just bought a farm here and drifts into town to get his teeth looked at, and after Dillon gets through with him, you'll see him edging around to Westlake and McGanum, every time!"

Carol reached for her blouse, which hung on a chair by the bed. She draped it about her shoulders, and sat up studying Kennicott, her chin in her hands. In the gray light from the small electric bulb down the hall she could see that he was frowning.

"Will, this is—I must get this straight. Some one said to me the other day that in towns like this, even more than in cities, all the doctors hate each other, because of the money——"

"Who said that?"

"It doesn't matter."

"I'll bet a hat it was your Vida Sherwin. She's a brainy woman, but she'd be a damn sight brainier if she kept her mouth shut and didn't let so much of her brains ooze out that way."

"Will! O Will! That's horrible! Aside from the vulgarity —— Some ways, Vida is my best friend. Even if she *had* said it. Which, as a matter of fact, she didn't."

He reared up his thick shoulders, in absurd pink and green flannelette pajamas. He sat straight, and irritatingly snapped his fingers, and growled:

"Well, if she didn't say it, let's forget her. Doesn't make any difference who said it, anyway. The point is that you believe it. God! To think you don't understand me any better than that! Money!"

("This is the first real quarrel we've ever had," she was agonizing.)

He thrust out his long arm and snatched his wrinkly vest from a chair. He took out a cigar, a match. He tossed the vest on the floor. He lighted the cigar and puffed savagely. He broke up the match and snapped the fragments at the foot-board.

She suddenly saw the foot-board of the bed as the foot-stone of the grave of love.

The room was drab-colored and ill-ventilated—Kennicott did not "believe in opening the windows so darn wide that you heat all outdoors." The stale air seemed never to change. In the light from the hall they were two lumps of bedclothes with shoulders and tousled heads attached.

She begged, "I didn't mean to wake you up, dear. And

please don't smoke. You've been smoking so much. Please go back to sleep. I'm sorry."

"Being sorry's all right, but I'm going to tell you one or two things. This falling for anybody's say-so about medical jealousy and competition is simply part and parcel of your usual willingness to think the worst you possibly can of us poor dubs in Gopher Prairie. Trouble with women like you is, you always want to *argue*. Can't take things the way they are. Got to argue. Well, I'm not going to argue about this in any way, shape, manner, or form. Trouble with you is, you don't make any effort to appreciate us. You're so damned superior, and think the city is such a hell of a lot finer place, and you want us to do what *you* want, all the time——"

"That's not true! It's I who make the effort. It's they— it's you—who stand back and criticize. I have to come over to the town's opinion; I have to devote myself to their interests. They can't even *see* my interests, to say nothing of adopting them. I get ever so excited about their old Lake Minniemashie and the cottages, but they simply guffaw (in that lovely friendly way you advertise so much) if I speak of wanting to see Taormina also."

"Sure, Tormina, whatever that is—some nice expensive millionaire colony, I suppose. Sure; that's the idea; champagne taste and beer income; and make sure that we never will have more than a beer income, too!"

"Are you by any chance implying that I am not economical?"

"Well, I hadn't intended to, but since you bring it up yourself, I don't mind saying the grocery bills are about twice what they ought to be."

"Yes, they probably are. I'm not economical. I can't be. Thanks to you!"

"Where d' you get that 'thanks to you'?"

"Please don't be quite so colloquial—or shall I say *vulgar?*"

"I'll be as damn colloquial as I want to. How do you get that 'thanks to you'? Here about a year ago you jump me for not remembering to give you money. Well, I'm reasonable. I didn't blame you, and I *said* I was to blame. But have I ever forgotten it since—practically?"

"No. You haven't—practically! But that isn't it. I ought to have an allowance. I will, too! I must have an agreement for a regular stated amount, every month."

"Fine idea! Of course a doctor gets a regular stated amount! Sure! A thousand one month—and lucky if he makes a hundred the next."

"Very well then, a percentage. Or something else. No matter how much you vary, you can make a rough average for——"

"But what's the idea? What are you trying to get at? Mean to say I'm unreasonable? Think I'm so unreliable and tightwad that you've got to tie me down with a contract? By God, that hurts! I thought I'd been pretty generous and decent, and I took a lot of pleasure—thinks I, 'she'll be tickled when I hand her over this twenty'—or fifty, or whatever it was; and now seems you been wanting to make it a kind of alimony. Me, like a poor fool, thinking I was liberal all the while, and you——"

"Please stop pitying yourself! You're having a beautiful time feeling injured. I admit all you say. Certainly. You've given me money both freely and amiably. Quite as if I were your mistress!"

"Carrie!"

"I mean it! What was a magnificent spectacle of generosity to you was humiliation to me. You *gave* me money—gave it to your mistress, if she was complaisant, and then you——"

"Carrie!"

"(Don't interrupt me!)—then you felt you'd discharged all obligation. Well, hereafter I'll refuse your money, as a gift. Either I'm your partner, in charge of the household department of our business, with a regular budget for it, or else I'm nothing. If I'm to be a mistress, I shall choose my lovers. Oh, I hate it—I hate it—this smirking and hoping for money—and then not even spending it on jewels as a mistress has a right to, but spending it on double-boilers and socks for you! Yes indeed! You're generous! You give me a dollar, right out—the only proviso is that I must spend it on a tie for you! And you give it when and as you wish. How can I be anything but uneconomical?"

"Oh well, of course, looking at it that way——"

"I can't shop around, can't buy in large quantities, have to stick to stores where I have a charge account, good deal of the time, can't plan because I don't know how much money I can depend on. That's what I pay for your charming sentimentalities about giving so generously. You make me——"

"Wait! Wait! You know you're exaggerating. You never thought about that mistress stuff till just this minute! Matter of fact, you never have 'smirked and hoped for money.' But all the same, you may be right. You ought to run the household as a business. I'll figure out a definite plan tomorrow, and hereafter you'll be on a regular amount or percentage, with your own checking account."

"Oh, that *is* decent of you!" She turned toward him, trying to be affectionate. But his eyes were pink and unlovely in the flare of the match with which he lighted his dead and malodorous cigar. His head drooped, and a ridge of flesh scattered with pale small bristles bulged out under his chin.

She sat in abeyance till he croaked:

"No. 'Tisn't especially decent. It's just fair. And God knows I want to be fair. But I expect others to be fair, too. And you're so high and mighty about people. Take Sam Clark; best soul that ever lived, honest and loyal and a damn good fellow——"

("Yes, and a good shot at ducks, don't forget that!")

("Well, and he is a good shot, too!) Sam drops around in the evening to sit and visit, and by golly just because he takes a dry smoke and rolls his cigar around in his mouth, and maybe spits a few times, you look at him as if he was a hog. Oh, you didn't know I was onto you, and I certainly hope Sam hasn't noticed it, but I never miss it."

"I have felt that way. Spitting—ugh! But I'm sorry you caught my thoughts. I tried to be nice; I tried to hide them."

"Maybe I catch a whole lot more than you think I do!"

"Yes, perhaps you do."

"And d' you know why Sam doesn't light his cigar when he's here?"

"Why?"

"He's so darn afraid you'll be offended if he smokes. You scare him. Every time he speaks of the weather you jump him because he ain't talking about poetry or Gertie—Goethe? —or some other highbrow junk. You've got him so leery he scarcely dares to come here."

"Oh, I *am* sorry. (Though I'm sure it's you who are exaggerating now.")

"Well now, I don't know as I am! And I can tell you one thing: if you keep on you'll manage to drive away every friend I've got."

"That would be horrible of me. You *know* I don't mean to—— Will, what is it about me that frightens Sam—if I do frighten him."

"Oh, you do, all right! 'Stead of putting his legs up on another chair, and unbuttoning his vest, and telling a good story or maybe kidding me about something, he sits on the edge of his chair and tries to make conversation about politics, and he doesn't even cuss, and Sam's never real comfortable unless he can cuss a little!"

"In other words, he isn't comfortable unless he can behave like a peasant in a mud hut!"

"Now that'll be about enough of that! You want to know how you scare him? First you deliberately fire some question at him that you know darn well he can't answer—any fool could see you were experimenting with him—and then you shock him by talking of mistresses or something, like you were doing just now——"

"Of course the pure Samuel never speaks of such erring ladies in his private conversations?"

"Not when there's ladies around! You can bet your life on that!"

"So the impurity lies in failing to pretend that——"

"Now we won't go into that—eugenics or whatever damn fad you choose to call it. As I say, first you shock him, and then you become so darn flighty that nobody can follow you. Either you want to dance, or you bang the piano, or else you get moody as the devil and don't want to talk or anything else. If you must be temperamental, why can't you be that way by yourself?"

"My dear man, there's nothing I'd like better than to be by myself occasionally! To have a room of my own! I suppose you expect me to sit here and dream delicately and satisfy my 'temperamentality' while you wander in from the bathroom with lather all over your face, and shout, 'Seen my brown pants?' "

"Huh!" he did not sound impressed. He made no answer. He turned out of bed, his feet making one solid thud on the floor. He marched from the room, a grotesque figure in baggy union-pajamas. She heard him drawing a drink of water at the bathroom tap. She was furious at the contemptuousness of his exit. She snuggled down in bed, and looked away from him as he returned. He ignored her. As he flumped into bed he yawned, and casually stated:

"Well, you'll have plenty of privacy when we build a new house."

"When!"

"Oh, I'll build it all right, don't you fret! But of course I don't expect any credit for it."

Now it was she who grunted "Huh!" and ignored him, and felt independent and masterful as she shot up out of bed, turned her back on him, fished a lone and petrified chocolate out of her glove-box in the top right-hand drawer of the bureau, gnawed at it, found that it had cocoanut filling, said "Damn!" wished that she had not said it, so that she might be superior to his colloquialism, and hurled the chocolate into the wastebasket, where it made an evil and mocking clatter among the débris of torn linen collars and toothpaste box. Then, in great dignity and self-dramatization, she returned to bed.

All this time he had been talking on, embroidering his assertion that he "didn't expect any credit." She was reflecting that he was a rustic, that she hated him, that she had been insane to marry him, that she had married him only because she was tired of work, that she must get her long gloves cleaned, that she would never do anything more for him, and that she mustn't forget his hominy for breakfast. She was roused to attention by his storming:

"I'm a fool to think about a new house. By the time I get it built you'll probably have succeeded in your plan to get me completely in Dutch with every friend and every patient I've got."

She sat up with a bounce. She said coldly, "Thank you very much for revealing your real opinion of me. If that's the way you feel, if I'm such a hindrance to you, I can't stay under this roof another minute. And I am perfectly well able to earn my own living. I will go at once, and you may get a divorce at your pleasure! What you want is a nice sweet cow of a woman who will enjoy having your dear friends talk about the weather and spit on the floor!"

"Tut! Don't be a fool!"

"You will very soon find out whether I'm a fool or not! I mean it! Do you think I'd stay here one second after I found out that I was injuring you? At least I have enough sense of justice not to do that."

"Please stop flying off at tangents, Carrie. This——"

"Tangents? *Tangents!* Let me tell you——"

"——isn't a theater-play; it's a serious effort to have us get together on fundamentals. We've both been cranky, and said a lot of things we didn't mean. I wish we were a couple o' bloomin' poets and just talked about roses and moonshine, but we're human. All right. Let's cut out jabbing at each other. Let's admit we both do fool things. See here: You *know* you feel superior to folks. You're not as bad as I say, but you're not as good as you say—not by a long shot! What's the reason you're so superior? Why can't you take folks as they are?"

Her preparations for stalking out of the Doll's House were not yet visible. She mused:

"I think perhaps it's my childhood." She halted. When she went on her voice had an artificial sound, her words the bookish quality of emotional meditation. "My father was the tenderest man in the world, but he did feel superior to ordinary people. Well, he was! And the Minnesota Valley—— I used to sit there on the cliffs above Mankato for hours at a time, my chin in my hand, looking way down the valley, wanting to write poems. The shiny tilted roofs below me, and the river, and beyond it the level fields in the mist, and the rim of palisades across—— It held my thoughts in. I *lived*, in the valley. But the prairie—all my thoughts go flying off into the big space. Do you think it might be that?"

"Um, well, maybe, but—— Carrie, you always talk so much about getting all you can out of life, and not letting the years slip by, and here you deliberately go and deprive yourself of a lot of real good home pleasure by not enjoying people unless they wear frock coats and trot out——"

("Morning clothes. Oh. Sorry. Didn't mean t' interrupt you.")

"——to a lot of tea-parties. Take Jack Elder. You think Jack hasn't got any ideas about anything but manufacturing and the tariff on lumber. But do you know that Jack is nutty about music? He'll put a grand-opera record on the phonograph and sit and listen to it and close his eyes—— Or you take Lym Cass. Ever realize what a well-informed man he is?"

"But *is* he? Gopher Prairie calls anybody 'well-informed' who's been through the State Capitol and heard about Gladstone."

"Now I'm telling you! Lym reads a lot—solid stuff—history. Or take Mart Mahoney, the garageman. He's got a lot of Perry prints of famous pictures in his office. Or old Bingham Playfair, that died here 'bout a year ago—lived seven miles out. He was a captain in the Civil War, and knew

General Sherman, and they say he was a miner in Nevada
right alongside of Mark Twain. You'll find these characters
in all these small towns, and a pile of savvy in every single
one of them, if you just dig for it."

"I know. And I do love them. Especially people like Champ
Perry. But I can't be so very enthusiastic over the smug
cits like Jack Elder."

"Then I'm a smug cit, too, whatever that is."

"No, you're a scientist. Oh, I will try and get the music
out of Mr. Elder. Only, why can't he let it *come* out, instead
of being ashamed of it, and always talking about hunting
dogs? But I will try. Is it all right now?"

"Sure. But there's one other thing. You might give me some
attention, too!"

"That's unjust! You have everything I am!"

"No, I haven't. You think you respect me—you always
hand out some spiel about my being so 'useful.' But you
never think of me as having ambitions, just as much as you
have!"

"Perhaps not. I think of you as being perfectly satisfied."

"Well, I'm not, not by a long shot! I don't want to be a
plug general practitioner all my life, like Westlake, and die
in harness because I can't get out of it, and have 'em say,
'He was a good fellow, but he couldn't save a cent.' Not that
I care a whoop what they say, after I've kicked in and can't
hear 'em, but I want to put enough money away so you and
I can be independent some day, and not have to work unless I feel like it, and I want to have a good house—by golly,
I'll have as good a house as anybody in *this* town!—and if we
want to travel and see your Tormina or whatever it is, why
we can do it, with enough money in our jeans so we won't
have to take anything off anybody, or fret about our old
age. You never worry about what might happen if we got
sick and didn't have a good fat wad salted away, do you!"

"I don't suppose I do."

"Well then, I have to do it for you. And if you think for
one moment I want to be stuck in this burg all my life, and
not have a chance to travel and see the different points of
interest and all that, then you simply don't get me. I want
to have a squint at the world, much's you do. Only, I'm practical about it. First place, I'm going to make the money—
I'm investing in good safe farmlands. Do you understand
why now?"

"Yes."

"Will you try and see if you can't think of me as something more than just a dollar-chasing roughneck?"

"Oh, my dear, I haven't been just! I *am* difficile. And I won't call on the Dillons! And if Dr. Dillon is working for Westlake and McGanum, I hate him!"

chapter 15

THAT December she was in love with her husband. She romanticized herself not as a great reformer but as the wife of a country physician. The realities of the doctor's household were colored by her pride.

Late at night, a step on the wooden porch, heard through her confusion of sleep; the storm-door opened; fumbling over the inner door-panels; the buzz of the electric bell. Kennicott muttering "Gol darn it," but patiently creeping out of bed, remembering to draw the covers up to keep her warm, feeling for slippers and bathrobe, clumping downstairs.

From below, half-heard in her drowsiness, a colloquy in the pidgin-German of the farmers who have forgotten the Old Country language without learning the new:

"Hello, Barney, *wass willst du?*"

"*Morgen,* doctor. *Die Frau ist ja* awful sick. All night she been having an awful pain in de belly."

"How long she been this way? *Wie lang,* eh?"

"I dunno, maybe two days."

"Why didn't you come for me yesterday, instead of waking me up out of a sound sleep? Here it is two o'clock! *So spät— warum,* eh?"

"*Nun aber,* I know it, but she soch a lot vorse last evening. I t'ought maybe all de time it go avay, but it got a lot vorse."

"Any fever?"

"Vell *ja,* I t'ink she got fever."

"Which side is the pain on?"

"Huh?"

"*Das Schmertz—die Weh*—which side is it on? Here?"

"So. Right here it is."

"Any rigidity there?"

"Huh?"

"Is it rigid—stiff—I mean, does the belly feel hard to the fingers?"

"I dunno. She ain't said yet."

"What she been eating?"

"Vell, I t'ink about vot ve alwis eat, maybe corn beef and cabbage and sausage, *und so weiter.* Doc, *sie weint immer,* all the time she holler like hell. I vish you come."

"Well, all right, but you call me earlier, next time. Look here, Barney, you better install a 'phone—telephone *haben.* Some of you Dutchmen will be dying one of these days before you can fetch the doctor."

The door closing. Barney's wagon—the wheels silent in the snow, but the wagon-body rattling. Kennicott clicking the receiver-hook to rouse the night telephone-operator, giving a number, waiting, cursing mildly, waiting again, and at last growling, "Hello, Gus, this is the doctor. Say, uh, send me up a team. Guess snow's too thick for a machine. Going eight miles south. All right. Huh? The hell I will! Don't *you* go back to sleep. Huh? Well, that's all right now, you didn't wait so very darn long. All right, Gus; shoot her along. By!"

His steps on the stairs; his quiet moving about the frigid room while he dressed; his abstracted and meaningless cough. She was supposed to be asleep; she was too exquisitely drowsy to break the charm by speaking. On a slip of paper laid on the bureau—she could hear the pencil grinding against the marble slab—he wrote his destination. He went out, hungry, chilly, unprotesting; and she, before she fell asleep again, loved him for his sturdiness, and saw the drama of his riding by night to the frightened household on the distant farm; pictured children standing at a window, waiting for him. He suddenly had in her eyes the heroism of a wireless operator on a ship in a collision; of an explorer, fever-clawed, deserted by his bearers, but going on—jungle—going——

At six, when the light faltered in as through ground glass and bleakly identified the chairs as gray rectangles, she heard his step on the porch; heard him at the furnace: the rattle of shaking the grate, the slow grinding removal of ashes, the shovel thrust into the coal-bin, the abrupt clatter of the coal as it flew into the fire-box, the fussy regulation of drafts—the daily sounds of a Gopher Prairie life, now first appealing to her as something brave and enduring, many-colored and free. She visioned the fire-box: flames turned to lemon and metallic gold as the coal-dust sifted over them; thin twisty flutters of purple, ghost flames which gave no light, slipping up between the dark banked coals.

It was luxurious in bed, and the house would be warm for her when she rose, she reflected. What a worthless cat she was! What were her aspirations beside his capability?

She awoke again as he dropped into bed.

"Seems just a few minutes ago that you started out!"

"I've been away four hours. I've operated a woman for appendicitis, in a Dutch kitchen. Came awful close to losing her, too, but I pulled her through all right. Close squeak. Barney says he shot ten rabbits last Sunday."

He was instantly asleep—one hour of rest before he had to be up and ready for the farmers who came in early. She marveled that in what was to her but a night-blurred moment, he should have been in a distant place, have taken charge of a strange house, have slashed a woman, saved a life.

What wonder he detested the lazy Westlake and McGanum! How could the easy Guy Pollock understand this skill and endurance?

Then Kennicott was grumbling, "Seven-fifteen! Aren't you ever going to get up for breakfast?" and he was not a hero-scientist but a rather irritable and commonplace man who needed a shave. They had coffee, griddle-cakes, and sausages, and talked about Mrs. McGanum's atrocious alligator-hide belt. Night witchery and morning disillusion were alike forgotten in the march of realities and days.

II

Familiar to the doctor's wife was the man with an injured leg, driven in from the country on a Sunday afternoon and brought to the house. He sat in a rocker in the back of a lumber-wagon, his face pale from the anguish of the jolting. His leg was thrust out before him, resting on a starch-box and covered with a leather-bound horse-blanket. His drab courageous wife drove the wagon, and she helped Kennicott support him as he hobbled up the steps, into the house.

"Fellow cut his leg with an ax—pretty bad gash—Halvor Nelson, nine miles out," Kennicott observed.

Carol fluttered at the back of the room, childishly excited when she was sent to fetch towels and a basin of water.

Kennicott lifted the farmer into a chair and chuckled, "There we are, Halvor! We'll have you out fixing fences and drinking *aquavit* in a month." The farmwife sat on the couch, expressionless, bulky in a man's dogskin coat and unplumbed layers of jackets. The flowery silk handkerchief which she had worn over her head now hung about her seamed neck. Her white wool gloves lay in her lap.

Kennicott drew from the injured leg the thick red "German sock," the innumerous other socks of gray and white wool, then the spiral bandage. The leg was of an unwholesome dead white, with the black hairs feeble and thin and flattened, and the scar a puckered line of crimson. Surely, Carol shuddered, this was not human flesh, the rosy shining tissue of the amorous poets.

Kennicott examined the scar, smiled at Halvor and his wife, chanted, "Fine, b' gosh! Couldn't be better!"

The Nelsons looked deprecating. The farmer nodded a cue to his wife and she mourned:

"Vell, how much ve going to owe you, doctor?"

"I guess it'll be—— Let's see: one drive out and two calls. I guess it'll be about eleven dollars in all, Lena."

"I dunno ve can pay you yoost a little w'ile, doctor."

Kennicott lumbered over to her, patted her shoulder, roared, "Why, Lord love you, sister, I won't worry if I never get it! You pay me next fall, when you get your crop. . . . Carrie! Suppose you or Bea could shake up a cup of coffee and some cold lamb for the Nelsons? They got a long cold drive ahead."

III

He had been gone since morning; her eyes ached with reading; Vida Sherwin could not come to tea. She wandered through the house, empty as the bleary street without. The problem of "Will the doctor be home in time for supper, or shall I sit down without him?" was important in the household. Six was the rigid, the canonical supper-hour, but at half-past six he had not come. Much speculation with Bea: Had the obstetrical case taken longer than he had expected? Had he been called somewhere else? Was the snow much heavier out in the country, so that he should have taken a buggy, or even a cutter, instead of the car? Here in town it *had* melted a lot, but still——

A honking, a shout, the motor engine raced before it was shut off.

She hurried to the window. The car was a monster at rest after furious adventures. The headlights blazed on the clots of ice in the road so that the tiniest lumps gave mountainous shadows, and the taillight cast a circle of ruby on the snow behind. Kennicott was opening the door, crying, "Here we are, old girl! Got stuck couple times, but we made it, by golly, we made it, and here we be! Come on! Food! Eatin's!"

She rushed to him, patted his fur coat, the long hairs smooth but chilly to her fingers. She joyously summoned Bea, "All right! He's here! We'll sit right down!"

IV

There were, to inform the doctor's wife of his successes, no clapping audiences nor book-reviews nor honorary degrees. But there was a letter written by a German farmer recently moved from Minnesota to Saskatchewan:

> Dear sor, as you haf bin treading mee for a fue Weaks dis Somer and seen wat is rong wit mee so in Regarding to dat i wont to tank you. the Doctor heir say wat shot bee rong wit mee and day give mee som Madsin but it diten halp mee like wat you dit. Now day glaim dat i Woten Neet aney Madsin ad all wat you tink?
>
> Well i haven ben tacking aney ting for about one &½ Mont but i dont get better so i like to heir Wat you tink about it i feel like dis Disconfebil feeling around the Stomac after eating and dat Pain around Heard and down the arm and about 3 to 3½ Hour after Eating i feel weeak like and dissy and a dull Hadig. Now you gust lett mee know Wat you tink about mee, i do Wat you say.

V

She encountered Guy Pollock at the drug store. He looked at her as though he had a right to; he spoke softly. "I haven't seen you, the last few days."

"No. I've been out in the country with Will several times. He's so—— Do you know that people like you and me can never understand people like him? We're a pair of hyper-critical loafers, you and I, while he quietly goes and does things."

She nodded and smiled and was very busy about purchasing boric acid. He stared after her, and slipped away.

When she found that he was gone she was slightly disconcerted.

She could—at times—agree with Kennicott that the shav-
ing-and-corsets familiarity of married life was not dreary
vulgarity but a wholesome frankness; that artificial reticences
might merely be irritating. She was not much disturbed when
for hours he sat about the living-room in his honest socks.
But she would not listen to his theory that "all this romance
stuff is simply moonshine—elegant when you're courting,
but no use busting yourself keeping it up all your life."

She thought of surprises, games, to vary the days. She
knitted an astounding purple scarf, which she hid under his
supper plate. (When he discovered it he looked embarrassed,
and gasped, "Is today an anniversary or something? Gosh,
I'd forgotten it!")

Once she filled a thermos bottle with hot coffee, a corn-
flakes box with cookies just baked by Bea, and bustled to his
office at three in the afternoon. She hid her bundles in the
hall and peeped in.

The office was shabby. Kennicott had inherited it from a
medical predecessor, and changed it only by adding a white
enameled operating-table, a sterilizer, a Roentgen-ray apparatus, and a small portable typewriter. It was a suite of
two rooms: a waiting-room with straight chairs, shaky pine
table, and those coverless and unknown magazines which are
found only in the offices of dentists and doctors. The room
beyond, looking on Main Street, was business-office, con-
sulting-room, operating-room, and, in an alcove, bacterio-
logical and chemical laboratory. The wooden floors of both
rooms were bare; the furniture was brown and scaly.

Waiting for the doctor were two women, as still as though
they were paralyzed, and a man in a railroad brakeman's
uniform, holding his bandaged right hand with his tanned
left. They stared at Carol. She sat modestly in a stiff chair,
feeling frivolous and out of place.

Kennicott appeared at the inner door, ushering out a
bleached man with a trickle of wan beard, and consoling
him, "All right, Dad. Be careful about the sugar, and mind
the diet I gave you. Get the prescription filled, and come in
and see me next week. Say, uh, better, uh, better not drink
too much beer. All right, Dad."

His voice was artificially hearty. He looked absently at

Carol. He was a medical machine now, not a domestic machine. "What is it, Carrie?" he droned.

"No hurry. Just wanted to say hello."

"Well——"

Self-pity because he did not divine that this was a surprise party rendered her sad and interesting to herself, and she had the pleasure of the martyrs in saying bravely to him, "It's nothing special. If you're busy long I'll trot home."

While she waited she ceased to pity and began to mock herself. For the first time she observed the waiting-room. Oh yes, the doctor's family had to have obi panels and a wide couch and an electric percolator, but any hole was good enough for sick tired common people who were nothing but the one means and excuse for the doctor's existing! No. She couldn't blame Kennicott. He was satisfied by the shabby chairs. He put up with them as his patients did. It was her neglected province—she who had been going about talking of rebuilding the whole town!

When the patients were gone she brought in her bundles.

"What's those?" wondered Kennicott.

"Turn your back! Look out of the window!"

He obeyed—not very much bored. When she cried "Now!" a feast of cookies and small hard candies and hot coffee was spread on the roll-top desk in the inner room.

His broad face lighted. "That's a new one on me! Never was more surprised in my life! And, by golly, I believe I am hungry. Say, this is fine."

When the first exhilaration of the surprise had declined she demanded, "Will! I'm going to refurnish your waiting-room!"

"What's the matter with it? It's all right."

"It is not! It's hideous. We can afford to give your patients a better place. And it would be good business." She felt tremendously politic.

"Rats! I don't worry about the business. You look here now: As I told you—— Just because I like to tuck a few dollars away, I'll be switched if I'll stand for your thinking I'm nothing but a dollar-chasing——"

"Stop it! Quick! I'm not hurting your feelings! I'm not criticizing! I'm the adoring least one of thy harem. I just mean——"

Two days later, with pictures, wicker chairs, a rug, she had made the waiting-room habitable; and Kennicott admitted,

"Does look a lot better. Never thought much about it. Guess I need being bullied."

She was convinced that she was gloriously content in her career as doctor's-wife.

VII

She tried to free herself from the speculation and disillusionment which had been twitching at her; sought to dismiss all the opinionation of an insurgent era. She wanted to shine upon the veal-faced bristly-bearded Lyman Cass as much as upon Miles Bjornstam or Guy Pollock. She gave a reception for the Thanatopsis Club. But her real acquiring of merit was in calling upon that Mrs. Bogart whose gossipy good opinion was so valuable to a doctor.

Though the Bogart house was next door she had entered it but three times. Now she put on her new moleskin cap, which made her face small and innocent, she rubbed off the traces of a lip-stick—and fled across the alley before her admirable resolution should sneak away.

The age of houses, like the age of men, has small relation to their years. The dull-green cottage of the good Widow Bogart was twenty years old, but it had the antiquity of Cheops, and the smell of mummy-dust. Its neatness rebuked the street. The two stones by the path were painted yellow; the outhouse was so overmodestly masked with vines and lattice that it was not concealed at all; the last iron dog remaining in Gopher Prairie stood among whitewashed conchshells upon the lawn. The hallway was dismayingly scrubbed: the kitchen was an exercise in mathematics, with problems worked out in equidistant chairs.

The parlor was kept for visitors. Carol suggested, "Let's sit in the kitchen. Please don't trouble to light the parlor stove."

"No trouble at all! My gracious, and you coming so seldom and all, and the kitchen is a perfect sight, I try to keep it clean, but Cy will track mud all over it, I've spoken to him about it a hundred times if I've spoken once, no, you sit right there, dearie, and I'll make a fire, no trouble at all, practically no trouble at all."

Mrs. Bogart groaned, rubbed her joints, and repeatedly dusted her hands while she made the fire, and when Carol tried to help she lamented, "Oh, it doesn't matter; guess I ain't good for much but toil and workin' anyway; seems as though that's what a lot of folks think."

The parlor was distinguished by an expanse of rag carpet from which, as they entered, Mrs. Bogart hastily picked one sad dead fly. In the center of the carpet was a rug depicting a red Newfoundland dog, reclining in a green and yellow daisy field and labeled "Our Friend." The parlor organ, tall and thin, was adorned with a mirror partly circular, partly square, and partly diamond-shaped, and with brackets holding a pot of geraniums, a mouth-organ, and a copy of "The Old-time Hymnal." On the center table was a Sears-Roebuck mail-order catalogue, a silver frame with photographs of the Baptist Church and of an elderly clergyman, and an aluminum tray containing a rattlesnake's rattle and a broken spectacle-lens.

Mrs. Bogart spoke of the eloquence of the Reverend Mr. Zitterel, the coldness of cold days, the price of poplar wood, Dave Dyer's new hair-cut, and Cy Bogart's essential piety. "As I said to his Sunday School teacher, Cy may be a little wild, but that's because he's got so much better brains than a lot of these boys, and this farmer that claims he caught Cy stealing 'beggies, is a liar, and I ought to have the law on him."

Mrs. Bogart went thoroughly into the rumor that the girl waiter at Billy's Lunch was not all she might be—or, rather, was quite all she might be.

"My lands, what can you expect when everybody knows what her mother was? And if these traveling salesmen would let her alone she would be all right, though I certainly don't believe she ought to be allowed to think she can pull the wool over our eyes. The sooner she's sent to the school for incorrigible girls down at Sauk Centre, the better for all and—— Won't you just have a cup of coffee, Carol dearie, I'm sure you won't mind old Aunty Bogart calling you by your first name when you think how long I've known Will, and I was such a friend of his dear lovely mother when she lived here and—was that fur cap expensive? But—— Don't you think it's awful, the way folks talk in this town?"

Mrs. Bogart hitched her chair nearer. Her large face, with its disturbing collection of moles and lone black hairs, wrinkled cunningly. She showed her decayed teeth in a reproving smile, and in the confidential voice of one who scents stale bedroom scandal she breathed:

"I just don't see how folks can talk and act like they do.

You don't know the things that go on under cover. This town—why it's only the religious training I've given Cy that's kept him so innocent of—things. Just the other day— I never pay no attention to stories, but I heard it mighty good and straight that Harry Haydock is carrying on with a girl that clerks in a store down in Minneapolis, and poor Juanita not knowing anything about it—though maybe it's the judgment of God, because before she married Harry she acted up with more than one boy—— Well, I don't like to say it, and maybe I ain't up-to-date, like Cy says, but I always believed a lady shouldn't even give names to all sorts of dreadful things, but just the same I know there was at least one case where Juanita and a boy—well, they were just dreadful. And—and—— Then there's that Ole Jenson the grocer, that thinks he's so plaguey smart, and I know he made up to a farmer's wife and—— And this awful man Bjornstam that does chores, and Nat Hicks and——"

There was, it seemed, no person in town who was not living a life of shame except Mrs. Bogart, and naturally she resented it.

She knew. She had always happened to be there. Once, she whispered, she was going by when an indiscreet window-shade had been left up a couple of inches. Once she had noticed a man and woman holding hands, and right at a Methodist sociable!

"Another thing—— Heaven knows I never want to start trouble, but I can't help what I see from my back steps, and I notice your hired girl Bea carrying on with the grocery boys and all——"

"Mrs. Bogart! I'd trust Bea as I would myself!"

"Oh, dearie, you don't understand me! I'm sure she's a good girl. I mean she's green, and I hope that none of these horrid young men that there are around town will get her into trouble! It's their parents' fault, letting them run wild and hear evil things. If I had my way there wouldn't be none of them, not boys nor girls neither, allowed to know anything about—about things till they was married. It's terrible the bald way that some folks talk. It just shows and gives away what awful thoughts they got inside them, and there's nothing can cure them except coming right to God and kneeling down like I do at prayer-meeting every Wednesday evening, and saying, 'O God, I would be a miserable sinner except for thy grace.'

"I'd make every last one of these brats go to Sunday School

and learn to think about nice things 'stead of about cigarettes
and goings-on—and these dances they have at the lodges are
the worst thing that ever happened to this town, lot of young
men squeezing girls and finding out—— Oh, it's dreadful.
I've told the mayor he ought to put a stop to them and——
There was one boy in this town, I don't want to be suspicious
or uncharitable but——"

It was half an hour before Carol escaped.

She stopped on her own porch and thought viciously:

"If that woman is on the side of the angels, then I have
no choice; I must be on the side of the devil. But—isn't she
like me? She too wants to 'reform the town'! She too criti-
cizes everybody! She too thinks the men are vulgar and lim-
ited! *Am I like her?* This is ghastly!"

That evening she did not merely consent to play cribbage
with Kennicott; she urged him to play; and she worked up
a hectic interest in land-deals and Sam Clark.

VIII

In courtship days Kennicott had shown her a photograph
of Nels Erdstrom's baby and log cabin, but she had never
seen the Erdstroms. They had become merely "patients of
the doctor." Kennicott telephoned her on a mid-December
afternoon, "Want to throw your coat on and drive out to
Erdstrom's with me? Fairly warm. Nels got the jaundice."

"Oh yes!" She hastened to put on woolen stockings, high
boots, sweater, muffler, cap, mittens.

The snow was too thick and the ruts frozen too hard for
the motor. They drove out in a clumsy high carriage. Tucked
over them was a blue woolen cover, prickly to her wrists,
and outside of it a buffalo robe, humble and moth-eaten
now, used ever since the bison herds had streaked the prairie
a few miles to the west.

The scattered houses between which they passed in town
were small and desolate in contrast to the expanse of huge
snowy yards and wide street. They crossed the railroad
tracks, and instantly were in the farm country. The big pie-
bald horses snorted clouds of steam, and started to trot. The
carriage squeaked in rhythm. Kennicott drove with clucks
of "There boy, take it easy!" He was thinking. He paid no
attention to Carol. Yet it was he who commented, "Pretty
nice, over there," as they approached an oak-grove where

shifty winter sunlight quivered in the hollow between two
snow-drifts.

They drove from the natural prairie to a cleared district
which twenty years ago had been forest. The country seemed
to stretch unchanging to the North Pole: low hill, brush-
scraggly bottom, reedy creek, muskrat mound, fields with
frozen brown clods thrust up through the snow.

Her ears and nose were pinched; her breath frosted her
collar; her fingers ached.

"Getting colder," she said.

"Yup."

That was all their conversation for three miles. Yet she
was happy.

They reached Nels Erdstrom's at four, and with a throb
she recognized the courageous venture which had lured her
to Gopher Prairie: the cleared fields, furrows among stumps,
a log cabin chinked with mud and roofed with dry hay. But
Nels had prospered. He used the log cabin as a barn; and
a new house reared up, a proud, unwise, Gopher Prairie
house, the more naked and ungraceful in its glossy white
paint and pink trimmings. Every tree had been cut down. The
house was so unsheltered, so battered by the wind, so bleakly
thrust out into the harsh clearing, that Carol shivered. But
they were welcomed warmly enough in the kitchen, with its
crisp new plaster, its black and nickel range, its cream separator in a corner.

Mrs. Erdstrom begged her to sit in the parlor, where there
was a phonograph and an oak and leather davenport, the
prairie farmer's proofs of social progress, but she dropped
down by the kitchen stove and insisted, "Please don't
mind me." When Mrs. Erdstrom had followed the doctor out
of the room Carol glanced in a friendly way at the grained
pine cupboard, the framed Lutheran *Konfirmations Attest,*
the traces of fried eggs and sausages on the dining table
against the wall, and a jewel among calendars, presenting not
only a lithographic young woman with cherry lips, and a
Swedish advertisement of Axel Egge's grocery, but also a
thermometer and a match-holder.

She saw that a boy of four or five was staring at her from
the hall; a boy in gingham shirt and faded corduroy trousers,
but large-eyed, firm-mouthed, wide-browed. He vanished,
then peeped in again, biting his knuckles, turning his shoulder
toward her in shyness.

Didn't she remember—what was it?—Kennicott sitting beside her at Fort Snelling, urging, "See how scared that baby is. Needs some woman like you."

Magic had fluttered about her then—magic of sunset and cool air and the curiosity of lovers. She held out her hands as much to that sanctity as to the boy.

He edged into the room, doubtfully sucking his thumb.

"Hello," she said. "What's your name?"

"Hee, hee, hee!"

"You're quite right. I agree with you. Silly people like me always ask children their names."

"Hee, hee, hee!"

"Come here and I'll tell you the story of—well, I don't know what it will be about, but it will have a slim heroine and a Prince Charming."

He stood stoically while she spun nonsense. His giggling ceased. She was winning him. Then the telephone bell—two long rings, one short.

Mrs. Erdstrom galloped into the room, shrieked into the transmitter, "Vell? Yes, yes, dis is Erdstrom's place! Heh? Oh, you vant de doctor?"

Kennicott appeared, growled into the telephone:

"Well, what do you want? Oh, hello Dave; what do you want? Which Morgenroth's? Adolph's? All right. Amputation? Yuh, I see. Say, Dave, get Gus to harness up and take my surgical kit down there—and have him take some chloroform. I'll go straight down from here. May not get home tonight. You can get me at Adolph's. Huh? No, Carrie can give the anesthetic, I guess. G'-by. Huh? No; tell me about that tomorrow—too damn many people always listening in on this farmers' line."

He turned to Carol. "Adolph Morgenroth, farmer ten miles southwest of town, got his arm crushed—fixing his cow-shed and a post caved in on him—smashed him up pretty bad—may have to amputate, Dave Dyer says. Afraid we'll have to go right from here. Darn sorry to drag you clear down there with me——"

"Please do. Don't mind me a bit."

"Think you could give the anesthetic? Usually have my driver do it."

"If you'll tell me how."

"All right. Say, did you hear me putting one over on these goats that are always rubbering in on party-wires? I hope they heard me! Well. . . . Now, Bessie, don't you worry about Nels. He's getting along all right. Tomorrow you or one of the neighbors drive in and get this prescription filled at Dyer's. Give him a teaspoonful every four hours. Good-by. Hel-lo! Here's the little fellow! My Lord, Bessie, it ain't possible this is the fellow that used to be so sickly? Why, say, he's a great big strapping Svenska now—going to be bigger 'n his daddy!"

Kennicott's bluffness made the child squirm with a delight which Carol could not evoke. It was a humble wife who followed the busy doctor out to the carriage, and her ambition was not to play Rachmaninoff better, nor to build town halls, but to chuckle at babies.

The sunset was merely a flush of rose on a dome of silver, with oak twigs and thin poplar branches against it, but a silo on the horizon changed from a red tank to a tower of violet misted over with gray. The purple road vanished, and without lights, in the darkness of a world destroyed, they swayed on—toward nothing.

It was a bumpy cold way to the Morgenroth farm, and she was asleep when they arrived.

Here was no glaring new house with a proud phonograph, but a low whitewashed kitchen smelling of cream and cabbage. Adolph Morgenroth was lying on a couch in the rarely used dining-room. His heavy work-scarred wife was·shaking her hands in anxiety.

Carol felt that Kennicott would do something magnificent and startling. But he was casual. He greeted the man, "Well, well, Adolph, have to fix you up, eh?" Quietly, to the wife, "*Hat die* drug store my *schwartze* bag *hier geschickt? So— schön. Wie viel Uhr ist 's? Sieben? Nun, lassen uns ein wenig* supper *zuerst haben.* Got any of that good beer left— *giebt's noch Bier?*"

He had supped in four minutes. His coat off, his sleeves rolled up, he was scrubbing his hands in a tin basin in the sink, using the bar of yellow kitchen soap.

Carol had not dared to look into the farther room while she labored over the supper of beer, rye bread, moist corn-beef and cabbage, set on the kitchen table. The man in there was groaning. In her one glance she had seen that his blue flannel shirt was open at a corded tobacco-brown neck, the hollows of which were sprinkled with thin black and gray hairs. He was covered with a sheet, like a corpse, and outside the sheet was his right arm, wrapped in towels stained with blood.

But Kennicott strode into the other room gaily, and she followed him. With surprising delicacy in his large fingers he unwrapped the towels and revealed an arm which, below the elbow, was a mass of blood and raw flesh. The man bellowed. The room grew thick about her; she was very seasick; she fled to a chair in the kitchen. Through the haze of nausea she heard Kennicott grumbling, "Afraid it will have to come off, Adolph. What did you do? Fall on a reaper blade? We'll fix it right up. Carrie! *Carol!*"

She couldn't—she couldn't get up. Then she was up, her knees like water, her stomach revolving a thousand times a second, her eyes filmed, her ears full of roaring. She couldn't reach the dining-room. She was going to faint. Then she was in the dining-room, leaning against the wall, trying to smile, flushing hot and cold along her chest and sides, while Kennicott mumbled, "Say, help Mrs. Morgenroth and me carry him in on the kitchen table. No, first go out and shove those two tables together, and put a blanket on them and a clean sheet."

It was salvation to push the heavy tables, to scrub them, to be exact in placing the sheet. Her head cleared; she was able to look calmly in at her husband and the farmwife while they undressed the wailing man, got him into a clean nightgown, and washed his arm. Kennicott came to lay out his instruments. She realized that, with no hospital facilities, yet with no worry about it, her husband—*her husband*—was going to perform a surgical operation, that miraculous boldness of which one read in stories about famous surgeons.

She helped them to move Adolph into the kitchen. The man was in such a funk that he would not use his legs. He was heavy, and smelled of sweat and the stable. But she put her arm about his waist, her sleek head by his chest; she tugged at him; she clicked her tongue in imitation of Kennicott's cheerful noises.

When Adolph was on the table Kennicott laid a hemispheric steel and cotton frame on his face; suggested to Carol, "Now you sit here at his head and keep the ether dripping—about this fast, see? I'll watch his breathing. Look who's here! Real anesthetist! Ochsner hasn't got a better one! Class, eh? . . . Now, now, Adolph, take it easy. This won't hurt you a bit. Put you all nice and asleep and it won't hurt a bit. *Schweig' mal! Bald schlaft man grat wie ein Kind. So! So! Bald geht's besser!*"

As she let the ether drip, nervously trying to keep the

rhythm that Kennicott had indicated, Carol stared at her husband with the abandon of hero-worship.

He shook his head. "Bad light—bad light. Here, Mrs. Morgenroth, you stand right here and hold this lamp. *Hier, und dieses—dieses* lamp *halten—so!*"

By that streaky glimmer he worked, swiftly, at ease. The room was still. Carol tried to look at him, yet not look at the seeping blood, the crimson slash, the vicious scalpel. The ether fumes were sweet, choking. Her head seemed to be floating away from her body. Her arm was feeble.

It was not the blood but the grating of the surgical saw on the living bone that broke her, and she knew that she had been fighting off nausea, that she was beaten. She was lost in dizziness. She heard Kennicott's voice:

"Sick? Trot outdoors couple minutes. Adolph will stay under now."

She was fumbling at a door-knob which whirled in insulting circles; she was on the stoop, gasping, forcing air into her chest, her head clearing. As she returned she caught the scene as a whole: the cavernous kitchen, two milk-cans a leaden patch by the wall, hams dangling from a beam, bars of light at the stove door, and in the center, illuminated by a small glass lamp held by a frightened stout woman, Dr. Kennicott bending over a body which was humped under a sheet—the surgeon, his bare arms daubed with blood, his hands, in pale-yellow rubber gloves, loosening the tourniquet, his face without emotion save when he threw up his head and clucked at the farmwife, "Hold that light steady just a second more—*noch blos ein wenig.*"

"He speaks a vulgar, common, incorrect German of life and death and birth and the soil. I read the French and German of sentimental lovers and Christmas garlands. And I thought that it was I who had the culture!" she worshiped as she returned to her place.

After a time he snapped, "That's enough. Don't give him any more ether." He was concentrated on tying an artery. His gruffness seemed heroic to her.

As he shaped the flap of flesh she murmured, "Oh, you *are* wonderful!"

He was surprised. "Why, this is a cinch. Now if it had been like last week—— Get me some more water. Now last week I had a case with an ooze in the peritoneal cavity, and by golly if it wasn't a stomach ulcer that I hadn't suspected and—— There. Say, I certainly am sleepy. Let's turn in here. Too late to drive home. And tastes to me like a storm coming."

IX

They slept on a feather bed with their fur coats over them; in the morning they broke ice in the pitcher—the vast flowered and gilt pitcher.

Kennicott's storm had not come. When they set out it was hazy and growing warmer. After a mile she saw that he was studying a dark cloud in the north. He urged the horses to the run. But she forgot his unusual haste in wonder at the tragic landscape. The pale snow, the prickles of old stubble, and the clumps of ragged brush faded into a gray obscurity. Under the hillocks were cold shadows. The willows about a farmhouse were agitated by the rising wind, and the patches of bare wood where the bark had peeled away were white as the flesh of a leper. The snowy slews were of a harsh flatness. The whole land was cruel, and a climbing cloud of slate-edged blackness dominated the sky.

"Guess we're about in for a blizzard," speculated Kennicott. "We can make Ben McGonegal's, anyway."

"Blizzard? Really? Why—— But still we used to think they were fun when I was a girl. Daddy had to stay home from court, and we'd stand at the window and watch the snow."

"Not much fun on the prairie. Get lost. Freeze to death. Take no chances." He chirruped at the horses. They were flying now, the carriage rocking on the hard ruts.

The whole air suddenly crystallized into large damp flakes. The horses and the buffalo robe were covered with snow; her face was wet; the thin butt of the whip held a white ridge. The air became colder. The snowflakes were harder; they shot in level lines, clawing at her face.

She could not see a hundred feet ahead.

Kennicott was stern. He bent forward, the reins firm in his coonskin gauntlets. She was certain that he would get through. He always got through things.

Save for his presence, the world and all normal living disappeared. They were lost in the boiling snow. He leaned close to bawl, "Letting the horses have their heads. They'll get us home."

With a terrifying bump they were off the road, slanting with two wheels in the ditch, but instantly they were jerked back as the horses fled on. She gasped. She tried to, and did not, feel brave as she pulled the woolen robe up about her chin.

They were passing something like a dark wall on the right. "I know that barn!" he yelped. He pulled at the reins. Peeping from the covers she saw his teeth pinch his lower lip, saw him scowl as he slackened and sawed and jerked sharply again at the racing horses.

They stopped.

"Farmhouse there. Put robe around you and come on," he cried.

It was like diving into icy water to climb out of the carriage, but on the ground she smiled at him, her face little and childish and pink above the buffalo robe over her shoulders. In a swirl of flakes which scratched at their eyes like a maniac darkness, he unbuckled the harness. He turned and plodded back, a ponderous furry figure, holding the horses' bridles, Carol's hand dragging at his sleeve.

They came to the cloudy bulk of a barn whose outer wall was directly upon the road. Feeling along it, he found a gate, led them into a yard, into the barn. The interior was warm. It stunned them with its languid quiet.

He carefully drove the horses into stalls.

Her toes were coals of pain. "Let's run for the house," she said.

"Can't. Not yet. Might never find it. Might get lost ten feet away from it. Sit over in this stall, near the horses. We'll rush for the house when the blizzard lifts."

"I'm so stiff! I can't walk!"

He carried her into the stall, stripped off her overshoes and boots, stopping to blow on his purple fingers as he fumbled at her laces. He rubbed her feet, and covered her with the buffalo robe and horse-blankets from the pile on the feed-box. She was drowsy, hemmed in by the storm. She sighed:

"You're so strong and yet so skilful and not afraid of blood or storm or——"

"Used to it. Only thing that's bothered me was the chance the ether fumes might explode, last night."

"I don't understand."

"Why, Dave, the darn fool, sent me ether, instead of chloroform like I told him, and you know ether fumes are mighty inflammable, especially with that lamp right by the table. But I had to operate, of course—wound chuck-full of barnyard filth that way."

"You knew all the time that—— Both you and I might have been blown up? You knew it while you were operating?" "Sure. Didn't you? Why, what's the matter?"

chapter 16

KENNICOTT was heavily pleased by her Christmas presents, and he gave her a diamond bar-pin. But she could not persuade herself that he was much interested in the rites of the morning, in the tree she had decorated, the three stockings she had hung, the ribbons and gilt seals and hidden messages. He said only:

"Nice way to fix things, all right. What do you say we go down to Jack Elder's and have a game of five hundred this afternoon?"

She remembered her father's Christmas fantasies: the sacred old rag doll at the top of the tree, the score of cheap presents, the punch and carols, the roast chestnuts by the fire, and the gravity with which the judge opened the children's scrawly notes and took cognizance of demands for sled-rides, for opinions upon the existence of Santa Claus. She remembered him reading out a long indictment of himself for being a sentimentalist, against the peace and dignity of the State of Minnesota. She remembered his thin legs twinkling before their sled——

She muttered unsteadily, "Must run up and put on my shoes—slippers so cold." In the not very romantic solitude of the locked bathroom she sat on the slippery edge of the tub and wept.

II

Kennicott had five hobbies: medicine, land-investment, Carol, motoring, and hunting. It is not certain in what order he preferred them. Solid though his enthusiasms were in the matter of medicine—his admiration of this city surgeon, his condemnation of that for tricky ways of persuading country practitioners to bring in surgical patients, his indignation about fee-splitting, his pride in a new X-ray apparatus—none of these beatified him as did motoring.

He nursed his two-year-old Buick even in winter, when it was stored in the stable-garage behind the house. He filled the grease-cups, varnished a fender, removed from beneath the back seat the débris of gloves, copper washers, crumpled maps, dust, and greasy rags. Winter noons he wandered out and stared owlishly at the car. He became excited over a fabulous "trip we might take next summer." He galloped to the station, brought home railway maps, and traced motor-routes from Gopher Prairie to Winnipeg or Des Moines or Grand Marais, thinking aloud and expecting her to be effusive about such academic questions as "Now I wonder if we could stop at Baraboo and break the jump from La Crosse to Chicago?"

To him motoring was a faith not to be questioned, a high-church cult, with electric sparks for candles, and piston-rings possessing the sanctity of altar-vessels. His liturgy was composed of intoned and metrical road-comments: "They say there's a pretty good hike from Duluth to International Falls."

Hunting was equally a devotion, full of metaphysical concepts veiled from Carol. All winter he read sporting-catalogues, and thought about remarkable past shots: " 'Member that time when I got two ducks on a long chance, just at sunset?" At least once a month he drew his favorite repeating shotgun, his "pump gun," from its wrapper of greased canton flannel; he oiled the trigger, and spent silent ecstatic moments aiming at the ceiling. Sunday mornings Carol heard him trudging up to the attic and there, an hour later, she found him turning over boots, wooden duck-decoys, lunch-boxes, or reflectively squinting at old shells, rubbing their brass caps with his sleeve and shaking his head as he thought about their uselessness.

He kept the loading-tool he had used as a boy: a capper for shot-gun shells, a mold for lead bullets. When once, in a housewifely frenzy for getting rid of things, she raged, "Why don't you give these away?" he solemnly defended them, "Well, you can't tell; they might come in handy some day."

She flushed. She wondered if he was thinking of the child they would have when, as he put it, they were "sure they could afford one."

Mysteriously aching, nebulously sad, she slipped away, half-convinced but only half-convinced that it was horrible and unnatural, this postponement of release of mother-affection, this sacrifice to her opinionation and to his cautious desire for prosperity.

"But it would be worse if he were like Sam Clark—insisted on having children," she considered; then, "If Will were the Prince, wouldn't I *demand* his child?"

Kennicott's land-deals were both financial advancement and favorite game. Driving through the country, he noticed which farms had good crops; he heard the news about the restless farmer who was "thinking about selling out here and pulling his freight for Alberta." He asked the veterinarian about the value of different breeds of stock; he inquired of Lyman Cass whether or not Einar Gyseldson really had had a yield of forty bushels of wheat to the acre. He was always consulting Julius Flickerbaugh, who handled more real estate than law, and more law than justice. He studied township maps, and read notices of auctions.

Thus he was able to buy a quarter-section of land for one hundred and fifty dollars an acre, and to sell it in a year or two, after installing a cement floor in the barn and running water in the house, for one hundred and eighty or even two hundred.

He spoke of these details to Sam Clark. . . . rather often.

In all his games, cars and guns and land, he expected Carol to take an interest. But he did not give her the facts which might have created interest. He talked only of the obvious and tedious aspects; never of his aspirations in finance, nor of the mechanical principles of motors.

This month of romance she was eager to understand his hobbies. She shivered in the garage while he spent half an hour in deciding whether to put alcohol or patent non-freezing liquid into the radiator, or to drain out the water entirely. "Or no, then I wouldn't want to take her out if it turned warm—still, of course, I could fill the radiator again—wouldn't take so awful long—just take a few pails of water—still, if it turned cold on me again before I drained it——Course there's some people that put in kerosene, but they say it rots the hose-connections and—— Where did I put that lug-wrench?"

It was at this point that she gave up being a motorist and retired to the house.

In their new intimacy he was more communicative about his practise; he informed her, with the invariable warning not to tell, that Mrs. Sunderquist had another baby coming, that the "hired girl at Howland's was in trouble." But when she

asked technical questions he did not know how to answer;
when she inquired, "Exactly what is the method of taking out
the tonsils?" he yawned, "Tonsilectomy? Why you just——
If there's pus, you operate. Just take 'em out. Seen the newspaper? What the devil did Bea do with it?"

She did not try again.

III

They had gone to the "movies." The movies were almost
as vital to Kennicott and the other solid citizens of Gopher
Prairie as land-speculation and guns and automobiles.

The feature film portrayed a brave young Yankee who conquered a South American republic. He turned the natives
from their barbarous habits of singing and laughing to the
vigorous sanity, the Pep and Punch and Go, of the North;
he taught them to work in factories, to wear Klassy Kollege
Klothes, and to shout, "Oh, you baby doll, watch me gather
in the mazuma." He changed nature itself. A mountain which
had borne nothing but lilies and cedars and loafing clouds
was by his Hustle so inspirited that it broke out in long
wooden sheds, and piles of iron ore to be converted into
steamers to carry iron ore to be converted into steamers to
carry iron ore.

The intellectual tension induced by the master film was
relieved by a livelier, more lyric and less philosophical
drama: Mack Schnarken and the Bathing Suit Babes in a
comedy of manners entitled "Right on the Coco." Mr. Schnarken was at various high moments a cook, a life-guard, a
burlesque actor, and a sculptor. There was a hotel hallway
up which policemen charged, only to be stunned by plaster
busts hurled upon them from the innumerous doors. If the
plot lacked lucidity, the dual motif of legs and pie was clear
and sure. Bathing and modeling were equally sound occasions
for legs; the wedding-scene was but an approach to the
thunderous climax when Mr. Schnarken slipped a piece of
custard pie into the clergyman's rear pocket.

The audience in the Rosebud Movie Palace squealed and
wiped their eyes; they scrambled under the seats for overshoes, mittens, and mufflers, while the screen announced
that next week Mr. Schnarken might be seen in a new, riproaring, extra-special superfeature of the Clean Comedy
Corporation entitled, "Under Mollie's Bed."

"I'm glad," said Carol to Kennicott as they stooped before

the northwest gale which was torturing the barren street, "that this is a moral country. We don't allow any of these beastly frank novels."

"Yump. Vice Society and Postal Department won't stand for them. The American people don't like filth."

"Yes. It's fine. I'm glad we have such dainty romances as 'Right on the Coco' instead."

"Say what in heck do you think you're trying to do? Kid me?"

He was silent. She awaited his anger. She meditated upon his gutter patois, the Bœotian dialect characteristic of Gopher Prairie. He laughed puzzlingly. When they came into the glow of the house he laughed again. He condescended:

"I've got to hand it to you. You're consistent, all right. I'd of thought that after getting this look-in at a lot of good decent farmers, you'd get over this high-art stuff, but you hang right on."

"Well——" To herself: "He takes advantage of my trying to be good."

"Tell you, Carrie: There's just three classes of people: folks that haven't got any ideas at all; and cranks that kick about everything; and Regular Guys, the fellow with stick-tuitiveness, that boost and get the world's work done."

"Then I'm probably a crank." She smiled negligently.

"No. I won't admit it. You do like to talk, but at a show-down you'd prefer Sam Clark to any damn long-haired artist."

"Oh—well——"

"Oh well!" mockingly. "My, we're just going to change everything, aren't we! Going to tell fellows that have been making movies for ten years how to direct 'em; and tell architects how to build towns; and make the magazines publish nothing but a lot of highbrow stories about old maids, and about wives that don't know what they want. Oh, we're a terror! . . . Come on now, Carrie; come out of it; wake up! You've got a fine nerve, kicking about a movie because it shows a few legs! Why, you're always touting these Greek dancers, or whatever they are, that don't even wear a shimmy!"

"But, dear, the trouble with that film—it wasn't that it got in so many legs, but that it giggled coyly and promised to show more of them, and then didn't keep the promise. It was Peeping Tom's idea of humor."

"I don't get you. Look here now——"

She lay awake, while he rumbled with sleep.

"I must go on. My 'crank ideas,' he calls them. I thought that adoring him, watching him operate, would be enough. It isn't. Not after the first thrill.

"I don't want to hurt him. But I must go on.

"It isn't enough, to stand by while he fills an automobile radiator and chucks me bits of information.

"If I stood by and admired him long enough, I would be content. I would become a 'nice little woman.' The Village Virus. Already—— I'm not reading anything. I haven't touched the piano for a week. I'm letting the days drown in worship of 'a good deal, ten plunks more per acre.' I won't! I won't succumb!

"How? I've failed at everything: the Thanatopsis, parties, pioneers, city hall, Guy and Vida. But—— It doesn't *matter!* I'm not trying to 'reform the town' now. I'm not trying to organize Browning Clubs, and sit in clean white kids yearning up at lecturers with ribbony eyeglasses. I am trying to save my soul.

"Will Kennicott, asleep there, trusting me, thinking he holds me. And I'm leaving him. All of me left him when he laughed at me. It wasn't enough for him that I admired him; I must change myself and grow like him. He takes advantage. No more. It's finished. I will go on."

IV

Her violin lay on top of the upright piano. She picked it up. Since she had last touched it the dried strings had snapped, and upon it lay a gold and crimson cigar-band.

V

She longed to see Guy Pollock, for the confirming of the brethren in the faith. But Kennicott's dominance was heavy upon her. She could not determine whether she was checked by fear or him, or by inertia—by dislike of the emotional labor of the "scenes" which would be involved in asserting independence. She was like the revolutionist at fifty: not afraid of death, but bored by the probability of bad steaks and bad breaths and sitting up all night on windy barricades.

The second evening after the movies she impulsively summoned Vida Sherwin and Guy to the house for pop-corn and cider. In the living-room Vida and Kennicott debated "the

value of manual training in grades below the eighth," while
Carol sat beside Guy at the dining table, buttering pop-corn.
She was quickened by the speculation in his eyes. She mur-
mured:

"Guy, do you want to help me?"

"My dear! How?"

"I don't know!"

He waited.

"I think I want you to help me find out what has made the
darkness of the women. Gray darkness and shadowy trees.
We're all in it, ten million women, young married women
with good prosperous husbands, and business women in linen
collars, and grandmothers that gad out to teas, and wives of
underpaid miners, and farmwives who really like to make
butter and go to church. What is it we want—and need? Will
Kennicott there would say that we need lots of children and
hard work. But it isn't that. There's the same discontent in
women with eight children and one more coming—always
one more coming! And you find it in stenographers and wives
who scrub, just as much as in girl college-graduates who
wonder how they can escape their kind parents. What do
we want?"

"Essentially, I think, you are like myself, Carol; you want
to go back to an age of tranquillity and charming manners.
You want to enthrone good taste again."

"Just good taste? Fastidious people? Oh—no! I believe all
of us want the same things—we're all together, the industrial
workers and the women and the farmers and the Negro race
and the Asiatic colonies, and even a few of the Respectables.
It's all the same revolt, in all the classes that have waited
and taken advice. I think perhaps we want a more conscious
life. We're tired of drudging and sleeping and dying. We're
tired of seeing just a few people able to be individualists.
We're tired of always deferring hope till the next generation.
We're tired of hearing the politicians and priests and cautious
reformers (and the husbands!) coax us, 'Be calm! Be patient!
Wait! We have the plans for a Utopia already made; just
give us a bit more time and we'll produce it; trust us; we're
wiser than you.' For ten thousand years they've said that.
We want our Utopia now—and we're going to try our hands
at it. All we want is—everything for all of us! For every
housewife and every longshoreman and every Hindu nation-
alist and every teacher. We want everything. We sha'n't get
it. So we sha'n't ever be content——"

She wondered why he was wincing. He broke in:

"See here, my dear, I certainly hope you don't class your-self with a lot of trouble-making labor-leaders! Democracy is all right theoretically, and I'll admit there are industrial in-justices, but I'd rather have them than see the world reduced to a dead level of mediocrity. I refuse to believe that you have anything in common with a lot of laboring men rowing for bigger wages so that they can buy wretched flivvers and hideous player-pianos and——"

At this second, in Buenos Aires, a newspaper editor broke his routine of being bored by exchanges to assert, "Any in-justice is better than seeing the world reduced to a gray level of scientific dullness." At this second a clerk standing at the bar of a New York saloon stopped milling his secret fear of his nagging office-manager long enough to growl at the chauffeur beside him, "Aw, you socialists make me sick! I'm an individualist. I ain't going to be nagged by no bureaus and take orders off labor-leaders. And mean to say a hobo's as good as you and me?"

At this second Carol realized that for all Guy's love of dead elegances his timidity was as depressing to her as the bulkiness of Sam Clark. She realized that he was not a mys-tery, as she had excitedly believed; not a romantic messenger from the World Outside on whom she could count for escape. He belonged to Gopher Prairie, absolutely. She was snatched back from a dream of far countries, and found herself on Main Street.

He was completing his protest, "You don't want to be mixed up in all this orgy of meaningless discontent?"

She soothed him. "No, I don't. I'm not heroic. I'm scared by all the fighting that's going on in the world. I want no-bility and adventure, but perhaps I want still more to curl on the hearth with some one I love."

"Would you——"

He did not finish it. He picked up a handful of pop-corn, let it run through his fingers, looked at her wistfully.

With the loneliness of one who has put away a possible love Carol saw that he was a stranger. She saw that he had never been anything but a frame on which she had hung shining garments. If she had let him diffidently make love to her, it was not because she cared, but because she did not care, because it did not matter.

She smiled at him with the exasperating tactfulness of a woman checking a flirtation; a smile like an airy pat on the arm. She sighed, "You're a dear to let me tell you my imaginary troubles." She bounced up, and trilled, "Shall we take the pop-corn in to them now?"

Guy looked after her desolately.

While she teased Vida and Kennicott she was repeating, "I must go on."

VI

Miles Bjornstam, the pariah "Red Swede," had brought his circular saw and portable gasoline engine to the house, to cut the cords of poplar for the kitchen range. Kennicott had given the order; Carol knew nothing of it till she heard the ringing of the saw, and glanced out to see Bjornstam, in black leather jacket and enormous ragged purple mittens, pressing sticks against the whirling blade, and flinging the stove-lengths to one side. The red irritable motor kept up a red irritable "tip-tip-tip-tip-tip-tip." The whine of the saw rose till it simulated the shriek of a fire-alarm whistle at night, but always at the end it gave a lively metallic clang, and in the stillness she heard the flump of the cut stick falling on the pile.

She threw a motor robe over her, ran out. Bjornstam welcomed her, "Well, well, well! Here's old Miles, fresh as ever. Well say, that's all right; he ain't even begun to be cheeky yet; next summer he's going to take you out on his horse-trading trip, clear into Idaho."

"Yes, and I may go!"

"How's tricks? Crazy about the town yet?"

"No, but I probably shall be, some day."

"Don't let 'em get you. Kick 'em in the face!"

He shouted at her while he worked. The pile of stove-wood grew astonishingly. The pale bark of the poplar sticks was mottled with lichens of sage-green and dusty gray; the newly sawed ends were fresh-colored, with the agreeable roughness of a woolen muffler. To the sterile winter air the wood gave a scent of March sap.

Kennicott telephoned that he was going into the country. Bjornstam had not finished his work at noon, and she invited him to have dinner with Bea in the kitchen. She wished that she were independent enough to dine with these her guests. She considered their friendliness, she sneered at "social distinctions," she raged at her own taboos—and she continued to regard them as retainers and herself as a lady. She sat in the dining-room and listened through the door to Bjornstam's booming and Bea's giggles. She was the more absurd to herself in that, after the rite of dining alone, she could go out to the kitchen, lean against the sink, and talk to them.

They were attracted to each other; a Swedish Othello and Desdemona, more useful and amiable than their prototypes. Bjornstam told his scapes: selling horses in a Montana mining-camp, breaking a log-jam, being impertinent to a "two-fisted" millionaire lumberman. Bea gurgled "Oh my!" and kept his coffee cup filled.

He took a long time to finish the wood. He had frequently to go into the kitchen to get warm. Carol heard him confiding to Bea, "You're a darn nice Swede girl. I guess if I had a woman like you I wouldn't be such a sorehead. Gosh, your kitchen is clean; makes an old bach feel sloppy. Say, that's nice hair you got. Huh? Me fresh? Saaaay, girl, if I ever do get fresh, you'll know it. Why, I could pick you up with one finger, and hold you in the air long enough to read Robert J. Ingersoll clean through. Ingersoll? Oh, he's a religious writer. Sure. You'd like him fine."

When he drove off he waved to Bea; and Carol, lonely at the window above, was envious of their pastoral.

"And I—— But I will go on."

$$chapter\ 17$$

THEY were driving down the lake to the cottages that moonlit January night, twenty of them in the bob-sled. They sang "Toy Land" and "Seeing Nelly Home"; they leaped from the low back of the sled to race over the slippery snow ruts; and when they were tired they climbed on the runners for a lift. The moon-tipped flakes kicked up by the horses settled over the revelers and dripped down their necks, but they laughed, yelped, beat their leather mittens against their chests. The harness rattled, the sleigh-bells were frantic, Jack Elder's setter sprang beside the horses, barking.

For a time Carol raced with them. The cold air gave fictive power. She felt that she could run on all night, leap twenty feet at a stride. But the excess of energy tired her, and she was glad to snuggle under the comforters which covered the hay in the sled-box.

In the midst of the babel she found enchanted quietude. Along the road the shadows from oak-branches were inked on the snow like bars of music. Then the sled came out on the surface of Lake Minniemashie. Across the thick ice was a veritable road, a short-cut for farmers. On the glaring expanse of the lake—levels of hard crust, flashes of green ice blown clear, chains of drifts ribbed like the sea-beach—the moonlight was overwhelming. It stormed on the snow, it turned the woods ashore into crystals of fire. The night was tropical and voluptuous. In that drugged magic there was no difference between heavy heat and insinuating cold.

Carol was dream-strayed. The turbulent voices, even Guy Pollock being connotative beside her, were nothing. She repeated:

Deep on the convent-roof the snows
Are sparkling to the moon.

The words and the light blurred into one vast indefinite happiness, and she believed that some great thing was coming to her. She withdrew from the clamor into a worship of incomprehensible gods. The night expanded, she was conscious of the universe, and all mysteries stooped down to her.

She was jarred out of her ecstasy as the bob-sled bumped up the steep road to the bluff where stood the cottages.

They dismounted at Jack Elder's shack. The interior walls of unpainted boards, which had been grateful in August, were forbidding in the chill. In fur coats and mufflers tied over caps they were a strange company, bears and walruses talking. Jack Elder lighted the shavings waiting in the belly of a cast-iron stove which was like an enlarged bean-pot. They piled their wraps high on a rocker, and cheered the rocker as it solemnly tipped over backward.

Mrs. Elder and Mrs. Sam Clark made coffee in an enormous blackened tin pot; Vida Sherwin and Mrs. McGanum unpacked doughnuts and gingerbread; Mrs. Dave Dyer warmed up "hot dogs"—frankfurters in rolls; Dr. Terry Gould, after announcing, "Ladies and gents, prepare to be shocked; shock line forms on the right," produced a bottle of bourbon whisky.

The others danced, muttering "Ouch!" as their frosted feet struck the pine planks. Carol had lost her dream. Harry

Haydock lifted her by the waist and swung her. She laughed. The gravity of the people who stood apart and talked made her the more impatient for frolic.

Kennicott, Sam Clark, Jackson Elder, young Dr. McGanum, and James Madison Howland, teetering on their toes near the stove, conversed with the sedate pomposity of the commercialist. In details the men were unlike, yet they said the same things in the same hearty monotonous voices. You had to look at them to see which was speaking.

"Well, we made pretty good time coming up," from one— any one.

"Yump, we hit it up after we struck the good going on the lake."

"Seems kind of slow though, after driving an auto."

"Yump, it does, at that. Say, how'd you make out with that Sphinx tire you got?"

"Seems to hold out fine. Still, I don't know's I like it any better than the Roadeater Cord."

"Yump, nothing better than a Roadeater. Especially the cord. The cord's lots better than the fabric."

"Yump, you said something—— Roadeater's a good tire."

"Say, how'd you come out with Pete Garsheim on his payments?"

"He's paying up pretty good. That's a nice piece of land he's got."

"Yump, that's a dandy farm."

"Yump, Pete's got a good place there."

They glided from these serious topics into the jocose insults which are the wit of Main Street. Sam Clark was particularly apt at them. "What's this wild-eyed sale of summer caps you think you're trying to pull off?" he clamored at Harry Haydock. "Did you steal 'em, or are you just overcharging us, as usual? . . . Oh say, speaking about caps, d'I ever tell you the good one I've got on Will? The doc thinks he's a pretty good driver, fact, he thinks he's almost got human intelligence, but one time he had his machine out in the rain, and the poor fish, he hadn't put on chains, and thinks I——"

Carol had heard the story rather often. She fled back to the dancers, and at Dave Dyer's masterstroke of dropping an icicle down Mrs. McGanum's back she applauded hysterically.

They sat on the floor, devouring the food. The men giggled amiably as they passed the whisky bottle, and laughed, "There's a real sport!" when Juanita Haydock took a sip.

Carol tried to follow; she believed that she desired to be drunk and riotous; but the whisky choked her and as she saw Kennicott frown she handed the bottle on repentantly. Somewhat too late she remembered that she had given up domesticity and repentance.

"Let's play charades!" said Raymie Wutherspoon.

"Oh yes, do let us," said Ella Stowbody.

"That's the caper," sanctioned Harry Haydock.

They interpreted the word "making" as May and King. The crown was a red flannel mitten cocked on Sam Clark's broad pink bald head. They forgot they were respectable. They made-believe. Carol was stimulated to cry:

"Let's form a dramatic club and give a play! Shall we? It's been so much fun tonight!"

They looked affable.

"Sure," observed Sam Clark loyally.

"Oh, do let us! I think it would be lovely to present 'Romeo and Juliet'!" yearned Ella Stowbody.

"Be a whale of a lot of fun," Dr. Terry Gould granted.

"But if we did," Carol cautioned, "it would be awfully silly to have amateur theatricals. We ought to paint our own scenery and everything, and really do something fine. There'd be a lot of hard work. Would you—would we all be punctual at rehearsals, do you suppose?"

"You bet!" "Sure." "That's the idea." "Fellow ought to be prompt at rehearsals," they all agreed.

"Then let's meet next week and form the Gopher Prairie Dramatic Association!" Carol sang.

She drove home loving these friends who raced through moonlit snow, had Bohemian parties, and were about to create beauty in the theater. Everything was solved. She would be an authentic part of the town, yet escape the coma of the Village Virus. . . . She would be free of Kennicott again, without hurting him, without his knowing.

She had triumphed.

The moon was small and high now, and unheeding.

II

Though they had all been certain that they longed for the privilege of attending committee meetings and rehearsals, the dramatic association as definitely formed consisted only of Kennicott, Carol, Guy Pollock, Vida Sherwin, Ella Stowbody, the Harry Haydocks, the Dave Dyers, Raymie Wutherspoon,

Dr. Terry Gould and four new candidates: flirtatious Rita Simons, Dr. and Mrs. Harvey Dillon and Myrtle Cass, an uncomely but intense girl of nineteen. Of these fifteen only seven came to the first meeting. The rest telephoned their unparalleled regrets and engagements and illnesses, and announced that they would be present at all other meetings through eternity.

Carol was made president and director.

She had added the Dillons. Despite Kennicott's apprehension the dentist and his wife had not been taken up by the Westlakes but had remained as definitely outside really smart society as Willis Woodford, who was teller, bookkeeper, and janitor in Stowbody's bank. Carol had noted Mrs. Dillon dragging past the house during a bridge of the Jolly Seventeen, looking in with pathetic lips at the splendor of the accepted. She impulsively invited the Dillons to the dramatic association meeting, and when Kennicott was brusque to them she was unusually cordial, and felt virtuous.

That self-approval balanced her disappointment at the smallness of the meeting, and her embarrassment during Raymie Wutherspoon's repetitions of "The stage needs uplifting," and "I believe that there are great lessons in some plays."

Ella Stowbody, who was a professional, having studied elocution in Milwaukee, disapproved of Carol's enthusiasm for recent plays. Miss Stowbody expressed the fundamental principle of the American drama: the only way to be artistic is to present Shakespeare. As no one listened to her she sat back and looked like Lady Macbeth.

III

The Little Theaters, which were to give piquancy to American drama three or four years later, were only in embryo. But of this fast coming revolt Carol had premonitions. She knew from some lost magazine article that in Dublin were innovators called The Irish Players. She knew confusedly that a man named Gordon Craig had painted scenery—or had he written plays? She felt that in the turbulence of the drama she was discovering a history more important than the commonplace chronicles which dealt with senators and their pompous puerilities. She had a sensation of familiarity; a dream of sitting in a Brussels café and going afterward to a tiny gay theater under a cathedral wall.

The advertisement in the Minneapolis paper leaped from the page to her eyes:

The Cosmos School of Music, Oratory, and Dramatic Art announces a program of four one-act plays by Schnitzler, Shaw, Yeats, and Lord Dunsany.

She had to be there! She begged Kennicott to "run down to the Cities" with her.

"Well, I don't know. Be fun to take in a show, but why the deuce do you want to see those darn foreign plays, given by a lot of amateurs? Why don't you wait for a regular play, later on? There's going to be some corkers coming: 'Lottie of Two-Gun Rancho,' and 'Cops and Crooks'—real Broadway stuff, with the New York casts. What's this junk you want to see? Hm. 'How He Lied to Her Husband.' That doesn't listen so bad. Sounds racy. And, uh, well, I could go to the motor show, I suppose. I'd like to see this new Hup roadster. Well——"

She never knew which attraction made him decide.

She had four days of delightful worry—over the hole in her one good silk petticoat, the loss of a string of beads from her chiffon and brown velvet frock, the catsup stain on her best georgette crêpe blouse. She wailed, "I haven't a single solitary thing that's fit to be seen in," and enjoyed herself very much indeed.

Kennicott went about casually letting people know that he was "going to run down to the Cities and see some shows."

As the train plodded through the gray prairie, on a windless day with the smoke from the engine clinging to the fields in giant cotton-rolls, in a low and writhing wall which shut off the snowy fields, she did not look out of the window. She closed her eyes and hummed, and did not know that she was humming.

She was the young poet attacking fame and Paris.

In the Minneapolis station the crowd of lumberjacks, farmers, and Swedish families with innumerous children and grandparents and paper parcels, their foggy crowding and their clamor confused her. She felt rustic in this once familiar city, after a year and a half of Gopher Prairie. She was certain that Kennicott was taking the wrong trolley-car. By dusk, the liquor warehouses, Hebraic clothing-shops, and lodging-houses on lower Hennepin Avenue were smoky, hideous, ill-tempered. She was battered by the noise and shuttling of the rush-hour traffic. When a clerk in an overcoat too closely fitted at the waist stared at her, she moved nearer to Kennicott's arm. The clerk was flippant and urban. He was a superior person, used to this tumult. Was he laughing at her?

For a moment she wanted the secure quiet of Gopher Prairie.

In the hotel-lobby she was self-conscious. She was not used to hotels; she remembered with jealousy how often Juanita Haydock talked of the famous hotels in Chicago. She could not face the traveling salesmen, baronial in large leather chairs. She wanted people to believe that her husband and she were accustomed to luxury and chill elegance; she was faintly angry at him for the vulgar way in which, after signing the register "Dr. W. P. Kennicott & wife," he bellowed at the clerk, "Got a nice room with bath for us, old man?" She gazed about haughtily, but as she discovered that no one was interested in her she felt foolish, and ashamed of her irritation.

She asserted, "This silly lobby is too florid," and simultaneously she admired it: the onyx columns with gilt capitals, the crown-embroidered velvet curtains at the restaurant door, the silk-roped alcove where pretty girls perpetually waited for mysterious men, the two-pound boxes of candy and the variety of magazines at the news-stand. The hidden orchestra was lively. She saw a man who looked like a European diplomat, in a loose top-coat and a Homburg hat. A woman with a broadtail coat, a heavy lace veil, pearl earrings, and a close black hat entered the restaurant. "Heavens! That's the first really smart woman I've seen in a year!" Carol exulted. She felt metropolitan.

But as she followed Kennicott to the elevator the coat-check girl, a confident young woman, with cheeks powdered like lime, and a blouse low and thin and furiously crimson, inspected her, and under that supercilious glance Carol was shy again. She unconsciously waited for the bellboy to precede her into the elevator. When he snorted "Go ahead!" she was mortified. He thought she was a hayseed, she worried.

The moment she was in their room, with the bellboy safely out of the way, she looked critically at Kennicott. For the first time in months she really saw him.

His clothes were too heavy and provincial. His decent gray suit, made by Nat Hicks of Gopher Prairie, might have been of sheet iron; it had no distinction of cut, no easy grace like the diplomat's Burberry. His black shoes were blunt and not well polished. His scarf was a stupid brown. He needed a shave.

But she forgot her doubt as she realized the ingenuities of the room. She ran about, turning on the taps of the bathtub, which gushed instead of dribbling like the taps at home, snatching the new wash-rag out of its envelope of oiled paper, trying the rose-shaded light between the twin beds, pulling out the drawers of the kidney-shaped walnut desk to examine the engraved stationery, planning to write on it to every one she knew, admiring the claret-colored velvet arm-chair and the blue rug, testing the ice-water tap, and squealing happily when the water really did come out cold. She flung her arms about Kennicott, kissed him.

"Like it, old lady?"

"It's adorable. It's so amusing. I love you for bringing me. You really are a dear!"

He looked blankly indulgent, and yawned, and condescended, "That's a pretty slick arrangement on the radiator, so you can adjust it at any temperature you want. Must take a big furnace to run this place. Gosh, I hope Bea remembers to turn off the drafts tonight."

Under the glass cover of the dressing-table was a menu with the most enchanting dishes: breast of guinea hen De Vitresse, pommes de terre à la Russe, meringue Chantilly, gâteaux Bruxelles.

"Oh, let's—— I'm going to have a hot bath, and put on my new hat with the wool flowers, and let's go down and eat for hours, and we'll have a cocktail!" she chanted.

While Kennicott labored over ordering it was annoying to see him permit the waiter to be impertinent, but as the cocktail elevated her to a bridge among colored stars, as the oysters came in—not canned oysters in the Gopher Prairie fashion, but on the half-shell—she cried, "If you only knew how wonderful it is not to have had to plan this dinner, and order it at the butcher's and fuss and think about it, and then watch Bea cook it! I feel so free. And to have new kinds of food, and different patterns of dishes and linen, and not worry about whether the pudding is being spoiled! Oh, this is a great moment for me!"

IV

They had all the experiences of provincials in a metropolis. After breakfast Carol bustled to a hair-dresser's, bought gloves and a blouse, and importantly met Kennicott in front of an optician's, in accordance with plans laid down, revised, and verified. They admired the diamonds and furs and frosty silverware and mahogany chairs and polished morocco sewing-boxes in shop-windows, and were abashed by the throngs in the department-stores, and were bullied by a clerk into buying too many shirts for Kennicott, and gaped at the "clever novelty perfumes—just in from New York." Carol got three books on the theater, and spent an exultant hour in warning herself that she could not afford this rajah-silk frock, in thinking how envious it would make Juanita Haydock, in closing her eyes, and buying it. Kennicott went from shop to shop, earnestly hunting down a felt-covered device to keep the windshield of his car clear of rain.

They dined extravagantly at their hotel at night, and next morning sneaked round the corner to economize at a Childs' Restaurant. They were tired by three in the afternoon, and dozed at the motion-pictures and said they wished they were back in Gopher Prairie—and by eleven in the evening they were again so lively that they went to a Chinese restaurant that was frequented by clerks and their sweethearts on paydays. They sat at a teak and marble table eating Eggs Fooyung, and listened to a brassy automatic piano, and were altogether cosmopolitan.

On the street they met people from home—the McGanums. They laughed, shook hands repeatedly, and exclaimed, "Well, this is quite a coincidence!" They asked when the McGanums had come down, and begged for news of the town they had left two days before. Whatever the McGanums were at home, here they stood out as so superior to all the undistinguishable strangers absurdly hurrying past that the Kennicotts held them as long as they could. The McGanums said good-by as though they were going to Tibet instead of to the station to catch No. 7 north.

They explored Minneapolis. Kennicott was conversational and technical regarding gluten and cockle-cylinders and No. 1 Hard, when they were shown through the gray stone hulks and new cement elevators of the largest flour-mills in the world. They looked across Loring Park and the Parade to the towers of St. Mark's and the Procathedral, and the red roofs of houses climbing Kenwood Hill. They drove about the chain of garden-circled lakes, and viewed the houses of the millers and lumbermen and real estate peers—the potentates of the expanding city. They surveyed the small eccentric

bungalows with pergolas, the houses of pebbledash and tapestry brick with sleeping-porches above sun-parlors, and one
vast incredible château fronting the Lake of the Isles. They
tramped through a shining-new section of apartment-houses;
not the tall bleak apartments of Eastern cities but low structures of cheerful yellow brick, in which each flat had its
glass-enclosed porch with swinging couch and scarlet
cushions and Russian brass bowls. Between a waste of tracks
and a raw gouged hill they found poverty in staggering
shanties.

They saw miles of the city which they had never known in
their days of absorption in college. They were distinguished
explorers, and they remarked, in great mutual esteem, "I bet
Harry Haydock's never seen the City like this! Why, he'd
never have sense enough to study the machinery in the mills,
or go through all these outlying districts. Wonder folks in
Gopher Prairie wouldn't use their legs and explore, the way
we do!"

They had two meals with Carol's sister, and were bored, and
felt that intimacy which beatifies married people when they
suddenly admit that they equally dislike a relative of either
of them.

So it was with affection but also with weariness that they
approached the evening on which Carol was to see the plays
at the dramatic school. Kennicott suggested not going. "So
darn tired from all this walking; don't know but what we
better turn in early and get rested up." It was only from duty
that Carol dragged him and herself out of the warm hotel,
into a stinking trolley, up the brownstone steps of the converted residence which lugubriously housed the dramatic
school.

v

They were in a long whitewashed hall with a clumsy draw-
curtain across the front. The folding chairs were filled with
people who looked washed and ironed: parents of the pupils,
girl students, dutiful teachers.

"Strikes me it's going to be punk. If the first play isn't
good, let's beat it," said Kennicott hopefully.

"All right," she yawned. With hazy eyes she tried to read
the lists of characters, which were hidden among lifeless advertisements of pianos, music-dealers, restaurants, candy.

She regarded the Schnitzler play with no vast interest. The

actors moved and spoke stiffly. Just as its cynicism was beginning to rouse her village-dulled frivolity, it was over.

"Don't think a whale of a lot of that. How about taking a sneak?" petitioned Kennicott.

"Oh, let's try the next one, 'How He Lied to Her Husband.' "

The Shaw conceit amused her, and perplexed Kennicott:

"Strikes me it's darn fresh. Thought it would be racy. Don't know as I think much of a play where a husband actually claims he wants a fellow to make love to his wife. No husband ever did that! Shall we shake a leg?"

"I want to see this Yeats thing, 'Land of Heart's Desire.' I used to love it in college." She was awake now, and urgent. "I know you didn't care so much for Yeats when I read him aloud to you, but you just see if you don't adore him on the stage."

Most of the cast were as unwieldy as oak chairs marching, and the setting was an arty arrangement of batik scarfs and heavy tables, but Maire Bruin was slim as Carol, and larger-eyed, and her voice was a morning bell. In her, Carol lived, and on her lifting voice was transported from this sleepy small-town husband and all the rows of polite parents to the stilly loft of a thatched cottage where in a green dimness, beside a window caressed by linden branches, she bent over a chronicle of twilight women and the ancient gods.

"Well—gosh—nice kid played that girl—good-looker," said Kennicott. "Want to stay for the last piece? Heh?"

She shivered. She did not answer.

The curtain was again drawn aside. On the stage they saw nothing but long green curtains and a leather chair. Two young men in brown robes like furniture-covers were gesturing vacuously and droning cryptic sentences full of repetitions.

It was Carol's first hearing of Dunsany. She sympathized with the restless Kennicott as he felt in his pocket for a cigar and unhappily put it back.

Without understanding when or how, without a tangible change in the stilted intoning of the stage-puppets, she was conscious of another time and place.

Stately and aloof among vainglorious tiring-maids, a queen in robes that murmured on the marble floor, she trod the gallery of a crumbling palace. In the courtyard, elephants trumpeted, and swart men with beards dyed crimson stood with blood-stained hands folded upon their hilts, guarding the caravan from El Sharnak, the camels with Tyrian stuffs of topaz and cinnabar. Beyond the turrets of the outer wall the jungle glared and shrieked, and the sun was furious above drenched orchids. A youth came striding through the steel-bossed doors, the sword-bitten doors that were higher than ten tall men. He was in flexible mail, and under the rim of his planished morion were amorous curls. His hand was out to her; before she touched it she could feel its warmth——

"Gosh all hemlock! What the dickens is all this stuff about, Carrie?"

She was no Syrian queen. She was Mrs. Dr. Kennicott. She fell with a jolt into a whitewashed hall and sat looking at two scared girls and a young man in wrinkled tights.

Kennicott fondly rambled as they left the hall:

"What the deuce did that last spiel mean? Couldn't make head or tail of it. If that's highbrow drama, give me a cow-puncher movie, every time! Thank God, that's over, and we can get to bed. Wonder if we wouldn't make time by walking over to Nicollet to take a car? One thing I will say for that dump: they had it warm enough. Must have a big hot-air furnace, I guess. Wonder how much coal it takes to run 'em through the winter?"

In the car he affectionately patted her knee, and he was for a second the striding youth in armor; then he was Doc Kennicott of Gopher Prairie, and she was recaptured by Main Street. Never, not all her life, would she behold jungles and the tombs of kings. There were strange things in the world, they really existed; but she would never see them.

She would recreate them in plays!

She would make the dramatic association understand her aspiration. They would, surely they would——

She looked doubtfully at the impenetrable reality of yawning trolley conductor and sleepy passengers and placards advertising soap and underwear.

chapter 18

SHE hurried to the first meeting of the play-reading committee. Her jungle romance had faded, but she retained a religious fervor, a surge of half-formed thought about the creation of beauty by suggestion.

A Dunsany play would be too difficult for the Gopher Prairie association. She would let them compromise on Shaw —on "Androcles and the Lion," which had just been published.

The committee was composed of Carol, Vida Sherwin, Guy Pollock, Raymie Wutherspoon, and Juanita Haydock. They were exalted by the picture of themselves as being simultaneously business-like and artistic. They were entertained by Vida in the parlor of Mrs. Elisha Gurrey's boarding-house, with its steel engraving of Grant at Appomattox, its basket of stereoscopic views, and its mysterious stains on the gritty carpet.

Vida was an advocate of culture-buying and efficiency-systems. She hinted that they ought to have (as at the committee-meetings of the Thanatopsis) a "regular order of business," and "the reading of the minutes," but as there were no minutes to read, and as no one knew exactly what was the regular order of the business of being literary, they had to give up efficiency.

Carol, as chairman, said politely, "Have you any ideas about what play we'd better give first?" She waited for them to look abashed and vacant, so that she might suggest "Androcles."

Guy Pollock answered with disconcerting readiness, "I'll tell you: since we're going to try to do something artistic, and not simply fool around, I believe we ought to give something classic. How about 'The School for Scandal'?"

"Why—— Don't you think that has been done a good deal?"

"Yes, perhaps it has."

Carol was ready to say, "How about Bernard Shaw?" when he treacherously went on, "How would it be then to give a Greek drama—say 'Œdipus Tyrannus'?"

212

"Why, I don't believe——"

Vida Sherwin intruded, "I'm sure that would be too hard for us. Now I've brought something that I think would be awfully jolly."

She held out, and Carol incredulously took, a thin gray pamphlet entitled "McGinerty's Mother-in-law." It was the sort of farce which is advertised in "school entertainment" catalogues as:

Riproaring knock-out, 5 m. 3 f., time 2 hrs., interior set, popular with churches and all high-class occasions.

Carol glanced from the scabrous object to Vida, and realized that she was not joking.

"But this is—this is—why, it's just a—— Why, Vida, I thought you appreciated—well—appreciated art."

Vida snorted, "Oh. Art. Oh yes. I do like art. It's very nice. But after all, what does it matter what kind of play we give as long as we get the association started? The thing that matters is something that none of you have spoken of, that is: what are we going to do with the money, if we make any? I think it would be awfully nice if we presented the high school with a full set of Stoddard's travel-lectures!"

Carol moaned, "Oh, but Vida dear, do forgive me but this farce—— Now what I'd like us to give is something distinguished. Say Shaw's 'Androcles.' Have any of you read it?"

"Yes. Good play," said Guy Pollock.

Then Raymie Wutherspoon astoundingly spoke up:

"So have I. I read through all the plays in the public library, so's to be ready for this meeting. And—— But I don't believe you grasp the irreligious ideas in this 'Androcles,' Mrs. Kennicott. I guess the feminine mind is too innocent to understand all these immoral writers. I'm sure I don't want to criticize Bernard Shaw; I understand he is very popular with the highbrows in Minneapolis; but just the same—— As far as I can make out, he's downright improper! The things he *says*—— Well, it would be a very risky thing for our young folks to see. It seems to me that a play that doesn't leave a nice taste in the mouth and that hasn't any message is nothing but—nothing but—— Well, whatever it may be, it isn't art. So—— Now I've found a play that is clean, and there's some awfully funny scenes in it, too. I laughed out loud, reading it. It's called 'His Mother's Heart,' and it's about a young man in college who gets in with a lot of free-thinkers and boozers and everything, but in the end his mother's influence——"

Juanita Haydock broke in with a derisive, "Oh rats, Raymie! Can the mother's influence! I say let's give something with some class to it. I bet we could get the rights to 'The Girl from Kankakee,' and that's a real show. It ran for eleven months in New York!"

"That would be lots of fun, if it wouldn't cost too much," reflected Vida.

Carol's was the only vote cast against "The Girl from Kankakee."

II

She disliked "The Girl from Kankakee" even more than she had expected. It narrated the success of a farm-lassie in clearing her brother of a charge of forgery. She became secretary to a New York millionaire and social counselor to his wife; and after a well-conceived speech on the discomfort of having money, she married his son.

There was also a humorous office-boy.

Carol discerned that both Juanita Haydock and Ella Stowbody wanted the lead. She let Juanita have it. Juanita kissed her and in the exuberant manner of a new star presented to the executive committee her theory, "What we want in a play is humor and pep. There's where American playwrights put it all over these darn old European glooms."

As selected by Carol and confirmed by the committee, the persons of the play were:

John Grimm, a millionaire .	Guy Pollock
His wife	Miss Vida Sherwin
His son	Dr. Harvey Dillon
His business rival . . .	Raymond T. Wutherspoon
Friend of Mrs. Grimm . .	Miss Ella Stowbody
The girl from Kankakee . .	Mrs. Harold C. Haydock
Her brother	Dr. Terence Gould
Her mother	Mrs. David Dyer
Stenographer	Miss Rita Simons
Office-boy	Miss Myrtle Cass
Maid in the Grimms' home .	Mrs. W. P. Kennicott
Directon of Mrs. Kennicott	

Among the minor lamentations was Maud Dyer's "Well of course I suppose I look old enough to be Juanita's mother,

even if Juanita is eight months older than I am, but I don't
know as I care to have everybody noticing it and——"

Carol pleaded, "Oh, my *dear!* You two look exactly the
same age. I chose you because you have such a darling complexion, and you know with powder and a white wig, anybody
looks twice her age, and I want the mother to be sweet, no
matter who else is."

Ella Stowbody, the professional, perceiving that it was because of a conspiracy of jealousy that she had been given a
small part, alternated between lofty amusement and Christian
patience.

Carol hinted that the play would be improved by cutting,
but as every actor except Vida and Guy and herself wailed
at the loss of a single line, she was defeated. She told herself
that, after all, a great deal could be done with direction and
settings.

Sam Clark had boastfully written about the dramatic association to his schoolmate, Percy Bresnahan, president of the
Velvet Motor Company of Boston. Bresnahan sent a check
for a hundred dollars; Sam added twenty-five and brought
the fund to Carol, fondly crying, "There! That'll give you a
start for putting the thing across swell!"

She rented the second floor of the city hall for two months.
All through the spring the association thrilled to its own
talent in that dismal room. They cleared out the bunting,
ballot-boxes, handbills, legless chairs. They attacked the
stage. It was a simple-minded stage. It was raised above the
floor, and it did have a movable curtain, painted with the
advertisement of a druggist dead these ten years, but otherwise it might not have been recognized as a stage. There were
two dressing-rooms, one for men, one for women, on either
side. The dressing-room doors were also the stage-entrances,
opening from the house, and many a citizen of Gopher
Prairie had for his first glimpse of romance the bare shoulders
of the leading woman.

There were three sets of scenery: a woodland, a Poor Interior, and a Rich Interior, the last also useful for railway
stations, offices, and as a background for the Swedish Quar-
tette from Chicago. There were three gradations of lighting:
full on, half on, and entirely off.

This was the only theater in Gopher Prairie. It was known
as the "op'ra house." Once, strolling companies had used it
for performances of "The Two Orphans," and "Nellie the
Beautiful Cloak Model," and "Othello" with specialties be-

tween acts, but now the motion-pictures had ousted the gipsy drama.

Carol intended to be furiously modern in constructing the office-set, the drawing-room for Mr. Grimm, and the Humble Home near Kankakee. It was the first time that any one in Gopher Prairie had been so revolutionary as to use enclosed scenes with continuous side-walls. The rooms in the op'ra house sets had separate wing-pieces for sides, which simplified dramaturgy, as the villain could always get out of the hero's way by walking out through the wall.

The inhabitants of the Humble Home were supposed to be amiable and intelligent. Carol planned for them a simple set with warm color. She could see the beginning of the play: all dark save the high settles and the solid wooden table. between them, which were to be illuminated by a ray from off-stage. The high light was a polished copper pot filled with primroses. Less clearly she sketched the Grimm drawing-room as a series of cool high white arches.

As to how she was to produce these effects she had no notion.

She discovered that, despite the enthusiastic young writers, the drama was not half so native and close to the soil as motor cars and telephones. She discovered that simple arts require sophisticated training. She discovered that to produce one perfect stage-picture would be as difficult as to turn all of Gopher Prairie into a Georgian garden.

She read all she could find regarding staging; she bought paint and light wood; she borrowed furniture and drapes unscrupulously; she made Kennicott turn carpenter. She collided with the problem of lighting. Against the protest of Kennicott and Vida she mortgaged the association by sending to Minneapolis for a baby spotlight, a strip light, a dimming device, and blue and amber bulbs; and with the gloating rapture of a born painter first turned loose among colors, she spent absorbed evenings in grouping, dimming—painting with lights.

Only Kennicott, Guy, and Vida helped her. They speculated as to how flats could be lashed together to form a wall; they hung crocus-yellow curtains at the windows; they blacked the sheet-iron stove; they put on aprons and swept. The rest of the association dropped into the theater every evening, and were literary and superior. They had borrowed Carol's manuals of play-production and had become extremely stagey in vocabulary.

Juanita Haydock, Rita Simons, and Raymie Wutherspoon sat on a sawhorse, watching Carol try to get the right position for a picture on the wall in the first scene.

"I don't want to hand myself anything but I believe I'll give a swell performance in this first act," confided Juanita. "I wish Carol wasn't so bossy though. She doesn't understand clothes. I want to wear, oh, a dandy dress I have—all scarlet—and I said to her, 'When I enter wouldn't it knock their eyes out if I just stood there at the door in this straight scarlet thing?' But she wouldn't let me."

Young Rita agreed, "She's so much taken up with her old details and carpentering and everything that she can't see the picture as a whole. Now I thought it would be lovely if we had an office-scene like the one in 'Little, But Oh My!' Because I *saw* that, in Duluth. But she simply wouldn't listen at all."

Juanita sighed, "I wanted to give one speech like Ethel Barrymore would, if she was in a play like this. (Harry and I heard her one time in Minneapolis—we had dandy seats, in the orchestra—I just know I could imitate her.) Carol didn't pay any attention to my suggestion. I don't want to criticize but I guess Ethel knows more about acting than Carol does!"

"Say, do you think Carol has the right dope about using a strip light behind the fireplace in the second act? I told her I thought we ought to use a bunch," offered Raymie. "And I suggested it would be lovely if we used a cyclorama outside the window in the first act, and what do you think she said? 'Yes, and it would be lovely to have Eleanora Duse play the lead,' she said, 'and aside from the fact that it's evening in the first act, you're a great technician,' she said. I must say I think she was pretty sarcastic. I've been reading up, and I know I could build a cyclorama, if she didn't want to run everything."

"Yes, and another thing, I think the entrance in the first act ought to be L. U. E., not L. 3 E.," from Juanita.

"And why does she just use plain white tormenters?"

"What's a tormenter?" blurted Rita Simons.

The savants stared at her ignorance.

III

Carol did not resent their criticisms, she didn't very much resent their sudden knowledge, so long as they let her make pictures. It was at rehearsals that the quarrels broke. No one understood that rehearsals were as real engagements as bridge-games or sociables at the Episcopal Church. They gaily came in half an hour late, or they vociferously came in ten minutes early, and they were so hurt that they whispered about resigning when Carol protested. They telephoned, "I don't think I'd better come out; afraid the dampness might start my toothache," or "Guess can't make it tonight; Dave wants me to sit in on a poker game."

When, after a month of labor, as many as nine-elevenths of the cast were often present at a rehearsal; when most of them had learned their parts and some of them spoke like human beings, Carol had a new shock in the realization that Guy Pollock and herself were very bad actors, and that Raymie Wutherspoon was a surprisingly good one. For all her visions she could not control her voice, and she was bored by the fiftieth repetition of her few lines as maid. Guy pulled his soft mustache, looked self-conscious, and turned Mr. Grimm into a limp dummy. But Raymie, as the villain, had no repressions. The tilt of his head was full of character; his drawl was admirably vicious.

There was an evening when Carol hoped she was going to make a play; a rehearsal during which Guy stopped looking abashed.

From that evening the play declined.

They were weary. "We know our parts well enough now; what's the use of getting sick of them?" they complained. They began to skylark; to play with the sacred lights; to giggle when Carol was trying to make the sentimental Myrtle Cass into a humorous office-boy; to act everything but "The Girl from Kankakee." After loafing through his proper part Dr. Terry Gould had great applause for his burlesque of "Hamlet." Even Raymie lost his simple faith, and tried to show that he could do a vaudeville shuffle.

Carol turned on the company. "See here, I want this nonsense to stop. We've simply got to get down to work."

Juanita Haydock led the mutiny: "Look here, Carol, don't be so bossy. After all, we're doing this play principally for the fun of it, and if we have fun out of a lot of monkeyshines, why then——"

"Ye-es," feebly.

"You said one time that folks in G. P. didn't get enough fun out of life. And now we are having a circus, you want us to stop!"

Carol answered slowly: "I wonder if I can explain what I mean? It's the difference between looking at the comic page and looking at Manet. I want fun out of this, of course. Only—— I don't think it would be less fun, but more, to produce as perfect a play as we can." She was curiously exalted; her voice was strained; she stared not at the company but at the grotesques scrawled on the backs of wing-pieces by forgotten stage-hands. "I wonder if you can understand the 'fun' of making a beautiful thing, the pride and satisfaction of it, and the holiness!"

The company glanced doubtfully at one another. In Gopher Prairie it is not good form to be holy except at a church, between ten-thirty and twelve on Sunday.

"But if we want to do it, we've got to work; we must have self-discipline."

They were at once amused and embarrassed. They did not want to affront this mad woman. They backed off and tried to rehearse. Carol did not hear Juanita, in front, protesting to Maud Dyer, "If she calls it fun and holiness to sweat over her darned old play—well, I don't!"

IV

Carol attended the only professional play which came to Gopher Prairie that spring. It was a "tent show, presenting snappy new dramas under canvas." The hard-working actors doubled in brass, and took tickets; and between acts sang about the moon in June, and sold Dr. Wintergreen's Surefire Tonic for Ills of the Heart, Lungs, Kidneys, and Bowels. They presented "Sunbonnet Nell: A Dramatic Comedy of the Ozarks," with J. Witherbee Boothby wringing the soul by his resonant "Yuh ain't done right by mah little gal, Mr. City Man, but yer a-goin' to find that back in these-yere hills there's honest folks and good shots!"

The audience, on planks beneath the patched tent, admired Mr. Boothby's beard and long rifle; stamped their feet in the dust at the spectacle of his heroism; shouted when the comedian aped the City Lady's use of a lorgnon by looking through a doughnut stuck on a fork; wept visibly over Mr. Boothby's Little Gal Nell, who was also Mr. Boothby's legal wife Pearl, and when the curtain went down, listened respectfully to Mr. Boothby's lecture on Dr. Wintergreen's Tonic as a cure for tape-worms, which he illustrated by horrible pallid objects curled in bottles of yellowing alcohol.

Carol shook her head. "Juanita is right. I'm a fool. Holiness of the drama! Bernard Shaw! The only trouble with 'The Girl from Kankakee' is that it's too subtle for Gopher Prairie!"

She sought faith in spacious banal phrases, taken from books: "the instinctive nobility of simple souls," "need only the opportunity, to appreciate fine things," and "sturdy exponents of democracy." But these optimisms did not sound so loud as the laughter of the audience at the funny-man's line, "Yes, by heckelum, I'm a smart fella." She wanted to give up the play, the dramatic association, the town. As she came out of the tent and walked with Kennicott down the dusty spring street, she peered at this straggling wooden village and felt that she could not possibly stay here through all of tomorrow.

It was Miles Bjornstam who gave her strength—he and the fact that every seat for "The Girl from Kankakee" had been sold.

Bjornstam was "keeping company" with Bea. Every night he was sitting on the back steps. Once when Carol appeared he grumbled. "Hope you're going to give this burg one good show. If you don't, reckon nobody ever will."

v

It was the great night; it was the night of the play. The two dressing-rooms were swirling with actors, panting, twitchy, pale. Del Snafflin the barber, who was as much a professional as Ella, having once gone on in a mob scene at a stock-company performance in Minneapolis, was making them up, and showing his scorn for amateurs with, "Stand still! For the love o' Mike, how do you expect me to get your eyelids dark if you keep a-wigglin'?" The actors were beseeching, "Hey, Del, put some red in my nostrils—you put some in Rita's—gee, you didn't hardly do anything to my face."

They were enormously theatric. They examined Del's make-up box, they sniffed the scent of grease-paint, every minute they ran out to peep through the hole in the curtain, they came back to inspect their wigs and costumes, they read on the whitewashed walls of the dressing-rooms the pencil inscriptions: "The Flora Flanders Comedy Company," and "This is a bum theater," and felt that they were companions of these vanished troupers.

Carol, smart in maid's uniform, coaxed the temporary stagehands to finish setting the first act, wailed at Kennicott, the electrician, "Now for heaven's sake remember the change in cue for the ambers in Act Two," slipped out to ask Dave

Dyer, the ticket-taker, if he could get some more chairs, warned the frightened Myrtle Cass to be sure to upset the waste-basket when John Grimm called, "Here you, Reddy."

Del Snafflin's orchestra of piano, violin, and cornet began to tune up and everyone behind the magic line of the proscenic arch was frightened into paralysis. Carol wavered to the hole in the curtain. There were so many people out there, staring so hard——

In the second row she saw Miles Bjornstam, not with Bea but alone. He really wanted to see the play! It was a good omen. Who could tell? Perhaps this evening would convert Gopher Prairie to conscious beauty.

She darted into the women's dressing-room, roused Maud Dyer from her fainting panic, pushed her to the wings, and ordered the curtain up.

It rose doubtfully, it staggered and trembled, but it did get up without catching—this time. Then she realized that Kennicott had forgotten to turn off the houselights. Some one out front was giggling.

She galloped round to the left wing, herself pulled the switch, looked so ferociously at Kennicott that he quaked, and fled back.

Mrs. Dyer was creeping out on the half-darkened stage. The play was begun.

And with that instant Carol realized that it was a bad play abominably acted.

Encouraging them with lying smiles, she watched her work go to pieces. The settings seemed flimsy, the lighting commonplace. She watched Guy Pollock stammer and twist his mustache when he should have been a bullying magnate; Vida Sherwin, as Grimm's timid wife, chatter at the audience as though they were her class in high-school English; Juanita, in the leading rôle, defy Mr. Grimm as though she were repeating a list of things she had to buy at the grocery this morning; Ella Stowbody remark "I'd like a cup of tea" as though she were reciting "Curfew Shall Not Ring Tonight"; and Dr. Gould, making love to Rita Simons, squeak, "My—my—you—are—a—won'erful—girl."

Myrtle Cass, as the office-boy, was so much pleased by the applause of her relatives, then so much agitated by the remarks of Cy Bogart, in the back row, in reference to her wearing trousers, that she could hardly be got off the stage. Only Raymie was so unsociable as to devote himself entirely to acting.

That she was right in her opinion of the play Carol was certain when Miles Bjornstam went out after the first act, and did not come back.

VI

Between the second and third acts she called the company together, and supplicated, "I want to know something, before we have a chance to separate. Whether we're doing well or badly tonight, it is a beginning. But will we take it as merely a beginning? How many of you will pledge yourselves to start in with me, right away, tomorrow, and plan for another play, to be given in September?"

They stared at her; they nodded at Juanita's protest: "I think one's enough for a while. It's going elegant tonight, but another play—— Seems to me it'll be time enough to talk about that next fall. Carol! I hope you don't mean to hint and suggest we're not doing fine tonight? I'm sure the applause shows the audience think it's just dandy!"

Then Carol knew how completely she had failed.

As the audience seeped out she heard B. J. Gougerling the banker say to Howland the grocer, "Well, I think the folks did splendid; just as good as professionals. But I don't care much for these plays. What I like is a good movie, with auto accidents and hold-ups, and some git to it, and not all this talky-talk."

Then Carol knew how certain she was to fail again.

She wearily did not blame them, company nor audience. Herself she blamed for trying to carve intaglios in good wholesome jack-pine.

"It's the worst defeat of all. I'm beaten. By Main Street. 'I must go on.' But I can't!"

She was not vastly encouraged by the *Gopher Prairie Dauntless*:

> . . . would be impossible to distinguish among the actors when all gave such fine account of themselves in difficult rôles of this well-known New York stage play. Guy Pollock as the old millionaire could not have been bettered for his fine impersonation of the gruff old millionaire; Mrs. Harry Haydock as the young lady from the West who so easily showed the New York four-flushers where they got off was a vision of loveliness and with fine stage presence. Miss Vida Sherwin the ever popular teacher in our high school pleased as Mrs. Grimm, Dr. Gould was well suited in the rôle of young lover—girls you better look out, re-

member the doc is a bachelor. The local Four Hundred also report that he is a great hand at shaking the light fantastic tootsies in the dance. As the stenographer Rita Simons was pretty as a picture, and Miss Ella Stowbody's long and intensive study of the drama and kindred arts in Eastern schools was seen in the fine finish of her part.

. . . to no one is greater credit to be given than to Mrs. Will Kennicott on whose capable shoulders fell the burden of directing.

"So kindly," Carol mused, "so well meant, so neighborly —and so confoundedly untrue. Is it really my failure, or theirs?"

She sought to be sensible; she elaborately explained to herself that it was hysterical to condemn Gopher Prairie because it did not foam over the drama. Its justification was in its service as a market-town for farmers. How bravely and generously it did its work, forwarding the bread of the world, feeding and healing the farmers!

Then, on the corner below her husband's office, she heard a farmer holding forth:

"Sure. Course I was beaten. The shipper and the grocers here wouldn't pay us a decent price for our potatoes, even though folks in the cities were howling for 'em. So we says, well, we'll get a truck and ship 'em right down to Minneapolis. But the commission merchants there were in cahoots with the local shipper here; they said they wouldn't pay us a cent more than he would, not even if they was nearer to the market. Well, we found we could get higher prices in Chicago, but when we tried to get freight cars to ship there, the railroads wouldn't let us have 'em—even though they had cars standing empty right here in the yards. There you got it— good market, and these towns keeping us from it. Gus, that's the way these towns work all the time. They pay what they want to for our wheat, but we pay what they want us to for their clothes. Stowbody and Dawson foreclose every mortgage they can, and put in tenant farmers. The *Dauntless* lies to us about the Nonpartisan League, the lawyers sting us, the machinery-dealers hate to carry us over bad years, and then their daughters put on swell dresses and look at us as if we were a bunch of hoboes. Man, I'd like to burn this town!"

Kennicott observed, "There's that old crank Wes Brannigan shooting off his mouth again. Gosh, but he loves to hear himself talk! They ought to run that fellow out of town!"

She felt old and detached through high-school commencement week, which is the fête of youth in Gopher Prairie; through baccalaureate sermon, senior parade, junior entertainment, commencement address by an Iowa clergyman who asserted that he believed in the virtue of virtuousness, and the procession of Decoration Day, when the few Civil War veterans followed Champ Perry, in his rusty forage-cap, along the spring-powdered road to the cemetery. She met Guy; she found that she had nothing to say to him. Her head ached in an aimless way. When Kennicott rejoiced, "We'll have a great time this summer; move down to the lake early and wear old clothes and act natural," she smiled, but her smile creaked.

In the prairie heat she trudged along unchanging ways, talked about nothing to tepid people, and reflected that she might never escape from them.

She was startled to find that she was using the word "escape."

Then, for three years which passed like one curt paragraph, she ceased to find anything interesting save the Bjornstams and her baby.

chapter 19

I

IN three years of exile from herself Carol had certain experiences chronicled as important by the *Dauntless*, or discussed by the Jolly Seventeen, but the event unchronicled, undiscussed, and supremely controlling, was her slow admission of longing to find her own people.

II

Bea and Miles Bjornstam were married in June, a month after "The Girl from Kankakee." Miles had turned respectable. He had renounced his criticisms of state and society;

he had given up roving as horse-trader, and wearing red mackinaws in lumber-camps; he had gone to work as engineer in Jackson Elder's planing-mill; he was to be seen upon the streets endeavoring to be neighborly with suspicious men whom he had taunted for years.

Carol was the patroness and manager of the wedding. Juanita Haydock mocked, "You're a chump to let a good hired girl like Bea go. Besides! How do you know it's a good thing, her marrying a sassy bum like this awful Red Swede person? Get wise! Chase the man off with a mop, and hold onto your Svenska while the holding's good. Huh? Me go to their Scandahoofian wedding? Not a chance!"

The other matrons echoed Juanita. Carol was dismayed by the causalness of their cruelty, but she persisted. Miles had exclaimed to her, "Jack Elder says maybe he'll come to the wedding! Gee, it would be nice to have Bea meet the Boss as a reg'lar married lady. Some day I'll be so well off that Bea can play with Mrs. Elder—and you! Watch us!"

There was an uneasy knot of only nine guests at the service in the unpainted Lutheran Church—Carol, Kennicott, Guy Pollock, and the Champ Perrys, all brought by Carol; Bea's frightened rustic parents, her cousin Tina, and Pete, Miles's ex-partner in horse-trading, a surly, hairy man who had bought a black suit and come twelve hundred miles from Spokane for the event.

Miles continuously glanced back at the church door. Jackson Elder did not appear. The door did not once open after the awkward entrance of the first guests. Miles's hand closed on Bea's arm.

He had, with Carol's help, made his shanty over into a cottage with white curtains and a canary and a chintz chair.

Carol coaxed the powerful matrons to call on Bea. They half scoffed, half promised to go.

Bea's successor was the oldish, broad, silent Oscarina, who was suspicious of her frivolous mistress for a month, so that Juanita Haydock was able to crow, "There, smarty, I told you you'd run into the Domestic Problem!" But Oscarina adopted Carol as a daughter, and with her as faithful to the kitchen as Bea had been, there was nothing changed in Carol's life.

III

She was unexpectedly appointed to the town library-board by Ole Jenson, the new mayor. The other members were

Dr. Westlake, Lyman Cass, Julius Flickerbaugh the attorney, Guy Pollock, and Martin Mahoney, former livery-stable keeper and now owner of a garage. She was delighted. She went to the first meeting rather condescendingly, regarding herself as the only one besides Guy who knew anything about books or library methods. She was planning to revolutionize the whole system.

Her condescension was ruined and her humility wholesomely increased when she found the board, in the shabby room on the second floor of the house which had been converted into the library, not discussing the weather and longing to play checkers, but talking about books. She discovered that amiable old Dr. Westlake read everyting in verse and "light fiction"; that Lyman Cass, the veal-faced, bristly-bearded owner of the mill, had tramped through Gibbon, Hume, Grote, Prescott, and the other thick historians; that he could repeat pages from them—and did. When Dr. Westlake whispered to her, "Yes, Lym is a very well-informed man, but he's modest about it," she felt uninformed and immodest, and scolded at herself that she had missed the human potentialities in this vast Gopher Prairie. When Dr. Westlake quoted the "Paradiso," "Don Quixote," "Wilhelm Meister," and the Koran, she reflected that no one she knew, not even her father, had read all four.

She came diffidently to the second meeting of the board. She did not plan to revolutionize anything. She hoped that the wise elders might be so tolerant as to listen to her suggestions about changing the shelving of the juveniles.

Yet after four sessions of the library-board she was where she had been before the first session. She had found that for all their pride in being reading men, Westlake and Cass and even Guy had no conception of making the library familiar to the whole town. They used it, they passed resolutions about it, and they left it as dead as Moses. Only the Henty books and the Elsie books and the latest optimisms by moral female novelists and virile clergymen were in general demand, and the board themselves were interested only in old, stilted volumes. They had no tenderness for the noisiness of youth discovering great literature.

If she was egotistic about her tiny learning, they were at least as much so regarding theirs. And for all their talk of the need of additional library-tax none of them was willing to risk censure by battling for it, though they now had so small a fund that, after paying for rent, heat, light, and Miss

Villets's salary, they had only a hundred dollars a year for the purchase of books.

The Incident of the Seventeen Cents killed her none too enduring interest.

She had come to the board-meeting singing with a plan. She had made a list of thirty European novels of the past ten years, with twenty important books on psychology, education, and economics which the library lacked. She had made Kennicott promise to give fifteen dollars. If each of the board would contribute the same, they could have the books.

Lym Cass looked alarmed, scratched himself, and protested, "I think it would be a bad precedent for the board-members to contribute money—uh—not that I mind, but it wouldn't be fair—establish precedent. Gracious! They don't pay us a cent for our services! Certainly can't expect us to pay for the privilege of serving!"

Only Guy looked sympathetic, and he stroked the pine table and said nothing.

The rest of the meeting they gave to a bellicose investigation of the fact that there was seventeen cents less than there should be in the Fund. Miss Villets was summoned; she spent half an hour in explosively defending herself; the seventeen cents were gnawed over, penny by penny; and Carol, glancing at the carefully inscribed list which had been so lovely and exciting an hour before, was silent, and sorry for Miss Villets, and sorrier for herself.

She was reasonably regular in attendance till her two years were up and Vida Sherwin was appointed to the board in her place, but she did not try to be revolutionary. In the plodding course of her life there was nothing changed, and nothing new.

IV

Kennicott made an excellent land-deal, but as he told her none of the details, she was not greatly exalted or agitated. What did agitate her was his announcement, half whispered and half blurted, half tender and half coldly medical, that they "ought to have a baby, now they could afford it." They had so long agreed that "perhaps it would be just as well not to have any children for a while yet," the childlessness had come to be natural. Now, she feared and longed and did not know; she hesitatingly assented, and wished that she had not assented.

As there appeared no change in their drowsy relations, she forgot all about it, and life was planless.

V

Idling on the porch of their summer cottage at the lake, on afternoons when Kennicott was in town, when the water was glazed and the whole air languid, she pictured a hundred escapes: Fifth Avenue in a snow-storm, with limousines, golden shops, a cathedral spire. A reed hut on fantastic piles above the mud of a jungle river. A suite in Paris, immense high grave rooms, with lambrequins and a balcony. The Enchanted Mesa. An ancient stone mill in Maryland, at the turn of the road, between rocky brook and abrupt hills. An upland moor of sheep and flitting cool sunlight. A clanging dock where steel cranes unloaded steamers from Buenos Aires and Tsing-tao. A Munich concert-hall, and a famous 'cellist playing—playing to her.

One scene had a persistent witchery:

She stood on a terrace overlooking a boulevard by the warm sea. She was certain, though she had no reason for it, that the place was Mentone. Along the drive below her swept barouches, with a mechanical tlot-tlot, tlot-tlot, tlot-tlot, and great cars with polished black hoods and engines quiet as the sigh of an old man. In them were women erect, slender, enameled, and expressionless as marionettes, their small hands upon parasols, their unchanging eyes always forward, ignoring the men beside them, tall men with gray hair and distinguished faces. Beyond the drive were painted sea and painted sands, and blue and yellow pavilions. Nothing moved except the gliding carriages, and the people were small and wooden, spots in a picture drenched with gold and hard bright blues. There was no sound of sea or winds; no softness of whispers nor of falling petals; nothing but yellow and cobalt and staring light, and the never-changing tlot-tlot, tlot-tlot——

She startled. She whimpered. It was the rapid ticking of the clock which had hypnotized her into hearing the steady hoofs. No aching color of the sea and pride of supercilious people, but the reality of a round-bellied nickel alarm-clock on a shelf against a fuzzy unplaned pine wall, with a stiff gray wash-rag hanging above it and a kerosene-stove standing below.

A thousand dreams governed by the fiction she had read,

drawn from the pictures she had envied, absorbed her drowsy lake afternoons, but always in the midst of them Kennicott came out from town, drew on khaki trousers which were plastered with dry fish-scales, asked, "Enjoying yourself?" and did not listen to her answer.

And nothing was changed, and there was no reason to believe that there ever would be change.

VI

Trains!

At the lake cottage she missed the passing of the trains. She realized that in town she had depended upon them for assurance that there remained a world beyond.

The railroad was more than a means of transportation to Gopher Prairie. It was a new god; a monster of steel limbs, oak ribs, flesh of gravel, and a stupendous hunger for freight; a deity created by man that he might keep himself respectful to Property, as elsewhere he had elevated and served as tribal gods the mines, cotton-mills, motor-factories, colleges, army.

The East remembered generations when there had been no railroad, and had no awe of it; but here the railroads had been before time was. The towns had been staked out on barren prairie as convenient points for future train-halts; and back in 1860 and 1870 there had been much profit, much opportunity to found aristocratic families, in the possession of advance knowledge as to where the towns would arise.

If a town was in disfavor, the railroad could ignore it, cut it off from commerce, slay it. To Gopher Prairie the tracks were eternal verities, and boards of railroad directors an omnipotence. The smallest boy or the most secluded grandam could tell you whether No. 32 had a hot-box last Tuesday, whether No. 7 was going to put on an extra day-coach; and the name of the president of the road was familiar to every breakfast table.

Even in this new era of motors the citizens went down to the station to see the trains go through. It was their romance; their only mystery besides mass at the Catholic Church; and from the trains came lords of the outer world—traveling salesmen with piping on their waistcoats, and visiting cousins from Milwaukee.

Gopher Prairie had once been a "division-point." The roundhouse and repair-shops were gone, but two conductors still retained residence, and they were persons of distinction, men who traveled and talked to strangers, who wore uniforms with brass buttons, and knew all about these crooked games of con-men. They were a special caste, neither above nor below the Haydocks, but apart, artists and adventurers.

The night telegraph-operator at the railroad station was the most melodramatic figure in town: awake at three in the morning, alone in a room hectic with clatter of the telegraph key. All night he "talked" to operators twenty, fifty, a hundred miles away. It was always to be expected that he would be held up by robbers. He never was, but round him was a suggestion of masked faces at the window, revolvers, cords binding him to a chair, his struggle to crawl to the key before he fainted.

During blizzards everything about the railroad was melodramatic. There were days when the town was completely shut off, when they had no mail, no express, no fresh meat, no newspapers. At last the rotary snow-plow came through, bucking the drifts, sending up a geyser, and the way to the Outside was open again. The brakemen, in mufflers and fur caps, running along the tops of ice-coated freight-cars; the engineers scratching frost from the cab windows and looking out, inscrutable, self-contained, pilots of the prairie sea—they were heroism, they were to Carol the daring of the quest in a world of groceries and sermons.

To the small boys the railroad was a familiar playground. They climbed the iron ladders on the sides of the box-cars; built fires behind piles of old ties; waved to favorite brakemen. But to Carol it was magic.

She was motoring with Kennicott, the car lumping through darkness, the lights showing mud-puddles and ragged weeds by the road. A train coming! A rapid chuck-a-chuck, chuck-a-chuck, chuck-a-chuck. It was hurling past—the Pacific Flyer, an arrow of golden flame. Light from the fire-box splashed the under side of the trailing smoke. Instantly the vision was gone; Carol was back in the long darkness; and Kennicott was giving his version of that fire and wonder: "No. 19. Must be 'bout ten minutes late."

In town, she listened from bed to the express whistling in the cut a mile north. Uuuuuuu!—faint, nervous, distrait, horn of the free night riders journeying to the tall towns where were laughter and banners and the sound of bells— Uuuuu! Uuuuu!—the world going by—Uuuuuuu!—fainter, more wistful, gone.

Down here there were no trains. The stillness was very great. The prairie encircled the lake, lay round her, raw, dusty, thick. Only the train could cut it. Some day she would take a train; and that would be a great taking.

VII

She turned to the Chautauqua as she had turned to the dramatic association, to the library-board.

Besides the permanent Mother Chautauqua, in New York, there are, all over these States, commercial Chautauqua companies which send out to every smallest town troupes of lecturers and "entertainers" to give a week of culture under canvas. Living in Minneapolis, Carol had never encountered the ambulant Chautauqua, and the announcement of its coming to Gopher Prairie gave her hope that others might be doing the vague things which she had attempted. She pictured a condensed university course brought to the people. Mornings when she came in from the lake with Kennicott she saw placards in every shop-window, and strung on a cord across Main Street, a line of pennants alternately worded "The Boland Chautauqua COMING!" and "A solid week of inspiration and enjoyment!" But she was disappointed when she saw the program. It did not seem to be a tabloid university; it did not seem to be any kind of a university; it seemed to be a combination of vaudeville performance, Y. M. C. A. lecture, and the graduation exercises of an elocution class.

She took her doubt to Kennicott. He insisted, "Well, maybe it won't be so awful darn intellectual, the way you and I might like it, but it's a whole lot better than nothing." Vida Sherwin added, "They have some splendid speakers. If the people don't carry off so much actual information, they do get a lot of new ideas, and that's what counts."

During the Chautauqua Carol attended three evening meetings, two afternoon meetings, and one in the morning. She was impressed by the audience: the sallow women in skirts and blouses, eager to be made to think, the men in vests and shirt-sleeves, eager to be allowed to laugh, and the wriggling children, eager to sneak away. She liked the plain benches, the portable stage under its red marquee, the great tent over all, shadowy above strings of incandescent bulbs at night and by day casting an amber radiance on the patient crowd. The scent of dust and trampled grass and sun-baked wood gave her an illusion of Syrian caravans; she forgot the speakers while she listened to noises outside the tent: two farmers talking hoarsely, a wagon creaking down Main Street, the crow of a rooster. She was content. But it was the contentment of the lost hunter stopping to rest.

For from the Chautauqua itself she got nothing but wind and chaff and heavy laughter, the laughter of yokels at old jokes, a mirthless and primitive sound like the cries of beasts on a farm.

These were the several instructors in the condensed university's seven-day course:

Nine lecturers, four of them ex-ministers, and one an ex-congressman, all of them delivering "inspirational addresses." The only facts or opinions which Carol derived from them were: Lincoln was a celebrated president of the United States, but in his youth extremely poor. James J. Hill was the best-known railroad-man of the West, and in his youth extremely poor. Honesty and courtesy in business are preferable to boorishness and exposed trickery, but this is not to be taken personally, since all persons in Gopher Prairie are known to be honest and courteous. London is a large city. A distinguished statesman once taught Sunday School.

Four "entertainers" who told Jewish stories, Irish stories, German stories, Chinese stories, and Tennessee mountaineer stories, most of which Carol had heard.

A "lady elocutionist" who recited Kipling and imitated children.

A lecturer with motion-pictures of an Andean exploration; excellent pictures and a halting narrative.

Three brass-bands, a company of six opera-singers, a Hawaiian sextette, and four youths who played saxophones and guitars disguised as wash-boards. The most applauded pieces were those, such as the "Lucia" inevitability, which the audience had heard most often.

The local superintendent, who remained through the week while the other enlighteners went to other Chautauquas for their daily performances. The superintendent was a bookish, underfed man who worked hard at rousing artificial enthusiasm, at trying to make the audience cheer by dividing them into competitive squads and telling them that they were intelligent and made splendid communal noises. He gave most of the morning lectures, droning with equal unhappy facility about poetry, the Holy Land, and the injustice to employers in any system of profit-sharing.

The final item was a man who neither lectured, inspired, nor entertained; a plain little man with his hands in his pockets. All the other speakers had confessed, "I cannot keep from telling the citizens of your beautiful city that none of the talent on this circuit have found a more charming spot or more enterprising and hospitable people." But the little man suggested that the architecture of Gopher Prairie was haphazard, and that it was sottish to let the lake-front be monopolized by the cinder-heaped wall of the railroad embankment. Afterward the audience grumbled, "Maybe that guy's got the right dope, but what's the use of looking on the dark side of things all the time? New ideas are first-rate, but not all this criticism. Enough trouble in life without looking for it!"

Thus the Chautauqua, as Carol saw it. After it, the town felt proud and educated.

VIII

Two weeks later the Great War smote Europe.

For a month Gopher Prairie had the delight of shuddering, then, as the war settled down to a business of trench-fighting, they forgot.

When Carol talked about the Balkans, and the possibility of a German revolution, Kennicott yawned, "Oh yes, it's a great old scrap, but it's none of our business. Folks out here are too busy growing corn to monkey with any fool war that those foreigners want to get themselves into."

It was Miles Bjornstam who said, "I can't figure it out. I'm opposed to wars, but still, seems like Germany has got to be licked because them Junkers stands in the way of progress."

She was calling on Miles and Bea, early in autumn. They had received her with cries, with dusting of chairs, and a running to fetch water for coffee. Miles stood and beamed at her. He fell often and joyously into his old irreverence about the lords of Gopher Prairie, but always—with a certain difficulty—he added something decorous and appreciative.

"Lots of people have come to see you, haven't they?" Carol hinted.

"Why, Be's cousin Tina comes in right along, and the foreman at the mill, and—— Oh, we have good times. Say, take a look at that Be! Wouldn't you think she was a canary-bird, to listen to her, and to see that Scandahoofian tow-head of hers? But say, know what she is? She's a mother

hen! Way she fusses over me—way she makes old Miles wear
a necktie! Hate to spoil her by letting her hear it, but she's
one pretty darn nice—nice—— Hell! What do we care if
none of the dirty snobs come and call? We've got each other."

Carol worried about their struggle, but she forgot it in the
stress of sickness and fear. For that autumn she knew that a
baby was coming, that at last life promised to be interesting in
the peril of the great change.

chapter 20

THE baby was coming. Each morning she was nauseated,
chilly, bedraggled, and certain that she would never
again be attractive; each twilight she was afraid. She did not
feel exalted, but unkempt and furious. The period of daily
sickness crawled into an endless time of boredom. It became difficult for her to move about, and she raged that she,
who had been slim and light-footed, should have to lean on a
stick, and be heartily commented upon by street gossips. She
was encircled by greasy eyes. Every matron hinted, "Now
that you're going to be a mother, dearie, you'll get over all
these ideas of yours and settle down." She felt that willy-nilly
she was being initiated into the assembly of housekeepers;
with the baby for hostage, she would never escape; presently
she would be drinking coffee and rocking and talking about
diapers.

"I could stand fighting them. I'm used to that. But this
being taken in, being taken as a matter of course, I can't
stand it—and I must stand it!"

She alternately detested herself for not appreciating the
kindly women, and detested them for their advice: lugubrious
hints as to how much she would suffer in labor, details of
baby-hygiene based on long experience and total misunder-
standing, superstitious cautions about the things she must eat
and read and look at in prenatal care for the baby's soul, and
always a pest of simpering baby-talk. Mrs. Champ Perry
bustled in to lend "Ben Hur," as a preventive of future infant
immorality. The Widow Bogart appeared trailing pinkish ex-

clamations, "And how is our lovely 'ittle muzzy today! My, ain't it just like they always say: being in a Family Way does make the girlie so lovely, just like a Madonna. Tell me—" Her whisper was tinged with salaciousness—"does oo feel the dear itsy one stirring, the pledge of love? I remember with Cy, of course he was so big——"

"I do not look lovely, Mrs. Bogart. My complexion is rotten, and my hair is coming out, and I look like a potato-bag, and I think my arches are falling, and he isn't a pledge of love, and I'm afraid he *will* look like us, and I don't believe in mother-devotion, and the whole business is a confounded nuisance of a biological process," remarked Carol.

Then the baby was born, without unusual difficulty: a boy with straight back and strong legs. The first day she hated him for the tides of pain and hopeless fear he had caused; she resented his raw ugliness. After that she loved him with all the devotion and instinct at which she had scoffed. She marveled at the perfection of the miniature hands as noisily as did Kennicott; she was overwhelmed by the trust with which the baby turned to her; passion for him grew with each un-poetic irritating thing she had to do for him.

He was named Hugh, for her father.

Hugh developed into a thin healthy child with a large head and straight delicate hair of a faint brown. He was thoughtful and casual—a Kennicott.

For two years nothing else existed. She did not, as the cynical matrons had prophesied, "give up worrying about the world and other folks' babies soon as she got one of her own to fight for." The barbarity of that willingness to sacrifice other children so that one child might have too much was impossible to her. But she would sacrifice herself. She understood consecration—she who answered Kennicott's hints about having Hugh christened: "I refuse to insult my baby and myself by asking an ignorant young man in a frock coat to sanction him, to permit me to have him! I refuse to subject him to any devil-chasing rites! If I didn't give my baby—*my baby*—enough sanctification in those nine hours of hell, then he can't get any more out of the Reverend Mr. Zitterel!"

"Well, Baptists hardly ever christen kids. I was kind of thinking more about Reverend Warren," said Kennicott.

Hugh was her reason for living, promise of accomplishment in the future, shrine of adoration—and a diverting toy.

"I though I'd be a dilettante mother, but I'm as dismayingly natural as Mrs. Bogart," she boasted.

For two years Carol was a part of the town; as much one of Our Young Mothers as Mrs. McGanum. Her opinionation seemed dead; she had no apparent desire for escape; her brooding centered on Hugh. While she wondered at the pearl texture of his ear she exulted, "I feel like an old woman, with a skin like sandpaper, beside him, and I'm glad of it! He is perfect. He shall have everything. He sha'n't always stay here in Gopher Prairie. . . . I wonder which is really the best, Harvard or Yale or Oxford?"

II

The people who hemmed her in had been brilliantly reinforced by Mr. and Mrs. Whittier N. Smail—Kennicott's Uncle Whittier and Aunt Bessie.

The true Main Streetite defines a relative as a person to whose house you go uninvited, to stay as long as you like. If you hear that Lym Cass on his journey East has spent all his time "visiting" in Oyster Center, it does not mean that he prefers that village to the rest of New England, but that he has relatives there. It does not mean that he has written to the relatives these many years, nor that they have ever given signs of a desire to look upon him. But "you wouldn't expect a man to go and spend good money at a hotel in Boston, when his own third cousins live right in the same state, would you?"

When the Smails sold their creamery in North Dakota they visited Mr. Smail's sister, Kennicott's mother, at Lac-qui-Meurt, then plodded on to Gopher Prairie to stay with their nephew. They appeared unannounced, before the baby was born, took their welcome for granted, and immediately began to complain of the fact that their room faced north.

Uncle Whittier and Aunt Bessie assumed that it was their privilege as relatives to laugh at Carol, and their duty as Christians to let her know how absurd her "notions" were. They objected to the food, to Oscarina's lack of friendliness, to the wind, the rain, and the immodesty of Carol's maternity gowns. They were strong and enduring; for an hour at a time they could go on heaving questions about her father's income, about her theology, and about the reason why she had not put on her rubbers when she had gone across the street. For fussy discussion they had a rich, full genius, and their example developed in Kennicott a tendency to the same form of affectionate flaying.

If Carol was so indiscreet as to murmur that she had a small headache, instantly the two Smails and Kennicott were at it. Every five minutes, every time she sat down or rose or spoke to Oscarina, they twanged, "Is your head better now? Where does it hurt? Don't you keep hartshorn in the house? Didn't you walk too far today? Have you tried hartshorn? Don't you keep some in the house so it will be handy? Does it feel better now? How does it feel? Do your eyes hurt, too? What time do you usually get to bed? As late as *that?* Well! How does it feel now?"

In her presence Uncle Whittier snorted at Kennicott, "Carol get these headaches often? Huh? Be better for her if she didn't go gadding around to all these bridge-whist parties, and took some care of herself one in a while!"

They kept it up, commenting, questioning, commenting, questioning, till her determination broke and she bleated, "For heaven's *sake,* don't dis-*cuss* it! My head's all *right!"*

She listened to the Smails and Kennicott trying to determine by dialectics whether the copy of the *Dauntless,* which Aunt Bessie wanted to send to her sister in Alberta, ought to have two or four cents postage on it. Carol would have taken it to the drug store and weighed it, but then she was a dreamer, while they were practical people (as they frequently admitted). So they sought to evolve the postal rate from their inner consciousnesses, which, combined with entire frankness in thinking aloud, was their method of settling all problems.

The Smails did not "believe in all this nonsense" about privacy and reticence. When Carol left a letter from her sister on the table, she was astounded to hear from Uncle Whittier, "I see your sister says her husband is doing fine. You ought to go see her oftener. I asked Will and he says you don't go see her very often. My! You ought to go see her oftener!"

If Carol was writing a letter to a classmate, or planning the week's menus, she could be certain that Aunt Bessie would pop in and titter, "Now don't let me disturb you, I just wanted to see where you were, don't stop, I'm not going to stay only a second. I just wondered if you could possibly have thought that I didn't eat the onions this noon because I didn't think they were properly cooked, but that wasn't the reason at all, it wasn't because I didn't think they were well cooked, I'm sure that everything in your house is always very dainty and nice, though I do think that Oscarina is careless about some things, she doesn't appreciate the big wages you pay her, and she is so cranky, all these Swedes are so cranky, I don't really see why you have a Swede, but—— But that wasn't it, I didn't eat them not because I didn't think they weren't cooked proper, it was just—I find that onions don't agree with me, it's very strange, ever since I had an attack of biliousness one time, I have found that onions, either fried onions or raw ones, and Whittier does love raw onions with vinegar and sugar on them——"

It was pure affection.

Carol was discovering that the one thing that can be more disconcerting than intelligent hatred is demanding love.

She supposed that she was being gracefully dull and standardized in the Smails' presence, but they scented the heretic, and with forward-stooping delight they sat and tried to drag out her ludicrous concepts for their amusement. They were like the Sunday-afternoon mob starting at monkeys in the Zoo, poking fingers and making faces and giggling at the resentment of the more dignified race.

With a loose-lipped, superior, village smile Uncle Whittier hinted, "What's this I hear about your thinking Gopher Prairie ought to be all tore down and rebuilt, Carrie? I don't know where folks get these new-fangled ideas. Lots of farmers in Dakota getting 'em these days. About co-operation. Think they can run stores better 'n storekeepers! Huh!"

"Whit and I didn't need no co-operation as long as we was farming!" triumphed Aunt Bessie. "Carrie, tell your old auntie now: don't you ever go to church on Sunday? You do go sometimes? But you ought to go every Sunday! When you're as old as I am, you'll learn that no matter how smart folks think they are, God knows a whole lot more than they do, and then you'll realize and be glad to go and listen to your pastor!"

In the manner of one who has just beheld a two-headed calf they repeated that they had "never *heard* such funny ideas!" They were staggered to learn that a real tangible person, living in Minnesota, and married to their own flesh-and-blood relation, could apparently believe that divorce may not always be immoral; that illegitimate children do not bear any special and guaranteed form of curse; that there are ethical authorities outside of the Hebrew Bible; that men have drunk wine yet not died in the gutter; that the capitalistic system of distribution and the Baptist wedding-ceremony were not known in the Garden of Eden; that mushrooms are as edible as corn-beef hash; that the word "dude" is no longer frequently used; that there are Ministers of the Gospel who accept evolution; that some persons of apparent intelligence and business ability do not always vote the Republican ticket straight; that it is not a universal custom to wear scratchy flannels next the skin in winter; that a violin is not inherently more immoral than a chapel organ; that some poets do not have long hair; and that Jews are not always pedlers or pants-makers.

"Where does she get all them the'ries?" marveled Uncle Whittier Smail; while Aunt Bessie inquired, "Do you suppose there's many folks got notions like hers? My! If there are," and her tone settled the fact that there were not, "I just don't know what the world's coming to!"

Patiently—more or less—Carol awaited the exquisite day when they would announce departure. After three weeks Uncle Whittier remarked, "We kinda like Gopher Prairie. Guess maybe we'll stay here. We'd been wondering what we'd do, now we've sold the creamery and my farms. So I had a talk with Ole Jenson about his grocery, and I guess I'll buy him out and storekeep for a while."

He did.

Carol rebelled. Kennicott soothed her: "Oh, we won't see much of them. They'll have their own house."

She resolved to be so chilly that they would stay away. But she had no talent for conscious insolence. They found a house, but Carol was never safe from their appearance with a hearty, "Thought we'd drop in this evening and keep you from being lonely. Why, you ain't had them curtains washed yet!" Invariably, whenever she was touched by the realization that it was they who were lonely, they wrecked her pitying affection by comments—questions—comments—advice.

They immediately became friendly with all of their own race, with the Luke Dawsons, the Deacon Piersons, and Mrs. Bogart; and brought them along in the evening. Aunt Bessie was a bridge over whom the older women, bearing gifts of counsel and the ignorance of experience, poured into Carol's island of reserve. Aunt Bessie urged the good Widow Bogart, "Drop in and see Carrie real often. Young folks today don't understand housekeeping like we do."

Mrs. Bogart showed herself perfectly willing to be an associate relative.

Carol was thinking up protective insults when Kennicott's

mother came down to stay with Brother Whittier for two months. Carol was fond of Mrs. Kennicott. She could not carry out her insults.

She felt trapped.

She had been kidnapped by the town. She was Aunt Bessie's niece, and she was to be a mother. She was expected, she almost expected herself, to sit forever talking of babies, cooks, embroidery stitches, the price of potatoes, and the tastes of husbands in the matter of spinach.

She found a refuge in the Jolly Seventeen. She suddenly understood that they could be depended upon to laugh with her at Mrs. Bogart, and she now saw Juanita Haydock's gossip not as vulgarity but as gaiety and remarkable analysis.

Her life had changed, even before Hugh appeared. She looked forward to the next bridge of the Jolly Seventeen, and the security of whispering with her dear friends Maud Dyer and Juanita and Mrs. McGanum.

She was part of the town. Its philosophy and its feuds dominated her.

III

She was no longer irritated by the cooing of the matrons, nor by their opinion that diet didn't matter so long as the Little Ones had plenty of lace and moist kisses, but she concluded that in the care of babies as in politics, intelligence was superior to quotations about pansies. She liked best to talk about Hugh to Kennicott, Vida, and the Bjornstams. She was happily domestic when Kennicott sat by her on the floor, to watch baby make faces. She was delighted when Miles, speaking as one man to another, admonished Hugh, "I wouldn't stand them skirts if I was you. Come on. Join the union and strike. Make 'em give you pants."

As a parent, Kennicott was moved to establish the first child-welfare week held in Gopher Prairie. Carol helped him weigh babies and examine their throats, and she wrote out the diets for mute German and Scandinavian mothers.

The aristocracy of Gopher Prairie, even the wives of the rival doctors, took part, and for several days there was community spirit and much uplift. But this reign of love was overthrown when the prize for Best Baby was awarded not to decent parents but to Bea and Miles Bjornstam! The good matrons glared at Olaf Bjornstam, with his blue eyes, his honey-colored hair, and magnificent back, and they remarked,

"Well, Mrs. Kennicott, maybe that Swede brat is as healthy as your husband says he is, but let me tell you I hate to think of the future that awaits any boy with a hired girl for a mother and an awful irreligious socialist for a pa!"

She raged, but so violent was the current of their respectability, so persistent was Aunt Bessie in running to her with their blabber, that she was embarrassed when she took Hugh to play with Olaf. She hated herself for it, but she hoped that no one saw her go into the Bjornstam shanty. She hated herself and the town's indifferent cruelty when she saw Bea's radiant devotion to both babies alike; when she saw Miles staring at them wistfully.

He had saved money, had quit Elder's planing-mill and started a dairy on a vacant lot near his shack. He was proud of his three cows and sixty chickens, and got up nights to nurse them.

"I'll be a big farmer before you can bat an eye! I tell you that young fellow Olaf is going to go East to college along with the Haydock kids. Uh—— Lots of folks dropping in to chin with Bea and me now. Say! Ma Bogart come in one day! She was—— I liked the old lady fine. And the mill foreman comes in right along. Oh, we got lots of friends. You bet!"

IV

Though the town seemed to Carol to change no more than the surrounding fields, there was a constant shifting, these three years. The citizen of the prairie drifts always westward. It may be because he is the heir of ancient migrations—and it may be because he finds within his own spirit so little adventure that he is driven to seek it by changing his horizon. The towns remain unvaried, yet the individual faces alter like classes in college. The Gopher Prairie jeweler sells out, for no discernible reason, and moves on to Alberta or the state of Washington, to open a shop precisely like his former one, in a town precisely like the one he has left. There is, except among professional men and the wealthy, small permanence either of residence or occupation. A man becomes farmer, grocer, town policeman, garageman, restaurant-owner, postmaster, insurance-agent, and farmer all over again, and the community more or less patiently suffers from his lack of knowledge in each of his experiments.

Ole Jenson the grocer and Dahl the butcher moved on to

South Dakota and Idaho. Luke and Mrs. Dawson picked up ten thousand acres of prairie soil, in the magic portable form of a small check book, and went to Pasadena, to a bungalow and sunshine and cafeterias. Chet Dashaway sold his furniture and undertaking business and wandered to Los Angeles, where, the *Dauntless* reported, "Our good friend Chester has accepted a fine position with a real-estate firm, and his wife has in the charming social circles of the Queen City of the Southwestland that same popularity which she enjoyed in our own society sets."

Rita Simons was married to Terry Gould, and rivaled Juanita Haydock as the gayest of the Young Married Set. But Juanita also acquired merit. Harry's father died, Harry became senior partner in the Bon Ton Store, and Juanita was more acidulous and shrewd and cackling than ever. She bought an evening frock, and exposed her collar-bone to the wonder of the Jolly Seventeen, and talked of moving to Minneapolis.

To defend her position against the new Mrs. Terry Gould she sought to attach Carol to her faction by giggling that "*some* folks might call Rita innocent, but I've got a hunch that she isn't half as ignorant of things as brides are supposed to be—and of course Terry isn't one-two-three as a doctor alongside of your husband."

Carol herself would glady have followed Mr. Ole Jenson, and migrated even to another Main Street; flight from familiar tedium to new tedium would have for a time the outer look and promise of adventure. She hinted to Kennicott of the probable medical advantages of Montana and Oregon. She knew that he was satisfied with Gopher Prairie, but it gave her vicarious hope to think of going, to ask for railroad folders at the station, to trace the maps with a restless forefinger.

Yet to the casual eye she was not discontented, she was not an abnormal and distressing traitor to the faith of Main Street.

The settled citizen believes that the rebel is constantly in a stew of complaining and, hearing of a Carol Kennicott, he gasps, "What an awful person! She must be a Holy Terror to live with! Glad *my* folks are satisfied with things way they are!" Actually, it was not so much as five minutes a day that Carol devoted to lonely desires. It is probable that the agitated citizen has within his circle at least one inarticulate rebel with aspirations as wayward as Carol's.

The presence of the baby had made her take Gopher

Prairie and the brown house seriously, as natural places of residence. She pleased Kennicott by being friendly with the complacent maturity of Mrs. Clark and Mrs. Elder, and when she had often enough been in conference upon the Elders' new Cadillac car, or the job which the oldest Clark boy had taken in the office of the flour-mill, these topics became important, things to follow up day by day.

With nine-tenths of her emotion concentrated upon Hugh, she did not criticize shops, streets, acquaintances . . . this year or two. She hurried to Uncle Whittier's store for a package of corn-flakes, she abstractedly listened to Uncle Whittier's denunciation of Martin Mahoney for asserting that the wind last Tuesday had been south and not southwest, she came back along streets that held no surprises nor the startling faces of strangers. Thinking of Hugh's teething all the way, she did not reflect that this store, these drab blocks, made up all her background. She did her work, and she triumphed over winning from the Clarks at five hundred.

V

The most considerable event of the two years after the birth of Hugh occurred when Vida Sherwin resigned from the high school and was married. Carol was her attendant, and as the wedding was at the Episcopal Church, all the women wore new kid slippers and long white kid gloves, and looked refined.

For years Carol had been little sister to Vida, and had never in the least known to what degree Vida loved her and hated her and in curious strained ways was bound to her.

chapter 21

GRAY steel that seems unmoving because it spins so fast in the balanced fly-wheel, gray snow in an avenue of elms, gray dawn with the sun behind it—this was the gray of Vida Sherwin's life at thirty-six.

She was small and active and sallow; her yellow hair was

faded, and looked dry; her blue silk blouses and modest lace collars and high black shoes and sailor hats were as literal and uncharming as a schoolroom desk; but her eyes determined her appearance, revealed her as a personage and a force, indicated her faith in. the goodness and purpose of everything. They were blue, and they were never still; they expressed amusement, pity, enthusiasm. If she had been seen in sleep, with the wrinkles beside her eyes stilled and the creased lids hiding the radiant irises, she would have lost her potency.

She was born in a hill-smothered Wisconsin village where her father was a prosy minister; she labored through a sanctimonious college; she taught for two years in an iron-range town of blurry-faced Tatars and Montenegrins, and wastes of ore, and when she came to Gopher Prairie, its trees and the shining spaciousness of the wheat prairie made her certain that she was in paradise.

She admitted to her fellow-teachers that the schoolbuilding was slightly damp, but she insisted that the rooms were "arranged so conveniently—and then that bust of President McKinley at the head of the stairs, it's a lovely art-work, and isn't it an inspiration to have the brave, honest, martyr president to think about!" She taught French, English, and history, and the Sophomore Latin class, which dealt in matters of a metaphysical nature called Indirect Discourse and the Ablative Absolute. Each year she was reconvinced that the pupils were beginning to learn more quickly. She spent four winters in building up the Debating Society, and when the debate really was lively one Friday afternoon, and the speakers of pieces did not forget their lines, she felt rewarded.

She lived an engrossed useful life, and seemed as cool and simple as an apple. But secretly she was creeping among fears, longing, and guilt. She knew what it was, but she dared not name it. She hated even the sound of the word "sex." When she dreamed of being a woman of the harem, with great white,warm limbs, she awoke to shudder, defenseless in the dusk of her room. She prayed to Jesus, always to the Son of God, offering him the terrible power of her adoration, addressing him as the eternal lover, growing passionate, exalted, large, as she contemplated his splendor. Thus she mounted to endurance and surcease.

By day, rattling about in many activities, she was able to ridicule her blazing nights of darkness. With spurious cheerfulness she announced everywhere, "I guess I'm a born spinster," and "No one will ever marry a plain schoolma'am like me," and "You men, great big noisy bothersome creatures, we women wouldn't have you round the place, dirtying up nice clean rooms, if it wasn't that you have to be petted and guided. We just ought to say 'Scat!' to all of you!"

But when a man held her close at a dance, even when "Professor" George Edwin Mott patted her hand paternally as they considered the naughtiness of Cy Bogart, she quivered, and reflected how superior she was to have kept her virginity.

In the autumn of 1911, a year before Dr. Will Kennicott was married, Vida was his partner at a five-hundred tournament. She was thirty-four then; Kennicott about thirty-six. To her he was a superb, boyish, diverting creature; all the heroic qualities in a manly magnificent body. They had been helping the hostess to serve the Waldorf salad and coffee and gingerbread. They were in the kitchen, side by side on a bench, while the others ponderously supped in the room beyond.

Kennicott was masculine and experimental. He stroked Vida's hand, he put his arm carelessly about her shoulder.

"Don't!" she said sharply.

"You're a cunning thing," he offered, patting the back of her shoulder in an exploratory manner.

While she strained away, she longed to move nearer to him. He bent over, looked at her knowingly. She glanced down at his left hand as it touched her knee. She sprang up, started noisily and needlessly to wash the dishes. He helped her. He was too lazy to adventure further—and too used to women in his profession. She was grateful for the impersonality of his talk. It enabled her to gain control. She knew that she had skirted wild thoughts.

A month after, on a sleighing-party, under the buffalo robes in the bob-sled, he whispered, "You pretend to be a grown-up schoolteacher, but you're nothing but a kiddie." His arm was about her. She resisted.

"Don't you like the poor lonely bachelor?" he yammered in a fatuous way.

"No, I don't! You don't care for me in the least. You're just practising on me."

"You're so mean! I'm terribly fond of you."

"I'm not of you. And I'm not going to let myself be fond of you, either."

He persistently drew her toward him. She clutched his arm. Then she threw off the robe, climbed out of the sled, raced after it with Harry Haydock. At the dance which followed the sleigh-ride Kennicott was devoted to the watery prettiness of Maud Dyer, and Vida was noisily interested in getting up a Virginia Reel. Without seeming to watch Kennicott, she knew that he did not once look at her.

That was all of her first love-affair.

He gave no sign of remembering that he was "terribly fond." She waited for him; she reveled in longing, and in a sense of guilt because she longed. She told herself that she did not want part of him; unless he gave her all his devotion she would never let him touch her; and when she found that she was probably lying, she burned with scorn. She fought it out in prayer. She knelt in a pink flannel nightgown, her thin hair down her back, her forehead as full of horror as a mask of tragedy, while she identified her love for the Son of God with her love for a mortal, and wondered if any other woman had ever been so sacrilegious. She wanted to be a nun and observe perpetual adoration. She bought a rosary, but she had been so bitterly reared as a Protestant that she could not bring herself to use it.

Yet none of her intimates in the school and in the boardinghouse knew of her abyss of passion. They said she was "so optimistic."

When she heard that Kennicott was to marry a girl, pretty, young, and imposingly from the Cities, Vida despaired. She congratulated Kennicott; carelessly ascertained from him the hour of marriage. At that hour, sitting in her room, Vida pictured the wedding in St. Paul. Full of an ecstasy which horrified her, she followed Kennicott and the girl who had stolen her place, followed them to the train, through the evening, the night.

She was relieved when she had worked out a belief that she wasn't really shameful, that there was a mystical relation between herself and Carol, so that she was vicariously yet veritably with Kennicott, and had the right to be.

She saw Carol during the first five minutes in Gopher Prairie. She stared at the passing motor, at Kennicott and the girl beside him. In that fog world of transference of emotion Vida had no normal jealousy but a conviction that, since through Carol she had received Kennicott's love, then Carol was a part of her, an astral self, a heightened and more beloved self. She was glad of the girl's charm, of the smooth black hair, the airy head and young shoulders. But she was suddenly angry. Carol glanced at her for a quarter-second, but looked past her, at an old roadside barn. If she had made the great sacrifice, at least she expected gratitude and recognition, Vida raged, while her conscious schoolroom mind fussily begged her to control this insanity.

During her first call half of her wanted to welcome a fellow reader of books; the other half itched to find out whether Carol knew anything about Kennicott's former interest in herself. She discovered that Carol was not aware that he had ever touched another woman's hand. Carol was an amusing, naive, curiously learned child. While Vida was most actively describing the glories of the Thanatopsis, and complimenting this librarian on her training as a worker, she was fancying that this girl was the child born of herself and Kennicott; and out of that symbolizing she had a comfort she had not known for months.

When she came home, after supper with the Kennicotts and Guy Pollock, she had a sudden and rather pleasant backsliding from devotion. She bustled into her room, she slammed her hat on the bed, and chattered, "I don't *care!* I'm a lot like her—except a few years older. I'm light and quick, too, and I can talk just as well as she can, and I'm sure—— Men are such fools. I'd be ten times as sweet to make love to as that dreamy baby. And I *am* as good-looking!"

But as she sat on the bed and stared at her thin thighs, defiance oozed away. She mourned:

"No. I'm not. Dear God, how we fool ourselves! I pretend I'm 'spiritual.' I pretend my legs are graceful. They aren't. They're skinny. Old-maidish. I hate it! I hate that impertinent young woman! A selfish cat, taking his love for granted. . . . No, she's adorable. . . . I don't think she ought to be so friendly with Guy Pollock."

For a year Vida loved Carol, longed to and did not pry into the details of her relations with Kennicott, enjoyed her spirit of play as expressed in childish tea-parties, and, with the mystic bond between them forgotten, was healthily vexed by Carol's assumption that she was a sociological messiah come to save Gopher Prairie. This last facet of Vida's thought was the one which, after a year, was most often turned to the light. In a testy way she brooded, "These people that want to change everything all of a sudden without doing any work, make me tired! Here I have to go and work for four years, picking out the pupils for debates, and drill-

ing them, and nagging at them to get them to look up references, and begging them to choose their own subjects—four
years, to get up a couple of good debates! And she comes
rushing in, and expects in one year to change the whole town
into a lollypop paradise with everybody stopping everything
else to grow tulips and drink tea. And it's a comfy homey
old town, too!"

She had such an outburst after each of Carol's campaigns
—for better Thanatopsis programs, for Shavian plays, for
more human schools—but she never betrayed herself, and
always she was penitent.

Vida was, and always would be, a reformer, a liberal.
She believed that details could excitingly be altered, but that
things-in-general were comely and kind and immutable. Carol
was, without understanding or accepting it, a revolutionist,
a radical, and therefore possessed of "constructive ideas,"
which only the destroyer can have, since the reformer believes that all the essential constructing has already been
done. After years of intimacy it was this unexpressed opposi-
tion more than the fancied loss of Kennicott's love which
held Vida irritably fascinated.

But the birth of Hugh revived the transcendental emotion.
She was indignant that Carol should not be utterly fulfilled
in having borne Kennicott's child. She admitted that Carol
seemed to have affection and immaculate care for the baby,
but she began to identify herself now with Kennicott, and
in this phase to feel that she had endured quite too much
from Carol's instability.

She recalled certain other women who had come from
the Outside and had not appreciated Gopher Prairie. She
remembered, the rector's wife who had been chilly to callers
and who was rumored throughout the town to have said,
"Re-ah-ly I cawn't endure this bucolic heartiness in the re-
sponses." The woman was positively known to have worn
handkerchiefs in her bodice as padding—oh, the town had
simply roared at her. Of course the rector and she were
got rid of in a few months.

Then there was the mysterious woman with the dyed hair
and penciled eyebrows, who wore tight English dresses, like
basques, who smelled of stale musk, who flirted with the
men and got them to advance money for her expenses in a
lawsuit, who laughed at Vida's reading at a school-entertain-
ment, and went off owing a hotel-bill and the three hundred
dollars she had borrowed.

Vida insisted that she loved Carol, but with some satisfaction she compared her to these traducers of the town.

II

Vida had enjoyed Raymie Wutherspoon's singing in the Episcopal choir; she had thoroughly reviewed the weather with him at Methodist sociables and in the Bon Ton. But she did not really know him till she moved to Mrs. Gurrey's boardinghouse. It was five years after her affair with Kennicott. She was thirty-nine, Raymie perhaps a year younger.

She said to him, and sincerely, "My! You can do anything, with your brains and tact and that heavenly voice. You were so good in 'The Girl from Kankakee.' You made me feel terribly stupid. If you'd gone on the stage, I believe you'd be just as good as anybody in Minneapolis. But still, I'm not sorry you stuck to business. It's such a constructive career."

"Do you really think so?" yearned Raymie, across the apple-sauce.

It was the first time that either of them had found a dependable intellectual companionship. They looked down on Willis Woodford the bank-clerk, and his anxious babycentric wife, the silent Lyman Casses, the slangy traveling man, and the rest of Mrs. Gurrey's unenlightened guests. They sat opposite, and they sat late. They were exhilarated to find that they agreed in confession of faith:

"People like Sam Clark and Harry Haydock aren't earnest about music and pictures and eloquent sermons and really refined movies, but then, on the other hand, people like Carol Kennicott put too much stress on all this art. Folks ought to appreciate lovely things, but just the same, they got to be practical and—they got to look at things in a practical way."

Smiling, passing each other the pressed-glass pickle-dish, seeing Mrs. Gurrey's linty supper-cloth irradiated by the light of intimacy, Vida and Raymie talked about Carol's rose-colored turban, Carol's sweetness, Carol's new low shoes, Carol's erroneous theory that there was no need of strict discipline in school, Carol's amiability in the Bon Ton, Carol's flow of wild ideas, which, honestly, just simply made you nervous trying to keep track of them;

About the lovely display of gents' shirts in the Bon Ton window as dressed by Raymie, about Raymie's offertory last Sunday, the fact that there weren't any of these new solos as nice as "Jerusalem the Golden," and the way Raymie stood

up to Juanita Haydock when she came into the store and tried
to run things and he as much as told her that she was so
anxious to have folks think she was smart and bright that
she said things she didn't mean, and anyway, Raymie was
running the shoe-department, and if Juanita, or Harry
either, didn't like the way he ran things, they could go get
another man;

About Vida's new jabot which made her look thirty-two
(Vida's estimate) or twenty-two (Raymie's estimate), Vida's
plan to have the high-school Debating Society give a playlet,
and the difficulty of keeping the younger boys well behaved
on the playground when a big lubber like Cy Bogart acted
up so;

About the picture post-card which Mrs. Dawson had sent
to Mrs. Cass from Pasadena, showing roses growing right
outdoors in February, the change in time on No. 4, the reckless way Dr. Gould always drove his auto, the reckless way
almost all these people drove their autos, the fallacy of supposing that these socialists could carry on a government for
as much as six months if they ever did have a chance to try
out their theories, and the crazy way in which Carol jumped
from subject to subject.

Vida had once beheld Raymie as a thin man with spectacles,
mournful drawn-out face, and colorless stiff hair. Now she
noted that his jaw was square, that his long hands moved
quickly and were bleached in a refined manner, and that his
trusting eyes indicated that he had "led a clean life." She
began to call him "Ray," and to bounce in defense of his un-
selfishness and thoughtfulness every time Juanita Haydock
or Rita Gould giggled about him at the Jolly Seventeen.

On a Sunday afternoon of late autumn they walked down
to Lake Minniemashie. Ray said that he would like to see the
ocean; it must be a grand sight; it must be much grander than
a lake, even a great big lake. Vida had seen it, she stated
modestly; she had seen it on a summer trip to Cape Cod.

"Have you been clear to Cape Cod? Massachusetts? I
knew you'd traveled, but I never realized you'd been that
far!"

Made taller and younger by his interest she poured out,
"Oh my yes. It was a wonderful trip. So many points of interest through Massachusetts—historical. There's Lexington
where we turned back the redcoats, and Longfellow's home
at Cambridge, and Cape Cod—just everything—fishermen
and whaleships and sand-dunes and everything."

She wished that she had a little cane to carry. He broke off a willow branch.

"My, you're strong!" she said.

"No, not very. I wish there was a Y. M. C. A. here, so I could take up regular exercise. I used to think I could do pretty good acrobatics, if I had a chance."

"I'm sure you could. You're unusually lithe, for a large man."

"Oh no, not so very. But I wish we had a Y. M. It would be dandy to have lectures and everything, and I'd like to take a class in improving the memory—I believe a fellow ought to go on educating himself and improving his mind even if he is in business, don't you, Vida—I guess I'm kind of fresh to call you 'Vida'!"

"I've been calling you 'Ray' for weeks!"

He wondered why she sounded tart.

He helped her down the bank to the edge of the lake but dropped her hand abruptly, and as they sat on a willow log and he brushed her sleeve, he delicately moved over and murmured, "Oh, excuse me—accident."

She stared at the mud-browned chilly water, the floating gray reeds.

"You look so thoughtful," he said.

She threw out her hands. "I am! Will you kindly tell me what's the use of—anything! Oh, don't mind me. I'm a moody old hen. Tell me about your plan for getting a partnership in the Bon Ton. I do think you're right: Harry Haydock and that mean old Simons ought to give you one."

He hymned the old unhappy wars in which he had been Achilles and the mellifluous Nestor, yet gone his righteous ways unheeded by the cruel kings. . . . "Why, if I've told 'em once, I've told 'em a dozen times to get in a side-line of light-weight pants for gents' summer wear, and of course here they go and let a cheap kike like Rifkin beat them to it and grab the trade right off 'em, and then Harry said—you know how Harry is, maybe he don't mean to be grouchy, but he's such a sore-head——"

He gave her a hand to rise. "If you don't *mind*. I think a fellow is awful if a lady goes on a walk with him and she can't trust him and he tries to flirt with her and all."

"I'm sure you're highly trustworthy!" she snapped, and she sprang up without his aid. Then, smiling excessively, "Uh—don't you think Carol sometimes fails to appreciate Dr. Will's ability?"

III

Ray habitually asked her about his window-trimming, the display of the new shoes, the best music for the entertainment at the Eastern Star, and (though he was recognized as a professional authority on what the town called "gents' furnishings") about his own clothes. She persuaded him not to wear the small bow ties which made him look like an elongated Sunday School scholar. Once she burst out:

"Ray, I could shake you! Do you know you're too apologetic? You always appreciate other people too much. You fuss over Carol Kennicott when she has some crazy theory that we all ought to turn anarchists or live on figs and nuts or something. And you listen when Harry Haydock tries to show off and talk about turnovers and credits and things you know lots better than he does. Look folks in the eye! Glare at 'em! Talk deep! You're the smartest man in town, if you only knew it. You *are!*"

He could not believe it. He kept coming back to her for confirmation. He practised glaring and talking deep, but he circuitously hinted to Vida that when he had tried to look Harry Haydock in the eye, Harry had inquired, "What's the matter with you, Raymie? Got a pain?" But afterward Harry had asked about Kantbeatum socks in a manner which, Ray felt, was somehow different from his former condescension.

They were sitting on the squat yellow satin settee in the boarding-house parlor. As Ray reannounced that he simply wouldn't stand it many more years if Harry didn't give him a partnership, his gesticulating hand touched Vida's shoulders.

"Oh, excuse me!" he pleaded.

"It's all right. Well, I think I must be running up to my room. Headache," she said briefly.

IV

Ray and she had stopped in at Dyer's for a hot chocolate on their way home from the movies, that March evening. Vida speculated, "Do you know that I may not be here next year?"

"What do you mean?"

With her fragile narrow nails she smoothed the glass slab which formed the top of the round table at which they sat. She peeped through the glass at the perfume-boxes of black and gold and citron in the hollow table. She looked about at shelves of red rubber water-bottles, pale yellow sponges, washrags with blue borders, hair-brushes of polished cherry backs. She shook her head like a nervous medium coming out of a trance, stared at him unhappily, demanded:

"Why should I stay here? And I must make up my mind. Now. Time to renew our teaching-contracts for next year. I think I'll go teach in some other town. Everybody here is tired of me. I might as well go. Before folks come out and *say* they're tired of me. I have to decide tonight. I might as well—— Oh, no matter. Come. Let's skip. It's late."

She sprang up, ignoring his wail of "Vida! Wait! Sit down! Gosh! I'm flabbergasted! Gee! Vida!" She marched out. While he was paying his check she got ahead. He ran after her, blubbering, "Vida! Wait!" In the shade of the lilacs in front of the Gougerling house he came up with her, stayed her flight by a hand on her shoulder.

"Oh, don't! Don't! What does it matter?" she begged. She was sobbing, her soft wrinkly lids soaked with tears. "Who cares for my affection or help? I might as well drift on, forgotten. O Ray, please don't hold me. Let me go. I'll just decide not to renew my contract here, and—and drift—way off——"

His hand was steady on her shoulder. She dropped her head. rubbed the back of his hand with her cheek.

They were married in June.

V

They took the Ole Jenson house. "It's small," said Vida, "but it's got the dearest vegetable garden, and I love having time to get near to Nature for once."

Though she became Vida Wutherspoon technically, and though she certainly had no ideals about the independence of keeping her name, she continued to be known as Vida Sherwin.

She had resigned from the school, but she kept up one class in English. She bustled about on every committee of the Thanatopsis; she was always popping into the rest-room to make Mrs. Nodelquist sweep the floor; she was appointed to the library-board to succeed Carol; she taught the Senior Girls' Class in the Episcopal Sunday School, and tried to revive the King's Daughters. She exploded into self-confidence and happiness; her draining thoughts were by marriage turned into energy. She became daily and visibly more plump, and though she chattered as eagerly, she was less obviously admiring of marital bliss, less sentimental about babies, sharper in demanding that the entire town share her reforms—the purchase of a park, the compulsory cleaning of back-yards.

She penned Harry Haydock at his desk in the Bon Ton; she interrupted his joking; she told him that it was Ray who had built up the shoe-department and men's department; she demanded that he be made a partner. Before Harry could answer she threatened that Ray and she would start a rival shop. "I'll clerk behind the counter myself, and a Certain Party is all ready to put up the money."

She rather wondered who the Certain Party was.

Ray was made a one-sixth partner.

He became a glorified floor-walker, greeting the men with new poise, no longer coyly subservient to pretty women. When he was not affectionately coercing people into buying things they did not need, he stood at the back of the store, glowing, abstracted, feeling masculine as he recalled the tempestuous surprises of love revealed by Vida.

The only remnant of Vida's identification of herself with Carol was a jealousy when she saw Kennicott and Ray together, and reflected that some people might suppose that Kennicott was his superior. She was sure that Carol thought so, and she wanted to shriek, "You needn't try to gloat! I wouldn't have your pokey old husband. He hasn't one single bit of Ray's spiritual nobility."

chapter 22

THE greatest mystery about a human being is not his reaction to sex or praise, but the manner in which he contrives to put in twenty-four hours a day. It is this which puzzles the longshoreman about the clerk, the Londoner about the bushman. It was this which puzzled Carol in regard to the married Vida. Carol herself had the baby, a larger house to care for, all the telephone calls for Kennicott when he was away; and she read everything, while Vida was satisfied with newspaper headlines.

But after detached brown years in boarding-houses, Vida was hungry for housework, for the most pottering detail of it. She had no maid, nor wanted one. She cooked, baked, swept, washed supper-cloths, with the triumph of a chemist in a new laboratory. To her the hearth was veritably the altar. When she went shopping she hugged the cans of soup, and she bought a mop or a side of bacon as though she were preparing for a reception. She knelt beside a bean sprout and crooned, "I raised this with my own hands—I brought this new life into the world."

"I love her for being so happy," Carol brooded. "I ought to be that way. I worship the baby, but the housework—— Oh, I suppose I'm fortunate; so much better off than farm-women on a new clearing, or people in a slum."

It has not yet been recorded that any human being has gained a very large or permanent contentment from meditation upon the fact that he is better off than others.

In Carol's own twenty-four hours a day she got up, dressed the baby, had breakfast, talked to Oscarina about the day's shopping, put the baby on the porch to play, went to the butcher's to choose between steak and pork chops, bathed the baby, nailed up a shelf, had dinner, put the baby to bed for a nap, paid the iceman, read for an hour, took the baby out for a walk, called on Vida, had supper, put the baby to bed, darned socks, listened to Kennicott's yawning comment on what a fool Dr. McGanum was to try to use that cheap X-ray outfit of his on an epithelioma, repaired a frock, drowsily heard Kennicott stoke the furnace, tried to read a page of Thorstein Veblen—and the day was gone.

Except when Hugh was vigorously naughty, or whiney, or laughing, or saying "I like my chair" with thrilling maturity, she was always enfeebled by loneliness. She no longer felt superior about that misfortune. She would gladly have been converted to Vida's satisfaction in Gopher Prairie and mopping the floor.

II

Carol drove through an astonishing number of books from the public library and from city shops. Kennicott was at first uncomfortable over her disconcerting habit of buying them. A book was a book, and if you had several thousand of them right here in the library, free, why the dickens should you spend your good money? After worrying about it for two or three years, he decided that this was one of the Funny Ideas which she had caught as a librarian and from which she would never entirely recover.

The authors whom she read were most of them frightfully annoyed by the Vida Sherwins. They were young American sociologists, young English realists, Russian horrorists; Anatole France, Rolland, Nexo, Wells, Shaw, Key, Edgar Lee Masters, Theodore Dreiser, Sherwood Anderson, Henry Mencken, and all the other subversive philosophers and artists whom women were consulting everywhere, in batik-curtained studios in New York, in Kansas farmhouses, San Francisco drawing-rooms, Alabama schools for Negroes. From them she got the same confused desire which the million other women felt; the same determination to be class-conscious without discovering the class of which she was to be conscious.

Certainly her reading precipitated her observations of Main Street, of Gopher Prairie and of the several adjacent Gopher Prairies which she had seen on drives with Kennicott. In her fluid thought certain convictions appeared, jaggedly, a fragment of an impression at a time, while she was going to sleep, or manicuring her nails, or waiting for Kennicott.

These convictions she presented to Vida Sherwin—Vida Wutherspoon—beside a radiator, over a bowl of not very good walnuts and pecans from Uncle Whittier's grocery, on an evening when both Kennicott and Raymie had gone out of town with the other officers of the Ancient and Affiliated Order of Spartans, to inaugurate a new chapter at Wakamin. Vida had come to the house for the night. She helped in putting Hugh to bed, sputtering the while about his soft skin. Then they talked till midnight.

What Carol said that evening, what she was passionately thinking, was also emerging in the minds of women in ten thousand Gopher Prairies. Her formulatons were not pat solutions but visions of a tragic futility. She did not utter them so compactly that they can be given in her words, they were roughened with "Well, you see" and "if you get what I mean" and "I don't know that I'm making myself clear." But they were definite enough, and indignant enough.

III

In reading popular stories and seeing plays, asserted Carol, she had found only two traditions of the American small town. The first tradition, repeated in scores of magazines every month, is that the American village remains the one sure abode of friendship, honesty, and clean sweet marriageable girls. Therefore all men who succeed in painting in Paris or in finance in New York at last become weary of smart women, return to their native towns, assert that cities are vicious, marry their childhood sweethearts and, presumably, joyously abide in those towns until death.

The other tradition is that the significant features of all villages are whiskers, iron dogs upon lawns, gold bricks, checkers, jars of gilded cat-tails, and shrewd comic old men who are known as "hicks" and who ejaculate "Waal I swan." This altogether admirable tradition rules the vaudeville stage, facetious illustrators, and syndicated newspaper humor, but out of actual life it passed forty years ago. Carol's small town thinks not in hoss-swapping but in cheap motor cars, telephones, ready-made clothes, silos, alfalfa, kodaks, phonographs, leather-upholstered Morris chairs, bridge-prizes, oil-stocks, motion-pictures, land-deals, unread sets of Mark Twain, and a chaste version of national politics.

With such a small-town life a Kennicott or a Champ Perry is content, but there are also hundreds of thousands, particularly women and young men, who are not at all content. The more intelligent young people (and the fortunate widows!) flee to the cities with agility and, despite the fictional tradition, resolutely stay there, seldom returning even for holidays. The most protesting patriots of the towns leave them in old age, if they can afford it, and go to live in California or in the cities.

The reason, Carol insisted, is not a whiskered rusticity. It is nothing so amusing!

It is an unimaginatively standardized background, a sluggishness of speech and manners, a rigid ruling of the spirit by the desire to appear respectable. It is contentment . . . the contentment of the quiet dead, who are scornful of the living for their restless walking. It is negation canonized as the one positive virtue. It is the prohibition of happiness. It is slavery self-sought and self-defended. It is dullness made God.

A savorless people, gulping tasteless food, and sitting afterward, coatless and thoughtless, in rocking-chairs prickly with inane decorations, listening to mechanical music, saying mechanical things about the excellence of Ford automobiles, and viewing themselves as the greatest race in the world.

IV

She had inquired as to the effect of this dominating dullness upon foreigners. She remembered the feeble exotic quality to be found in the first-generation Scandinavians; she recalled the Norwegian Fair at the Lutheran Church, to which Bea had taken her. There, in the *bondestue*, the replica of a Norse farm kitchen, pale women in scarlet jackets embroidered with gold thread and colored beads, in black skirts with a line of blue, green-striped aprons, and ridged caps very pretty to set off a fresh face, had served *rommegrod og lefse*—sweet cakes and sour milk pudding spiced with cinnamon. For the first time in Gopher Prairie Carol had found novelty. She reveled in the mild foreignness of it.

But she saw these Scandinavian women zealously exchanging their spiced puddings and red jackets for fried pork chops and congealed white blouses, trading the ancient Christmas hymns of the fjords for "She's My Jazzland Cutie," being Americanized into uniformity, and in less than a generation losing in the grayness whatever pleasant new customs they might have added to the life of the town. Their sons finished the process. In ready-made clothes and ready-made highschool phrases they sank into propriety, and the sound American customs had absorbed without one trace of pollution another alien invasion.

And along with these foreigners, she felt herself being ironed into glossy mediocrity, and she rebelled, in fear.

The respectability of the Gopher Prairies, said Carol, is reinforced by vows of poverty and chastity in the matter of knowledge. Except for half a dozen in each town the citizens are proud of that achievement of ignorance which it is so easy to come by. To be "intellectual" or "artistic" or, in their own word, to be "highbrow," is to be priggish and of dubious virtue.

Large experiments in politics and in co-operative distribution, ventures requiring knowledge, courage, and imagination, do originate in the West and Middlewest, but they are not of the towns, they are of the farmers. If these heresies

are supported by the townsmen it is only by occasional
teachers, doctors, lawyers, the labor unions, and workmen
like Miles Bjornstam, who are punished by being mocked as
"cranks," as "half-baked parlor socialists." The editor and the
rector preach at them. The cloud of serene ignorance sub-
merges them in unhappiness and futility.

V

Here Vida observed, "Yes—well—— Do you know,
I've always thought that Ray would have made a wonderful
rector. He has what I call an essentially religious soul. My!
He'd have read the service beautifully! I suppose it's too late
now, but as I tell him, he can also serve the world by selling
shoes and—— I wonder if we oughtn't to have family-
prayers?"

VI

Doubtless all small towns, in all countries, in all ages,
Carol admitted, have a tendency to be not only dull but
mean, bitter, infested with curiosity. In France or Tibet quite
as much as in Wyoming or Indiana these timidities are in-
herent in isolation.

But a village in a country which is taking pains to become
altogether standardized and pure, which aspires to succeed
Victorian England as the chief mediocrity of the world, is no
longer merely provincial, no longer downy and restful in its
leaf-shadowed ignorance. It is a force seeking to dominate
the earth, to drain the hills and sea of color, to set Dante at
boosting Gopher Prairie, and to dress the high gods in
Klassy Kollege Klothes. Sure of itself, it bullies other civiliza-
tions, as a traveling salesman in a brown derby conquers the
wisdom of China and tacks advertisements of cigarettes over
arches for centuries dedicate to the sayings of Confucius.

Such a society functions admirably in the large production
of cheap automobiles, dollar watches, and safety razors. But
it is not satisfied until the entire world also admits that the
end and joyous purpose of living is to ride in flivvers, to make
advertising-pictures of dollar watches, and in the twilight to
sit talking not of love and courage but of the convenience
of safety razors.

And such a society, such a nation, is determined by the
Gopher Prairies. The greatest manufacturer is but a busier

Sam Clark, and all the rotund senators and presidents are village lawyers and bankers grown nine feet tall.

Though a Gopher Prairie regards itself as a part of the Great World, compares itself to Rome and Vienna, it will not acquire the scientific spirit, the international mind, which would make it great. It picks at information which will visibly procure money or social distinction. Its conception of a community ideal is not the grand manner, the noble aspiration, the fine aristocratic pride, but cheap labor for the kitchen and rapid increase in the price of land. It plays at cards on greasy oil-cloth in a shanty, and does not know that prophets are walking and talking on the terrace.

If all the provincials were as kindly as Champ Perry and Sam Clark there would be no reason for desiring the town to seek great traditions. It is the Harry Haydocks, the Dave Dyers, the Jackson Elders, small busy men crushingly powerful in their common purpose, viewing themselves as men of the world but keeping themselves men of the cash-register and the comic film, who make the town a sterile oligarchy.

VII

She had sought to be definite in analyzing the surface ugliness of the Gopher Prairies. She asserted that it is a matter of universal similarity; of flimsiness of construction, so that the towns resemble frontier camps; of neglect of natural advantages, so that the hills are covered with brush, the lakes shut off by railroads, and the creeks lined with dumping-grounds; of depressing sobriety of color; rectangularity of buildings; and excessive breadth and straightness of the gashed streets, so that there is no escape from gales and from sight of the grim sweep of land, nor any windings to coax the loiterer along, while the breadth which would be majestic in an avenue of palaces makes the low shabby shops creeping down the typical Main Street the more mean by comparison.

The universal similarity—that is the physical expression of the philosophy of dull safety. Nine-tenths of the American towns are so alike that it is the completest boredom to wander from one to another. Always, west of Pittsburgh, and often, east of it, there is the same lumber yard, the same railroad station, the same Ford garage, the same creamery, the same box-like houses and two-story shops. The new, more conscious houses are alike in their very attempts at diversity: the same bungalows, the same square houses of stucco or tapestry brick. The shops show the same standardized nationally advertised wares; the newspapers of sections three thousand miles apart have the same "syndicated features"; the boy in Arkansas displays just such a flamboyant ready-made suit as is found on just such a boy in Delaware, both of them iterate the same slang phrases from the same sporting-pages, and if one of them is in college and the other is a barber, no one may surmise which is which.

If Kennicott were snatched from Gopher Prairie and instantly conveyed to a town leagues away, he would not realize it. He would go down apparently the same Main Street (almost certainly it would be called Main Street); in the same drug store he would see the same young man serving the same ice-cream soda to the same young woman with the same magazines and phonograph records under her arm. Not till he had climbed to his office and found another sign on the door, another Dr. Kennicott inside, would he understand that something curious had presumably happened.

Finally, behind all her comments, Carol saw the fact that the prairie towns no more exist to serve the farmers who are their reason of existence than do the great capitals; they exist to fatten on the farmers, to provide for the townsmen large motors and social preferment; and, unlike the capitals, they do not give to the district in return for usury a stately and permanent center, but only this ragged camp. It is a "parasitic Greek civilization"—minus the civilization.

"There we are then," said Carol. "The remedy? Is there any? Criticism, perhaps, for the beginning of the beginning. Oh, there's nothing that attacks the Tribal God Mediocrity that doesn't help a little . . . and probably there's nothing that helps very much. Perhaps some day the farmers will build and own their market-towns. (Think of the club they could have!) But I'm afraid I haven't any 'reform program.' Not any more! The trouble is spiritual, and no League or Party can enact a preference for gardens rather than dumping-grounds. . . . There's my confession. *Well?*"

"In other words, all you want is perfection?"

"Yes! Why not?"

"How you hate this place! How can you expect to do anything with it if you haven't any sympathy?"

"But I have! And affection. Or else I wouldn't fume so. I've learned that Gopher Prairie isn't just an eruption on the prairie, as I thought first, but as large as New York. In

New York I wouldn't know more than forty or fifty people, and I know that many here. Go on! Say what you're thinking."

"Well, my dear, if I *did* take all your notions seriously, it would be pretty discouraging. Imagine how a person would feel, after working hard for years and helping to build up a nice town, to have you airily flit in and simply say 'Rotten!' Think that's fair?"

"Why not? It must be just as discouraging for the Gopher Prairieite to see Venice and make comparisons."

"It would not! I imagine gondolas are kind of nice to ride in, but we've got better bath-rooms! But—— My dear, you're not the only person in this town who has done some thinking for herself, although (pardon my rudeness) I'm afraid you think so. I'll admit we lack some things. Maybe our theater isn't as good as shows in Paris. All right! I don't want to see any foreign culture suddenly forced on us— whether it's street-planning or table-manners or crazy communistic ideas."

Vida sketched what she termed "practical things that will make a happier and prettier town, but that do belong to our life, that actually are being done." Of the Thanatopsis Club she spoke; of the rest-room, the fight against mosquitos, the campaign for more gardens and shade-trees and sewers— matters not fantastic and nebulous and distant, but immediate and sure.

Carol's answer was fantastic and nebulous enough:

"Yes. . . . Yes. . . . I know. They're good. But if I could put through all those reforms at once, I'd still want startling, exotic things. Life is comfortable and clean enough here already. And so secure. What it needs is to be less secure, more eager. The civic improvements which I'd like the Thanatopsis to advocate are Strindberg plays, and classic dancers—exquisite legs beneath tulle—and (I can see him so clearly!) a thick, black-bearded, cynical Frenchman who would sit about and drink and sing opera and tell bawdy stories and laugh at our proprieties and quote Rabelais and not be ashamed to kiss my hand!"

"Huh! Not sure about the rest of it but I guess that's what you and all the other discontented young women really want: some stranger kissing your hand!" At Carol's gasp, the old squirrel-like Vida darted out and cried, "Oh, my dear, don't take that too seriously. I just meant——"

"I know. You just meant it. Go on. Be good for my soul.

Isn't it funny: here we all are—me trying to be good for Gopher Prairie's soul, and Gopher Prairie trying to be good for my soul. What are my other sins?"

"Oh, there's plenty of them. Possibly some day we shall have your fat cynical Frenchman (horrible, sneering, tobacco-stained object, ruining his brains and his digestion with vile liquor!) but, thank heaven, for a while we'll manage to keep busy with our lawns and pavements! You see, these things really are coming! The Thanatopsis is getting somewhere. And you——" Her tone italicized the words—"to my great disappointment, are doing less, not more, than the people you laugh at! Sam Clark, on the school-board, is working for better school ventilation. Ella Stowbody (whose elocuting you always think is so absurd) has persuaded the railroad to share the expense of a parked space at the station, to do away with that vacant lot.

"You sneer so easily. I'm sorry, but I do think there's something essentially cheap in your attitude. Especially about religion.

"If you must know, you're not a sound reformer at all. You're an impossibilist. And you give up too easily. You gave up on the new city hall, the anti-fly campaign, club papers, the library-board, the dramatic association—just because we didn't graduate into Ibsen the very first thing. You want perfection all at once. Do you know what the finest thing you've done is—aside from bringing Hugh into the world? It was the help you gave Dr. Will during baby-welfare week. You didn't demand that each baby be a philosopher and artist before you weighed him, as you do with the rest of us.

"And now I'm afraid perhaps I'll hurt you. We're going to have a new schoolbuilding in this town—in just a few years—and we'll have it without one bit of help or interest from you!

"Professor Mott and I and some others have been dinging away at the moneyed men for years. We didn't call on you because you would never stand the pound-pound-pounding year after year without one bit of encouragement. And we've won! I've got the promise of everybody who counts that just as soon as war-conditions permit, they'll vote the bonds for the schoolhouse. And we'll have a wonderful building—lovely brown brick, with big windows, and agricultural and manual-training departments. When we get it, that'll be my answer to all your theories!"

"I'm glad. And I'm ashamed I haven't had any part in

getting it. But—— Please don't think I'm unsympathetic if
I ask one question: Will the teachers in the hygienic new
building go on informing the children that Persia is a yellow
spot on the map, and 'Cæsar' the title of a book of gram-
matical puzzles?"

VIII

Vida was indignant; Carol was apologetic; they talked for
another hour, the eternal Mary and Martha—an immoralist
Mary and a reformist Martha. It was Vida who conquered.

The fact that she had been left out of the campaign for
the new schoolbuilding disconcerted Carol. She laid her
dreams of perfection aside. When Vida asked her to take
charge of a group of Camp Fire Girls, she obeyed, and had
definite pleasure out of the Indian dances and ritual and
costumes. She went more regularly to the Thanatopsis.
With Vida as lieutenant and unofficial commander she cam-
paigned for a village nurse to attend poor families, raised
the fund herself, saw to it that the nurse was young and
strong and amiable and intelligent.

Yet all the while she beheld the burly cynical Frenchman
and the diaphanous dancers as clearly as the child sees its
air-born playmates; she relished the Camp Fire Girls not
because, in Vida's words, "this Scout training will help so
much to make them Good Wives," but because she hoped
that the Sioux dances would bring subversive color into their
dinginess.

She helped Ella Stowbody to set out plants in the tiny
triangular park at the railroad station; she squatted in the
dirt, with a small curved trowel and the most decorous of
gardening gauntlets; she talked to Ella about the public-
spiritedness of fuchsias and cannas; and she felt that she was
scrubbing a temple deserted by the gods and empty even of
incense and the sound of chanting. Passengers looking from
trains saw her as a village woman of fading prettiness, in-
corruptible virtue, and no abnormalities; the baggageman
heard her say, "Oh yes, I do think it will be a good example
for the children"; and all the while she saw herself running
garlanded through the streets of Babylon.

Planting led her to botanizing. She never got much farther
than recognizing the tiger lily and the wild rose, but she rediscovered Hugh. "What does the buttercup say, mummy?"
he cried, his hand full of straggly grasses, his cheek gilded

with pollen. She knelt to embrace him; she affirmed that he made life more than full; she was altogether reconciled . . . for an hour.

But she awoke at night to hovering death. She crept away from the hump of bedding that was Kennicott; tiptoed into the bathroom and, by the mirror in the door of the medicine-cabinet, examined her pallid face.

Wasn't she growing visibly older in ratio as Vida grew plumper and younger? Wasn't her nose sharper? Wasn't her neck granulated? She stared and choked. She was only thirty. But the five years since her marriage—had they not gone by as hastily and stupidly as though she had been under ether; would time not slink past till death? She pounded her fist on the cool enameled rim of the bathtub and raged mutely against the indifferent gods:

"I don't care! I won't endure it! They lie so—Vida and Will and Aunt Bessie—they tell me I ought to be satisfied with Hugh and a good home and planting seven nasturtiums in a station garden! I am I! When I die the world will be annihilated, as far as I'm concerned. I am I! I'm not content to leave the sea and the ivory towers to others. I want them for me! Damn Vida! Damn all of them! Do they think they can make me believe that a display of potatoes at Howland & Gould's is enough beauty and strangeness?"

chapter 23

WHEN America entered the Great European War, Vida sent Raymie off to an officers' training-camp—less than a year after her wedding. Raymie was diligent and rather strong. He came out a first lieutenant of infantry, and was one of the earliest sent abroad.

Carol grew definitely afraid of Vida as Vida transferred the passion which had been released in marriage to the cause of the war; as she lost all tolerance. When Carol was touched by the desire for heroism in Raymie and tried tactfully to express it, Vida made her feel like an impertinent child.

By enlistment and draft, the sons of Lyman Cass, Nat

Hicks, Sam Clark joined the army. But most of the soldiers
were the sons of German and Swedish farmers unknown to
Carol. Dr. Terry Gould and Dr. McGanum became captains
in the medical corps, and were stationed at camps in Iowa
and Georgia. They were the only officers, besides Raymie,
from the Gopher Prairie district. Kennicott wanted to go
with them, but the several doctors of the town forgot medical
rivalry and, meeting in council, decided that he would do
better to wait and keep the town well till he should be needed.
Kennicott was forty-two now; the only youngish doctor left
in a radius of eighteen miles. Old Dr. Westlake, who loved
comfort like a cat, protestingly rolled out at night for country calls, and hunted through his collar-box for his G.A.R.
button.

Carol did not quite know what she thought about Kennicott's going. Certainly she was no Spartan wife. She knew
that he wanted to go; she knew that this longing was always
in him, behind his unchanged trudging and remarks about
the weather. She felt for him an admiring affection—and she
was sorry that she had nothing more than affection.

Cy Bogart was the spectacular warrior of the town. Cy
was no longer the weedy boy who had sat in the loft speculating about Carol's egotism and the mysteries of generation.
He was nineteen now, tall, broad, busy, the "town sport,"
famous for his ability to drink beer, to shake dice, to tell
undesirable stories, and, from his post in front of Dyer's drug
store, to embarrass the girls by "jollying" them as they
passed. His face was at once peach-bloomed and pimply.

Cy was to be heard publishing it abroad that if he couldn't
get the Widow Bogart's permission to enlist, he'd run away
and enlist without it. He shouted that he "hated every dirty
Hun; by gosh, if he could just poke a bayonet into one big
fat Heinie and learn him some decency and democracy,
he'd die happy." Cy got much reputation by whipping a
farmboy named Adolph Pochbauer for being a "damn hy-
phenated German." . . . This was the younger Pochbauer,
who was killed in the Argonne, while he was trying to bring
the body of his Yankee captain back to the lines. At this
time Cy Bogart was still dwelling in Gopher Prairie and
planning to go to war.

II

Everywhere Carol heard that the war was going to bring a
basic change in psychology, to purify and uplift everything

from marital relations to national politics, and she tried to
exult in it. Only she did not find it. She saw the women who
made bandages for the Red Cross giving up bridge, and
laughing at having to do without sugar, but over the sur-
gical-dressings they did not speak of God and the souls of
men, but of Miles Bjornstam's impudence, of Terry Gould's
scandalous carryings-on with a farmer's daughter four years
ago, of cooking cabbage, and of altering blouses. Their references to the war touched atrocities only. She herself was
punctual, and efficient at making dressings, but she could not,
like Mrs. Lyman Cass and Mrs. Bogart, fill the dressings with
hate for enemies.

When she protested to Vida, "The young do the work while
these old ones sit around and interrupt us and gag with hate
because they're too feeble to do anything but hate," then
Vida turned on her:

"If you can't be reverent, at least don't be so pert and
opinionated, now when men and women are dying. Some of
us—we have given up so much, and we're glad to. At least
we expect that you others sha'n't try to be witty at our
expense."

There was weeping.

Carol did desire to see the Prussian autocracy defeated;
she did persuade herself that there were no autocracies save
that of Prussia; she did thrill to motion-pictures of troops
embarking in New York; and she was uncomfortable when
she met Miles Bjornstam on the street and he croaked:

"How's tricks? Things going fine with me; got two new
cows. Well, have you become a patriot? Eh? Sure, they'll
bring democracy—the democracy of death. Yes, sure, in
every war since the Garden of Eden the workmen have gone
out to fight each other for perfectly good reasons—handed
to them by their bosses. Now me, I'm wise. I'm so wise that
I know I don't know anything about the war."

It was not a thought of the war that remained with her
after Miles's declamation but a perception that she and Vida
and 'all of the good-intentioners who wanted to "do something for the common people" were insignificant, because the
"common people" were able to do things for themselves, and
highly likely to, as soon as they learned the fact. The
conception of millions of workmen like Miles taking control
frightened her, and she scuttled rapidly away from the
thought of a time when she might no longer retain the posi-

tion of Lady Bountiful to the Bjornstams and Beas and Oscarinas whom she loved—and patronized.

III

It was in June, two months after America's entrance into the war, that the momentous event happened—the visit of the great Percy Bresnahan, the millionaire president of the Velvet Motor Car Company of Boston, the one native son who was always to be mentioned to strangers.

For two weeks there were rumors. Sam Clark cried to Kennicott, "Say, I hear Perce Bresnahan is coming! By golly it'll be great to see the old scout, eh?" Finally the *Dauntless* printed, on the front page with a No. 1 head, a letter from Bresnahan to Jackson Elder:

> DEAR JACK:
>   Well, Jack, I find I can make it. I'm to go to Washington as a dollar a year man for the government, in the aviation motor section, and tell them how much I don't know about carburetors. But before I start in being a hero I want to shoot out and catch me a big black bass and cuss out you and Sam Clark and Harry Haydock and Will Kennicott and the rest of you pirates. I'll land in G.P. on June 7, on No. 7 from Mpls. Shake a day-day. Tell Bert Tybee to save me a glass of beer.
> Sincerely yours,
> PERCE.

All members of the social, financial, scientific, literary, and sporting sets were at No. 7 to meet Bresnahan; Mrs. Lyman Cass was beside Del Snafflin the barber, and Juanita Haydock almost cordial to Miss Villets the librarian. Carol saw Bresnahan laughing down at them from the train vestibule—big, immaculate, overjawed, with the eye of an executive. In the voice of the professional Good Fellow he bellowed, "Howdy, folks!" As she was introduced to him (not he to her) Bresnahan looked into her eyes, and his handshake was warm, unhurried.

He declined the offers of motors; he walked off, his arm about the shoulder of Nat Hicks the sporting tailor, with the elegant Harry Haydock carrying one of his enormous pale leather bags, Del Snafflin the other, Jack Elder bearing an overcoat, and Julius Flickerbaugh the fishing-tackle. Carol noted that though Bresnahan wore spats and a stick, no small boy jeered. She decided, "I must have Will get a double-breasted blue coat and a wing collar and a dotted bow-tie like his."

That evening, when Kennicott was trimming the grass along the walk with sheep-shears, Bresnahan rolled up, alone. He was now in corduroy trousers, khaki shirt open at the throat, a white boating hat, and marvelous canvas-and-leather shoes. "On the job there, old Will! Say, my Lord, this is living, to come back and get into a regular man-sized pair of pants. They can talk all they want to about the city, but my idea of a good time is to loaf around and see you boys and catch a gamey bass!"

He hustled up the walk and blared at Carol, "Where's that little fellow? I hear you've got one fine big he-boy that you're holding out on me!"

"He's gone to bed," rather briefly.

"I know. And rules are rules, these days. Kids get routed through the shop like a motor. But look here, sister; I'm one great hand at busting rules. Come on now, let Uncle Perce have a look at him. Please now, sister?"

He put his arm about her waist; it was a large, strong, sophisticated arm, and very agreeable; he grinned at her with a devastating knowingness, while Kennicott glowed inanely. She flushed; she was alarmed by the ease with which the big-city man invaded her guarded personality. She was glad, in retreat, to scamper ahead of the two men up-stairs to the hall-room in which Hugh slept. All the way Kennicott muttered, "Well, well, say, gee whittakers but it's good to have you back, certainly is good to see you!"

Hugh lay on his stomach, making an earnest business of sleeping. He burrowed his eyes in the dwarf blue pillow to escape the electric light, then sat up abruptly, small and frail in his woolly nightdrawers, his floss of brown hair wild, the pillow clutched to his breast. He wailed. He stared at the stranger, in a manner of patient dismissal. He explained confidentially to Carol, "Daddy wouldn't let it be morning yet. What does the pillow say?"

Bresnahan dropped his arm caressingly on Carol's shoulder; he pronounced, "My Lord, you're a lucky girl to have a fine young husk like that. I figure Will knew what he was doing when he persuaded you to take a chance on an old bum like him! They tell me you come from St. Paul. We're going to get you to come to Boston some day." He leaned over the bed. "Young man, you're the slickest sight I've seen this side of Boston. With your permission, may we present you with a slight token of our regard and appreciation of your long service?"

He held out a red rubber Pierrot. Hugh remarked, "Gimme it," hid it under the bedclothes, and stared at Bresnahan as though he had never seen the man before.

For once Carol permitted herself the spiritual luxury of not asking "Why, Hugh dear, what do you say when some one gives you a present?" The great man was apparently waiting. They stood in inane suspense till Bresnahan led them out, rumbling, "How about planning a fishing-trip, Will?"

He remained for half an hour. Always he told Carol what a charming person she was; always he looked at her knowingly.

"Yes. He probably would make a woman fall in love with him. But it wouldn't last a week. I'd get tired of his confounded buoyancy. His hypocrisy. He's a spiritual bully. He makes me rude to him in self-defense. Oh yes, he is glad to be here. He does like us. He's so good an actor that he convinces his own self. . . . I'd *hate* him in Boston. He'd have all the obvious big-city things. Limousines. Discreet evening-clothes. Order a clever dinner at a smart restaurant. Drawing-room decorated by the best firm—but the pictures giving him away. I'd rather talk to Guy Pollock in his dusty office. . . . How I lie! His arm coaxed my shoulder and his eyes dared me not to admire him. I'd be afraid of him. I hate him! . . . Oh, the inconceivable egotistic imagination of women! All this stew of analysis about a man, a good, decent, friendly, efficient man, because he was kind to me, as Will's wife!"

IV

The Kennicotts, the Elders, the Clarks, and Bresnahan went fishing at Red Squaw Lake. They drove forty miles to the lake in Elder's new Cadillac. There was much laughter and bustle at the start, much storing of lunch baskets and jointed poles, much inquiry as to whether it would *really* bother Carol to sit with her feet up on a roll of shawls. When they were ready to go Mrs. Clark lamented, "Oh, Sam, I forgot my magazine," and Bresnahan bullied, "Come on now, if you women think you're going to be literary, you can't go with us tough guys!" Every one laughed a great deal, and as they drove on Mrs. Clark explained that though prob-

ably she would not have read it, still, she might have wanted
to, while the other girls had a nap in the afternoon, and she
was right in the middle of a serial—it was an awfully exciting story—it seems that this girl was a Turkish dancer
(only she was really the daughter of an American lady and
a Russian prince) and men kept running after her, just disgustingly, but she remained pure, and there was a scene——

While the men floated on the lake, casting for black bass,
the women prepared lunch and yawned. Carol was a little
resentful of the manner in which the men assumed that they
did not care to fish. "I don't want to go with them, but I
would like the privilege of refusing."

The lunch was long and pleasant. It was a background
for the talk of the great man come home, hints of cities
and large imperative affairs and famous people, jocosely
modest admissions that, yes, their friend Perce was doing
about as well as most of these "Boston swells that think so
much of themselves because they come from rich old families
and went to college and everything. Believe me, it's us new
business men that are running Beantown today, and not a lot
of fussy old bucks snoozing in their clubs!"

Carol realized that he was not one of the sons of Gopher
Prairie who, if they do not actually starve in the East, are
invariably spoken of as "highly successful"; and she found
behind his too incessant flattery a genuine affection for his
mates. It was in the matter of the war that he most favored
and thrilled them. Dropping his voice while they bent nearer
(there was no one within two miles to overhear), he disclosed the fact that in both Boston and Washington he'd been
getting a lot of inside stuff on the war—right straight from
headquarters—he was in touch with some men—couldn't
name them but they were darn high up in both the War and
State Departments—and he would say—only for Pete's sake
they mustn't breathe one word of this; it was strictly on the
Q.T. and not generally known outside of Washington—but
just between ourselves—and they could take this for gospel
—Spain had finally decided to join the Entente allies in the
Grand Scrap. Yes, sir, there'd be two million fully equipped
Spanish soldiers fighting with us in France in one month
now. Some surprise for Germany, all right!

"How about the prospects for revolution in Germany?"
reverently asked Kennicott.

The authority grunted. "Nothing to it. The one thing you
can bet on is that no matter what happens to the German

people, win or lose, they'll stick by the Kaiser till hell
freezes over. I got that absolutely straight, from a fellow who's
on the inside of the inside in Washington. No, sir! I don't
pretend to know much about international affairs but one
thing you can put down as settled is that Germany will be a
Hohenzollern empire for the next forty years. At that, I
don't know as it's so bad. The Kaiser and the Junkers keep a
firm hand on a lot of these red agitators who'd be worse
than a king if they could get control."

"I'm terribly interested in this uprising that overthrew
the Czar in Russia," suggested Carol. She had finally been
conquered by the man's wizard knowledge of affairs.

Kennicott apologized for her: "Carrie's nuts about this
Russian revolution. Is there much to it, Perce?"

"There is not!" Bresnahan said flatly. "I can speak by the
book there. Carol, honey, I'm surprised to find you talking
like a New York Russian Jew, or one of these long-hairs! I
can tell you, only you don't need to let every one in on it,
this is confidential, I got it from a man who's close to
the State Department, but as a matter of fact the Czar will be
back in power before the end of the year. You read a lot
about his retiring and about his being killed, but I know he's
got a big army back of him, and he'll show these damn agitators, lazy beggars hunting for a soft berth bossing the poor
goats that fall for 'em, he'll show 'em where they get off!"

Carol was sorry to hear that the Czar was coming back,
but she said nothing. The others had looked vacant at the
mention of a country so far away as Russia. Now they edged
in and asked Bresnahan what he thought about the Packard
car, investments in Texas oil-wells, the comparative merits of
young men born in Minnesota and in Massachusetts, the question of prohibition, the future cost of motor tires, and wasn't
it true that American aviators put it all over these French-
men?

They were glad to find that he agreed with them on every
point.

As she heard Bresnahan announce, "We're perfectly willing to talk to any committee the men may choose, but we're
not going to stand for some outside agitator butting in and
telling us how we're going to run our plant!" Carol remembered that Jackson Elder (now meekly receiving New Ideas)
had said the same thing in the same words.

While Sam Clark was digging up from his memory a long
and immensely detailed story of the crushing things he had

said to a Pullman porter, named George, Bresnahan hugged his knees and rocked and watched Carol. She wondered if he did not understand the laboriousness of the smile with which she listened to Kennicott's account of the "good one he had on Carrie," that marital, coyly improper, ten-times-told tale of how she had forgotten to attend to Hugh because she was "all het up pounding the box"—which may be translated as "eagerly playing the piano." She was certain that Bresnahan saw through her when she pretended not to hear Kennicott's invitation to join a game of cribbage. She feared the comments he might make; she was irritated by her fear.

She was equally irritated, when the motor returned through Gopher Prairie, to find that she was proud of sharing in Bresnahan's kudos as people waved, and Juanita Haydock leaned from a window. She said to herself, "As though I cared whether I'm seen with this fat phonograph!" and simultaneously, "Everybody has noticed how much Will and I are playing with Mr. Bresnahan."

The town was full of his stories, his friendliness, his memory for names, his clothes, his trout-flies, his generosity. He had given a hundred dollars to Father Klubok the priest, and a hundred to the Reverend Mr. Zitterel the Baptist minister, for Americanization work.

At the Bon Ton, Carol heard Nat Hicks the tailor exulting:

"Old Perce certainly pulled a good one on this fellow Bjornstam that always is shooting off his mouth. He's supposed to of settled down since he got married, but Lord, those fellows that think they know it all, they never change. Well, the Red Swede got the grand razz handed to him, all right. He had the nerve to breeze up to Perce, at Dave Dyer's, and he said, he said to Perce, 'I've always wanted to look at a man that was so useful that folks would pay him a million dollars for existing,' and Perce gave him the once-over and come right back, 'Have, eh?' he says. 'Well,' he says, 'I've been looking for a man so useful sweeping floors that I could pay him four dollars a day. Want the job, my friend?' Ha, ha, ha! Say, you know how lippy Bjornstam is? Well for once he didn't have a thing to say. He tried to get fresh, and tell what a rotten town this is, and Perce come right back at him, 'If you don't like this country, you better get out of it and go back to Germany, where you belong!' Say, maybe us fellows didn't give Bjornstam the horse-laugh though! Oh, Perce is the white-haired boy in this burg, all rightee!"

V

Bresnahan had borrowed Jackson Elder's motor; he stopped at the Kennicotts'; he bawled at Carol, rocking with Hugh on the porch, "Better come for a ride."

She wanted to snub him. "Thanks so much, but I'm being maternal."

"Bring him along! Bring him along!" Bresnahan was out of the seat, stalking up the sidewalk, and the rest of her protests and dignities were feeble.

She did not bring Hugh along.

Bresnahan was silent for a mile, in words, But he looked at her as though he meant her to know that he understood everything she thought.

She observed how deep was his chest.

"Lovely fields over there," he said.

"You really like them? There's no profit in them."

He chuckled. "Sister, you can't get away with it. I'm onto you. You consider me a big bluff. Well, maybe I am. But so are you, my dear—and pretty enough so that I'd try to make love to you, if I weren't afraid you'd slap me."

"Mr. Bresnahan, do you talk that way to your wife's friends? And do you call them 'sister'?"

"As a matter of fact, I do! And I make 'em like it. Score two!" But his chuckle was not so rotund, and he was very attentive to the ammeter.

In a moment he was cautiously attacking: "That's a wonderful boy, Will Kennicott. Great work these country practitioners are doing. The other day, in Washington, I was talking to a big scientific shark, a professor in Johns Hopkins medical school, and he was saying that no one has ever sufficiently appreciated the general practitioner and the sympathy and help he gives folks. These crack specialists, the young scientific fellows, they're so cocksure and so wrapped up in their laboratories that they miss the human element. Except in the case of a few freak diseases that no respectable human being would waste his time having, it's the old doc that keeps a community well, mind and body. And strikes me that Will is one of the steadiest and clearest-headed country practitioners I've ever met. Eh?"

"I'm sure he is. He's a servant of reality."

"Come again? Um. Yes. All of that, whatever that is. . . .

Say, child, you don't care a whole lot for Gopher Prairie, if
I'm not mistaken."

"Nope."

"There's where you're missing a big chance. There's nothing to these cities. Believe me, I *know!* This is a good
town, as they go. You're lucky to be here. I wish I could
stay on!"

"Very well, why don't you?"

"Huh? Why—Lord—can't get away fr——"

"You don't have to stay. I do! So I want to change it. Do
you know that men like you, prominent men, do quite a
reasonable amount of harm by insisting that your native
towns and native states are perfect? It's you who encourage
the denizens not to change. They quote you, and go on
believing that they live in paradise, and——" She clenched
her fist. "The incredible dullness of it!"

"Suppose you were right. Even so, don't you think you
waste a lot of thundering on one poor scared little town?
Kind of mean!"

"I tell you it's dull. *Dull!*"

"The folks don't find it dull. These couples like the Haydocks have a high old time; dances and cards——"

"They don't. They're bored. Almost every one here is.
Vacuousness and bad manners and spiteful gossip—that's what
I hate."

"Those things—course they're here. So are they in Boston!
And every place else! Why, the faults you find in this town
are simply human nature, and never will be changed."

"Perhaps. But in a Boston all the good Carols (I'll admit
I have no faults) can find one another and play. But here—
I'm alone, in a stale pool—except as it's stirred by the great
Mr. Bresnahan!"

"My Lord, to hear you tell it, a fellow 'd think that all
the denizens, as you impolitely call 'em, are so confoundedly
unhappy that it's a wonder they don't all up and commit
suicide. But they seem to struggle along somehow!"

"They don't know what they miss. And anybody can endure anything. Look at men in mines and in prisons."

He drew up on the south shore of Lake Minniemashie. He
glanced across the reeds reflected on the water, the quiver
of wavelets like crumpled tinfoil, the distant shores patched
with dark woods, silvery oats and deep yellow wheat. He
patted her hand. "Sis—— Carol, you're a darling girl, but
you're difficult. Know what I think?"

"Yes."

"Humph. Maybe you do, but—— My humble (not too humble!) opinion is that you like to be different. You like to think you're peculiar. Why, if you knew how many tens of thousands of women, especially in New York, say just what you do, you'd lose all the fun of thinking you're a lone genius and you'd be on the band-wagon whooping it up for Gopher Prairie and a good decent family life. There's always about a million young women just out of college who want to teach their grandmothers how to suck eggs."

"How proud you are of that homely rustic metaphor! You use it at 'banquets' and directors' meetings, and boast of your climb from a humble homestead."

"Huh! You may have my number. I'm not telling. But look here: You're so prejudiced against Gopher Prairie that you overshoot the mark; you antagonize those who might be inclined to agree with you in some particulars but—— Great guns, the town can't be all wrong!"

"No, it isn't. But it could be. Let me tell you a fable. Imagine a cavewoman complaining to her mate. She doesn't like one single thing; she hates the damp cave, the rats running over her bare legs, the stiff skin garments, the eating of half-raw meat, her husband's bushy face, the constant battles, and the worship of the spirits who will hoodoo her unless she gives the priests her best claw necklace. Her man protests, 'But it can't all be wrong!' and he thinks he has reduced her to absurdity. Now you assume that a world which produces a Percy Bresnahan and a Velvet Motor Company must be civilized. It is? Aren't we only about half-way along in barbarism? I suggest Mrs. Bogart as a test. And we'll continue in barbarism just as long as people as nearly intelligent as you continue to defend things as they are because they are."

"You're a fair spieler, child. But, by golly, I'd like to see you try to design a new manifold, or run a factory and keep a lot of your fellow reds from Czech-slovenski-magyar-godknowswheria on the job! You'd drop your theories so darn quick! I'm not any defender of things as they are. Sure. They're rotten. Only I'm sensible."

He preached his gospel: love of outdoors, Playing the Game, loyalty to friends. She had the neophyte's shock of discovery that, outside of tracts, conservatives do not tremble and find no answer when an iconoclast turns on them, but retort with agility and confusing statistics.

He was so much the man, the worker, the friend, that she liked him when she most tried to stand out against him; he was so much the successful executive that she did not want him to despise her. His manner of sneering at what he called "parlor socialists" (though the phrase was not overwhelmingly new) had a power which made her wish to placate his company of well-fed, speed-loving administrators. When he demanded, "Would you like to associate with nothing but a lot of turkey-necked, horn-spectacled nuts that have adenoids and need a hair-cut, and that spend all their time kicking about 'conditions' and never do a lick of work?" she said, "No, but just the same——" When he asserted, "Even if your cavewoman was right in knocking the whole works, I bet some red-blooded Regular Fellow, some real He-man, found her a nice dry cave, and not any whining criticizing radical," she wriggled her head feebly, between a nod and a shake.

His large hands, sensual lips, easy voice supported his self-confidence. He made her feel young and soft—as Kennicott had once made her feel. She had nothing to say when he bent his powerful head and experimented, "My dear, I'm sorry I'm going away from this town. You'd be a darling child to play with. You *are* pretty! Some day in Boston I'll show you how we buy a lunch. Well, hang it, got to be starting back."

The only answer to his gospel of beef which she could find, when she was home, was a wail of "But just the same——"

She did not see him again before he departed for Washington.

His eyes remained. His glances at her lips and hair and shoulders had revealed to her that she was not a wife-and-mother alone, but a girl; that there still were men in the world, as there had been in college days.

That admiration led her to study Kennicott, to tear at the shroud of intimacy, to perceive the strangeness of the most familiar.

$$\text{chapter } 24$$

ALL that midsummer month Carol was sensitive to Kennicott. She recalled a hundred grotesqueries: her comic dismay at his having chewed tobacco, the evening when she had tried to read poetry to him; matters which had seemed to vanish with no trace or sequence. Always she repeated that he had been heroically patient in his desire to join the army. She made much of her consoling affection for him in little things. She liked the homeliness of his tinkering about the house; his strength and handiness as he tightened the hinges of a shutter; his boyishness when he ran to her to be comforted because he had found rust in the barrel of his pumpgun. But at the highest he was to her another Hugh, without the glamor of Hugh's unknown future.

There was, late in June, a day of heat-lightning.

Because of the work imposed by the absence of the other doctors the Kennicotts had not moved to the lake cottage but remained in town, dusty and irritable. In the afternoon, when she went to Oleson & McGuire's (formerly Dahl & Oleson's), Carol was vexed by the assumption of the youthful clerk, recently come from the farm, that he had to be neighborly and rude. He was no more brusquely familiar than a dozen other clerks of the town, but her nerves were heat-scorched.

When she asked for codfish, for supper, he grunted, "What d'you want that darned old dry stuff for?"

"I like it!"

"Punk! Guess the doc can afford something better than that. Try some of the new wienies we got in. Swell. The Haydocks use 'em."

She exploded. "My dear young man, it is not your duty to instruct me in housekeeping, and it doesn't particularly concern me what the Haydocks condescend to approve!"

He was hurt. He hastily wrapped up the leprous fragment of fish; he gaped as she trailed out. She lamented, "I shouldn't

278

have spoken so. He didn't mean anything. He doesn't know when he is being rude."

Her repentance was not proof against Uncle Whittier when she stopped in at his grocery for salt and a package of safety matches. Uncle Whittier, in a shirt collarless and soaked with sweat in a brown streak down his back, was whining at a clerk, "Come on now, get a hustle on and lug that pound cake up to Mis' Cass's. Some folks in this town think a storekeeper ain't got nothing to do but chase out 'phone-orders. . . . Hello, Carrie. That dress you got on looks kind of low in the neck to me. May be decent and modest—I suppose I'm old-fashioned—but I never thought much of showing the whole town a woman's bust! Hee, hee, hee! . . . Afternoon, Mrs. Hicks. Sage? Just out of it. Lemme sell you some other spices. Heh?" Uncle Whittier was nasally indignant. "*Certainly!* Got *plenty* other spices jus' good as sage for any purp'se whatever! What's the matter with—well, with allspice?" When Mrs. Hicks had gone, he raged, "Some folks don't know what they want!"

"Sweating sanctimonious bully—my husband's uncle!" thought Carol.

She crept into Dave Dyer's. Dave held up his arms with, "Don't shoot! I surrender!" She smiled, but it occurred to her that for nearly five years Dave had kept up this game of pretending that she threatened his life.

As she went dragging through the prickly-hot street she reflected that a citizen of Gopher Prairie does not have jests—he has a jest. Every cold morning for five winters Lyman Cass had remarked, "Fair to middlin' chilly—get worse before it gets better." Fifty times had Ezra Stowbody informed the public that Carol had once asked, "Shall I indorse this check on the back?" Fifty times had Sam Clark called to her, "Where'd you steal that hat?" Fifty times had the mention of Barney Cahoon, the town drayman, like a nickel in a slot produced from Kennicott the apocryphal story of Barney's directing a minister, "Come down to the depot and get your case of religious books—they're leaking!"

She came home by the unvarying route. She knew every house-front, every street-crossing, every billboard, every tree, every dog. She knew every blackened banana-skin and empty cigarette-box in the gutters. She knew every greeting. When Jim Howland stopped and gaped at her there was no possibility that he was about to confide anything but his grudging, "Well, haryuh t'day?"

All her future life, this same red-labeled bread-crate in front of the bakery, this same thimble-shaped crack in the sidewalk a quarter of a block beyond Stowbody's granite hitching-post——

She silently handed her purchases to the silent Oscarina. She sat on the porch, rocking, fanning, twitchy with Hugh's whining.

Kennicott came home, grumbled, "What the devil is the kid yapping about?"

"I guess you can stand it ten minutes if I can stand it all day!"

He came to supper in his shirt sleeves, his vest partly open, revealing discolored suspenders.

"Why don't you put on your nice Palm Beach suit, and take off that hideous vest?" she complained.

"Too much trouble. Too hot to go up-stairs."

She realized that for perhaps a year she had not definitely looked at her husband. She regarded his table-manners. He violently chased fragments of fish about his plate with a knife and licked the knife after gobbling them. She was slightly sick. She asserted, "I'm ridiculous. What do these things matter! Don't be so simple!" But she knew that to her they did matter, these solecisms and mixed tenses of the table.

She realized that they found little to say; that, incredibly, they were like the talked-out couples whom she had pitied at restaurants.

Bresnahan would have spouted in a lively, exciting, unreliable manner. . . .

She realized that Kennicott's clothes were seldom pressed. His coat was wrinkled; his trousers would flap at the knees when he arose. His shoes were unblacked, and they were of an elderly shapelessness. He refused to wear soft hats; cleaved to a hard derby, as a symbol of virility and prosperity; and sometimes he forgot to take it off in the house. She peeped at his cuffs. They were frayed in prickles of starched linen. She had turned them once; she clipped them every week; but when she had begged him to throw the shirt away, last Sunday morning at the crisis of the weekly bath, he had uneasily protested, "Oh, it'll wear quite a while yet."

He was shaved (by himself or more socially by Del Snafflin) only three times a week. This morning had not been one of the three times.

Yet he was vain of his new turn-down collars and sleek ties; he often spoke of the "sloppy dressing" of Dr. McGanum; and he laughed at old men who wore detachable cuffs or Gladstone collars.

Carol did not care much for the creamed codfish that evening.

She noted that his nails were jagged and ill-shaped from his habit of cutting them with a pocket-knife and despising a nail-file as effeminate and urban. That they were invariably clean, that his were the scoured fingers of the surgeon, made his stubborn untidiness the more jarring. They were wise hands, kind hands, but they were not the hands of love.

She remembered him in the days of courtship. He had tried to please her, then; had touched her by sheepishly wearing a colored band on his straw hat. Was it possible that those days of fumbling for each other were gone so completely? He had read books, to impress her; had said (she recalled it ironically) that she was to point out his every fault; had insisted once, as they sat in the secret place beneath the walls of Fort Snelling——

She shut the door on her thoughts. That was sacred ground. But it *was* a shame that——

She nervously pushed away her cake and stewed apricots.

After supper, when they had been driven in from the porch by mosquitos, when Kennicott had for the two-hundredth time in five years commented, "We must have a new screen on the porch—lets all the bugs in," they sat reading, and she noted, and detested herself for noting, and noted again his habitual awkwardness. He slumped down in one chair, his legs up on another, and he explored the recesses of his left ear with the end of his little finger—she could hear the faint smack—he kept it up—he kept it up——

He blurted, "Oh. Forgot tell you. Some of the fellows coming in to play poker this evening. Suppose we could have some crackers and cheese and beer?"

She nodded.

"He might have mentioned it before. Oh well, it's his house."

The poker-party straggled in: Sam Clark, Jack Elder, Dave Dyer, Jim Howland. To her they mechanically said, " 'Devenin'," but to Kennicott, in a heroic male manner, "Well well, shall we start playing? Got a hunch I'm going to lick somebody real bad." No one suggested that she join them. She told herself that it was her own fault, because she was not more friendly; but she remembered that they never asked Mrs. Sam Clark to play.

Bresnahan would have asked her.

She sat in the living-room, glancing across the hall at the men as they humped over the dining table.

They were in shirt sleeves; smoking, chewing, spitting incessantly; lowering their voices for a moment so that she did not hear what they said and afterward giggling hoarsely; using over and over the canonical phrases: "Three to dole," "I raise you a finif," "Come on now, ante up; what do you think this is, a pink tea?" The cigar-smoke was acrid and pervasive. The firmness with which the men mouthed their cigars made the lower part of their faces expressionless, heavy, unappealing. They were like politicians cynically dividing appointments.

How could they understand her world?

Did that faint and delicate world exist? Was she a fool? She doubted her world, doubted herself, and was sick in the acid, smoke-stained air.

She slipped back into brooding upon the habituality of the house.

Kennicott was as fixed in routine as an isolated old man. At first he had amorously deceived himself into liking her experiments with food—the one medium in which she could express imagination—but now he wanted only his round of favorite dishes: steak, roast beef, boiled pig's-feet, oatmeal, baked apples. Because at some more flexible period he had advanced from oranges to grape-fruit he considered himself an epicure.

During their first autumn she had smiled over his affection for his hunting-coat, but now that the leather had come unstitched in dribbles of pale yellow thread, and tatters of canvas, smeared with dirt of the fields and grease from gun-cleaning, hung in a border of rags, she hated the thing.

Wasn't her whole life like that hunting-coat?

She knew every nick and brown spot on each piece of the set of china purchased by Kennicott's mother in 1895—discreet china with a pattern of washed-out forget-me-nots, rimmed with blurred gold: the gravy-boat, in a saucer which did not match, the solemn and evangelical covered vegetable-dishes, the two platters.

Twenty times had Kennicott sighed over the fact that Bea had broken the other platter—the medium-sized one.

The kitchen.

Damp black iron sink, damp whitey-yellow drain-board
with shreds of discolored wood which from long scrubbing
were as soft as cotton thread, warped table, alarm clock,
stove bravely blackened by Oscarina but an abomination in
its loose doors and broken drafts and oven that never would
keep an even heat.

Carol had done her best by the kitchen: painted it white,
put up curtains, replaced a six-year-old calendar by a color
print. She had hoped for tiling, and a kerosene range for
summer cooking, but Kennicott always postponed these expenses.

She was better acquainted with the utensils in the kitchen
than with Vida Sherwin or Guy Pollock. The can-opener,
whose soft gray metal handle was twisted from some ancient
effort to pry open a window, was more pertinent to her than
all the cathedrals in Europe; and more significant than the
future of Asia was the never-settled weekly question as to
whether the small kitchen knife with the unpainted handle or
the second-best buckhorn carving-knife was better for cutting up cold chicken for Sunday supper.

II

She was ignored by the males till midnight. Her husband
called, "Suppose we could have some eats, Carrie?" As she
passed through the dining-room the men smiled on her, belly-
smiles. None of them noticed her while she was serving the
crackers and cheese and sardines and beer. They were de-
termining the exact psychology of Dave Dyer in standing
pat, two hours before.

When they were gone she said to Kennicott, "Your friends
have the manners of a barroom. They expect me to wait on
them like a servant. They're not so much interested in me as
they would be in a waiter, because they don't have to tip me.
Unfortunately! Well, good night."

So rarely did she nag in this petty, hot-weather fashion
that he was astonished rather than angry. "Hey! Wait! What's
the idea? I must say I don't get you. The boys—— Barroom?
Why, Perce Bresnahan was saying there isn't a finer bunch
of royal good fellows anywhere than just the crowd that
were here tonight!"

They stood in the lower hall. He was too shocked to go on
with his duties of locking the front door and winding his
watch and the clock.

"Bresnahan! I'm sick of him!" She meant nothing in particular.

"Why, Carrie, he's one of the biggest men in the country! Boston just eats out of his hand!"

"I wonder if it does? How do we know but that in Boston among well-bred people, he may be regarded as an absolute lout? The way he calls women 'Sister,' and the way——"

"Now look here! That'll do! Of course I know you don't mean it—you're simply hot and tired, and trying to work off your peeve on me. But just the same, I won't stand your jumping on Perce. You—— It's just like your attitude toward the war—so darn afraid that America will become militaristic——"

"But you are the pure patriot!"

"By God, I am!"

"Yes, I heard you talking to Sam Clark tonight about ways of avoiding the income tax!"

He had recovered enough to lock the door; he clumped up-stairs ahead of her, growling, "You don't know what you're talking about. I'm perfectly willing to pay my full tax—fact, I'm in favor of the income tax—even though I do think it's a penalty on frugality and enterprise—fact, it's an unjust, darn-fool tax. But just the same, I'll pay it. Only, I'm not idiot enough to pay more than the government makes me pay, and Sam and I were just figuring out whether all automobile expenses oughtn't to be exemptions. I'll take a lot off you, Carrie, but I don't propose for one second to stand your saying I'm not patriotic. You know mighty well and good that I've tried to get away and join the army. And at the beginning of the whole fracas I said—I've said right along that we ought to have entered the war the minute Germany invaded Belgium. You don't get me at all. You can't appreciate a man's work. You're abnormal. You've fussed so much with these fool novels and books and all this highbrow junk—— You like to argue!"

It ended, a quarter of an hour later, in his calling her a "neurotic" before he turned away and pretended to sleep.

For the first time they had failed to make peace.

"There are two races of people, only two, and they live side by side. His calls mine 'neurotic'; mine calls his 'stupid.' We'll never understand each other, never; and it's madness for us to debate—to lie together in a hot bed in a creepy room—enemies, yoked."

III

It clarified in her the longing for a place of her own. "While it's so hot, I think I'll sleep in the spare room," she said next day.

"Not a bad idea." He was cheerful and kindly.

The room was filled with a lumbering double bed and a cheap pine bureau. She stored the bed in the attic; replaced it by a cot which, with a denim cover, made a couch by day; put in a dressing-table, a rocker transformed by a cretonne cover; had Miles Bjornstam build book-shelves.

Kennicott slowly understood that she meant to keep up her seclusion. In his queries, "Changing the whole room?" "Putting your books in there?" she caught his dismay. But it was so easy, once her door was closed, to shut out his worry. That hurt her—the ease of forgetting him.

Aunt Bessie Smail sleuthed out this anarchy. She yammered, "Why, Carrie, you ain't going to sleep all alone by yourself? I don't believe in that. Married folks should have the same room, of course! Don't go getting silly notions. No telling what a thing like that might lead to. Suppose I up and told your Uncle Whit that I wanted a room of my own!"

Carol spoke of recipes for corn-pudding.

But from Mrs. Dr. Westlake she drew encouragement. She had made an afternoon call on Mrs. Westlake. She was for the first time invited up-stairs, and found the suave old woman sewing in a white and mahogany room with a small bed.

"Oh, do you have your own royal apartments, and the doctor his?" Carol hinted.

"Indeed I do! The doctor says it's bad enough to have to stand my temper at meals. Do——" Mrs. Westlake looked at her sharply. "Why, don't you do the same thing?"

"I've been thinking about it." Carol laughed in an embarrassed way. "Then you wouldn't regard me as a complete hussy if I wanted to be by myself now and then?"

"Why, child, every woman ought to get off by herself and turn over her thoughts—about children, and God, and how bad her complexion is, and the way men don't really understand her, and how much work she finds to do in the house, and how much patience it takes to endure some things in a man's love."

"Yes!" Carol said it in a gasp, her hands twisted together.
She wanted to confess not only her hatred for the Aunt
Bessies but her covert irritation toward those she best loved:
her alienation from Kennicott, her disappointment in Guy
Pollock, her uneasiness in the presence of Vida. She had
enough self-control to confine herself to, "Yes. Men! The
dear blundering souls, we do have to get off and laugh at
them."

"Of course we do. Not that you have to laugh at Dr.
Kennicott so much, but *my* man, heavens, now there's a
rare old bird! Reading story-books when he ought to be tending to business! 'Marcus Westlake,' I say to him, 'you're a
romantic old fool.' And does he get angry? He does not! He
chuckles and says, 'Yes, my beloved, folks do say that married people grow to resemble each other!' Drat him!" Mrs.
Westlake laughed comfortably.

After such a disclosure what could Carol do but return the
courtesy by remarking that as for Kennicott, he wasn't
romantic enough—the darling. Before she left she had babbled to Mrs. Westlake her dislike for Aunt Bessie, the fact
that Kennicott's income was now more than five thousand a
year, her view of the reason why Vida had married Raymie
(which included some thoroughly insincere praise of Raymie's
"kind heart"), her opinion of the library-board, just what
Kennicott had said about Mrs. Carthal's diabetes, and what
Kennicott thought of the several surgeons in the Cities.

She went home soothed by confession, inspirited by finding a new friend.

IV

The tragicomedy of the "domestic situation."

Oscarina went back home to help on the farm, and Carol
had a succession of maids, with gaps between. The lack of
servants was becoming one of the most cramping problems of
the prairie town. Increasingly the farmers' daughters rebelled
against village dullness, and against the unchanged attitude
of the Juanitas toward "hired girls." They went off to city
kitchens, or to city shops and factories, that they might be
free and even human after hours.

The Jolly Seventeen were delighted at Carol's desertion by
the loyal Oscarina. They reminded her that she had said,
"I don't have any trouble with maids; see how Oscarina
stays on."

Between incumbencies of Finn maids from the North Woods, Germans from the prairies, occasional Swedes and Norwegians and Icelanders, Carol did her own work—and endured Aunt Bessie's skittering in to tell her how to dampen a broom for fluffy dust, how to sugar doughnuts, how to stuff a goose. Carol was deft, and won shy praise from Kennicott, but as her shoulder blades began to sting, she wondered how many millions of women had lied to themselves during the death-rimmed years through which they had pretended to enjoy the puerile methods persisting in housework.

She doubted the convenience and, as a natural sequent, the sanctity of the monogamous and separate home which she had regarded as the basis of all decent life.

She considered her doubts vicious. She refused to remember how many of the women of the Jolly Seventeen nagged their husbands and were nagged by them.

She energetically did not whine to Kennicott. But her eyes ached; she was not the girl in breeches and a flannel shirt who had cooked over a camp-fire in the Colorado mountains five years ago. Her ambition was to get to bed at nine; her strongest emotion was resentment over rising at half-past six to care for Hugh. The back of her neck ached as she got out of bed. She was cynical about the joys of a simple laborious life. She understood why workmen and workmen's wives are not grateful to their kind employers.

At mid-morning, when she was momentarily free from the ache in her neck and back, she was glad of the reality of work. The hours were living and nimble. But she had no desire to read the eloquent little newspaper essays in praise of labor which are daily written by the white-browed journalistic prophets. She felt independent and (though she hid it) a bit surly.

In cleaning the house she pondered upon the maid's-room. It was a slant-roofed, small-windowed hole above the kitchen, oppressive in summer, frigid in winter. She saw that while she had been considering herself an unusually good mistress, she had been permitting her friends Bea and Oscarina to live in a sty. She complained to Kennicott. "What's the matter with it?" he growled, as they stood on the perilous stairs dodging up from the kitchen. She commented upon the sloping roof of unplastered boards stained in brown rings by the rain, the uneven floor, the cot and its tumbled discouraged-looking quilts, the broken rocker, the distorting mirror.

"Maybe it ain't any Hotel Radisson parlor, but still, it's

so much better than anything these hired girls are accustomed to at home that they think it's fine. Seems foolish to spend money when they wouldn't appreciate it."

But that night he drawled, with the casualness of a man who wishes to be surprising and delightful, "Carrie, don't know but we might begin to think about building a new house, one of these days. How'd you like that?"

"W-why——"

"I'm getting to the point now where I feel we can afford one—and a corker! I'll show this burg something like a real house! We'll put one over on Sam and Harry! Make folks sit up an' take notice!"

"Yes," she said.

He did not go on.

Daily he returned to the subject of the new house, but as to time and mode he was indefinite. At first she believed. She babbled of a low stone house with lattice windows and tulip-beds, of colonial brick, of a white frame cottage with green shutters and dormer windows. To her enthusiasms he answered, "Well, ye-es, might be worth thinking about. Remember where I put my pipe?" When she pressed him he fidgeted, "I don't know; seems to me those kind of houses you speak of have been overdone."

It proved that what he wanted was a house exactly like Sam Clark's, which was exactly like every third new house in every town in the country: a square, yellow stolidity with immaculate clapboards, a broad screened porch, tidy grass-plots, and concrete walks; a house resembling the mind of a merchant who votes the party ticket straight and goes to church once a month and owns a good car.

He admitted, "Well, yes, maybe it isn't so darn artistic but—— Matter of fact, though, I don't want a place just like Sam's. Maybe I would cut off that fool tower he's got, and I think probably it would look better painted a nice cream color. That yellow on Sam's house is too kind of flashy. Then there's another kind of house that's mighty nice and substantial-looking, with shingles, in a nice brown stain, instead of clapboards—seen some in Minneapolis. You're way off your base when you say I only like one kind of house!"

Uncle Whittier and Aunt Bessie came in one evening when Carol was sleepily advocating a rose-garden cottage.

"You've had a lot of experience with housekeeping, aunty, and don't you think," Kennicott appealed, "that it would be sensible to have a nice square house, and pay more attention to getting a crackajack furnace than to all this architecture and doodads?"

Aunt Bessie worked her lips as though they were an elastic band. "Why of course! I know how it is with young folks like you, Carrie; you want towers and bay-windows and pianos and heaven knows what all, but the thing to get is closets and a good furnace and a handy place to hang out the washing, and the rest don't matter."

Uncle Whittier dribbled a little, put his face near to Carol's, and sputtered, "Course it don't! What d'you care what folks think about the outside of your house? It's the inside you're living in. None of my business, but I must say you young folks that'd rather have cakes than potatoes get me riled."

She reached her room before she became savage. Below, dreadfully near, she could hear the broom-swish of Aunt Bessie's voice, and the mop-pounding of Uncle Whittier's grumble. She had a reasonless dread that they would intrude on her, then a fear that she would yield to Gopher Prairie's conception of duty toward an Aunt Bessie and go down-stairs to be "nice." She felt the demand for standardized behavior coming in waves from all the citizens who sat in their sitting-rooms watching her with respectable eyes, waiting, demanding, unyielding. She snarled, "Oh, all right, I'll go!" She powdered her nose, straightened her collar, and coldly marched down-stairs. The three elders ignored her. They had advanced from the new house to agreeable general fussing. Aunt Bessie was saying, in a tone like the munching of dry toast:

"I do think Mr. Stowbody ought to have had the rain-pipe fixed at our store right away. I went to see him on Tuesday morning before ten, no, it was couple minutes after ten, but anyway, it was long before noon—I know because I went right from the bank to the meat market to get some steak—my! I think it's outrageous, the prices Oleson & McGuire charge for their meat, and it isn't as if they gave you a good cut either, but just any old thing, and I had time to get it, and I stopped in at Mrs. Bogart's to ask about her rheumatism——"

Carol was watching Uncle Whittier. She knew from his taut expression that he was not listening to Aunt Bessie but herding his own thoughts, and that he would interrupt her bluntly. He did:

"Will, where c'n I get an extra pair of pants for this coat and vest? D' want to pay too much."

"Well, guess Nat Hicks could make you up a pair. But if I were you, I'd drop into Ike Rifkin's—his prices are lower than the Bon Ton's."

"Humph. Got the new stove in your office yet?"

"No, been looking at some at Sam Clark's but——"

"Well y' ought get 't in. Don't do to put off getting a stove all summer, and then have it come cold on you in the fall."

Carol smiled upon them ingratiatingly. "Do you dears mind if I slip up to bed? I'm rather tired—cleaned the up-stairs today."

She retreated. She was certain that they were discussing her, and foully forgiving her. She lay awake till she heard the distant creak of a bed which indicated that Kennicott had retired. Then she felt safe.

It was Kennicott who brought up the matter of the Smails at breakfast. With no visible connection he said, "Uncle Whit is kind of clumsy, but just the same, he's a pretty wise old coot. He's certainly making good with the store."

Carol smiled, and Kennicott was pleased that she had come to her senses. "As Whit says, after all the first thing is to have the inside of a house right, and darn the people on the outside looking in!"

It seemed settled that the house was to be a sound example of the Sam Clark school.

Kennicott made much of erecting it entirely for her and the baby. He spoke of closets for her frocks, and "a comfy sewing-room." But when he drew on a leaf from an old account-book (he was a paper-saver and a string-picker) the plans for the garage, he gave much more attention to a cement floor and a work-bench and a gasoline-tank than he had to sewing-rooms.

She sat back and was afraid.

In the present rookery there were odd things—a step up from the hall to the dining-room, a picturesqueness in the shed and bedraggled lilac bush. But the new place would be smooth, standardized, fixed. It was probable, now that Kennicott was past forty, and settled, that this would be the last venture he would ever make in building. So long as she stayed in this ark, she would always have a possibility of change, but once she was in the new house, there she would sit for all the rest of her life—there she would die. Desperately she wanted to put it off, against the chance of miracles.

While Kennicott was chattering about a patent swing-door for the garage she saw the swing-doors of a prison. She never voluntarily returned to the project. Aggrieved, Kennicott stopped drawing plans, and in ten days the new house was forgotten.

V

Every year since their marriage Carol had longed for a trip through the East. Every year Kennicott had talked of attending the American Medical Association convention, "and then afterwards we could do the East up brown. I know New York clean through—spent pretty near a week there—but I would like to see New England and all these historic places and have some sea-food." He talked of it from February to May, and in May he invariably decided that coming confinement-cases or land-deals would prevent his "getting away from home-base for very long *this* year—and no sense going till we can do it right."

The weariness of dish-washing had increased her desire to go. She pictured herself looking at Emerson's manse, bathing in a surf of jade and ivory, wearing a *trottoir* and a summer fur, meeting an aristocratic Stranger. In the spring Kennicott had pathetically volunteered, "S'pose you'd like to get in a good long tour this summer, but with Gould and Mac away and so many patients depending on me, don't see how I can make it. By golly, I feel like a tightwad though, not taking you." Through all this restless July after she had tasted Bresnahan's disturbing flavor of travel and gaiety, she wanted to go, but she said nothing. They spoke of and postponed a trip to the Twin Cities. When she suggested, as though it were a tremendous joke, "I think baby and I might up and leave you, and run off to Cape Cod by ourselves!" his only reaction was "Golly, don't know but what you may almost have to do that, if we don't get in a trip next year."

Toward the end of July he proposed, "Say, the Beavers are holding a convention in Joralemon, street fair and everything. We might go down tomorrow. And I'd like to see Dr. Calibree about some business. Put in the whole day. Might help some to make up for our trip. Fine fellow, Dr. Calibree."

Joralemon was a prairie town of the size of Gopher Prairie.

Their motor was out of order, and there was no passenger-train at an early hour. They went down by freight-train,

after the weighty and conversational business of leaving Hugh
with Aunt Bessie. Carol was exultant over this irregular
jaunting. It was the first unusual thing, except the glance of
Bresnahan, that had happened since the weaning of Hugh.
They rode in the caboose, the small red cupola-topped car
jerked along at the end of the train. It was a roving shanty,
the cabin of a land schooner, with black oilcloth seats along
the side, and for desk, a pine board to be let down on hinges.
Kennicott played seven-up with the conductor and two brakemen. Carol liked the blue silk kerchiefs about the brakemen's
throats; she liked their welcome to her, and their air of friendly independence. Since there were no sweating passengers
crammed in beside her, she reveled in the train's slowness. She
was part of these lakes and tawny wheatfields. She liked
the smell of hot earth and clean grease; and the leisurely chug-
a-chug, chug-a-chug of the trucks was a song of contentment
in the sun.

She pretended that she was going to the Rockies. When they
reached Joralemon she was radiant with holiday-making.

Her eagerness began to lessen the moment they stopped at
a red frame station exactly like the one they had just left at
Gopher Prairie, and Kennicott yawned, "Right on time. Just
in time for dinner at the Calibrees'. I 'phoned the doctor from
G. P. that we'd be here. 'We'll catch the freight that gets in
before twelve,' I told him. He said he'd meet us at the depot
and take us right up to the house for dinner. Calibree is a
good man, and you'll find his wife is a mighty brainy little
woman, bright as a dollar. By golly, there he is."

Dr. Calibree was a squat, clean-shaven, conscientious-
looking man of forty. He was curiously like his own brown-
painted motor car, with eye-glasses for windshield. "Want
you to meet my wife, doctor—Carrie, make you 'quainted
with Dr. Calibree," said Kennicott. Calibree bowed quietly
and shook her hand, but before he had finished shaking it
he was concentrating upon Kennicott with, "Nice to see you,
doctor. Say, don't let me forget to ask you about what you
did in that exophthalmic goiter case—that Bohemian woman
at Wahkeenyan."

The two men, on the front seat of the car, chanted goiters
and ignored her. She did not know it. She was trying to feed
her illusion of adventure by staring at unfamiliar houses . . .
drab cottages, artificial stone bungalows, square painty stolidi-

ties with immaculate clapboards and broad screened porches and tidy grass-plots.

Calibree handed her over to his wife, a thick woman who called her "dearie," and asked if she was hot and, visibly searching for conversation, produced, "Let's see, you and the doctor have a Little One, haven't you?" At dinner Mrs. Calibree served the corned beef and cabbage and looked steamy, looked like the steamy leaves of cabbage. The men were oblivious of their wives as they gave the social passwords of Main Street, the orthodox opinions on weather, crops, and motor cars, then flung away restraint and gyrated in the debauch of shop-talk. Stroking his chin, drawling in the ecstasy of being erudite, Kennicott inquired, "Say, doctor, what success have you had with thyroid for treatment of pains in the legs before child-birth?"

Carol did not resent their assumption that she was too ignorant to be admitted to masculine mysteries. She was used to it. But the cabbage and Mrs. Calibree's monotonous "I don't know what we're coming to with all this difficulty getting hired girls" were gumming her eyes with drowsiness. She sought to clear them by appealing to Calibree, in a manner of exaggerated liveliness, "Doctor, have the medical societies in Minnesota ever advocated legislation for help to nursing mothers?"

Calibree slowly revolved toward her. "Uh—I've never—uh—never looked into it. I don't believe much in getting mixed up in politics." He turned squarely from her and, peering earnestly at Kennicott, resumed, "Doctor, what's been your experience with unilateral pyelonephritis? Buckburn of Baltimore advocates decapsulation and nephrotomy, but seems to me——"

Not till after two did they rise. In the lee of the stonily mature trio Carol proceeded to the street fair which added mundane gaiety to the annual rites of the United and Fraternal Order of Beavers. Beavers, human Beavers, were everywhere: thirty-second degree Beavers in gray sack suits and decent derbies, more flippant Beavers in crash summer coats and straw hats, rustic Beavers in shirt sleeves and frayed suspenders; but whatever his caste-symbols, every Beaver was distinguished by an enormous shrimp-colored ribbon lettered in silver, "Sir Knight and Brother, U. F. O. B., Annual State Convention." On the motherly shirtwaist of each of their wives was a badge, "Sir Knight's Lady." The Duluth delegation had brought their famous Beaver amateur band, in Zouave costumes of green velvet jacket, blue trousers, and scarlet fez. The strange thing was that beneath their scarlet pride the Zouaves' faces remained those of American business-men, pink, smooth, eye-glassed; and as they stood playing in a circle, at the corner of Main Street and Second, as they tootled on fifes or with swelling cheeks blew into cornets, their eyes remained as owlish as though they were sitting at desks under the sign "This Is My Busy Day."

Carol had supposed that the Beavers were average citizens organized for the purposes of getting cheap life-insurance and playing poker at the lodge-rooms every second Wednesday, but she saw a large poster which proclaimed:

B E A V E R S
U. F. O. B.

The greatest influence for good citizenship in the country. The jolliest aggregation of red-blooded, open-handed, hustle-em-up good fellows in the world. Joralemon welcomes you to her hospitable city.

Kennicott read the poster and to Calibree admired, "Strong lodge, the Beavers. Never joined. Don't know but what I will."

Calibree adumbrated, "They're a good bunch. Good strong lodge. See that fellow there that's playing the snare drum? He's the smartest wholesale grocer in Duluth, they say. Guess it would be worth joining. Oh say, are you doing much insurance examining?"

They went on to the street fair.

Lining one block of Main Street were the "attractions"— two hot-dog stands, a lemonade and pop-corn stand, a merry-go-round, and booths in which balls might be thrown at rag dolls, if one wished to throw balls at rag dolls. The dignified delegates were shy of the booths, but country boys with brick-red necks and pale-blue ties and bright-yellow shoes, who had brought sweethearts into town in somewhat dusty and listed Fords, were wolfing sandwiches, drinking strawberry pop out of bottles, and riding the revolving crimson and gold horses. They shrieked and giggled; peanut-roasters whistled; the merry-go-round pounded out monotonous music; the barkers bawled, "Here's your chance—here's your chance—come on here, boy—come on here—give that girl a good time—give her a swell time—here's your chance to win a genuwine gold watch for five cents, half a dime, the twentieth part of a dollah!" The prairie sun jabbed the unshaded street with shafts that were like poisonous thorns; the tinny cornices above the brick stores were glaring; the dull breeze scattered dust on sweaty Beavers who crawled along in tight scorching new shoes, up two blocks and back, up two blocks and back, wondering what to do next, working at having a good time.

Carol's head ached as she trailed behind the unsmiling Calibrees along the block of booths. She chirruped at Kennicott, "Let's be wild! Let's ride on the merry-go-round and grab a gold ring!"

Kennicott considered it, and mumbled to Calibree, "Think you folks would like to stop and try a ride on the merry-go-round?"

Calibree considered it, and mumbled to his wife, "Think you'd like to stop and try a ride on the merry-go-round?"

Mrs. Calibree smiled in a washed-out manner, and sighed, "Oh no, I don't believe I care to much, but you folks go ahead and try it."

Calibree stated to Kennicott, "No, I don't believe we care to a whole lot, but you folks go ahead and try it."

Kennicott summarized the whole case against wildness: "Let's try it some other time, Carrie."

She gave it up. She looked at the town. She saw that in adventuring from Main Street, Gopher Prairie, to Main Street, Joralemon, she had not stirred. There were the same two-story brick groceries with lodge-signs above the awnings; the same one-story wooden millinery shop; the same fire-brick garages; the same prairie at the open end of the wide street; the same people wondering whether the levity of eating a hot-dog sandwich would break their taboos.

They reached Gopher Prairie at nine in the evening.

"You look kind of hot," said Kennicott.

"Yes."

"Joralemon is an enterprising town, don't you think so?" She broke. "No! I think it's an ash-heap."

"Why, Carrie!"

He worried over it for a week. While he ground his plate with his knife as he energetically pursued fragments of bacon, he peeped at her.

chapter 25

C ARRIE'S all right. She's finicky, but she'll get over it. But I wish she'd hurry up about it! What she can't understand is that a fellow practising medicine in a small town like this has got to cut out the highbrow stuff, and not spend all his time going to concerts and shining his shoes. (Not but what he might be just as good at all these intellectual and art things as some other folks, if he had the time for it!)" Dr. Will Kennicott was brooding in his office, during a free moment toward the end of the summer afternoon. He hunched down in his tilted desk-chair, undid a button of his shirt, glanced at the state news in the back of the *Journal of the American Medical Association*, dropped the magazine, leaned back with his right thumb hooked in the arm-hole of his vest and his left thumb stroking the back of his hair.

"By golly, she's taking an awful big chance, though. You'd expect her to learn by and by that I won't be a parlor lizard. She says we try to 'make her over.' Well, she's always trying to make me over, from a perfectly good M. D. into a damn poet with a socialist necktie! She'd have a fit if she knew how many women would be willing to cuddle up to Friend Will and comfort him, if he'd give 'em the chance! There's still a few dames that think the old man isn't so darn unattractive! I'm glad I've ducked all that woman-game since I've been married but—— Be switched if sometimes I don't feel tempted to shine up to some girl that has sense enough to take life as it is; some frau that doesn't want to talk Longfellow all the time, but just hold my hand and say, 'You look all in, honey. Take it easy, and don't try to talk.'

"Carrie thinks she's such a whale at analyzing folks. Giving the town the once-over. Telling us where we get off. Why, she'd simply turn up her toes and croak if she found out how much she doesn't know about the high old times a wise guy could have in this burg on the Q.T., if he wasn't faithful to his wife. But I am. At that, no matter what faults she's

298

got, there's nobody here, no, nor in Minn'aplus either, that's as nice-looking and square and bright as Carrie. She ought to of been an artist or a writer or one of those things. But once she took a shot at living here, she ought to stick by it. Pretty—— Lord yes. But cold. She simply doesn't know what passion is. She simply hasn't got an í-dea how hard it is for a full-blooded man to go on pretending to be satisfied with just being endured. It gets awful tiresome, having to feel like a criminal just because I'm normal. She's getting so she doesn't even care for my kissing her. Well——

"I guess I can weather it, same as I did earning my way through school and getting started in practise. But I wonder how long I can stand being an outsider in my own home?"

He sat up at the entrance of Mrs. Dave Dyer. She slumped into a chair and gasped with the heat. He chuckled, "Well, well, Maud, this is fine. Where's the subscription-list? What cause do I get robbed for, this trip?"

"I haven't any subscription-list, Will. I want to see you professionally."

"And you a Christian Scientist? Have you given that up? What next? New Thought or Spiritualism?"

"No, I have not given it up!"

"Strikes me it's kind of a knock on the sisterhood, you coming to see a doctor!"

"No, it isn't. It's just that my faith isn't strong enough yet. So there now! And besides, you *are* kind of consoling, Will. I mean as a man, not just as a doctor. You're so strong and placid."

He sat on the edge of his desk, coatless, his vest swinging open with the thick gold line of his watch-chain across the gap, his hand in his trousers pockets, his big arms bent and easy. As she purred he cocked an interested eye. Maud Dyer was neurotic, religiocentric, faded; her emotions were moist, and her figure was unsystematic—splendid thighs and arms, with thick ankles, and a body that was bulgy in the wrong places. But her milky skin was delicious, her eyes were alive, her chestnut hair shone, and there was a tender slope from her ears to the shadowy place below her jaw.

With unusual solicitude he uttered his stock phrase, "Well, what seems to be the matter, Maud?"

"I've got such a backache all the time. I'm afraid the organic trouble that you treated me for is coming back."

"Any definite signs of it?"

"N-no, but I think you'd better examine me."

"Nope. Don't believe it's necessary, Maud. To be honest, between old friends, I think your troubles are mostly imaginary. I can't really advise you to have an examination."

She flushed, looked out of the window. He was conscious that his voice was not impersonal and even.

She turned quickly. "Will, you always say my troubles are imaginary. Why can't you be scientific? I've been reading an article about these new nerve-specialists, and they claim that lots of 'imaginary' ailments, yes, and lots of real pain, too, are what they call psychoses, and they order a change in a woman's way of living so she can get on a higher plane——"

"Wait! Wait! Whoa-up! Wait now! Don't mix up your Christian Science and your psychology! They're two entirely different fads! You'll be mixing in socialism next! You're as bad as Carrie, with your 'psychoses.' Why, Good Lord, Maud, I could talk about neuroses and psychoses and inhibitions and repressions and complexes just as well as any damn specialist, if I got paid for it, if I was in the city and had the nerve to charge the fees that those fellows do. If a specialist stung you for a hundred-dollar consultation-fee and told you to go to New York to duck Dave's nagging, you'd do it, to save the hundred dollars! But you know me— I'm your neighbor—you see me mowing the lawn—you figure I'm just a plug general practitioner. If I said, 'Go to New York,' Dave and you would laugh your heads off and say, 'Look at the airs Will is putting on. What does he think he is?'

"As a matter of fact, you're right. You have a perfectly well-developed case of repression of sex instinct, and it raises the old Ned with your body. What you need is to get away from Dave and travel, yes, and go to every dog-gone kind of New Thought and Bahai and Swami and Hooptedoodle meeting you can find. I know it, well's you do. But how can I advise it? Dave would be up here taking my hide off. I'm willing to be family physician and priest and lawyer and plumber and wet-nurse, but I draw the line at making Dave loosen up on money. Too hard a job in weather like this! So, savvy, my dear? Believe it will rain if this heat keeps——"

"But, Will, he'd never give it to me on *my* say-so. He'd never let me go away. You know how Dave is: so jolly and liberal in society, and oh, just *loves* to match quarters, and such a perfect sport if he loses! But at home he pinches a nickel till the buffalo drips blood. I have to nag him for every single dollar."

"Sure, I know, but it's your fight, honey. Keep after him. He'd simply resent my butting in."

He crossed over and patted her shoulder. Outside the window, beyond the fly-screen that was opaque with dust and cottonwood lint, Main Street was hushed except for the impatient throb of a standing motor car. She took his firm hand, pressed his knuckles against her cheek.

"O Will, Dave is so mean and little and noisy—the shrimp! You're so calm. When he's cutting up at parties I see you standing back and watching him—the way a mastiff watches a terrier."

He fought for professional dignity with "Dave's not a bad fellow."

Lingeringly she released his hand. "Will, drop round by the house this evening and scold me. Make me be good and sensible. And I'm so lonely."

"If I did, Dave would be there, and we'd have to play cards. It's his evening off from the store."

"No. The clerk just got called to Corinth—mother sick. Dave will be in the store till midnight. Oh, come on over. There's some lovely beer on the ice, and we can sit and talk and be all cool and lazy. That wouldn't be wrong of us, *would* it!"

"No, no, course it wouldn't be wrong. But still, oughtn't to——" He saw Carol, slim black and ivory, cool, scornful of intrigue.

"All right. But I'll be so lonely."

Her throat seemed young, above her loose blouse of muslin and machine-lace.

"Tell you, Maud: I'll drop in just for a minute, if I happen to be called down that way."

"If you'd like," demurely. "O Will, I just want comfort. I know you're all married, and my, such a proud papa, and of course now—— If I could just sit near you in the dusk, and be quiet, and forget Dave! You *will* come?"

"Sure I will!"

"I'll expect you. I'll be lonely if you don't come! Good-by."

He cursed himself: "Darned fool, what 'd I promise to go for? I'll have to keep my promise, or she'll feel hurt. She's a good, decent, affectionate girl, and Dave's a cheap skate, all right. She's got more life to her than Carol has. All my fault, anyway. Why can't I be more cagey, like Calibree and McGanum and the rest of the doctors? Oh, I am, but Maud's such a demanding idiot. Deliberately bamboozling me into going up there tonight. Matter of principle: ought not to let her get away with it. I won't go. I'll call her up and tell her I won't go. Me, with Carrie at home, finest little woman in the world, and a messy-minded female like Maud Dyer— no, *sir!* Though there's no need of hurting her feelings. I may just drop in for a second, to tell her I can't stay. All my fault anyway; ought never to have started in and jollied Maud along in the old days. If it's my fault, I've got no right to punish Maud. I could just drop in for a second and then pretend I had a country call and beat it. Damn nuisance, though, having to fake up excuses. Lord, why can't the women let you alone? Just because once or twice, seven hundred million years ago, you were a poor fool, why can't they let you forget it? Maud's own fault. I'll stay strictly away. Take Carrie to the movies, and forget Maud. . . . But it would be kind of hot at the movies tonight."

He fled from himself. He rammed on his hat, threw his coat over his arm, banged the door, locked it, tramped downstairs. "I won't go!" he said sturdily and, as he said it, he would have given a good deal to know whether he was going.

He was refreshed, as always, by the familiar windows and faces. It restored his soul to have Sam Clark trustingly bellow, "Better come down to the lake this evening and have a swim, doc. Ain't you going to open your cottage at all, this summer? By golly, we miss you." He noted the progress on the new garage. He had triumphed in the laying of every course of bricks; in them he had seen the growth of the town. His pride was ushered back to its throne by the respectfulness of Oley Sundquist: "Evenin,' doc! The woman is a lot better. That was swell medicine you gave her." He was calmed by the mechanicalness of the tasks at home: burning the gray web of a tent-worm on the wild cherry tree, sealing with gum a cut in the right front tire of the car, sprinkling the road before the house. The hose was cool to his hands. As the bright arrows fell with a faint puttering sound, a crescent of blackness was formed in the gray dust.

Dave Dyer came along.

"Where going, Dave?"

"Down to the store. Just had supper."

"But Thursday's your night off."

"Sure, but Pete went home. His mother's supposed to be sick. Gosh, these clerks you get nowadays—overpay 'em and then they won't work!"

"That's tough, Dave. You'll have to work clear up till twelve, then."

"Yup. Better drop in and have a cigar, if you're downtown."

"Well, I may, at that. May have to go down and see Mrs. Champ Perry. She's ailing. So long, Dave."

Kennicott had not yet entered the house. He was conscious that Carol was near him, that she was important, that he was afraid of her disapproval; but he was content to be alone. When he had finished sprinkling he strolled into the house, up to the baby's room, and cried to Hugh, "Story-time for the old man, eh?"

Carol was in a low chair, framed and haloed by the window behind her, an image in pale gold. The baby curled in her lap, his head on her arm, listening with gravity while she sang from Gene Field:

'Tis little Luddy-Dud in the morning—
'Tis little Luddy-Dud at night;
And all day long
'Tis the same dear song,
Of that growing, crowing, knowing little sprite.

Kennicott was enchanted.

"Maud Dyer? I should say not!"

When the current maid bawled up-stairs, "Supper on de table!" Kennicott was upon his back, flapping his hands in the earnest effort to be a seal, thrilled by the strength with which his son kicked him. He slipped his arm about Carol's shoulder; he went down to supper rejoicing that he was cleansed of perilous stuff. While Carol was putting the baby to bed he sat on the front steps. Nat Hicks, tailor and roué, came to sit beside him. Between waves of his hand as he drove off mosquitos, Nat whispered, "Say, doc, you don't feel like imagining you're a bacheldore again, and coming out for a Time tonight, do you?"

"As how?"

"You know this new dressmaker, Mrs. Swiftwaite?—swell dame with blondine hair? Well, she's a pretty good goer. Me and Harry Haydock are going to take her and that fat wren that works in the Bon Ton—nice kid, too—on an auto ride tonight. Maybe we'll drive down to that farm Harry bought. We're taking some beer, and some of the smoothest rye you ever laid tongue to. I'm not predicting none, but if we don't have a picnic, I'll miss my guess."

"Go to it. No skin off my ear, Nat. Think I want to be fifth wheel in the coach?"

"No, but look here: The little Swiftwaite has a friend with her from Winona, dandy looker and some gay bird, and Harry and me thought maybe you'd like to sneak off for one evening."

"No—no——"

"Rats now, doc, forget your everlasting dignity. You used to be a pretty good sport yourself, when you were foot-free."

It may have been the fact that Mrs. Swiftwaite's friend remained to Kennicott an ill-told rumor, it may have been Carol's voice, wistful in the pallid evening as she sang to Hugh, it may have been natural and commendable virtue, but certainly he was positive:

"Nope. I'm married for keeps. Don't pretend to be any saint. Like to get out and raise Cain and shoot a few drinks. But a fellow owes a duty—— Straight now, won't you feel like a sneak when you come back to the missus after your jamboree?"

"Me? My moral in life is, 'What they don't know won't hurt 'em none.' The way to handle wives, like the fellow says, is to catch 'em early, treat 'em rough, and tell 'em nothing!"

"Well, that's your business, I suppose. But I can't get away with it. Besides that—way I figure it, this illicit love-making is the one game that you always lose at. If you do lose, you feel foolish; and if you win, as soon as you find out how little it is that you've been scheming for, why then you lose worse than ever. Nature stinging us, as usual. But at that, I guess a lot of wives in this burg would be surprised if they knew everything that goes on behind their backs, eh, Nattie?"

"*Would* they! Say, boy! If the good wives knew what some of the boys get away with when they go down to the Cities, why, they'd throw a fit! Sure you won't come, doc? Think of getting all cooled off by a good long drive, and then the lov-e-ly Swiftwaite's white hand mixing you a good stiff highball!"

"Nope. Nope. Sorry. Guess I won't," grumbled Kennicott.

He was glad that Nat showed signs of going. But he was restless. He heard Carol on the stairs. "Come have a seat— have the whole earth!" he shouted jovially.

She did not answer his joviality. She sat on the porch, rocked silently, then sighed, "So many mosquitoes out here. You haven't had the screen fixed."

As though he was testing her he said quietly, "Head aching again?"

"Oh, not much, but—— This maid is *so* slow to learn. I have to show her everything. I had to clean most of the silver myself. And Hugh was so bad all afternoon. He whined so. Poor soul, he was hot, but he did wear me out."

"Uh—— You usually want to get out. Like to walk down to the lake shore? (The girl can stay home.) Or go to the movies? Come on, let's go to the movies! Or shall we jump in the car and run out to Sam's, for a swim?"

"If you don't mind, dear, I'm afraid I'm rather tired."

"Why don't you sleep down-stairs tonight, on the couch? Be cooler. I'm going to bring down my mattress. Come on! Keep the old man company. Can't tell—I might get scared of burglars. Lettin' little fellow like me stay all alone by himself!"

"It's sweet of you to think of it, but I like my own room so much. But you go ahead and do it, dear. Why don't you sleep on the couch, instead of putting your mattress on the floor? Well—— I believe I'll run in and read for just a second —want to look at the last *Vogue*—and then perhaps I'll go by-by. Unless you want me, dear? Of course if there's anything you really *want* me for——?"

"No. No. . . . Matter of fact, I really ought to run down and see Mrs. Champ Perry. She's ailing. So you skip in and—— May drop in at the drug store. If I'm not home when you get sleepy, don't wait up for me."

He kissed her, rambled off, nodded to Jim Howland, stopped indifferently to speak to Mrs. Terry Gould. But his heart was racing, his stomach was constricted. He walked more slowly. He reached Dave Dyer's yard. He glanced in. On the porch, sheltered by a wild-grape vine, was the figure of a woman in white. He heard the swing-couch creak as she sat up abruptly, peered, then leaned back and pretended to relax.

"Be nice to have some cool beer. Just drop in for a second," he insisted, as he opened the Dyer gate.

II

Mrs. Bogart was calling upon Carol, protected by Aunt Bessie Smail.

"Have you heard about this awful woman that's supposed to have come here to do dressmaking—a Mrs. Swiftwaite—awful peroxide blonde?" moaned Mrs. Bogart. "They say there's some of the awfullest goings-on at her house—mere boys and old gray-headed rips sneaking in there evenings and drinking licker and every kind of goings-on. We women can't never realize the carnal thoughts in the hearts of men. I tell you, even though I been acquainted with Will Kennicott almost since he was a mere boy, seems like, I wouldn't trust even him! Who knows what designin' women might tempt him! Especially a doctor, with women rushin' in to see him at his office and all! You know I never hint around, but haven't you felt that——"

Carol was furious. "I don't pretend that Will has no faults. But one thing I do know: He's as simple-hearted about what you call 'goings-on' as a babe. And if he ever were such a sad dog as to look at another woman, I certainly hope he'd have spirit enough to do the tempting, and not be coaxed into it, as in your depressing picture!"

"Why, what a wicked thing to say, Carrie!" from Aunt Bessie.

"No, I mean it! Oh, of course, I don't mean it! But—— I know every thought in his head so well that he couldn't hide anything even if he wanted to. Now this morning—— He was out late, last night; he had to go see Mrs. Perry, who is ailing, and then fix a man's hand, and this morning he was so quiet and thoughtful at breakfast and——" She leaned forward, breathed dramatically to the two perched harpies, "What do you suppose he was thinking of?"

"What?" trembled Mrs. Bogart.

"Whether the grass needs cutting, probably! There, there! Don't mind my naughtiness. I have some fresh-made raisin cookies for you."

chapter 26

C AROL'S liveliest interest was in her walks with the baby. Hugh wanted to know what the box-elder tree said, and what the Ford garage said, and what the big cloud said, and she told him, with a feeling that she was not in the least making up stories, but discovering the souls of things. They had an especial fondness for the hitching-post in front of the mill. It was a brown post, stout and agreeable; the smooth leg of it held the sunlight, while its neck, grooved by hitching-straps, tickled one's fingers. Carol had never been awake to the earth except as a show of changing color and great satisfying masses; she had lived in people and in ideas about having ideas; but Hugh's questions made her attentive to the comedies of sparrows, robins, blue jays, yellowhammers; she regained her pleasure in the arching flight of swallows, and added to it a solicitude about their nests and family squabbles.

She forgot her seasons of boredom. She said to Hugh, "We're two fat disreputable old minstrels roaming round the world," and he echoed her, "Roamin' round—roamin' round."

The high adventure, the secret place to which they both fled joyously, was the house of Miles and Bea and Olaf Bjornstam.

Kennicott steadily disapproved of the Bjornstams. He protested, "What do you want to talk to that crank for?" He hinted that a former "Swede hired girl" was low company for the son of Dr. Will Kennicott. She did not explain. She did not quite understand it herself; did not know that in the Bjornstams she found her friends, her club, her sympathy, and her ration of blessed cynicism. For a time the gossip of Juanita Haydock and the Jolly Seventeen had been a refuge from the droning of Aunt Bessie, but the relief had not continued. The young matrons made her nervous. They talked so loud, always so loud. They filled a room with clashing cackle; their jests and gags they repeated nine times over. Pollock, Vida, and every one save Mrs. Dr. Westlake and the friends whom she did not clearly know as friends—the Bjornstams.

To Hugh, the Red Swede was the most heroic and powerful person in the world. With unrestrained adoration he trotted after while Miles fed the cows, chased his one pig—an animal of lax and migratory instincts—or dramatically slaughtered a chicken. And to Hugh, Olaf was lord among mortal men, less stalwart than the old monarch, King Miles, but more understanding of the relations and values of things, of small sticks, lone playing-cards, and irretrievably injured hoops.

Carol saw, though she did not admit, that Olaf was not only more beautiful than her own dark child, but more gracious. Olaf was a Norse chieftain: straight, sunny-haired, large-limbed, resplendently amiable to his subjects. Hugh was a vulgarian; a bustling business man. It was Hugh that bounced and said "Let's play"; Olaf that opened luminous blue eyes and agreed "All right," in condescending gentleness. If Hugh batted him—and Hugh did bat him—Olaf was unafraid but shocked. In magnificent solitude he marched toward the house, while Hugh bewailed his sin and the overclouding of august favor.

The two friends played with an imperial chariot which Miles had made out of a starch-box and four red spools; together they stuck switches into a mouse-hole, with vast satisfaction though entirely without known results.

Bea, the chubby and humming Bea, impartially gave cookies and scoldings to both children, and if Carol refused a cup of coffee and a wafer of buttered *knäckebröd*, she was desolated.

Miles had done well with his dairy. He had six cows, two hundred chickens, a cream separator, a Ford truck. In the spring he had built a two-room addition to his shack. That illustrious building was to Hugh a carnival. Uncle Miles did the most spectacular, unexpected things: ran up the ladder; stood on the ridge-pole, waving a hammer and singing something about "To arms, my citizens"; nailed shingles faster than Aunt Bessie could iron handkerchiefs; and lifted a two-by-six with Hugh riding on one end and Olaf on the other. Uncle Miles's most ecstatic trick was to make figures not on paper but right on a new pine board, with the broadest softest pencil in the world. There was a thing worth seeing!

The tools! In his office Father had tools fascinating in their shininess and curious shapes, but they were sharp, they were something called sterized, and they distinctly were not for boys to touch. In fact it was a good dodge to volunteer "I must not touch," when you looked at the tools on the glass shelves in Father's office. But Uncle Miles, who was a person altogether superior to Father, let you handle all his kit except the saws. There was a hammer with a silver head; there was a metal thing like a big L; there was a magic instrument, very precious, made out of costly red wood and gold, with a tube which contained a drop—no, it wasn't a drop, it was a nothing, which lived in the water, but the nothing *looked* like a drop, and it ran in a frightened way up and down the tube, no matter how cautiously you tilted the magic instrument. And there were nails, very different and clever—big valiant spikes, middle-sized ones which were not very interesting, and shingle-nails much jollier than the fussed-up fairies in the yellow book.

II

While he had worked on the addition Miles had talked frankly to Carol. He admitted now that so long as he stayed in Gopher Prairie he would remain a pariah. Bea's Lutheran friends were as much offended by his agnostic gibes as the merchants by his radicalism. "And I can't seem to keep my mouth shut. I think I'm being a baa-lamb, and not springing any theories wilder than 'c-a-t spells cat,' but when folks have gone, I re'lize I've been stepping on their pet religious corns. Oh, the mill foreman keeps dropping in, and that Danish shoemaker, and one fellow from Elder's factory, and a few Svenskas, but you know Be: big good-hearted wench like her wants a lot of folks around—likes to fuss over 'em—never satisfied unless she's tiring herself out making coffee for somebody.

"Once she kidnapped me and drug me to the Methodist Church. I goes in, pious as Widow Bogart, and sits still and never cracks a smile while the preacher is favoring us with his misinformation on evolution. But afterwards, when the old stalwarts were pumphandling everybody at the door and calling 'em 'Brother' and 'Sister,' they let me sail right by with nary a clinch. They figure I'm the town badman. Always will be, I guess. It'll have to be Olaf who goes on. And sometimes—— Blamed if I don't feel like coming out and saying, 'I've been conservative. Nothing to it. Now I'm going to start something in these rotten one-horse lumber-

camps west of town.' But Be's got me hypnotized. Lord, Mrs.
Kennicott, do you re'lize what a jolly, square, faithful woman
she is? And I love Olaf—— Oh well, I won't go and get
sentimental on you.

"Course I've had thoughts of pulling up stakes and going
West. Maybe if they didn't know it beforehand, they wouldn't
find out I'd ever been guilty of trying to think for myself. But
—oh, I've worked hard, and built up this dairy business, and
I hate to start all over again, and move Be and the kid into
another one-room shack. That's how they get us! Encourage
us to be thrifty and own our own houses, and then, by
golly, they've got us; they know we won't dare risk everything by committing lez—what is it? lez majesty?—I mean
they know we won't be hinting around that if we had a co-
operative bank, we could get along without Stowbody.
Well——As long as I can sit and play pinochle with Be,
and tell whoppers to Olaf about his daddy's adventures in
the woods, and how he snared a wapaloosie and knew Paul
Bunyan, why, I don't mind being a bum. It's just for them
that I mind. Say! Say! Don't whisper a word to Be, but when
I get this addition done, I'm going to buy her a phonograph!"
He did.

While she was busy with the activities her work-hungry
muscles found—washing, ironing, mending, baking, dusting,
preserving, plucking a chicken, painting the sink; tasks
which, because she was Miles's full partner, were exciting and
creative—Bea listened to the phonograph records with rapture like that of cattle in a warm stable. The addition gave
her a kitchen with a bedroom above. The original one-room
shack was now a living-room, with the phonograph, a
genuine leather-upholstered golden-oak rocker, and a picture
of Governor John Johnson.

In late July Carol went to the Bjornstams' desirous of a
chance to express her opinion of Beavers and Calibrees and
Joralemons. She found Olaf abed, restless from a slight fever,
and Bea flushed and dizzy but trying to keep up her work.
She lured Miles aside and worried:

"They don't look at all well. What's the matter?"

"Their stomachs are out of whack. I wanted to call in Doc
Kennicott, but Be thinks the doc doesn't like us—she thinks
maybe he's sore because you come down here. But I'm getting worried."

"I'm going to call the doctor at once."

She yearned over Olaf. His lambent eyes were stupid, he moaned, he rubbed his forehead.

"Have they been eating something that's been bad for them?" she fluttered to Miles.

"Might be bum water. I'll tell you: We used to get our water at Oscar Eklund's place, over across the street, but Oscar kept dinging at me, and hinting I was a tightwad not to dig a well of my own. One time he said, 'Sure, you socialists are great on divvying up other folks' money—and water!' I knew if he kept it up there'd be a fuss, and I ain't safe to have around, once a fuss starts; I'm likely to forget myself and let loose with a punch in the snoot. I offered to pay Oscar but he refused—he'd rather have the chance to kid me. So I starts getting water down at Mrs. Fageros's, in the hollow there, and I don't believe it's real good. Figuring to dig my own well this fall."

One scarlet word was before Carol's eyes while she listened. She fled to Kennicott's office. He gravely heard her out, nodded, said, "Be right over."

He examined Bea and Olaf. He shook his head. "Yes. Looks to me like typhoid."

"Golly, I've seen typhoid in lumber-camps," groaned Miles, all the strength dripping out of him. "Have they got it very bad?"

"Oh, we'll take good care of them," said Kennicott, and for the first time in their acquaintance he smiled on Miles and clapped his shoulder.

"Won't you need a nurse?" demanded Carol.

"Why——" To Miles, Kennicott hinted, "Couldn't you get Bea's cousin, Tina?"

"She's down at the old folks', in the country."

"Then let me do it!" Carol insisted. "They need some one to cook for them, and isn't it good to give them sponge baths, in typhoid?"

"Yes. All right." Kennicott was automatic; he was the official, the physician. "I guess probably it would be hard to get a nurse here in town just now. Mrs. Stiver is busy with an obstetrical case, and that town nurse of yours is off on vacation, ain't she? All right, Bjornstam can spell you at night."

All week, from eight each morning till midnight, Carol fed them, bathed them, smoothed sheets, took temperatures. Miles refused to let her cook. Terrified, pallid, noiseless in stocking feet, he did the kitchen work and the sweeping, his

big red hands awkwardly careful. Kennicott came in three
times a day, unchangingly tender and hopeful in the sick-
room, evenly polite to Miles.

Carol understood how great was her love for her friends.
It bore her through; it made her arm steady and tireless to
bathe them. What exhausted her was the sight of Bea and
Olaf turned into flaccid invalids, uncomfortably flushed after
taking food, begging for the healing of sleep at night.

During the second week Olaf's powerful legs were
flabby. Spots of a viciously delicate pink came out on his chest
and back. His cheeks sank. He looked frightened. His tongue
was brown and revolting. His confident voice dwindled to
a bewildered murmur, ceaseless and racking.

Bea had stayed on her feet too long at the beginning. The
moment Kennicott had ordered her to bed she had begun to
collapse. One early evening she startled them by screaming,
in an intense abdominal pain, and within half an hour she
was in a delirium. Till dawn Carol was with her, and not all
of Bea's groping through the blackness of half-delirious
pain was so pitiful to Carol as the way in which Miles silently
peered into the room from the top of the narrow stairs.
Carol slept three hours next morning, and ran back. Bea was
altogether delirious but she muttered nothing save, "Olaf—
ve have such a good time——"

At ten, while Carol was preparing an ice-bag in the kitchen,
Miles answered a knock. At the front door she saw Vida
Sherwin, Maud Dyer, and Mrs. Zitterel, wife of the Baptist
pastor. They were carrying grapes, and women's-magazines,
magazines with high-colored pictures and optimistic fiction.

"We just heard your wife was sick. We've come to see
if there isn't something we can do," chirruped Vida.

Miles looked steadily at the three women. "You're too
late. You can't do nothing now. Bea's always kind of hoped
that you folks would come see her. She wanted to have a
chance and be friends. She used to sit waiting for somebody
to knock. I've seen her sitting here, waiting. Now—— Oh,
you ain't worth God-damning." He shut the door.

All day Carol watched Olaf's strength oozing. He was
emaciated. His ribs were grim clear lines, his skin was
clammy, his pulse was feeble but terrifyingly rapid. It beat
—beat—beat in a drum-roll of death. Late that afternoon
he sobbed, and died.

Bea did not know it. She was delirious. Next morning,
when she went, she did not know that Olaf would no longer

swing his lath sword on the door-step, no longer rule his subjects of the cattle-yard; that Miles's son would not go East to college.

Miles, Carol, Kennicott were silent. They washed the bodies together, their eyes veiled.

"Go home now and sleep. You're pretty tired. I can't ever pay you back for what you done," Miles whispered to Carol.

"Yes. But I'll be back here tomorrow. Go with you to the funeral," she said laboriously.

When the time for the funeral came, Carol was in bed, collapsed. She assumed that neighbors would go. They had not told her that word of Miles's rebuff to Vida had spread through town, a cyclonic fury.

It was only by chance that, leaning on her elbow in bed, she glanced through the window and saw the funeral of Bea and Olaf. There was no music, no carriages. There was only Miles Bjornstam, in his black wedding-suit, walking quite alone, head down, behind the shabby hearse that bore the bodies of his wife and baby.

An hour after, Hugh came into her room crying, and when she said as cheerily as she could, "What is it, dear?" he besought, "Mummy, I want to go play with Olaf."

That afternoon Juanita Haydock dropped in to brighten Carol. She said, "Too bad about this Bea that was your hired girl. But I don't waste any sympathy on that man of hers. Everybody says he drank too much, and treated his family awful, and that's how they got sick."

chapter 27

A LETTER from Raymie Wutherspoon, in France, said that he had been sent to the front, been slightly wounded, been made a captain. From Vida's pride Carol sought to draw a stimulant to rouse her from depression.

Miles had sold his dairy. He had several thousand dollars. To Carol he said good-by with a mumbled word, a harsh hand-shake, "Going to buy a farm in northern Alberta—far off from folks as I can get." He turned sharply away, but he did not walk with his former spring. His shoulders seemed old.

It was said that before he went he cursed the town. There was talk of arresting him, of riding him on a rail. It was rumored that at the station old Champ Perry rebuked him, "You better not come back here. We've got respect for your dead, but we haven't got any for a blasphemer and a traitor that won't do anything for his country and only bought one Liberty Bond."

Some of the people who had been at the station declared that Miles made some dreadful seditious retort: something about loving German workmen more than American bankers; but others asserted that he couldn't find one word with which to answer the veteran; that he merely sneaked up on the platform of the train. He must have felt guilty, everybody agreed, for as the train left town, a farmer saw him standing in the vestibule and looking out.

His house—with the addition which he had built four months ago—was very near the track on which his train passed.

When Carol went there, for the last time, she found Olaf's chariot with its red spool wheels standing in the sunny corner beside the stable. She wondered if a quick eye could have noticed it from a train.

That day and that week she went reluctantly to Red Cross work; she stitched and packed silently, while Vida read the war bulletins. And she said nothing at all when Kennicott commented, "From what Champ says, I guess Bjornstam was a bad egg, after all. In spite of Bea, don't know but what the citizens' committee ought to have forced him to be patriotic —let on like they could send him to jail if he didn't volunteer and come through for bonds and the Y.M.C.A. They've worked that stunt fine with all these German farmers."

II

She found no inspiration but she did find a dependable kindness in Mrs. Westlake, and at last she yielded to the old woman's receptivity and had relief in sobbing the story of Bea.

Guy Pollock she often met on the street, but he was merely a pleasant voice which said things about Charles Lamb and sunsets.

Her most positive experience was the revelation of Mrs.

Flickerbaugh, the tall, thin, twitchy wife of the attorney. Carol encountered her at the drug store.

"Walking?" snapped Mrs. Flickerbaugh.

"Why, yes."

"Humph. Guess you're the only female in this town that retains the use of her legs. Come home and have a cup o' tea with me."

Because she had nothing else to do, Carol went. But she was uncomfortable in the presence of the amused stares which Mrs. Flickerbaugh's raiment drew. Today, in reeking early August, she wore a man's cap, a skinny fur like a dead cat, a necklace of imitation pearls, a scabrous satin blouse, and a thick cloth skirt hiked up in front.

"Come in. Sit down. Stick the baby in that rocker. Hope you don't mind the house looking like a rat's nest. You don't like this town. Neither do I," said Mrs. Flickerbaugh.

"Why——"

"Course you don't!"

"Well then, I don't! But I'm sure that some day I'll find some solution. Probably I'm a hexagonal peg. Solution: find the hexagonal hole." Carol was very brisk.

"How do you know you ever will find it?"

"There's Mrs. Westlake. She's naturally a big-city woman—she ought to have a lovely old house in Philadelphia or Boston—but she escapes by being absorbed in reading."

"You be satisfied to never do anything but read?"

"No, but—— Heavens, one can't go on hating a town always!"

"Why not? I can! I've hated it for thirty-two years. I'll die here—and I'll hate it till I die. I ought to have been a business woman. I had a good deal of talent for tending to figures. All gone now. Some folks think I'm crazy. Guess I am. Sit and grouch. Go to church and sing hymns. Folks think I'm religious. Tut! Trying to forget washing and ironing and mending socks. Want an office of my own, and sell things. Julius never hear of it. Too late."

Carol sat on the gritty couch, and sank into fear. Could this drabness of life keep up forever, then? Would she some day so despise herself and her neighbors that she too would walk Main Street an old skinny eccentric woman in a mangy cat's-fur? As she crept home she felt that the trap had finally closed. She went into the house, a frail small woman, still winsome but hopeless of eye as she staggered with the weight of the drowsy boy in her arms.

She sat alone on the porch, that evening. It seemed that Kennicott had to make a professional call on Mrs. Dave Dyer.

Under the stilly boughs and the black gauze of dusk the street was meshed in silence. There was but the hum of motor tires crunching the road, the creak of a rocker on the Howlands' porch, the slap of a hand attacking a mosquito, a heat-weary conversation starting and dying, the precise rhythm of crickets, the thud of moths against the screen—sounds that were a distilled silence. It was a street beyond the end of the world, beyond the boundaries of hope. Though she should sit here forever, no brave procession, no one who was interesting, would be coming by. It was tediousness made tangible, a street builded of lassitude and of futility.

Myrtle Cass appeared, with Cy Bogart. She giggled and bounced when Cy tickled her ear in village love. They strolled with the half-dancing gait of lovers, kicking their feet out sideways or shuffling a dragging jig, and the concrete walk sounded to the broken two-four rhythm. Their voices had a dusky turbulence. Suddenly, to the woman rocking on the porch of the doctor's house, the night came alive, and she felt that everywhere in the darkness panted an ardent quest which she was missing as she sank back to wait for—— There must be something.

chapter 28

IT WAS at a supper of the Jolly Seventeen in August that Carol heard of "Elizabeth," from Mrs. Dave Dyer.

Carol was fond of Maud Dyer, because she had been particularly agreeable lately; had obviously repented of the nervous distaste which she had once shown. Maud patted her hand when they met, and asked about Hugh.

Kennicott said that he was "kind of sorry for the girl, some ways; she's too darn emotional, but still, Dave is sort of mean to her." He was polite to poor Maud when they all went down to the cottages for a swim. Carol was proud of that sympathy in him, and now she took pains to sit with their new friend.

Mrs. Dyer was bubbling, "Oh, have you folks heard about this young fellow that's just come to town that the boys call 'Elizabeth'? He's working in Nat Hicks's tailor shop. I bet he doesn't make eighteen a week, but my! isn't he the perfect lady though! He talks so refined, and oh, the lugs he puts on—belted coat, and piqué collar with a gold pin, and socks to match his necktie, and honest—you won't believe this, but I got it straight—this fellow, you know he's staying at Mrs. Gurrey's punk old boarding-house, and they say he asked Mrs. Gurrey if he ought to put on a dress-suit for supper! Imagine! Can you beat that? And him nothing but a Swede tailor—Erik Valborg his name is. But he used to be in a tailor shop in Minneapolis (they do say he's a smart needle-pusher, at that) and he tries to let on that he's a regular city fellow. They say he tries to make people think he's a poet—carries books around and pretends to read 'em. Myrtle Cass says she met him at a dance, and he was mooning around all over the place, and he asked her did she like flowers and poetry and music and everything; he spieled like he was a regular United States Senator; and Myrtle—she's a devil, that girl, ha! ha!—she kidded him along, and got him going, and honest, what d'you think he said? He said he didn't find any intellectual companionship in this town. Can you *beat* it? Imagine! And him a Swede tailor! My! And they say he's the most awful mollycoddle—looks just like a girl. The boys call him 'Elizabeth,' and they stop him and ask about the books he lets on to have read, and he goes and tells them, and they take it all in and jolly him terribly, and he never gets onto the fact they're kidding him. Oh, I think it's just *too* funny!"

The Jolly Seventeen laughed, and Carol laughed with them. Mrs. Jack Elder added that this Erik Valborg had confided to Mrs. Gurrey that he would "love to design clothes for women." Imagine! Mrs. Harvey Dillon had had a glimpse of him, but honestly, she'd thought he was awfully handsome. This was instantly controverted by Mrs. B. J. Gougerling, wife of the banker. Mrs. Gougerling had had, she reported, a good look at this Valborg fellow. She and B. J. had been motoring, and passed "Elizabeth" out by McGruder's Bridge. He was wearing the awfullest clothes, with the waist pinched in like a girl's. He was sitting on a rock doing nothing, but when he heard the Gougerling car coming he snatched a book out of his pocket, and as they went by he pretended to be reading it, to show off. And he wasn't really good-looking—just kind of soft, as B. J. had pointed out.

When the husbands came they joined in the exposé. "My name is Elizabeth. I'm the celebrated musical tailor. The skirts fall for me by the thou. Do I get some more veal loaf?" merrily shrieked Dave Dyer. He had some admirable stories about the tricks the town youngsters had played on Valborg. They had dropped a decaying perch into his pocket. They had pinned on his back a sign, "I'm the prize boob, kick me."

Glad of any laughter, Carol joined the frolic, and surprised them by crying, "Dave, I do think you're the dearest thing since you got your hair cut!" That was an excellent sally. Everybody applauded. Kennicott looked proud.

She decided that sometime she really must go out of her way to pass Hicks's shop and see this freak.

II

She was at Sunday morning service at the Baptist Church, in a solemn row with her husband, Hugh, Uncle Whittier, Aunt Bessie.

Despite Aunt Bessie's nagging the Kennicotts rarely attended church. The doctor asserted, "Sure, religion is a fine influence —got to have it to keep the lower classes in order—fact, it's the only thing that appeals to a lot of those fellows and makes 'em respect the rights of property. And I guess this theology is O.K.; lot of wise old coots figured it all out, and they knew more about it than we do." He believed in the Christian religion, and never thought about it; he believed in the church, and seldom went near it; he was shocked by Carol's lack of faith, and wasn't quite sure what was the nature of the faith that she lacked.

Carol herself was an uneasy and dodging agnostic.

When she ventured to Sunday School and heard the teachers droning that the genealogy of Shamsherai was a valuable ethical problem for children to think about; when she experimented with Wednesday prayer-meeting and listened to store-keeping elders giving their unvarying weekly testimony in primitive erotic symbols and such gory Chaldean phrases as "washed in the blood of the lamb" and "a vengeful God"; when Mrs. Bogart boasted that through his boyhood she had made Cy confess nightly upon the basis of the Ten

Commandments; then Carol was dismayed to find the Christian religion, in America, in the twentieth century, as abnormal as Zoroastrianism—without the splendor. But when she went to church suppers and felt the friendliness, saw the gaiety with which the sisters served cold ham and scalloped potatoes; when Mrs. Champ Perry cried to her, on an afternoon call, "My dear, if you just knew how happy it makes you to come into abiding grace," then Carol found the humanness behind the sanguinary and alien theology. Always she perceived that the churches—Methodist, Baptist, Congregational, Catholic, all of them—which had seemed so unimportant to the judge's home in her childhood, so isolated from the city struggle in St. Paul, were still, in Gopher Prairie, the strongest of the forces compelling respectability.

This August Sunday she had been tempted by the announcement that the Reverend Edmund Zitterel would preach on the topic "America, Face Your Problems!" With the great war, workmen in every nation showing a desire to control industries, Russia hinting a leftward revolution against Kerensky, woman suffrage coming, there seemed to be plenty of problems for the Reverend Mr. Zitterel to call on America to face. Carol gathered her family and trotted off behind Uncle Whittier.

The congregation faced the heat with informality. Men with highly plastered hair, so painfully shaved that their faces looked sore, removed their coats, sighed, and unbuttoned two buttons of their uncreased Sunday vests. Large-bosomed, white-bloused, hot-necked, spectacled matrons—the Mothers in Israel, pioneers and friends of Mrs. Champ Perry—waved their palm-leaf fans in a steady rhythm. Abashed boys slunk into the rear pews and giggled, while milky little girls, up front with their mothers, self-consciously kept from turning around.

The church was half barn and half Gopher Prairie parlor. The streaky brown wallpaper was broken in its dismal sweep only by framed texts, "Come unto Me" and "The Lord Is My Shepherd," by a list of hymns, and by a crimson and green diagram, staggeringly drawn upon hemp-colored paper, indicating the alarming ease with which a young man may descend from Palaces of Pleasure and the House of Pride to Eternal Damnation. But the varnished oak pews and the new red carpet and the three large chairs on the platform, behind the bare reading-stand, were all of a rocking-chair comfort.

Carol was civic and neighborly and commendable today. She beamed and bowed. She trolled out with the others the hymn:

> How pleasant 'tis on Sabbath morn
> To gather in the church,
> And there I'll have no carnal thoughts,
> Nor sin shall me besmirch.

With a rustle of starched linen skirts and stiff shirt-fronts, the congregation sat down, and gave heed to the Reverend Mr. Zitterel. The priest was a thin, swart, intense young man with a bang. He wore a black sack suit and a lilac tie. He smote the enormous Bible on the reading-stand, vociferated, "Come, let us reason together," delivered a prayer informing Almighty God of the news of the past week, and began to reason.

It proved that the only problems which America had to face were Mormonism and Prohibition:

"Don't let any of these self-conceited fellows that are always trying to stir up trouble deceive you with the belief that there's anything to all these smart-aleck movements to let the unions and the Farmers' Nonpartisan League kill all our initiative and enterprise by fixing wages and prices. There isn't any movement that amounts to a whoop without it's got a moral background. And let me tell you that while folks are fussing about what they call 'economics' and 'socialism' and 'science' and a lot of things that are nothing in the world but a disguise for atheism, the Old Satan is busy spreading his secret net and tentacles out there in Utah, under his guise of Joe Smith or Brigham Young or whoever their leaders happen to be today, it doesn't make any difference, and they're making game of the Old Bible that has led this American people through its manifold trials and tribulations to its firm position as the fulfilment of the prophecies and the recognized leader of all nations. 'Sit thou on my right hand till I make thine enemies the footstool of my feet,' said the Lord of Hosts, Acts II, the thirty-fourth verse—and let me tell you right now, you got to get up a good deal earlier in the morning than you get up even when you're going fishing, if you want to be smarter than the Lord, who has shown us the straight and narrow way, and he that passeth therefrom is in eternal peril and, to return to this vital and terrible subject of Mormonism—and as I say, it is terrible to realize how little attention is given to this evil right here in our midst and on

our very doorstep, as it were—it's a shame and a disgrace
that the Congress of these United States spends all its time
talking about inconsequential financial matters that ought
to be left to the Treasury Department, as I understand it, instead of arising in their might and passing a law that any
one admitting he is a Mormon shall simply be deported and
as it were kicked out of this free country in which we
haven't got any room for polygamy and the tyrannies of
Satan.

"And, to digress for a moment, especially as there are
more of them in this state than there are Mormons, though
you never can tell what will happen with this vain generation of young girls, that think more about wearing silk stockings than about minding their mothers and learning to bake
a good loaf of bread, and many of them listening to these
sneaking Mormon missionaries—and I actually heard one of
them talking right out on a street-corner in Duluth, a few
years ago, and the officers of the law not protesting—but still,
as they are a smaller but more immediate problem, let me
stop for just a moment to pay my respects to these Seventh-
Day Adventists. Not that they are immoral, I don't mean,
but when a body of men go on insisting that Saturday is the
Sabbath, after Christ himself has clearly indicated the new
dispensation, then I think the legislature ought to step in——"

At this point Carol awoke.

She got through three more minutes by studying the face of
a girl in the pew across: a sensitive unhappy girl whose
longing poured out with intimidating self-revelation as she
worshiped Mr. Zitterel. Carol wondered who the girl was. She
had seen her at church suppers. She considered how many of
the three thousand people in the town she did not know; to
how many of them the Thanatopsis and the Jolly Seventeen
were icy social peaks; how many of them might be toiling
through boredom thicker than her own—with greater courage.

She examined her nails. She read two hymns. She got some
satisfaction out of rubbing an itching knuckle. She pillowed
on her shoulder the head of the baby who, after killing time
in the same manner as his mother, was so fortunate as to
fall asleep. She read the introduction, title-page and acknowl-
edgment of copyrights, in the hymnal. She tried to evolve a
philosophy which would explain why Kennicott could never
tie his scarf so that it would reach the top of the gap in his
turn-down collar.

There were no other diversions to be found in the pew.

She glanced back at the congregation. She thought that it would be amiable to bow to Mrs. Champ Perry.

Her slow turning head stopped, galvanized.

Across the aisle, two rows back, was a strange young man who shone among the cud-chewing citizens like a visitant from the sun—amber curls, low forehead, fine nose, chin smooth but not raw from Sabbath shaving. His lips startled her. The lips of men in Gopher Prairie are flat in the face, straight and grudging. The stranger's mouth was arched, the upper lip short. He wore a brown jersey coat, a delft-blue bow, a white silk shirt, white flannel trousers. He suggested the ocean beach, a tennis court, anything but the sun-blistered utility of Main Street.

A visitor from Minneapolis, here for business? No. He wasn't a business man. He was a poet. Keats was in his face, and Shelley, and Arthur Upson, whom she had once seen in Minneapolis. He was at once too sensitive and too sophisticated to touch business as she knew it in Gopher Prairie.

With restrained amusement he was analyzing the noisy Mr. Zitterel. Carol was ashamed to have this spy from the Great World hear the pastor's maundering. She felt responsible for the town. She resented his gaping at their private rites. She flushed, turned away. But she continued to feel his presence.

How could she meet him? She must! For an hour of talk. He was all that she was hungry for. She could not let him get away without a word—and she would have to. She pictured, and ridiculed, herself as walking up to him and remarking, "I am sick with the Village Virus. Will you please tell me what people are saying and playing in New York?" She pictured, and groaned over, the expression of Kennicott if she should say, "Why wouldn't it be reasonable for you, my soul, to ask that complete stranger in the brown jersey coat to come to supper tonight?"

She brooded, not looking back. She warned herself that she was probably exaggerating; that no young man could have all these exalted qualities. Wasn't he too obviously smart, too glossy-new? Like a movie actor. Probably he was a traveling salesman who sang tenor and fancied himself in imitations of Newport clothes and spoke of "the swellest business proposition that ever came down the pike." In a panic she peered at him. No! This was no hustling salesman, this boy with the curving Grecian lips and the serious eyes.

She rose after the service, carefully taking Kennicott's arm and smiling at him in a mute assertion that she was devoted to him no matter what happened. She followed the Mystery's soft brown jersey shoulders out of the church.

Fatty Hicks, the shrill and puffy son of Nat, flapped his hand at the beautiful stranger and jeered, "How's the kid? All dolled up like a plush horse today, ain't we!"

Carol was exceeding sick. Her herald from the outside was Erik Valborg, "Elizabeth." Apprentice tailor! Gasoline and hot goose! Mending dirty jackets! Respectfully holding a tape-measure about a paunch!

And yet, she insisted, this boy was also himself.

III

They had Sunday dinner with the Smails, in a dining-room which centered about a fruit and flower piece and a crayon-enlargement of Uncle Whittier. Carol did not heed Aunt Bessie's fussing in regard to Mrs. Robert B. Schminke's bead necklace and Whittier's error in putting on the striped pants, day like this. She did not taste the shreds of roast pork. She said vacuously:

"Uh—Will, I wonder if that young man in the white flannel trousers, at church this morning, was this Valborg person that they're all talking about?"

"Yump. That's him. Wasn't that the darndest get-up he had on!" Kennicott scratched at a white smear on his hard gray sleeve.

"It wasn't so bad. I wonder where he comes from? He seems to have lived in cities a good deal. Is he from the East?"

"The East? Him? Why, he comes from a farm right up north here, just this side of Jefferson. I know his father slightly—Adolph Valborg—typical cranky old Swede farmer."

"Oh, really?" blandly.

"Believe he has lived in Minneapolis for quite some time, though. Learned his trade there. And I will say he's bright, some ways. Reads a lot. Pollock says he takes more books out of the library than anybody else in town. Huh! He's kind of like you in that!"

The Smails and Kennicott laughed very much at this sly jest. Uncle Whittier seized the conversation. "That fellow that's working for Hicks? Milksop, that's what he is. Makes me tired to see a young fellow that ought to be in the war, or anyway out in the fields earning his living honest, like I done when I was young, doing a woman's work and then come out and dress up like a show-actor! Why, when I was his age——"

Carol reflected that the carving-knife would make an excellent dagger with which to kill Uncle Whittier. It would slide in easily. The headlines would be terrible.

Kennicott said judiciously, "Oh, I don't want to be unjust to him. I believe he took his physical examination for military service. Got varicose veins—not bad, but enough to disqualify him. Though I will say he doesn't look like a fellow that would be so awful darn crazy to poke his bayonet into a Hun's guts."

"Will! *Please!*"

"Well, he don't. Looks soft to me. And they say he told Del Snafflin, when he was getting a hair-cut on Saturday, that he wished he could play the piano."

"Isn't it wonderful how much we all know about one another in a town like this," said Carol innocently.

Kennicott was suspicious, but Aunt Bessie, serving the floating island pudding, agreed, "Yes, it is wonderful. Folks can get away with all sorts of meannesses and sins in these terrible cities, but they can't here. I was noticing this tailor fellow this morning, and when Mrs. Riggs offered to share her hymn-book with him, he shook his head, and all the while we was singing he just stood there like a bump on a log and never opened his mouth. Everybody says he's got an idea that he's got so much better manners and all than what the rest of us have, but if that's what he calls good manners, I want to know!"

Carol again studied the carving-knife. Blood on the whiteness of a tablecloth might be gorgeous.

Then:

"Fool! Neurotic impossibilist! Telling yourself orchard fairy-tales—at thirty. . . . Dear Lord, am I really *thirty?* That boy can't be more than twenty-five."

IV

She went calling.

Boarding with the Widow Bogart was Fern Mullins, a girl of twenty-two who was to be teacher of English, French, and gymnastics in the high school this coming session. Fern Mullins had come to town early, for the six-weeks normal course for country teachers. Carol had noticed her on the street, had heard almost as much about her as about Erik

Valborg. She was tall, weedy, pretty, and incurably rakish. Whether she wore a low middy collar or dressed reticently for school in a black suit with a high-necked blouse, she was airy, flippant. "She looks like an absolute totty," said all the Mrs. Sam Clarks, disapprovingly, and all the Juanita Haydocks, enviously.

That Sunday evening, sitting in baggy canvas lawn-chairs beside the house, the Kennicotts saw Fern laughing with Cy Bogart who, though still a junior in high school, was now a lump of a man, only two or three years younger than Fern. Cy had to go downtown for weighty matters connected with the pool-parlor. Fern drooped on the Bogart porch, her chin in her hands.

"She looks lonely," said Kennicott.

"She does, poor soul. I believe I'll go over and speak to her. I was introduced to her at Dave's but I haven't called." Carol was slipping across the lawn, a white figure in the dimness, faintly brushing the dewy grass. She was thinking of Erik and of the fact that her feet were wet, and she was casual in her greeting: "Hello! The doctor and I wondered if you were lonely."

Resentfully, "I am!"

Carol concentrated on her. "My dear, you sound so! I know how it is. I used to be tired when I was on the job —I was a librarian. What was your college? I was Blodgett."

More interestedly, "I went to the U." Fern meant the University of Minnesota.

"You must have had a splendid time. Blodgett was a bit dull."

"Where were you a librarian?" challengingly.

"St. Paul—the main library."

"Honest? Oh dear, I wish I was back in the Cities! This is my first year of teaching, and I'm scared stiff. I did have the best time in college: dramatics and basket-ball and fussing and dancing—I'm simply crazy about dancing. And here, except when I have the kids in gymnasium class, or when I'm chaperoning the basket-ball team on a trip out-of-town, I won't dare to move above a whisper. I guess they don't care much if you put any pep into teaching or not, as long as you look like a Good Influence out of school-hours—and that means never doing anything you want to. This normal course is bad enough, but the regular school will be *fierce!* If it wasn't too late to get a job in the Cities, I swear I'd resign here. I bet I won't dare to go to a single dance all winter. If I cut loose and danced the way I like to, they'd think I was a perfect hellion—poor harmless me! Oh, I oughtn't to be talking like this. Fern, you never could be cagey!"

"Don't be frightened, my dear! . . . Doesn't that sound atrociously old and kind! I'm talking to you the way Mrs. Westlake talks to me! That's having a husband and a kitchen range, I suppose. But I feel young, and I want to dance like a —like a hellion?—too. So I sympathize."

Fern made a sound of gratitude. Carol inquired, "What experience did you have with college dramatics? I tried to start a kind of Little Theater here. It was dreadful. I must tell you about it——"

Two hours later, when Kennicott came over to greet Fern and to yawn, "Look here, Carrie, don't you suppose you better be thinking about turning in? I've got a hard day tomorrow," the two were talking so intimately that they constantly interrupted each other.

As she went respectably home, convoyed by a husband, and decorously holding up her skirts, Carol rejoiced, "Everything has changed! I have two friends, Fern and—— But who's the other? That's queer; I thought there was—— Oh, how absurd!"

V

She often passed Erik Valborg on the street; the brown jersey coat became unremarkable. When she was driving with Kennicott, in early evening, she saw him on the lake shore, reading a thin book which might easily have been poetry. She noted that he was the only person in the motorized town who still took long walks.

She told herself that she was the daughter of a judge, the wife of a doctor, and that she did not care to know a capering tailor. She told herself that she was not responsive to men . . . not even to Percy Bresnahàn. She told herself that a woman of thirty who heeded a boy of twenty-five was ridiculous. And on Friday, when she had convinced herself that the errand was necessary, she went to Nat Hicks's shop, bearing the not very romantic burden of a pair of her husband's trousers. Hicks was in the back room. She faced the Greek god who, in a somewhat ungodlike way, was stitching a coat on a scaley sewing-machine, in a room of smutted plaster walls.

She saw that his hands were not in keeping with a Hellenic face. They were thick, roughened with needle and hot iron and plow-handle. Even in the shop he persisted in his finery. He wore a silk shirt, a topaz scarf, thin tan shoes.

This she absorbed while she was saying curtly, "Can I get these pressed, please?"

Not rising from the sewing-machine he stuck out his hand, mumbled, "When do you want them?"

"Oh, Monday."

The adventure was over. She was marching out.

"What name?" he called after her.

He had risen and, despite the farcicality of Dr. Will Kennicott's bulgy trousers draped over his arm, he had the grace of a cat.

"Kennicott."

"Kennicott. Oh! Oh say, you're Mrs. Dr. Kennicott then, aren't you?"

"Yes." She stood at the door. Now that she had carried out her preposterous impulse to see what he was like, she was cold, she was as ready to detect familiarities as the virtuous Miss Ella Stowbody.

"I've heard about you. Myrtle Cass was saying you got up a dramatic club and gave a dandy play. I've always wished I had a chance to belong to a Little Theater, and give some European plays, or whimsical like Barrie, or a pageant."

He pronounced it "pagent"; he rhymed "pag" with "rag."

Carol nodded in the manner of a lady being kind to a tradesman, and one of her selves sneered, "Our Erik is indeed a lost John Keats."

He was appealing, "Do you suppose it would be possible to get up another dramatic club this coming fall?"

"Well, it might be worth thinking of." She came out of her several conflicting poses, and said sincerely, "There's a new teacher, Miss Mullins, who might have some talent. That would make three of us for a nucleus. If we could scrape up half a dozen we might give a real play with a small cast. Have you had any experience?"

"Just a bum club that some of us got up in Minneapolis when I was working there. We had one good man, an interior decorator—maybe he was kind of sis and effeminate, but he really was an artist, and we gave one dandy play. But I—— Of course I've always had to work hard, and study by myself, and I'm probably sloppy, and I'd love it if I had training in rehearsing—I mean, the crankier the director was, the better I'd like it. If you didn't want to use me as an actor, I'd love to design the costumes. I'm crazy about fabrics—textures and colors and designs."

She knew that he was trying to keep her from going, trying to indicate that he was something more than a person to whom one brought trousers for pressing. He besought:

"Some day I hope I can get away from this fool repairing, when I have the money saved up. I want to go East and work for some big dressmaker, and study art drawing, and become a high-class designer. Or do you think that's a kind of fiddlin' ambition for a fellow? I was brought up on a farm. And then monkeyin' round with silks! I don't know. What do you think? Myrtle Cass says you're awfully educated."

"I am. Awfully. Tell me: Have the boys made fun of your ambition?"

She was seventy years old, and sexless, and more advisory than Vida Sherwin.

"Well, they have, at that. They've jollied me a good deal, here and Minneapolis both. They say dressmaking is ladies' work. (But I was willing to get drafted for the war! I tried to get in. But they rejected me. But I did try!) I thought some of working up in a gents' furnishings store, and I had a chance to travel on the road for a clothing house, but somehow—I hate this tailoring, but I can't seem to get enthusiastic about salesmanship. I keep thinking about a room in gray oatmeal paper with prints in very narrow gold frames—or would it be better in white enamel paneling?—but anyway, it looks out on Fifth Avenue, and I'm designing a sumptuous——" He made it "sump-too-ous"—"robe of linden green chiffon over cloth of gold! You know—tileul. It's elegant. . . . What do you think?"

"Why not? What do you care for the opinion of city rowdies, or a lot of farm boys? But you mustn't, you really mustn't, let casual strangers like me have a chance to judge you."

"Well—— You aren't a stranger, one way. Myrtle Cass—Miss Cass, should say—she's spoken about you so often. I wanted to call on you—and the doctor—but I didn't quite have the nerve. One evening I walked past your house, but you and your husband were talking on the porch, and you looked so chummy and happy I didn't dare butt in."

Maternally, "I think it's extremely nice of you to want to be trained in—in enunciation by a stage-director. Perhaps I

could help you. I'm a thoroughly sound and uninspired
schoolma'am by instinct; quite hopelessly mature."

"Oh, you aren't *either!*"

She was not very successful at accepting his fervor with
the air of amused woman of the world, but she sounded
reasonably impersonal: "Thank you. Shall we see if we really
can get up a new dramatic club? I'll tell you: Come to the
house this evening, about eight. I'll ask Miss Mullins to come
over, and we'll talk about it."

VI

"He has absolutely no sense of humor. Less than Will. But
hasn't he—— What is a 'sense of humor'? Isn't the thing he
lacks the back-slapping jocosity that passes for humor here?
Anyway—— Poor lamb, coaxing me to stay and play with
him! Poor lonely lamb! If he could be free from Nat Hickses,
from people who say 'dandy' and 'bum,' would he develop?

"I wonder if Whitman didn't use Brooklyn back-street
slang, as a boy?

"No. Not Whitman. He's Keats—sensitive to silken things.
'Innumerable of stains and splendid dyes as are the tiger-
moth's deep-damask'd wings.' Keats, here! A bewildered spirit
fallen on Main Street. And Main Street laughs till it aches,
giggles till the spirit doubts his own self and tries to give up
the use of wings for the correct uses of a 'gents' furnishings
store.' Gopher Prairie with its celebrated eleven miles of
cement walk. . . . I wonder how much of the cement is made
out of the tombstones of John Keatses?"

VII

Kennicott was cordial to Fern Mullins, teased her, told her
he was a "great hand for running off with pretty schoolteachers," and promised that if the school-board should object to her dancing, he would "bat 'em one over the head and
tell 'em how lucky they were to get a girl with some go to
her, for once."

But to Erik Valborg he was not cordial. He shook hands
loosely, and said, "H' are yuh."

Nat Hicks was socially acceptable; he had been here for
years, and owned his shop; but this person was merely
Nat's workman, and the town's principle of perfect democracy was not meant to be applied indiscriminately.

The conference on a dramatic club theoretically included Kennicott, but he sat back, patting yawns, conscious of Fern's ankles, smiling amiably on the children at their sport.

Fern wanted to tell her grievances; Carol was sulky every time she thought of "The Girl from Kankakee"; it was Erik who made suggestions. He had read with astounding breadth, and astounding lack of judgment. His voice was sensitive to liquids, but he overused the word "glorious." He mispronounced a tenth of the words he had from books, but he knew it. He was insistent, but he was shy.

When he demanded, "I'd like to stage 'Suppressed Desires,' by Cook and Miss Glaspell," Carol ceased to be patronizing. He was not the yearner: he was the artist, sure of his vision. "I'd make it simple. Use a big window at the back, with a cyclorama of a blue that would simply hit you in the eye, and just one tree-branch, to suggest a park below. Put the breakfast table on a dais. Let the colors be kind of arty and tearoomy—orange chairs, and orange and blue table, and blue Japanese breakfast set, and some place, one big flat smear of black—bang! Oh. Another play I wish we could do is Tennyson Jesse's 'The Black Mask.' I've never seen it but—— Glorious ending, where this woman looks at the man with his face all blown away, and she just gives one horrible scream."

"Good God, is that your idea of a glorious ending?" bayed Kennicott.

"That sounds fierce! I do love artistic things, but not the horrible ones," moaned Fern Mullins.

Erik was bewildered; glanced at Carol. She nodded loyally.

At the end of the conference they had decided nothing.

chapter 29

SHE had walked up the railroad track with Hugh, this Sunday afternoon.

She saw Erik Valborg coming, in an ancient highwater suit, tramping sullenly and alone, striking at the rails with a stick. For a second she unreasoningly wanted to avoid him, but she kept on, and she serenely talked about God, whose voice, Hugh asserted, made the humming in the telegraph wires. Erik stared, straightened. They greeted each other with "Hello."

"Hugh, say how-do-you-do to Mr. Valborg."

"Oh, dear me, he's got a button unbuttoned," worried Erik, kneeling. Carol frowned, then noted the strength with which he swung the baby in the air.

"May I walk along a piece with you?"

"I'm tired. Let's rest on those ties. Then I must be trotting back."

They sat on a heap of discarded railroad ties, oak logs spotted with cinnamon-colored dry-rot and marked with metallic brown streaks where iron plates had rested. Hugh learned that the pile was the hiding-place of Injuns; he went gunning for them while the elders talked of uninteresting things.

The telegraph wires thrummed, thrummed, thrummed above them; the rails were glaring hard lines; the goldenrod smelled dusty. Across the track was a pasture of dwarf clover and sparse lawn cut by earthy cow-paths; beyond its placid narrow green, the rough immensity of new stubble, jagged with wheat-stacks like huge pineapples.

Erik talked of books; flamed like a recent convert to any faith. He exhibited as many titles and authors as possible, halting only to appeal, "Have you read his last book? Don't you think he's a terribly strong writer?"

She was dizzy. But when he insisted, "You've been a librarian; tell me; do I read too much fiction?" She advised him loftily, rather discursively. He had, she indicated, never studied. He had skipped from one emotion to another. Especially—she hesitated, then flung it at him—he must not guess at pronunciations; he must endure the nuisance of stopping to reach for the dictionary.

"I'm talking like a cranky teacher," she sighed.

"No! And I will study! Read the damned dictionary right through." He crossed his legs and bent over, clutching his ankle with both hands. "I know what you mean. I've been rushing from picture to picture, like a kid let loose in an art gallery for the first time. You see, it's so awful recent that I've found there was a world—well, a world where beautiful things counted. I was on the farm till I was nineteen. Dad is a good farmer, but nothing else. Do you know why he first sent me off to learn tailoring? I wanted to study drawing, and he had a cousin that'd made a lot of money tailoring out in Dakota, and he said tailoring was a lot like drawing, so he sent me down to a punk hole called Curlew, to work in a tailor shop. Up to that time I'd only had three months' schooling a year—walked to school two miles, through snow up to my knees—and Dad never would stand for my having a single book except schoolbooks.

"I never read a novel till I got 'Dorothy Vernon of Haddon Hall' out of the library at Curlew. I thought it was the loveliest thing in the world! Next I read 'Barriers Burned Away' and then Pope's translation of Homer. Some combination, all right! When I went to Minneapolis, just two years ago, I guess I'd read pretty much everything in that Curlew library, but I'd never heard of Rossetti or John Sargent or Balzac or Brahms. But—— Yump, I'll study. Look here! Shall I get out of this tailoring, this pressing and repairing?"

"I don't see why a surgeon should spend very much time cobbling shoes."

"But what if I find I can't really draw and design? After fussing around in New York or Chicago, I'd feel like a fool if I had to go back to work in a gents' furnishings store!"

"Please say 'haberdashery.' "

"Haberdashery? All right. I'll remember." He shrugged and spread his fingers wide.

She was humbled by his humility; she put away in her mind, to take out and worry over later, a speculation as to whether it was not she who was naive. She urged, "What if you do have to go back? Most of us do! We can't all be artists—myself, for instance. We have to darn socks, and yet we're not content to think of nothing but socks and darning-cotton. I'd demand all I could get—whether I finally settled down to designing frocks or building temples or pressing pants. What if you do drop back? You'll have had the adventure. Don't be too meek toward life! Go! You're young, you're unmarried. Try everything! Don't listen to Nat Hicks and Sam Clark and be a 'steady young man'—in order to help them make money. You're still a blessed innocent. Go and play till the Good People capture you!"

"But I don't just want to play. I want to make something beautiful. God! And I don't know enough. Do you get it? Do you understand? Nobody else ever has! Do you understand?"

"Yes."

"And so—— But here's what bothers me: I like fabrics; dinky things like that; little drawings and elegant words. But look over there at those fields. Big! New! Don't it seem kind of a shame to leave this and go back to the East and Europe, and do what all those people have been doing so long? Being careful about words, when there's millions of bushels of wheat here! Reading this fellow Pater, when I've helped Dad to clear fields!"

"It's good to clear fields. But it's not for you. It's one of our favorite American myths that broad plains necessarily make broad minds, and high mountains make high purpose. I thought that myself, when I first came to the prairie. 'Big— new.' Oh, I don't want to deny the prairie future. It will be magnificent. But equally I'm hanged if I want to be bullied by it, go to war on behalf of Main Street, be bullied and *bullied* by the faith that the future is already here in the present, and that all of us must stay and worship wheat-stacks and insist that this is 'God's Country'—and never, of course, do anything original or gay-colored that would help to make that future! Anyway, you don't belong here. Sam Clark and Nat Hicks, that's what our big newness has produced. Go! Before it's too late, as it has been for—for some of us. Young man, go East and grow up with the revolution! Then perhaps you may come back and tell Sam and Nat and me what to do with the land we've been clearing— if we'll listen—if we don't lynch you first!"

He looked at her reverently. She could hear him saying, "I've always wanted to know a woman who would talk to me like that."

Her hearing was faulty. He was saying nothing of the sort. He was saying:

"Why aren't you happy with your husband?"

"I—you——"

"He doesn't care for the 'blessed innocent' part of you, does he!"

"Erik, you mustn't——"

"First you tell me to go and be free, and then you say that I 'mustn't'!"

"I know. But you mustn't—— You must be more imper-sonal!"

He glowered at her like a downy young owl. She wasn't sure but she thought that he muttered, "I'm damned if I will." She considered with wholesome fear the perils of meddling with other people's destinies, and she said timidly, "Hadn't we better start back now?"

He mused, "You're younger than I am. Your lips are for songs about rivers in the morning and lakes at twilight. I don't see how anybody could ever hurt you. . . . Yes. We better go."

He trudged beside her, his eyes averted. Hugh experimentally took his thumb. He looked down at the baby seriously. He burst out, "All right. I'll do it. I'll stay here one year. Save. Not spend so much money on clothes. And then I'll go East, to art-school. Work on the side—tailor shop, dressmaker's. I'll learn what I'm good for: designing clothes, stage-settings, illustrating, or selling collars to fat men. All settled." He peered at her, unsmiling.

"Can you stand it here in town for a year?"

"With you to look at?"

"Please! I mean: Don't the people here think you're an odd bird? (They do me, I assure you!)"

"I don't know. I never notice much. Oh, they do kid me about not being in the army—especially the old warhorses, the old men that aren't going themselves. And this Bogart boy. And Mr. Hicks's son—he's a horrible brat. But probably he's licensed to say what he thinks about his father's hired man!"

"He's beastly!"

They were in town. They passed Aunt Bessie's house. Aunt Bessie and Mrs. Bogart were at the window, and Carol saw that they were staring so intently that they answered her wave only with the stiffly raised hands of automatons. In the next block Mrs. Dr. Westlake was gaping from her porch. Carol said with an embarrassed quaver:

"I want to run in and see Mrs. Westlake. I'll say good-by here."

She avoided his eyes.

Mrs. Westlake was affable. Carol felt that she was expected to explain; and while she was mentally asserting that she'd be hanged if she'd explain, she was explaining:

"Hugh captured that Valborg boy up the track. They became such good friends. And I talked to him for a while. I'd heard he was eccentric, but really, I found him quite intelligent. Crude, but he reads—reads almost the way Dr. Westlake does."

"That's fine. Why does he stick here in town? What's this I hear about his being interested in Myrtle Cass?"

"I don't know. Is he? I'm sure he isn't! He said he was quite lonely! Besides, Myrtle is a babe in arms!"

"Twenty-one if she's a day!"

"Well—— Is the doctor going to do any hunting this fall?"

II

The need of explaining Erik dragged her back into doubting. For all his ardent reading, and his ardent life, was he anything but a small-town youth bred on an illiberal farm and in cheap tailor shops? He had rough hands. She had been attracted only by hands that were fine and suave, like those of her father. Delicate hands and resolute purpose. But this boy—powerful seamed hands and flabby will.

"It's not appealing weakness like his, but sane strength that will animate the Gopher Prairies. Only—— Does that mean anything? Or am I echoing Vida? The world has always let 'strong' statesmen and soldiers—the men with strong voices—take control, and what have the thundering boobies done? What is 'strength'?

"This classifying of people! I suppose tailors differ as much as burglars or kings.

"Erik frightened me when he turned on me. Of course he didn't mean anything, but I mustn't let him be so personal.

"Amazing impertinence!

"But he didn't mean to be.

"His hands are *firm*. I wonder if sculptors don't have thick hands, too?

"Of course if there really is anything I can do to *help* the boy——

"Though I despise these people who interfere. He must be independent."

III

She wasn't altogether pleased, the week after, when Erik was independent and, without asking for her inspiration, planned the tennis tournament. It proved that he had learned to play in Minneapolis; that, next to Juanita Haydock, he had the best serve in town. Tennis was well spoken of in Gopher Prairie and almost never played. There were three courts: one belonging to Harry Haydock, one to the cottages at the lake, and one, a rough field on the outskirts, laid out by a defunct tennis association.

Erik had been seen in flannels and an imitation panama hat, playing on the abandoned court with Willis Woodford, the clerk in Stowbody's bank. Suddenly he was going about proposing the reorganization of the tennis association, and writing names in a fifteen-cent note-book bought for the purpose at Dyer's. When he came to Carol he was so excited over being an organizer that he did not stop to talk of himself and Aubrey Beardsley for more than ten minutes. He begged, "Will you get some of the folks to come in?" and she nodded agreeably.

He proposed an informal exhibition match to advertise the association; he suggested that Carol and himself, the Haydocks, the Woodfords, and the Dillons play doubles, and that the association be formed from the gathered enthusiasts. He had asked Harry Haydock to be tentative president. Harry, he reported, had promised, "All right. You bet. But you go ahead and arrange things, and I'll O.K. 'em." Erik planned that the match should be held Saturday afternoon, on the old public court at the edge of town. He was happy in being, for the first time, part of Gopher Prairie.

Through the week Carol heard how select an attendance there was to be.

Kennicott growled that he didn't care to go.

Had he any objections to her playing with Erik?

No; sure not; she needed the exercise.

Carol went to the match early. The court was in a meadow out on the New Antonia road. Only Erik was there. He was dashing about with a rake, trying to make the court somewhat less like a plowed field. He admitted that he had stage-fright at the thought of the coming horde. Willis and Mrs. Woodford arrived, Willis in home-made knickers and black sneakers through at the toe; then Dr. and Mrs. Harvey Dillon, people as harmless and grateful as the Woodfords.

Carol was embarrassed and excessively agreeable, like the bishop's lady trying not to feel out of place at a Baptist bazaar.

They waited.

The match was scheduled for three. As spectators there assembled one youthful grocery clerk, stopping his Ford delivery wagon to stare from the seat, and one solemn small boy, tugging a smaller sister who had a careless nose.

"I wonder where the Haydocks are? They ought to show up, at least," said Erik.

Carol smiled confidently at him, and peered down the empty road toward town. Only heat-waves and dust and dusty weeds.

At half-past three no one had come, and the grocery boy reluctantly got out, cranked his Ford, glared at them in a disillusioned manner, and rattled away. The small boy and his sister ate grass and sighed.

The players pretended to be exhilarated by practising service, but they startled at each dust-cloud from a motor car. None of the cars turned into the meadow—none till a quarter to four, when Kennicott drove in.

Carol's heart swelled. "How loyal he is! Depend on him! He'd come, if nobody else did. Even though he doesn't care for the game. The old darling!"

Kennicott did not alight. He called out, "Carrie! Harry Haydock 'phoned me that they've decided to hold the tennis matches, or whatever you call 'em, down at the cottages at the lake, instead of here. The bunch are down there now: Haydocks and Dyers and Clarks and everybody. Harry wanted to know if I'd bring you down. I guess I can take the time—come right back after supper."

Before Carol could sum it all up, Erik stammered, "Why, Haydock didn't say anything to me about the change. Of course he's the president, but——"

Kennicott looked at him heavily, and grunted, "I don't know a thing about it. . . . Coming, Carrie?"

"I am not! The match was to be here, and it will be here! You can tell Harry Haydock that he's beastly rude!" She rallied the five who had been left out, who would always be left out. "Come on! We'll toss to see which four of us play the Only and Original First Annual Tennis Tournament of Forest Hills, Del Monte, and Gopher Prairie!"

"Don't know as I blame you," said Kennicott. "We'll have supper at home then?" He drove off.

She hated him for his composure. He had ruined her defiance. She felt much less like Susan B. Anthony as she turned to her huddled followers.

Mrs. Dillon and Willis Woodford lost the toss. The others played out the game, slowly, painfully, stumbling on the rough earth, muffing the easiest shots, watched only by the small boy and his sniveling sister. Beyond the court stretched the eternal stubble-fields. The four marionettes, awkwardly going through exercises, insignificant in the hot sweep of contemptuous land, were not heroic; their voices did not ring out in the score, but sounded apologetic; and when the game was over they glanced about as though they were waiting to be laughed at.

They walked home. Carol took Erik's arm. Through her thin linen sleeve she could feel the crumply warmth of his familiar brown jersey coat. She observed that there were purple and red-gold threads interwoven with the brown. She remembered the first time she had seen it.

Their talk was nothing but improvisations on the theme: "I never did like this Haydock. He just considers his own convenience." Ahead of them, the Dillons and Woodfords spoke of the weather and B. J. Gougerling's new bungalow. No one referred to their tennis tournament. At her gate Carol shook hands firmly with Erik and smiled at him.

Next morning, Sunday morning, when Carol was on the porch, the Haydocks drove up.

"We didn't mean to be rude to you, dearie!" implored Juanita. "I wouldn't have you think that for anything. We planned that Will and you should come down and have supper at our cottage."

"No. I'm sure you didn't mean to be." Carol was super-neighborly. "But I do think you ought to apologize to poor Erik Valborg. He was terribly hurt."

"Oh. Valborg. I don't care so much what he thinks," objected Harry. "He's nothing but a conceited buttinsky. Juanita and I kind of figured he was trying to run this tennis thing too darn much anyway."

"But you asked him to make arrangements."

"I know, but I don't like him. Good Lord, you couldn't hurt his feelings! He dresses up like a chorus man—and, by golly, he looks like one!—but he's nothing but a Swede farm boy, and these foreigners, they all got hides like a covey of rhinoceroses."

"But he *is* hurt!"

"Well—— I don't suppose I ought to have gone off half-cocked, and not jollied him along. I'll give him a cigar. He'll——"

Juanita had been licking her lips and staring at Carol. She interrupted her husband, "Yes, I do think Harry ought to fix it up with him. You *like* him, *don't* you, Carol?"

Over and through Carol ran a frightened cautiousness. "Like him? I haven't an í-dea. He seems to be a very decent young man. I just felt that when he'd worked so hard on the plans for the match, it was a shame not to be nice to him."

"Maybe there's something to that," mumbled Harry; then, at sight of Kennicott coming round the corner tugging the red garden hose by its brass nozzle, he roared in relief, "What d' you think you're trying to do, doc?"

While Kennicott explained in detail all that he thought he was trying to do, while he rubbed his chin and gravely stated, "Struck me the grass was looking kind of brown in patches—didn't know but what I'd give it a sprinkling," and while Harry agreed that this was an excellent idea, Juanita made friendly noises and, behind the gilt screen of an affectionate smile, watched Carol's face.

IV

She wanted to see Erik. She wanted some one to play with! There wasn't even so dignified and sound an excuse as having Kennicott's trousers pressed; when she inspected them, all three pairs looked discouragingly neat. She probably would not have ventured on it had she not spied Nat Hicks in the pool-parlor, being witty over bottle-pool. Erik was alone! She fluttered toward the tailor shop, dashed into its slovenly heat with the comic fastidiousness of a humming bird dipping into a dry tiger-lily. It was after she had entered that she found an excuse.

Erik was in the back room, cross-legged on a long table, sewing a vest. But he looked as though he were doing this eccentric thing to amuse himself.

"Hello. I wonder if you couldn't plan a sports-suit for me?" she said breathlessly.

He stared at her; he protested, "No, I won't! God! I'm not going to be a tailor with you!"

"Why, Erik!" she said, like a mildly shocked mother.

It occurred to her that she did not need a suit, and that the order might have been hard to explain to Kennicott.

He swung down from the table. "I want to show you something." He rummaged in the roll-top desk on which Nat Hicks kept bills, buttons, calendars, buckles, thread-channeled wax, shotgun shells, samples of brocade for "fancy vests," fishing-reels, pornographic post-cards, shreds of buckram lining. He pulled out a blurred sheet of Bristol board and anxiously gave it to her. It was a sketch for a frock. It was not well drawn; it was too finicking; the pillars in the background were grotesquely squat. But the frock had an original back, very low, with a central triangular section from the waist to a string of jet beads at the neck.

"It's stunning. But how it would shock Mrs. Clark!"

"Yes, wouldn't it!"

"You must let yourself go more when you're drawing."

"Don't know if I can. I've started kind of late. But listen! What do you think I've done this two weeks? I've read almost clear through a Latin grammar, and about twenty pages of Cæsar."

"Splendid! You are lucky. You haven't a teacher to make you artificial."

"You're my teacher!"

There was a dangerous edge of personality to his voice. She was offended and agitated. She turned her shoulder on him, stared through the back window, studying this typical center of a typical Main Street block, a vista hidden from casual strollers. The backs of the chief establishments in town surrounded a quadrangle neglected, dirty, and incomparably dismal. From the front, Howland & Gould's grocery was smug enough, but attached to the rear was a lean-to of storm-streaked pine lumber with a sanded tar roof—a staggering doubtful shed behind which was a heap of ashes, splintered packing-boxes, shreds of excelsior, crumpled straw-board, broken olive-bottles, rotten fruit, and utterly disintegrated vegetables: orange carrots turning black, and potatoes with ulcers. The rear of the Bon Ton Store was grim with blistered black-painted iron shutters, under them a pile of once glossy red shirt-boxes, now a pulp from recent rain.

As seen from Main Street, Oleson & McGuire's Meat Market had a sanitary and virtuous expression with its new tile counter, fresh sawdust on the floor, and a hanging veal cut in rosettes. But she now viewed a back room with a home-made refrigerator of yellow smeared with black grease. A man in an apron spotted with dry blood was hoisting out a hard slab of meat.

Behind Billy's Lunch, the cook, in an apron which must long ago have been white, smoked a pipe and spat at the pest of sticky flies. In the center of the block, by itself, was the stable for the three horses of the drayman, and beside it a pile of manure.

The rear of Ezra Stowbody's bank was whitewashed, and back of it was a concrete walk and a three-foot square of grass, but the window was barred, and behind the bars she saw Willis Woodford cramped over figures in pompous books. He raised his head, jerkily rubbed his eyes, and went back to the eternity of figures.

The backs of the other shops were an impressionistic picture of dirty grays, drained browns, writhing heaps of refuse.

"Mine is a back-yard romance—with a journeyman tailor!"

She was saved from self-pity as she began to think through Erik's mind. She turned to him with an indignant, "It's disgusting that this is all you have to look at."

He considered it. "Outside there? I don't notice much. I'm learning to look inside. Not awful easy!"

"Yes. . . . I must be hurrying."

As she walked home—without hurrying—she remembered her father saying to a serious ten-year-old Carol, "Lady, only a fool thinks he's superior to beautiful bindings, but only a double-distilled fool reads nothing but bindings."

She was startled by the return of her father, startled by a sudden conviction that in this flaxen boy she had found the gray reticent judge who was divine love, perfect understanding. She debated it, furiously denied it, reaffirmed it, ridiculed it. Of one thing she was unhappily certain: there was nothing of the beloved father image in Will Kennicott.

v

She wondered why she sang so often, and why she found so many pleasant things—lamplight seen through trees on a cool evening, sunshine on brown wood, morning sparrows, black sloping roofs turned to plates of silver by moonlight. Pleasant things, small friendly things, and pleasant places— a field of goldenrod, a pasture by the creek—and suddenly a wealth of pleasant people. Vida was lenient to Carol at the surgical-dressing class; Mrs. Dave Dyer flattered her with questions about her health, baby, cook, and opinions on the war.

Mrs. Dyer seemed not to share the town's prejudice against Erik. "He's a nice-looking fellow; we must have him go on one of our picnics some time." Unexpectedly, Dave Dyer also liked him. The tight-fisted little farceur had a confused reverence for anything that seemed to him refined or clever. He answered Harry Haydock's sneers, "That's all right now! Elizabeth may doll himself up too much, but he's smart, and

don't you forget it! I was asking round trying to find out
where this Ukraine is, and darn if he didn't tell me. What's
the matter with his talking so polite? Hell's bells, Harry, no
harm in being polite. There's some regular he-men that are
just as polite as women, prett' near."

Carol found herself going about rejoicing, "How neighborly the town is!" She drew up with a dismayed "Am I falling in love with this boy? That's ridiculous! I'm merely interested in him. I like to think of helping him to succeed."

But as she dusted the living-room, mended a collar-band,
bathed Hugh, she was picturing herself and a young artist—
an Apollo nameless and evasive—building a house in the
Berkshires or in Virginia; exuberantly buying a chair with his
first check; reading poetry together, and frequently being
earnest over valuable statistics about labor; tumbling out of
bed early for a Sunday walk, and chattering (where Kennicott
would have yawned) over bread and butter by a lake. Hugh
was in her pictures, and he adored the young artist, who
made castles of chairs and rugs for him. Beyond these
playtimes she saw the "things I could do for Erik"—and she
admitted that Erik did partly make up the image of her altogether perfect artist.

In panic she insisted on being attentive to Kennicott, when
he wanted to be left alone to read the newspaper.

VI

She needed new clothes. Kennicott had promised, "We'll
have a good trip down to the Cities in the fall, and take
plenty of time for it, and you can get your new glad-rags
then." But as she examined her wardrobe she flung her ancient black velvet frock on the floor and raged, "They're
disgraceful. Everything I have is falling to pieces."

There was a new dressmaker and milliner, a Mrs. Swiftwaite. It was said that she was not altogether an elevating
influence in the way she glanced at men; that she would
as soon take away a legally appropriated husband as not;
that if there *was* any Mr. Swiftwaite, "it certainly was
strange that nobody seemed to know anything about him!"
But she had made for Rita Gould an organdy frock and hat
to match universally admitted to be "too cunning for words,"
and the matrons went cautiously, with darting eyes and excessive politeness, to the rooms which Mrs. Swiftwaite had
taken in the old Luke Dawson house, on Floral Avenue.

With none of the spiritual preparation which normally precedes the buying of new clothes in Gopher Prairie, Carol marched into Mrs. Swiftwaite's, and demanded, "I want to see a hat, and possibly a blouse."

In the dingy old front parlor which she had tried to make smart with a pier glass, covers from fashion magazines, anemic French prints, Mrs. Swiftwaite moved smoothly among the dress-dummies and hat-rests, spoke smoothly as she took up a small black and red turban. "I am sure the lady will find this extremely attractive."

"It's dreadfully tabby and small-towny," thought Carol, while she soothed, "I don't believe it quite goes with me."

"It's the choicest thing I have, and I'm sure you'll find it suits you beautifully. It has a great deal of *chic*. Please try it on," said Mrs. Swiftwaite, more smoothly than ever.

Carol studied the woman. She was as imitative as a glass diamond. She was the more rustic in her effort to appear urban. She wore a severe high-collared blouse with a row of small black buttons, which was becoming to her low-breasted slim neatness, but her skirt was hysterically checkered, her cheeks were too highly rouged, her lips too sharply penciled. She was magnificently a specimen of the illiterate divorcée of forty made up to look thirty, clever, and alluring.

While she was trying on the hat Carol felt very condescending. She took it off, shook her head, explained with the kind smile for inferiors, "I'm afraid it won't do, though it's unusually nice for so small a town as this."

"But it's really absolutely New-Yorkish."

"Well, it——"

"You see, I know my New York styles. I lived in New York for years, besides almost a year in Akron!"

"You did?" Carol was polite, and edged away, and went home unhappily. She was wondering whether her own airs were as laughable as Mrs. Swiftwaite's. She put on the eyeglasses which Kennicott had recently given to her for reading, and looked over a grocery bill. She went hastily up to her room, to her mirror. She was in a mood of self-depreciation. Accurately or not, this was the picture she saw in the mirror:

Neat rimless eye-glasses. Black hair clumsily tucked under a mauve straw hat which would have suited a spinster. Cheeks clear, bloodless. Thin nose. Gentle mouth and chin. A modest voile blouse with an edging of lace at the neck. A virginal sweetness and timorousness—no flare of gaiety, no suggestion of cities, music, quick laughter.

"I have become a small-town woman. Absolute. Typical. Modest and moral and safe. Protected from life. *Genteel!* The Village Virus—the village virtuousness. My hair—just scrambled together. What can Erik see in that wedded spinster there? He does like me! Because I'm the only woman who's decent to him! How long before he'll wake up to me? . . . I've waked up to myself. . . . Am I as old as—as old as I am?

"Not really old. Become careless. Let myself look tabby.

"I want to chuck every stitch I own. Black hair and pale cheeks—they'd go with a Spanish dancer's costume—rose behind my ear, scarlet mantilla over one shoulder, the other bare."

She seized the rouge sponge, daubed her cheeks, scratched at her lips with the vermilion pencil until they stung, tore open her collar. She posed with her thin arms in the attitude of the fandango. She dropped them sharply. She shook her head. "My heart doesn't dance," she said. She flushed as she fastened her blouse.

"At least I'm much more graceful than Fern Mullins."

"Heavens! When I came here from the Cities, girls imitated me. Now I'm trying to imitate a city girl."

chapter 30

FERN Mullins rushed into the house on a Saturday morning early in September and shrieked at Carol, "School starts next Tuesday. I've got to have one more spree before I'm arrested. Let's get up a picnic down the lake for this afternoon. Won't you come, Mrs. Kennicott, and the doctor? Cy Bogart wants to go—he's a brat but he's lively."

"I don't think the doctor can go," sedately. "He said something about having to make a country call this afternoon. But I'd love to."

"That's dandy! Who can we get?"

"Mrs. Dyer might be chaperon. She's been so nice. And maybe Dave, if he could get away from the store."

"How about Erik Valborg? I think he's got lots more

style than these town boys. You like him all right, don't you?"

So the picnic of Carol, Fern, Erik, Cy Bogart, and the Dyers was not only moral but inevitable.

They drove to the birch grove on the south shore of Lake Minniemashie. Dave Dyer was his most clownish self. He yelped, jigged, wore Carol's hat, dropped an ant down Fern's back, and when they went swimming (the women modestly changing in the car with the side curtains up, the men undressing behind the bushes, constantly repeating, "Gee, hope we don't run into poison ivy"), Dave splashed water on them and dived to clutch his wife's ankle. He infected the others. Erik gave an imitation of the Greek dancers he had seen in vaudeville, and when they sat down to picnic supper spread on a lap-robe on the grass, Cy climbed a tree to throw acorns at them.

But Carol could not frolic.

She had made herself young, with parted hair, sailor blouse and large blue bow, white canvas shoes and short linen skirt. Her mirror had asserted that she looked exactly as she had in college, that her throat was smooth, her collar-bone not very noticeable. But she was under restraint. When they swam she enjoyed the freshness of the water but she was irritated by Cy's tricks, by Dave's excessive good spirits. She admired Erik's dance; he could never betray bad taste, as Cy did, and Dave. She waited for him to come to her. He did not come. By his joyousness he had apparently endeared himself to the Dyers. Maud watched him and, after supper, cried to him, "Come sit down beside me, bad boy!" Carol winced at his willingness to be a bad boy and come and sit, at his enjoyment of a not very stimulating game in which Maud, Dave, and Cy snatched slices of cold tongue from one another's plates. Maud, it seemed, was slightly dizzy from the swim. She remarked publicly, "Dr. Kennicott has helped me so much by putting me on a diet," but it was to Erik alone that she gave the complete version of her peculiarity in being so sensitive, so easily hurt by the slightest cross word, that she simply had to have nice cheery friends.

Erik was nice and cheery.

Carol assured herself, "Whatever faults I may have, I certainly couldn't ever be jealous. I do like Maud; she's always so pleasant. But I wonder if she isn't just a bit fond of fishing for men's sympathy? Playing with Erik, and her married—— Well—— But she looks at him in that languishing, swooning, mid-Victorian way. Disgusting!"

Cy Bogart lay between the roots of a big birch, smoking his pipe and teasing Fern, assuring her that a week from now, when he was again a high-school boy and she his teacher, he'd wink at her in class. Maud Dyer wanted Erik to "come down to the beach to see the darling little minnies." Carol was left to Dave, who tried to entertain her with humorous accounts of Ella Stowbody's fondness for chocolate peppermints. She watched Maud Dyer put her hand on Erik's shoulder to steady herself.

"Disgusting!" she thought.

Cy Bogart covered Fern's nervous hand with his red paw, and when she bounced with half-anger and shrieked, "Let go, I tell you!" he grinned and waved his pipe—a gangling twenty-year-old satyr.

"Disgusting!"

When Maud and Erik returned and the grouping shifted, Erik muttered at Carol, "There's a boat on shore. Let's skip off and have a row."

"What will they think?" she worried. She saw Maud Dyer peer at Erik with moist possessive eyes. "Yes! Let's!" she said.

She cried to the party, with the canonical amount of sprightliness, "Good-by, everybody. We'll wireless you from China."

As the rhythmic oars plopped and creaked, as she floated on an unreality of delicate gray over which the sunset was poured out thin, the irritation of Cy and Maud slipped away. Erik smiled at her proudly. She considered him—coatless, in white thin shirt. She was conscious of his male differentness, of his flat masculine sides, his thin thighs, his easy rowing. They talked of the library, of the movies. He hummed and she softly sang "Swing Low, Sweet Chariot." A breeze shivered across the agate lake. The wrinkled water was like armor damascened and polished. The breeze flowed round the boat in a chill current. Carol drew the collar of her middy blouse over her bare throat.

"Getting cold. Afraid we'll have to go back," she said.

"Let's not go back to them yet. They'll be cutting up. Let's keep along the shore."

"But you enjoy the 'cutting up!' Maud and you had a beautiful time."

"Why! We just walked on the shore and talked about fishing!"

She was relieved, and apologetic to her friend Maud. "Of course. I was joking."

"I'll tell you! Let's land here and sit on the shore—that bunch of hazel-brush will shelter us from the wind—and watch the sunset. It's like melted lead. Just a short while! We don't want to go back and listen to them!"

"No, but——" She said nothing while he sped ashore. The keel clashed on the stones. He stood on the forward seat, holding out his hand. They were alone, in the ripple-lapping silence. She rose slowly, slowly stepped over the water in the bottom of the old boat. She took his hand confidently. Unspeaking they sat on a bleached log, in a russet twilight which hinted of autumn. Linden leaves fluttered about them.

"I wish—— Are you cold now?" he whispered.

"A little." She shivered. But it was not with cold.

"I wish we could curl up in the leaves there, covered all up, and lie looking out at the dark."

"I wish we could." As though it was comfortably understood that he did not mean to be taken seriously.

"Like what all the poets say—brown nymph and faun."

"No. I can't be a nymph any more. Too old—— Erik, am I old? Am I faded and small-towny?"

"Why, you're the youngest—— Your eyes are like a girl's. They're so—well, I mean, like you believed everything. Even if you do teach me, I feel a thousand years older than you, instead of maybe a year younger."

"Four or five years younger!"

"Anyway, your eyes are so innocent and your cheeks so soft—— Damn it, it makes me want to cry, somehow, you're so defenseless; and I want to protect you and—— There's nothing to protect you against!"

"Am I young? Am I? Honestly? Truly?" She betrayed for a moment the childish, mock-imploring tone that comes into the voice of the most serious woman when an agreeable man treats her as a girl; the childish tone and childish pursed-up lips and shy lift of the cheek.

"Yes, you are!"

"You're dear to believe it, Will—*Erik!*"

"Will you play with me? A lot?"

"Perhaps."

"Would you really like to curl in the leaves and watch the stars swing by overhead?"

"I think it's rather better to be sitting here!" He twined his fingers with hers. "And—— Erik, we must go back."

"Why?"

"It's somewhat late to outline all the history of social custom!"

"I know. We must. Are you glad we ran away though?"

"Yes." She was quiet, perfectly simple. But she rose. He circled her waist with a brusque arm. She did not resist. She did not care. He was neither a peasant tailor, a potential artist, a social complication, nor a peril. He was himself, and in him, in the personality flowing from him, she was unreasoningly content. In his nearness she caught a new view of his head; the last light brought out the planes of his neck, his flat ruddied cheeks, the side of his nose, the depression of his temples. Not as coy or uneasy lovers but as companions they walked to the boat, and he lifted her up on the prow.

She began to talk intently as he rowed: "Erik, you've got to work! You ought to be a personage. You're robbed of your kingdom. Fight for it! Take one of these correspondence courses in drawing—they mayn't be any good in themselves, but they'll make you try to draw and——"

As they reached the picnic ground she perceived that it was dark, that they had been gone for a long time.

"What will they say?" she wondered.

The others greeted them with the inevitable storm of humor and slight vexation: "Where the deuce do you think you've been?" "You're a fine pair, you are!" Erik and Carol looked self-conscious; failed in their effort to be witty. All the way home Carol was embarrassed. Once Cy winked at her. That Cy, the Peeping Tom of the garage-loft, should consider her a fellow-sinner—— She was furious and frightened and exultant by turns, and in all her moods certain that Kennicott would read her adventuring in her face.

She came into the house awkwardly defiant.

Her husband, half asleep under the lamp, greeted her, "Well, well, have a nice time?"

She could not answer. He looked at her. But his look did not sharpen. He began to wind his watch, yawning the old "Wellllll, guess it's about time to turn in."

That was all. Yet she was not glad. She was almost disappointed.

II

Mrs. Bogart called next day. She had a hen-like, crumb-pecking, diligent appearance. Her smile was too innocent. The pecking started instantly:

"Cy says you had lots of fun at the picnic yesterday. Did you enjoy it?"

"Oh yes. I raced Cy at swimming. He beat me badly. He's so strong, isn't he!"

"Poor boy, just crazy to get into the war, too, but—— This Erik Valborg was along, wa'n't he?"

"Yes."

"I think he's an awful handsome fellow, and they say he's smart. Do you like him?"

"He seems very polite."

"Cy says you and him had a lovely boat-ride. My, that must have been pleasant."

"Yes, except that I couldn't get Mr. Valborg to say a word. I wanted to ask him about the suit Mr. Hicks is making for my husband. But he insisted on singing. Still, it was restful, floating around on the water and singing. So happy and innocent. Don't you think it's a shame, Mrs. Bogart, that people in this town don't do more nice clean things like that, instead of all this horrible gossiping?"

"Yes. . . . Yes."

Mrs. Bogart sounded vacant. Her bonnet was awry; she was incomparably dowdy. Carol stared at her, felt contemptuous, ready at last to rebel against the trap, and as the rusty goodwife fished again, "Plannin' some more picnics?" she flung out, "I haven't the slightest idea! Oh. Is that Hugh crying? I must run up to him."

But up-stairs she remembered that Mrs. Bogart had seen her walking with Erik from the railroad track into town, and she was chilly with disquietude.

At the Jolly Seventeen, two days after, she was effusive to Maud Dyer, to Juanita Haydock. She fancied that every one was watching her, but she could not be sure, and in rare strong moments she did not care. She could rebel against the town's prying now that she had something, however indistinct, for which to rebel.

In a passionate escape there must be not only a place from which to flee but a place to which to flee. She had known that she would gladly leave Gopher Prairie, leave Main

Street and all that it signified, but she had had no destination. She had one now. That destination was not Erik Valborg and the love of Erik. She continued to assure herself that she wasn't in love with him but merely "fond of him, and interested in his success." Yet in him she had discovered both her need of youth and the fact that youth would welcome her. It was not Erik to whom she must escape, but universal and joyous youth, in class-rooms, in studios, in offices, in meetings to protest against Things in General. . . . But universal and joyous youth rather resembled Erik.

All week she thought of things she wished to say to him. High, improving things. She began to admit that she was lonely without him. Then she was afraid.

It was at the Baptist church supper, a week after the picnic, that she saw him again. She had gone with Kennicott and Aunt Bessie to the supper, which was spread on oilcloth-covered and trestle-supported tables in the church basement. Erik was helping Myrtle Cass to fill coffee cups for the waitresses. The congregation had doffed their piety. Children tumbled under the tables, and Deacon Pierson greeted the women with a rolling, "Where's Brother Jones, sister, where's Brother Jones? Not going to be with us tonight? Well, you tell Sister Perry to hand you a plate, and make 'em give you enough oyster pie!"

Erik shared in the cheerfulness. He laughed with Myrtle, jogged her elbow when she was filling cups, made deep mock bows to the waitresses as they came up for coffee. Myrtle was enchanted by his humor. From the other end of the room, a matron among matrons, Carol observed Myrtle, and hated her, and caught herself at it. "To be jealous of a wooden-faced village girl!" But she kept it up. She detested Erik; gloated over his gaucheries—his "breaks," she called them. When he was too expressive, too much like a Russian dancer, in saluting Deacon Pierson, Carol had the ecstasy of pain in seeing the deacon's sneer. When, trying to talk to three girls at once, he dropped a cup and effeminately wailed, "Oh dear!" she sympathized with—and ached over—the insulting secret glances of the girls.

From meanly hating him she rose to compassion as she saw that his eyes begged every one to like him. She perceived how inaccurate her judgments could be. At the picnic she had fancied that Maud Dyer looked upon Erik too sentimentally, and she had snarled, "I hate these married women who cheapen themselves and feed on boys." But at the supper Maud was one of the waitresses; she bustled with platters of cake, she was pleasant to old women; and to Erik she gave no attention at all. Indeed, when she had her own supper, she joined the Kennicotts, and how ludicrous it was to suppose that Maud was a gourmet of emotions Carol saw in the fact that she talked not to one of the town beaux but to the safe Kennicott himself.

When Carol glanced at Erik again she discovered that Mrs. Bogart had an eye on her. It was a shock to know that at last there was something which could make her afraid of Mrs. Bogart's spying.

"What am I doing? Am I in love with Erik? Unfaithful? *I?* I want youth but I don't want him—I mean, I don't want youth—enough to break up my life. I must get out of this. Quick."

She said to Kennicott on their way home, "Will! I want to run away for a few days. Wouldn't you like to skip down to Chicago?"

"Still be pretty hot there. No fun in a big city till winter. What do you want to go for?"

"People! To occupy my mind. I want stimulus."

"Stimulus?" He spoke good-naturedly. "Who's been feeding you meat? You got that 'stimulus' out of one of these fool stories about wives that don't know when they're well off. Stimulus! Seriously, though, to cut out the jollying, I can't get away."

"Then why don't I run off by myself?"

"Why—— 'Tisn't the money, you understand. But what about Hugh?"

"Leave him with Aunt Bessie. It would be just for a few days."

"I don't think much of this business of leaving kids around. Bad for 'em."

"So you don't think——"

"I'll tell you: I think we better stay put till after the war. Then we'll have a dandy long trip. No, I don't think you better plan much about going away now."

So she was thrown at Erik.

III

She awoke at ebb-time, at three of the morning, woke sharply and fully; and sharply and coldly as her father pronouncing sentence on a cruel swindler she gave judgment: "A pitiful and tawdry love-affair.

"No splendor, no defiance. A self-deceived little woman whispering in corners with a pretentious little man.

"No, he is not. He is fine. Aspiring. It's not his fault. His eyes are sweet when he looks at me. Sweet, so sweet."

She pitied herself that her romance should be pitiful; she sighed that in this colorless hour, to this austere self, it should seem tawdry.

Then, in a very great desire of rebellion and unleashing of all her hatreds, "The pettier and more tawdry it is, the more blame to Main Street. It shows how much I've been longing to escape. Any way out! Any humility so long as I can flee. Main Street has done this to me. I came here eager for nobilities, ready for work, and now—— Any way out.

"I came trusting them. They beat me with rods of dullness. They don't know, they don't understand how agonizing their complacent dullness is. Like ants and August sun on a wound.

"Tawdry! Pitiful! Carol—the clean girl that used to walk so fast!—sneaking and tittering in dark corners, being sentimental and jealous at church suppers!"

At breakfast-time her agonies were night-blurred, and persisted only as a nervous irresolution.

IV

Few of the aristocrats of the Jolly Seventeen attended the humble folk-meets of the Baptist and Methodist church suppers, where the Willis Woodfords, the Dillons, the Champ Perrys, Oleson the butcher, Brad Bemis the tinsmith, and Deacon Pierson found release from loneliness. But all of the smart set went to the lawn-festivals of the Episcopal Church, and were reprovingly polite to outsiders.

The Harry Haydocks gave the last lawn-festival of the season; a splendor of Japanese lanterns and card-tables and chicken patties and Neapolitan ice-cream. Erik was no longer entirely an outsider. He was eating his ice-cream with a group of the people most solidly "in"—the Dyers, Myrtle Cass, Guy Pollock, the Jackson Elders. The Haydocks themselves kept aloof, but the others tolerated him. He would never, Carol fancied, be one of the town pillars, because he was not orthodox in hunting and motoring and poker. But he was winning approbation by his liveliness, his gaiety—the qualities least important in him.

When the group summoned Carol she made several very well-taken points in regard to the weather.

Myrtle cried to Erik, "Come on! We don't belong with these old folks. I want to make you 'quainted with the jolliest girl, she comes from Wakamin, she's staying with Mary Howland."

Carol saw him being profuse to the guest from Wakamin. She saw him confidentially strolling with Myrtle. She burst out to Mrs. Westlake, "Valborg and Myrtle seem to have quite a crush on each other."

Mrs. Westlake glanced at her curiously before she mumbled, "Yes, don't they."

"I'm mad, to talk this way," Carol worried.

She had regained a feeling of social virtue by telling Juanita Haydock "how darling her lawn looked with the Japanese lanterns" when she saw that Erik was stalking her. Though he was merely ambling about with his hands in his pockets, though he did not peep at her, she knew that he was calling her. She sidled away from Juanita. Erik hastened to her. She nodded coolly (she was proud of her coolness).

"Carol! I've got a wonderful chance! Don't know but what some ways it might be better than going East to take art. Myrtle Cass says—— I dropped in to say howdy to Myrtle last evening, and had quite a long talk with her father, and he said he was hunting for a fellow to go to work in the flour mill and learn the whole business, and maybe become general manager. I know something about wheat from my farming, and I worked a couple of months in the flour mill at Curlew when I got sick of tailoring. What do you think? You said any work was artistic if it was done by an artist. And flour is so important. What do you think?"

"Wait! Wait!"

This sensitive boy would be very skilfully stamped into conformity by Lyman Cass and his sallow daughter; but did she detest the plan for this reason? "I must be honest. I mustn't tamper with his future to please my vanity." But she had no sure vision. She turned on him:

"How can I decide? It's up to you. Do you want to become a person like Lym Cass, or do you want to become a person like—yes, like me! Wait! Don't be flattering. Be honest. This is important."

"I know. I am a person like you now! I mean, I want to rebel."

"Yes. We're alike," gravely.

"Only I'm not sure I can put through my schemes. I really can't draw much. I guess I have pretty fair taste in fabrics, but since I've known you I don't like to think about fussing with dress-designing. But as a miller, I'd have the means—books, piano, travel."

"I'm going to be frank and beastly. Don't you realize that it isn't just because her papa needs a bright young man in the mill that Myrtle is amiable to you? Can't you understand what she'll do to you when she has you, when she sends you to church and makes you become respectable?"

He glared at her. "I don't know. I suppose so."

"You are thoroughly unstable!"

"What if I am? Most fish out of water are! Don't talk like Mrs. Bogart! How can I be anything but 'unstable'—wandering from farm to tailor shop to books, no training, nothing but trying to make books talk to me! Probably I'll fail. Oh, I know it; probably I'm uneven. But I'm not unstable in thinking about this job in the mill—and Myrtle. I know what I want. I want you!"

"Please, please, oh, please!"

"I do. I'm not a schoolboy any more. I want you. If I take Myrtle, it's to forget you."

"Please, please!"

"It's you that are unstable! You talk at things and play at things, but you're scared. Would I mind it if you and I went off to poverty, and I had to dig ditches? I would not! But you would. I think you would come to like me, but you won't admit it. I wouldn't have said this, but when you sneer at Myrtle and the mill—— If I'm not to have good sensible things like those, d' you think I'll be content with trying to become a damn dressmaker, after *you?* Are you fair? Are you?"

"No, I suppose not."

"Do you like me? Do you?"

"Yes—— No! Please! I can't talk any more."

"Not here. Mrs. Haydock is looking at us."

"No, nor anywhere. O Erik, I am fond of you, but I'm afraid."

"What of?"

"Of Them! Of my rulers—Gopher Prairie. . . . My dear boy, we are talking very foolishly. I am a normal wife and a good mother, and you are—oh, a college freshman."

"You do like me! I'm going to make you love me!"

She looked at him once, recklessly, and walked away with a serene gait that was a disordered flight.

Kennicott grumbled on their way home, "You and this Valborg fellow seem quite chummy."

"Oh, we are. He's interested in Myrtle Cass, and I was telling him how nice she is."

In her room she marveled, "I have become a liar. I'm snarled with lies and foggy analyses and desires—I who was clear and sure."

She hurried into Kennicott's room, sat on the edge of his bed. He flapped a drowsy welcoming hand at her from the expanse of quilt and dented pillows.

"Will, I really think I ought to trot off to St. Paul or Chicago or some place."

"I thought we settled all that, few nights ago! Wait till we can have a real trip." He shook himself out of his drowsiness. "You might give me a good-night kiss."

She did—dutifully. He held her lips against his for an intolerable time. "Don't you like the old man any more?" he coaxed. He sat up and shyly fitted his palm about the slimness of her waist.

"Of course. I like you very much indeed." Even to herself it sounded flat. She longed to be able to throw into her voice the facile passion of a light woman. She patted his cheek.

He sighed, "I'm sorry you're so tired. Seems like—— But of course you aren't very strong."

"Yes. . . . Then you don't think—you're quite sure I ought to stay here in town?"

"I told you so! I certainly do!"

She crept back to her room, a small timorous figure in white.

"I can't face Will down—demand the right. He'd be obstinate. And I can't even go off and earn my living again. Out of the habit of it. He's driving me—— I'm afraid of what he's driving me to. Afraid.

"That man in there, snoring in stale air, my husband? Could any ceremony make him my husband?

"No. I don't want to hurt him. I want to love him. I can't, when I'm thinking of Erik. Am I too honest—a funny topsy-turvy honesty—the faithfulness of unfaith? I wish I had a more compartmental mind, like men. I'm too monogamous—toward Erik!—my child Erik, who needs me.

"Is an illicit affair like a gambling debt—demands stricter

honor than the legitimate debt of matrimony, because it's not legally enforced?

"That's nonsense! I don't care in the least for Erik! Nor for any man. I want to be let alone, in a woman world—a world without Main Street, or politicians, or business men, or men with that sudden beastly hungry look, that glistening unfrank expression that wives know——

"If Erik were here, if he would just sit quiet and kind and talk, I could be still, I could go to sleep.

"I am so tired. If I could sleep——"

chapter 31

THEIR night came unheralded.

Kennicott was on a country call. It was cool but Carol huddled on the porch, rocking, meditating, rocking. The house was lonely and repellent, and though she sighed, "I ought to go in and read—so many things to read—ought to go in," she remained. Suddenly Erik was coming, turning in, swinging open the screen door, touching her hand.

"Erik!"

"Saw your husband driving out of town. Couldn't stand it."

"Well—— You mustn't stay more than five minutes."

"Couldn't stand not seeing you. Every day, towards evening, felt I had to see you—pictured you so clear. I've been good though, staying away, haven't I!"

"And you must go on being good."

"Why must I?"

"We better not stay here on the porch. The Howlands across the street are such window-peepers, and Mrs. Bo-gart——"

She did not look at him but she could divine his tremulousness as he stumbled indoors. A moment ago the night had been coldly empty; now it was incalculable, hot, treacherous. But it is women who are the calm realists once they discard the fetishes of the premarital hunt. Carol was serene as she murmured, "Hungry? I have some little honey-colored cakes. You may have two, and then you must skip home."

"Take me up and let me see Hugh asleep."

"I don't believe——"

"Just a glimpse!"

"Well——"

She doubtfully led the way to the hallroom-nursery. Their heads close, Erik's curls pleasant as they touched her cheek, they looked in at the baby. Hugh was pink with slumber. He had burrowed into his pillow with such energy that it was almost smothering him. Beside it was a celluloid rhinoceros; tight in his hand a torn picture of Old King Cole.

"Shhh!" said Carol, quite automatically. She tiptoed in to pat the pillow. As she returned to Erik she had a friendly sense of his waiting for her. They smiled at each other. She did not think of Kennicott, the baby's father. What she did think was that some one rather like Erik, an older and surer Erik, ought to be Hugh's father. The three of them would play—incredible imaginative games.

"Carol! You've told me about your own room. Let me peep in at it."

"But you mustn't stay, not a second. We must go downstairs."

"Yes."

"Will you be good?"

"R-reasonably!" He was pale, large-eyed, serious.

"You've got to be more than reasonably good!" She felt sensible and superior; she was energetic about pushing open the door.

Kennicott had always seemed out of place there but Erik surprisingly harmonized with the spirit of the room as he stroked the books, glanced at the prints. He held out his hands. He came toward her. She was weak, betrayed to a warm softness. Her head was tilted back. Her eyes were closed. Her thoughts were formless but many-colored. She felt his kiss, diffident and reverent, on her eyelid.

Then she knew that it was impossible. She shook herself. She sprang from him. "Please!" she said sharply.

He looked at her unyielding.

"I am fond of you," she said. "Don't spoil everything. Be my friend."

"How many thousands and millions of women must have said that! And now you! And it doesn't spoil everything. It glorifies everything."

"Dear, I do think there's a tiny streak of fairy in you—

whatever you do with it. Perhaps I'd have loved that once. But I won't. It's too late. But I'll keep a fondness for you. Impersonal—I will be impersonal! It needn't be just a thin talky fondness. You do need me, don't you? Only you and my son need me. I've wanted so to be wanted! Once I wanted love to be given to me. Now I'll be content if I can give. ... Almost content!

"We women, we like to do things for men. Poor men! We swoop on you when you're defenseless and fuss over you and insist on reforming you. But it's so pitifully deep in us. You'll be the one thing in which I haven't failed. Do something definite! Even if it's just selling cottons. Sell beautiful cottons—caravans from China——"

"Carol! Stop! You do love me!"

"I do not! It's just—— Can't you understand? Everything crushes in on me so, all the gaping dull people, and I look for a way out—— Please go. I can't stand any more. Please!"

He was gone. And she was not relieved by the quiet of the house. She was empty and the house was empty and she needed him. She wanted to go on talking, to get this threshed out, to build a sane friendship. She wavered down to the living-room, looked out of the bay-window. He was not to be seen. But Mrs. Westlake was. She was walking past, and in the light from the corner arc-lamp she quickly inspected the porch, the windows. Carol dropped the curtain, stood with movement and reflection paralyzed. Automatically, without reasoning, she mumbled, "I will see him again soon and make him understand we must be friends. But—— The house is so empty. It echoes so."

II

Kennicott had seemed nervous and absent-minded through that supper-hour, two evenings after. He prowled about the living-room, then growled:

"What the dickens have you been saying to Ma Westlake?"

Carol's book rattled. "What do you mean?"

"I told you that Westlake and his wife were jealous of us, and here you been chumming up to them and—— From what Dave tells me, Ma Westlake has been going around town saying you told her that you hate Aunt Bessie, and that you fixed up your own room because I snore, and you said Bjornstam was too good for Bea, and then, just recent, that you were sore on the town because we don't all go down on our knees and beg this Valborg fellow to come take supper with us. God only knows what else she says you said."

"It's not true, any of it! I did like Mrs. Westlake, and I've called on her, and apparently she's gone and twisted everything I've said——"

"Sure. Of course she would. Didn't I tell you she would? She's an old cat, like her pussyfooting, hand-holding husband. Lord, if I was sick, I'd rather have a faith-healer than Westlake, and she's another slice off the same bacon. What I can't understand though——"

She waited, taut.

"——is whatever possessed you to let her pump you, bright a girl as you are. I don't care what you told her—we all get peeved sometimes and want to blow off steam, that's natural —but if you wanted to keep it dark, why didn't you advertise it in the *Dauntless,* or get a megaphone and stand on top of the hotel and holler, or do anything besides spill it to her!"

"I know. You told me. But she was so motherly. And I didn't have any woman—— Vida's become so married and proprietary."

"Well, next time you'll have better sense."

He patted her head, flumped down behind his newspaper, said nothing more.

Enemies leered through the windows, stole on her from the hall. She had no one save Erik. This kind good man Kennicott—he was an elder brother. It was Erik; her fellow outcast, to whom she wanted to run for sanctuary. Through her storm she was, to the eye, sitting quietly with her fingers between the pages of a baby-blue book on home-dressmaking. But her dismay at Mrs. Westlake's treachery had risen to active dread. What had the woman said of her and Erik? What did she know? What had she seen? Who else would join in the baying hunt? Who else had seen her with Erik? What had she to fear from the Dyers, Cy Bogart, Juanita, Aunt Bessie? What precisely had she answered to Mrs. Bogart's questioning?

All next day she was too restless to stay home, yet as she walked the streets on fictitious errands she was afraid of every person she met. She waited for them to speak; waited with foreboding. She repeated, "I mustn't ever see Erik again." But the words did not register. She had no ecstatic indulgence in the sense of guilt which is, to the women of Main Street, the surest escape from blank tediousness.

At five, crumpled in a chair in the living-room, she started at the sound of the bell. Some one opened the door. She waited, uneasy. Vida Sherwin charged into the room. "Here's the one person I can trust!" Carol rejoiced.

Vida was serious but affectionate. She bustled at Carol with, "Oh, there you are, dearie, so glad t' find you in, sit down, want to talk to you."

Carol sat, obedient.

Vida fussily tugged over a large chair and launched out: "I've been hearing vague rumors you were interested in this Erik Valborg. I knew you couldn't be guilty, and I'm surer than ever of it now. Here we are, as blooming as a daisy."

"How does a respectable matron look when she feels guilty?"

Carol sounded resentful.

"Why—— Oh, it would show! Besides! I know that you, of all people, are the one that can appreciate Dr. Will."

"What have you been hearing?"

"Nothing, really. I just heard Mrs. Bogart say she'd seen you and Valborg walking together a lot." Vida's chirping slackened. She looked at her nails. "But—— I suspect you do like Valborg. Oh, I don't mean in any wrong way. But you're young; you don't know what an innocent liking might drift into. You always pretend to be so sophisticated and all, but you're a baby. Just because you are so innocent, you don't know what evil thoughts may lurk in that fellow's brain."

"You don't suppose Valborg could actually think about making love to me?"

Her rather cheap sport ended abruptly as Vida cried, with contorted face, "What do you know about the thoughts in hearts? You just play at reforming the world. You don't know what it means to suffer."

There are two insults which no human being will endure: the assertion that he hasn't a sense of humor, and the doubly impertinent assertion that he has never known trouble. Carol said furiously, "You think I don't suffer? You think I've always had an easy——"

"No, you don't. I'm going to tell you something I've never told a living soul, not even Ray." The dam of repressed imagination which Vida had builded for years, which now, with Raymie off at the wars, she was building again, gave way. "I was—I liked Will terribly well. One time at a party—oh, before he met you, of course—but we held hands, and we were so happy. But I didn't feel I was really suited to him. I let him go. Please don't think I still love him! I see now that Ray was predestined to be my mate. But because I liked him, I know how sincere and pure and noble Will is, and his thoughts never straying from the path of rectitude, and—— If I gave him to you, at least you've got to appreciate him! We danced together and laughed so, and I gave him up, but—— This *is* my affair. I'm *not* intruding! I see the whole thing as he does, because of all I've told you. Maybe it's shameless to bare my heart this way, but I do it for him—for him and you!"

Carol understood that Vida believed herself to have recited minutely and brazenly a story of intimate love; understood that, in alarm, she was trying to cover her shame as she struggled on, "Liked him in the most honorable way— simply can't help it if I still see things through his eyes—— If I gave him up, I certainly am not beyond my rights in demanding that you take care to avoid even the appearance of evil and——" She was weeping; an insignificant, flushed, ungracefully weeping woman.

Carol could not endure it. She ran to Vida, kissed her forehead, comforted her with a murmur of dove-like sounds, sought to reassure her with worn and hastily assembled gifts of words: "Oh, I appreciate it so much," and "You are so fine and splendid," and "Let me assure you there isn't a thing to what you've heard," and "Oh, indeed, I do know how sincere Will is, and as you say, so—so sincere."

Vida believed that she had explained many deep and devious matters. She came out of her hysteria like a sparrow shaking off rain-drops. She sat up, and took advantage of her victory:

"I don't want to rub it in, but you can see for yourself now, this is all a result of your being so discontented and not appreciating the dear good people here. And another thing: People like you and me, who want to reform things, have to be particularly careful about appearances. Think how much better you can criticize conventional customs if you yourself live up to them, scrupulously. Then people can't say you're attacking them to excuse your own infractions."

To Carol was given a sudden great philosophical understanding, an explanation of half the cautious reforms in history. "Yes. I've heard that plea. It's a good one. It sets revolts aside to cool. It keeps strays in the flock. To word it differently: 'You must live up to the popular code if you believe in it; but if you don't believe in it, then you *must* live up to it!' "

"I don't think so at all," said Vida vaguely. She began to look hurt, and Carol let her be oracular.

III

Vida had done her a service; had made all agonizing seem so fatuous that she ceased writhing and saw that her whole problem was simple as mutton: she was interested in Erik's aspiration; interest gave her a hesitating fondness for him; and the future would take care of the event. . . . But at night, thinking in bed, she protested, "I'm not a falsely accused innocent, though! If it were some one more resolute than Erik, a fighter, an artist with bearded surly lips—— They're only in books. Is that the real tragedy, that I never shall know tragedy, never find anything but blustery complications that turn out to be a farce?

"No one big enough or pitiful enough to sacrifice for. Tragedy in neat blouses; the eternal flame all nice and safe in a kerosene stove. Neither heroic faith nor heroic guilt. Peeping at love from behind lace curtains—on Main Street!"

Aunt Bessie crept in next day, tried to pump her, tried to prime the pump by again hinting that Kennicott might have his own affairs. Carol snapped, "Whatever I may do, I'll have you to understand that Will is only too safe!" She wished afterward that she had not been so lofty. How much would Aunt Bessie make of "Whatever I may do?"

When Kennicott came home he poked at things, and hemmed, and brought out, "Saw aunty, this afternoon. She said you weren't very polite to her."

Carol laughed. He looked at her in a puzzled way and fled to his newspaper.

IV

She lay sleepless. She alternately considered ways of leaving Kennicott, and remembered his virtues, pitied his bewilderment in face of the subtle corroding sicknesses which he could not dose nor cut out. Didn't he perhaps need her more than did the book-solaced Erik? Suppose Will were to die, suddenly. Suppose she never again saw him at breakfast, silent but amiable, listening to her chatter. Suppose he never again played elephant for Hugh. Suppose—— A country call, a slippery road, his motor skidding, the edge of the road crumbling, the car turning turtle, Will pinned beneath, suffering, brought home maimed, looking at her with spaniel eyes—or waiting for her, calling for her, while she was in Chicago, knowing nothing of it. Suppose he were sued by some vicious shrieking woman for malpractice. He tried to get witnesses; Westlake spread lies; his friends doubted him; his self-confidence was so broken that it was horrible to see the indecision of the decisive man; he was convicted, handcuffed, taken on a train——

She ran to his room. At her nervous push the door swung sharply in, struck a chair. He awoke, gasped, then in a steady voice: "What is it, dear? Anything wrong?" She darted to him, fumbled for the familiar harsh bristly cheek. How well she knew it, every seam, and hardness of bone, and roll of fat! Yet when he sighed, "This is a nice visit," and dropped his hand on her thin-covered shoulder, she said, too cheerily, "I thought I heard you moaning. So silly of me. Good night, dear."

V

She did not see Erik for a fortnight, save once at church and once when she went to the tailor shop to talk over the plans, contingencies, and strategy of Kennicott's annual campaign for getting a new suit. Nat Hicks was there, and he was not so deferential as he had been. With unnecessary jauntiness he chuckled, "Some nice flannels, them samples, heh?" Needlessly he touched her arm to call attention to the fashion-plates, and humorously he glanced from her to Erik. At home she wondered if the little beast might not be suggesting himself as a rival to Erik, but that abysmal bedragglement she would not consider.

She saw Juanita Haydock slowly walking past the house— as Mrs. Westlake had once walked past.

She met Mrs. Westlake in Uncle Whittier's store, and before that alert stare forgot her determination to be rude, and was shakily cordial.

She was sure that all the men on the street, even Guy Pollock and Sam Clark, leered at her in an interested hopeful way, as though she were a notorious divorcée. She felt as insecure as a shadowed criminal. She wished to see Erik, and wished that she had never seen him. She fancied that Kennicott was the only person in town who did not know all—

know incomparably more than there was to know—about herself and Erik. She crouched in her chair as she imagined men talking of her, thick-voiced, obscene, in barber shops and the tobacco-stinking pool parlor.

Through early autumn Fern Mullins was the only person who broke the suspense. The frivolous teacher had come to accept Carol as of her own youth, and though school had begun she rushed in daily to suggest dances, welsh-rabbit parties.

Fern begged her to go as chaperon to a barn-dance in the country, on a Saturday evening. Carol could not go. The next day, the storm crashed.

chapter 32

CAROL was on the back porch, tightening a bolt on the baby's go-cart, this Sunday afternoon. Through an open window of the Bogart house she heard a screeching, heard Mrs. Bogart's haggish voice:

". . . did too, and there's no use your denying it . . . no you don't, you march yourself right straight out of the house . . . never in my life heard of such . . . never had nobody talk to me like . . . walk in the ways of sin and nastiness . . . leave your clothes here, and heaven knows that's more than you deserve . . . any of your lip or I'll call the policeman."

The voice of the other interlocutor Carol did not catch, nor, though Mrs. Bogart was proclaiming that he was her confidant and present assistant, did she catch the voice of Mrs. Bogart's God.

"Another row with Cy," Carol inferred.

She trundled the go-cart down the back steps and tentatively wheeled it across the yard, proud of her repairs. She heard steps on the sidewalk. She saw not Cy Bogart but Fern Mullins, carrying a suit-case, hurrying up the street with her head low. The widow, standing on the porch with buttery arms akimbo, yammered after the fleeing girl:

"And don't you dare show your face on this block again.

You can send the drayman for your trunk. My house has been contaminated long enough. Why the Lord should afflict me——"

Fern was gone. The righteous widow glared, banged into the house, came out poking at her bonnet, marched away. By this time Carol was staring in a manner not visibly to be distinguished from the window-peeping of the rest of Gopher Prairie. She saw Mrs. Bogart enter the Howland house, then the Casses'. Not till suppertime did she reach the Kennicotts. The doctor answered her ring, and greeted her. "Well, well, how's the good neighbor?"

The good neighbor charged into the living-room, waving the most unctuous of black kid gloves and delightedly sputtering:

"You may well ask how I am! I really do wonder how I could go through the awful scenes of this day—and the impudence I took from that woman's tongue, that ought to be cut out——"

"Whoa! Whoa! Hold up!" roared Kennicott. "Who's the hussy, Sister Bogart? Sit down and take it cool and tell us about it."

"I can't sit down, I must hurry home, but I couldn't devote myself to my own selfish cares till I'd warned you, and heaven knows I don't expect any thanks for trying to warn the town against her, there's always so much evil in the world that folks simply won't see or appreciate your trying to safeguard them—— And forcing herself in here to get in with you and Carrie, many 's the time I've seen her doing it, and, thank heaven, she was found out in time before she could do any more harm, it simply breaks my heart and prostrates me to think what she may have done already, even if some of us that understand and know about things——"

"Whoa-up! Who are you talking about?"

"She's talking about Fern Mullins," Carol put in, not pleasantly.

"Huh?"

Kennicott was incredulous.

"I certainly am!" flourished Mrs. Bogart, "and good and thankful you may be that I found her out in time, before she could get *you* into something, Carol; because even if you are my neighbor and Will's wife and a cultured lady, let me tell you right now, Carol Kennicott, that you ain't always as respectful to—you ain't as reverent—you don't stick by the good old ways like they was laid down for us by God in the

Bible, and while of course there ain't a bit of harm in having
a good laugh, and I know there ain't any real wickedness in
you, yet just the same you don't fear God and hate the trans-
gressors of his commandments like you ought to, and you
may be thankful I found out this serpent I nourished in my
bosom—and oh yes! oh yes indeed! my lady must have two
eggs every morning for breakfast, and eggs sixty cents a
dozen, and wa'n't satisfied with one, like most folks—what
did she care how much they cost or if a person couldn't make
hardly nothing on her board and room, in fact I just took
her in out of charity and I might have known from the kind
of stockings and clothes that she sneaked into my house in
her trunk——"

Before they got her story she had five more minutes of
obscene wallowing. The gutter comedy turned into high
tragedy, with Nemesis in black kid gloves. The actual story
was simple, depressing, and unimportant. As to details Mrs.
Bogart was indefinite, and angry that she should be questioned.

Fern Mullins and Cy had, the evening before, driven alone
to a barn-dance in the country. (Carol brought out the admission that Fern had tried to get a chaperon.) At the dance
Cy had kissed Fern—she confessed that. Cy had obtained
a pint of whisky; he said that he didn't remember where he
had got it; Mrs. Bogart implied that Fern had given it to him;
Fern herself insisted that he had stolen it from a farmer's
overcoat—which, Mrs. Bogart raged, was obviously a lie.
He had become soggily drunk. Fern had driven him home;
deposited him, retching and wabbling, on the Bogart porch.

Never before had her boy been drunk, shrieked Mrs. Bogart. When Kennicott grunted, she owned, "Well, maybe once
or twice I've smelled licker on his breath." She also, with
an air of being only too scrupulously exact, granted that
sometimes he did not come home till morning. But he couldn't
ever have been drunk, for he always had the best excuses:
the other boys had tempted him to go down the lake spearing
pickerel by torchlight, or he had been out in a "machine that
ran out of gas." Anyway, never before had her boy fallen
into the hands of a "designing woman."

"What do you suppose Miss Mullins could design to do with
him?" insisted Carol.

Mrs. Bogart was puzzled, gave it up, went on. This morning, when she had faced both of them, Cy had manfully confessed that all of the blame was on Fern, because the teacher

—his own teacher—had dared him to take a drink. Fern had tried to deny it. "Then," gabbled Mrs. Bogart, "then that woman had the impudence to say to me, 'What purpose could I have in wanting the filthy pup to get drunk?' That's just what she called him—pup. 'I'll have no such nasty language in my house,' I says, 'and you pretending and pulling the wool over people's eyes and making them think you're educated and fit to be a teacher and look out for young people's morals—you're worse 'n any street-walker!' I says. I let her have it good. I wa'n't going to flinch from my bounden duty and let her think that decent folks had to stand for her vile talk. 'Purpose?' I says, 'Purpose? I'll tell you what purpose you had! Ain't I seen you making up to everything in pants that'd waste time and pay attention to your impert'nence? Ain't I seen you showing off your legs with them short skirts of yours, trying to make out like you was so girlish and la-de-da, running along the street?' "

Carol was very sick at this version of Fern's eager youth, but she was sicker as Mrs. Bogart hinted that no one could tell what had happened between Fern and Cy before the drive home. Without exactly describing the scene, by her power of lustful imagination the woman suggested dark country places apart from the lanterns and rude fiddling and banging dance-steps in the barn, then madness and harsh hateful conquest. Carol was too sick to interrupt. It was Kennicott who cried, "Oh, for God's sake quit it! You haven't any idea what happened. You haven't given us a single proof yet that Fern is anything but a rattle-brained youngster."

"I haven't, eh? Well, what do you say to this? I come straight out and I says to her, 'Did you or did you not taste the whisky Cy had?' and she says, 'I think I did take one sip—Cy made me,' she said. She owned up to that much, so you can imagine——"

"Does that prove her a prostitute?" asked Carol.

"Carrie! Don't you never use a word like that again!" wailed the outraged Puritan.

"Well, does it prove her to be a bad woman, that she took a taste of whisky? I've done it myself!"

"That's different. Not that I approve your doing it. What do the Scriptures tell us? 'Strong drink is a mocker'! But that's entirely different from a teacher drinking with one of her own pupils."

"Yes, it does sound bad. Fern was silly, undoubtedly. But

as a matter of fact she's only a year or two older than Cy, and probably a good many years younger in experience of vice."

"That's—not—true! She is plenty old enough to corrupt him!"

"The job of corrupting Cy was done by your sinless town, five years ago!"

Mrs. Bogart did not rage in return. Suddenly she was hopeless. Her head drooped. She patted her black kid gloves, picked at a thread of her faded brown skirt, and sighed, "He's a good boy, and awful affectionate if you treat him right. Some thinks he's terrible wild, but that's because he's young. And he's so brave and truthful—why, he was one of the first in town that wanted to enlist for the war, and I had to speak real sharp to him to keep him from running away. I didn't want him to get into no bad influences round these camps—and then," Mrs. Bogart rose from her pitifulness, recovered her pace, "then I go and bring into my own house a woman that's worse, when all's said and done, than any bad woman he could have met. You say this Mullins woman is too young and inexperienced to corrupt Cy. Well then, she's too young and inexperienced to teach him, too, one or t'other, you can't have your cake and eat it! So it don't make no difference which reason they fire her for, and that's practically almost what I said to the school-board."

"Have you been telling this story to the members of the school-board?"

"I certainly have! Every one of 'em! And their wives I says to them, ' 'Tain't my affair to decide what you should or should not do with your teachers,' I says, 'and I ain't presuming to dictate in any way, shape, manner, or form. I just want to know,' I says, 'whether you're going to go on record as keeping here in our schools, among a lot of innocent boys and girls, a woman that drinks, smokes, curses, uses bad language, and does such dreadful things as I wouldn't lay tongue to but you know what I mean,' I says, 'and if so, I'll just see to it that the town learns about it.' And that's what I told Professor Mott, too, being superintendent—and he's a righteous man, not going autoing on the Sabbath like the school-board members. And the professor as much as admitted he was suspicious of the Mullins woman himself."

II

Kennicott was less shocked and much less frightened than
Carol, and more articulate in his description of Mrs. Bogart,
when she had gone.

Maud Dyer telephoned to Carol and, after a rather improbable question about cooking lima beans with bacon,
demanded, "Have you heard the scandal about this Miss Mullins and Cy Bogart?"

"I'm sure it's a lie."

"Oh, probably is." Maud's manner indicated that the falsity
of the story was an insignificant flaw in its general delight-
fulness.

Carol crept to her room, sat with hands curled tight together
as she listened to a plague of voices. She could hear the town
yelping with it, every soul of them, gleeful at new details,
panting to win importance by having details of their own to
add. How well they would make up for what they had been
afraid to do by imagining it in another! They who had not
been entirely afraid (but merely careful and sneaky), all the
barber-shop roués and millinery-parlor mondaines, how
archly they were giggling (this second—she could hear them
at it); with what self-commendation they were cackling their
suavest wit: "You can't tell *me* she ain't a gay bird; I'm wise!"

And not one man in town to carry out their pioneer tradition of superb and contemptuous cursing, not one to verify
the myth that their "rough chivalry" and "rugged virtues" were
more generous than the petty scandal-picking of older lands,
not one dramatic frontiersman to thunder, with fantastic and
fictional oaths, "What are you hinting at? What are you
snickering at? What facts have you? What are these unheard-
of sins you condemn so much—and like so well?"

No one to say it. Not Kennicott nor Guy Pollock nor
Champ Perry.

Erik? Possibly. He would sputter uneasy protest.

She suddenly wondered what subterranean connection her
interest in Erik had with this affair. Wasn't it because they
had been prevented by her caste from bounding on her own
trail that they were howling at Fern?

III

Before supper she found, by half a dozen telephone calls,
that Fern had fled to the Minniemashie House. She hastened

there, trying not to be self-conscious about the people who
looked at her on the street. The clerk said indifferently that
he "guessed" Miss Mullins was up in Room 37, and left
Carol to find the way. She hunted along the stale-smelling
corridors with their wallpaper of cerise daisies and poison-
green rosettes, streaked in white spots from spilled water, their
frayed red and yellow matting, and rows of pine doors painted
a sickly blue. She could not find the number. In the darkness
at the end of a corridor she had to feel the aluminum figures
on the door-panels. She was startled once by a man's voice:
"Yep? Whadyuh want?" and fled. When she reached the
right door she stood listening. She made out a long sobbing.
There was no answer till her third knock; then an alarmed
"Who is it? Go away!"

Her hatred of the town turned resolute as she pushed open
the door.

Yesterday she had seen Fern Mullins in boots and tweed
skirt and canary-yellow sweater, fleet and self-possessed.
Now she lay across the bed, in crumpled lavender cotton and
shabby pumps, very feminine, utterly cowed. She lifted her
head in stupid terror. Her hair was in tousled strings and her
face was sallow, creased. Her eyes were a blur from weeping.

"I didn't! I didn't!" was all she would say at first, and she
repeated it while Carol kissed her cheek, stroked her hair,
bathed her forehead. She rested then, while Carol looked
about the room—the welcome to strangers, the sanctuary of
hospitable Main Street, the lucrative property of Kennicott's
friend, Jackson Elder. It smelled of old linen and decaying
carpet and ancient tobacco smoke. The bed was rickety, with
a thin knotty mattress; the sand-colored walls were scratched
and gouged; in every corner, under everything, were fluffy
dust and cigar ashes; on the tilted wash-stand was a
nicked and squatty pitcher; the only chair was a grim
straight object of spotty varnish; but there was an altogether
splendid gilt and rose cuspidor.

She did not try to draw out Fern's story; Fern insisted
on telling it.

She had gone to the party, not quite liking Cy but willing
to endure him for the sake of dancing, of escaping from Mrs.
Bogart's flow of moral comments, of relaxing after the first
strained weeks of teaching. Cy "promised to be good." He
was, on the way out. There were a few workmen from
Gopher Prairie at the dance, with many young farm-people.
Half a dozen squatters from a degenerate colony in a brush-

hidden hollow, planters of potatoes, suspected thieves, came in noisily drunk. They all pounded the floor of the barn in old-fashioned square dances, swinging their partners, skipping, laughing, under the incantations of Del Snafflin the barber, who fiddled and called the figures. Cy had two drinks from pocket-flasks. Fern saw him fumbling among the overcoats piled on the feed-box at the far end of the barn; soon after she heard a farmer declaring that some one had stolen his bottle. She taxed Cy with the theft; he chuckled, "Oh, it's just a joke; I'm going to give it back." He demanded that she take a drink. Unless she did, he wouldn't return the bottle.

"I just brushed my lips with it, and gave it back to him," moaned Fern. She sat up, glared at Carol. "Did you ever take a drink?"

"I have. A few. I'd love to have one right now! This contact with righteousness has about done me up!"

Fern could laugh then. "So would I! I don't suppose I've had five drinks in my life, but if I meet just one more Bogart and Son—— Well, I didn't really touch that bottle —horrible raw whisky—though I'd have loved some wine. I felt so jolly. The barn was almost like a stage scene—the high rafters, and the dark stalls, and tin lanterns swinging, and a silage-cutter up at the end like some mysterious kind of machine. And I'd been having lots of fun dancing with the nicest young farmer, so strong and nice, and awfully intelligent. But I got uneasy when I saw how Cy was. So I doubt if I touched two drops of the beastly stuff. Do you suppose God is punishing me for even wanting wine?"

"My dear, Mrs. Bogart's god may be—Main Street's god. But all the courageous intelligent people are fighting him ... though he slay us."

Fern danced again with the young farmer; she forgot Cy while she was talking with a girl who had taken the University agricultural course. Cy could not have returned the bottle; he came staggering toward her—taking time to make himself offensive to every girl on the way and to dance a jig. She insisted on their returning. Cy went with her, chuckling and jigging. He kissed her, outside the door. . . .
"And to think I used to think it was interesting to have men kiss you at a dance!" . . . She ignored the kiss, in the need of getting him home before he started a fight. A farmer helped her harness the buggy, while Cy snored in the seat.

He awoke before they set out; all the way home he alternately slept and tried to make love to her.

"I'm almost as strong as he is. I managed to keep him away while I drove—such a rickety buggy. I didn't feel like a girl; I felt like a scrubwoman—no, I guess I was too scared to have any feelings at all. It was terribly dark. I got home, somehow. But it was hard, the time I had to get out, and it was quite muddy, to read a sign-post—I lit matches that I took from Cy's coat pocket, and he followed me—he fell off the buggy step into the mud, and got up and tried to make love to me, and—— I was scared. But I hit him. Quite hard. And got in, and so he ran after the buggy, crying like a baby, and I let him in again, and right away again he was trying—— But no matter. I got him home. Up on the porch. Mrs. Bogart was waiting up. . . .

"You know, it was funny; all the time she was—oh, talking to me—and Cy was being terribly sick—I just kept thinking, 'I've still got to drive the buggy down to the livery stable. I wonder if the livery man will be awake?' But I got through somehow. I took the buggy down to the stable, and got to my room. I locked my door, but Mrs. Bogart kept saying things, outside the door. Stood out there saying things about me, dreadful things, and rattling the knob. And all the while I could hear Cy in the back yard—being sick. I don't think I'll ever marry any man. And then today——

"She drove me right out of the house. She wouldn't listen to me, all morning. Just to Cy. I suppose he's over his headache now. Even at breakfast he thought the whole thing was a grand joke. I suppose right this minute he's going around town boasting about his 'conquest.' You understand—oh, *don't* you understand? I *did* keep him away! But I don't see how I can face my school. They say country towns are fine for bringing up boys in, but—— I can't believe this is me, lying here and saying this. I don't *believe* what happened last night.

"Oh. This was curious: When I took off my dress last night—it was a darling dress, I loved it so, but of course the mud had spoiled it. I cried over it and—— No matter. But my white silk stockings were all torn, and the strange thing is, I don't know whether I caught my legs in the briers when I got out to look at the sign-post, or whether Cy scratched me when I was fighting him off."

IV

Sam Clark was president of the school-board. When Carol told him Fern's story Sam looked sympathetic and neighborly, and Mrs. Clark sat by cooing, "Oh, isn't that too bad." Carol was interrupted only when Mrs. Clark begged, "Dear, don't speak so bitter about 'pious' people. There's lots of sincere practising Christians that are real tolerant. Like the Champ Perrys."

"Yes. I know. Unfortunately there are enough kindly people in the churches to keep them going."

When Carol had finished, Mrs. Clark breathed, "Poor girl; I don't doubt her story a bit," and Sam rumbled, "Yuh, sure. Miss Mullins is young and reckless, but everybody in town, except Ma Bogart, knows what Cy is. But Miss Mullins was a fool to go with him."

"But not wicked enough to pay for it with disgrace?"

"N-no, but——" Sam avoided verdicts, clung to the entrancing horrors of the story. "Ma Bogart cussed her out all morning, did she? Jumped her neck, eh? Ma certainly is one hell-cat."

"Yes, you know how she is; so vicious."

"Oh no, her best style ain't her viciousness. What she pulls in our store is to come in smiling with Christian Fortitude and keep a clerk busy for one hour while she picks out half a dozen fourpenny nails. I remember one time——"

"Sam!" Carol was uneasy. "You'll fight for Fern, won't you? When Mrs. Bogart came to see you did she make definite charges?"

"Well, yes, you might say she did."

"But the school-board won't act on them?"

"Guess we'll more or less have to."

"But you'll exonerate Fern?"

"I'll do what I can for the girl personally, but you know what the board is. There's Reverend Zitterel; Sister Bogart about half runs his church, so of course he'll take her say-so; and Ezra Stowbody, as a banker he has to be all hell for morality and purity. Might 's well admit it, Carrie; I'm afraid there'll be a majority of the board against her. Not that any of us would believe a word Cy said, not if he swore it on a stack of Bibles, but still, after all this gossip, Miss Mullins wouldn't hardly be the party to chaperon our basket-ball team when it went out of town to play other high schools, would she?"

"Perhaps not, but couldn't some one else?"

"Why, that's one of the things she was hired for." Sam sounded stubborn.

"Do you realize that this isn't just a matter of a job, and hiring and firing; that it's actually sending a splendid girl out with a beastly stain on her, giving all the other Bogarts in the world a chance at her? That's what will happen if you discharge her."

Sam moved uncomfortably, looked at his wife, scratched his head, sighed, said nothing.

"Won't you fight for her on the board? If you lose, won't you, and whoever agrees with you, make a minority report?"

"No reports made in a case like this. Our rule is to just decide the thing and announce the final decision, whether it's unanimous or not."

"Rules! Against a girl's future! Dear God! Rules of a school-board! Sam! Won't you stand by Fern, and threaten to resign from the board if they try to discharge her?"

Rather testy, tired of so many subtleties, he complained, "Well, I'll do what I can, but I'll have to wait till the board meets."

And "I'll do what I can," together with the secret admission "Of course you and I know what Ma Bogart is," was all Carol could get from Superintendent George Edwin Mott, Ezra Stowbody, the Reverend Mr. Zitterel or any other member of the school-board.

Afterward she wondered whether Mr. Zitterel could have been referring to herself when he observed, "There's too much license in high places in this town, though, and the wages of sin is death—or anyway, bein' fired." The holy leer with which the priest said it remained in her mind.

She was at the hotel before eight next morning. Fern longed to go to school, to face the tittering, but she was too shaky. Carol read to her all day and, by reassuring her, convinced her own self that the school-board would be just. She was less sure of it that evening when, at the motion pictures, she heard Mrs. Gougerling exclaim to Mrs. Howland, "She may be so innocent and all, and I suppose she probably is, but still, if she drank a whole bottle of whisky at that dance, the way everybody says she did, she may have forgotten she was so innocent! Hee, hee, hee!" Maud Dyer, leaning back from her seat, put in, "That's what I've said all along. I don't want to roast anybody, but have you noticed the way she looks at men?"

"When will they have me on the scaffold?" Carol speculated.

Nat Hicks stopped the Kennicotts on their way home. Carol hated him for his manner of assuming that they two had a mysterious understanding. Without quite winking he seemed to wink at her as he gurgled, "What do you folks think about this Mullins woman? I'm not strait-laced, but I tell you we got to have decent women in our schools. D' you know what I heard? They say whatever she may of done afterwards, this Mullins dame took two quarts of whisky to the dance with her, and got stewed before Cy did! Some tank, that wren! Ha, ha, ha!"

"Rats, I don't believe it," Kennicott muttered.

He got Carol away before she was able to speak.

She saw Erik passing the house, late, alone, and she stared after him, longing for the lively bitterness of the things he would say about the town. Kennicott had nothing for her but "Oh, course, ev'body likes a juicy story, but they don't intend to be mean."

She went up to bed proving to herself that the members of the school-board were superior men.

It was Tuesday afternoon before she learned that the board had met at ten in the morning and voted to "accept Miss Fern Mullins's resignation." Sam Clark telephoned the news to her. "We're not making any charges. We're just letting her resign. Would you like to drop over to the hotel and ask her to write the resignation, now we've accepted it? Glad I could get the board to put it that way. It's thanks to you."

"But can't you see that the town will take this as proof of the charges?"

"We're—not—making—no—charges—whatever!" Sam was obviously finding it hard to be patient.

Fern left town that evening.

Carol went with her to the train. The two girls elbowed through a silent lip-licking crowd. Carol tried to stare them down but in face of the impishness of the boys and the bovine gaping of the men, she was embarrassed. Fern did not glance at them. Carol felt her arm tremble, though she was tearless, listless, plodding. She squeezed Carol's hand, said something unintelligible, stumbled up into the vestibule.

Carol remembered that Miles Bjornstam had also taken a train. What would be the scene at the station when she herself took departure?

She walked up-town behind two strangers.

One of them was giggling, "See that good-looking wench that got on here? The swell kid with the small black hat?

She's some charmer! I was here yesterday, before my jump to Ojibway Falls, and I heard all about her. Seems she was a teacher, but she certainly was a high-roller—O boy!—high, wide, and fancy! Her and couple of other skirts bought a whole case of whisky and went on a tear, and one night, darned if this bunch of cradle-robbers didn't get hold of some young kids, just small boys, and they all got lit up like a White Way, and went out to a roughneck dance, and they say——"

The narrator turned, saw a woman near and, not being a common person nor a coarse workman but a clever salesman and a householder, lowered his voice for the rest of the tale. During it the other man laughed hoarsely.

Carol turned off on a side-street.

She passed Cy Bogart. He was humorously narrating some achievement to a group which included Nat Hicks, Del Snafflin, Bert Tybee the bartender, and A. Tennyson O'Hearn the shyster lawyer. They were men far older than Cy but they accepted him as one of their own, and encouraged him to go on.

It was a week before she received from Fern a letter of which this was a part:

... & of course my family did not really believe the story but as they were sure I must have done something wrong they just lectured me generally, in fact jawed me till I have gone to live at a boarding house. The teachers' agencies must know the story, man at one almost slammed the door in my face when I went to ask about a job, & at another the woman in charge was beastly. Don't know what I will do. Don't seem to feel very well. May marry a fellow that's in love with me but he's so stupid that he makes me *scream*.

Dear Mrs. Kennicott you were the only one that believed me. I guess it's a joke on me, I was such a simp, I felt quite heroic while I was driving the buggy back that night & keeping Cy away from me. I guess I expected the people in Gopher Prairie to admire me. I did use to be admired for my athletics at the U.—just five months ago.

chapter 33

FOR a month which was one suspended moment of doubt she saw Erik only casually, at an Eastern Star dance, at the shop, where, in the presence of Nat Hicks, they conferred with immense particularity on the significance of having one or two buttons on the cuff of Kennicott's New Suit. For the benefit of beholders they were respectably vacuous.

Thus barred from him, depressed in the thought of Fern, Carol was suddenly and for the first time convinced that she loved Erik.

She told herself a thousand inspiriting things which he would say if he had the opportunity; for them she admired him, loved him. But she was afraid to summon him. He understood, he did not come. She forgot her every doubt of him, and her discomfort in his background. Each day it seemed impossible to get through the desolation of not seeing him. Each morning, each afternoon, each evening was a compartment divided from all other units of time, distinguished by a sudden "Oh! I want to see Erik!" which was as devastating as though she had never said it before.

There were wretched periods when she could not picture him. Usually he stood out in her mind in some little moment —glancing up from his preposterous pressing-iron, or running on the beach with Dave Dyer. But sometimes he had vanished; he was only an opinion. She worried then about his appearance: Weren't his wrists too large and red? Wasn't his nose a snub, like so many Scandinavians? Was he at all the graceful thing she had fancied? When she encountered him on the street she was as much reassuring herself as rejoicing in his presence. More disturbing than being unable to visualize him was the darting remembrance of some intimate aspect: his face as they had walked to the boat together at the picnic; the ruddy light on his temples, neck-cords, flat cheeks.

On a November evening when Kennicott was in the country she answered the bell and was confused to find Erik at the

door, stooped, imploring, his hands in the pockets of his top-
coat. As though he had been rehearsing his speech he instantly besought:

"Saw your husband driving away. I've got to see you. I
can't stand it. Come for a walk. I know! People might
see us. But they won't if we hike into the country. I'll wait
for you by the elevator. Take as long as you want to—oh,
come quick!"

"In a few minutes," she promised.

She murmured, "I'll just talk to him for a quarter of an
hour and come home." She put on her tweed coat and rubber
overshoes, considering how honest and hopeless are rubbers,
how clearly their chaperonage proved that she wasn't going
to a lovers' tryst.

She found him in the shadow of the grain-elevator, sulkily
kicking at a rail of the side-track. As she came toward him
she fancied that his whole body expanded. But he said nothing, nor she; he patted her sleeve, she returned the pat, and
they crossed the railroad tracks, found a road, clumped toward open country.

"Chilly night, but I like this melancholy gray," he said.

"Yes."

They passed a moaning clump of trees and splashed along
the wet road. He tucked her hand into the side-pocket of his
overcoat. She caught his thumb and, sighing, held it exactly
as Hugh held hers when they went walking. She thought about
Hugh. The current maid was in for the evening, but was it
safe to leave the baby with her? The thought was distant and
elusive.

Erik began to talk, slowly, revealingly. He made for her a
picture of his work in a large tailor shop in Minneapolis: the
steam and heat, and the drudgery; the men in darned vests
and crumpled trousers, men who "rushed growlers of beer"
and were cynical about women, who laughed at him and
played jokes on him. "But I didn't mind, because I could
keep away from them outside. I used to go to the Art
Institute and the Walker Gallery, and tramp clear around
Lake Harriet, or hike out to the Gates house and imagine it
was a château in Italy and I lived in it. I was a marquis
and collected tapestries—that was after I was wounded in
Padua. The only really bad time was when a tailor named
Finkelfarb found a diary I was trying to keep and he read
it aloud in the shop—it was a bad fight." He laughed. "I
got fined five dollars. But that's all gone now. Seems as

though you stand between me and the gas stoves—the long flames with mauve edges, licking up around the irons and making that sneering sound all day—aaaaah!"

Her fingers tightened about his thumb as she perceived the hot low room, the pounding of pressing-irons, the reek of scorched cloth, and Erik among giggling gnomes. His finger-tip crept through the opening of her glove and smoothed her palm. She snatched her hand away, stripped off her glove, tucked her hand back into his.

He was saying something about a "wonderful person." In her tranquillity she let the words blow by and heeded only the beating wings of his voice.

She was conscious that he was fumbling for impressive speech.

"Say, uh—Carol, I've written a poem about you."

"That's nice. Let's hear it."

"Damn it, don't be so casual about it! Can't you take me seriously?"

"My dear boy, if I took you seriously——! I don't want us to be hurt more than—more than we will be. Tell me the poem. I've never had a poem written about me!"

"It isn't really a poem. It's just some words that I love because it seems to me they catch what you are. Of course probably they won't seem so to anybody else, but—— Well——

> Little and tender and merry and wise
> With eyes that meet my eyes.

Do you get the idea the way I do?"

"Yes! I'm terribly grateful!" And she was grateful—while she impersonally noted how bad a verse it was.

She was aware of the haggard beauty in the lowering night. Monstrous tattered clouds sprawled round a forlorn moon; puddles and rocks glistened with inner light. They were passing a grove of scrub poplars, feeble by day but looming now like a menacing wall. She stopped. They heard the branches dripping, the wet leaves sullenly plumping on the soggy earth.

"Waiting—waiting—everything is waiting," she whispered. She drew her hand from his, pressed her clenched fingers against her lips. She was lost in the somberness. "I am happy—so we must go home, before we have time to become unhappy. But can't we sit on a log for a minute and just listen?"

"No. Too wet. But I wish we could build a fire, and you could sit on my overcoat beside it. I'm a grand fire-builder! My cousin Lars and me spent a week one time in a cabin way up in the Big Woods, snowed in. The fireplace was filled with a dome of ice when we got there, but we chopped it out, and jammed the thing full of pine-boughs. Couldn't we build a fire back here in the woods and sit by it for a while?"

She pondered, half-way between yielding and refusal. Her head ached faintly. She was in abeyance. Everything, the night, his silhouette, the cautious-treading future, was as undistinguishable as though she were drifting bodiless in a Fourth Dimension. While her mind groped, the lights of a motor car swooped round a bend in the road, and they stood farther apart. "What ought I to do?" she mused. "I think—— Oh. I won't be robbed! I *am* good! If I'm so enslaved that I can't sit by the fire with a man and talk, then I'd better be dead!"

The lights of the thrumming car grew magically; were upon them; abruptly stopped. From behind the dimness of the windshield a voice, annoyed, sharp: "Hello there!"

She realized that it was Kennicott.

The irritation in his voice smoothed out. "Having a walk?"

They made schoolboyish sounds of assent.

"Pretty wet, isn't it? Better ride back. Jump up in front here, Valborg."

His manner of swinging open the door was a command. Carol was conscious that Erik was climbing in, that she was apparently to sit in the back, and that she had been left to open the rear door for herself. Instantly the wonder which had flamed to the gusty skies was quenched, and she was Mrs. W. P. Kennicott of Gopher Prairie, riding in a squeaking old car, and likely to be lectured by her husband.

She feared what Kennicott would say to Erik. She bent toward them. Kennicott was observing, "Going to have some rain before the night's over, all right."

"Yes," said Erik.

"Been funny season this year, anyway. Never saw it with such a cold October and such a nice November. 'Member we had a snow way back on October ninth! But it certainly was nice up to the twenty-first, this month—as I remember it, not a flake of snow in November so far, has there been? But I shouldn't wonder if we'd be having some snow 'most any time now."

"Yes, good chance of it," said Erik.

"Wish I'd had more time to go after the ducks this fall. By golly, what do you think?" Kennicott sounded appealing. "Fellow wrote me from Man Trap Lake that he shot seven mallards and couple of canvas-back in one hour!"

"That must have been fine," said Erik.

Carol was ignored. But Kennicott was blustrously cheerful. He shouted to a farmer, as he slowed up to pass the frightened team, "There we are—*schon gut!*" She sat back, neglected, frozen, unheroic heroine in a drama insanely undramatic. She made a decision resolute and enduring. She would tell Kennicott—— What would she tell him? She could not say that she loved Erik. *Did* she love him? But she would have it out. She was not sure whether it was pity for Kennicott's blindness, or irritation at his assumption that he was enough to fill any woman's life, which prompted her, but she knew that she was out of the trap, that she could be frank; and she was exhilarated with the adventure of it . . . while in front he was entertaining Erik:

"Nothing like an hour on a duck-pass to make you relish your victuals and—— Gosh, this machine hasn't got the power of a fountain pen. Guess the cylinders are jam-cram-full of carbon again. Don't know but what maybe I'll have to put in another set of piston-rings."

He stopped on Main Street and clucked hospitably, "There, that'll give you just a block to walk. G' night."

Carol was in suspense. Would Erik sneak away?

He stolidly moved to the back of the car, thrust in his hand, muttered, "Good night—Carol. I'm glad we had our walk." She pressed his hand. The car was flapping on. He was hidden from her—by a corner drug store on Main Street!

Kennicott did not recognize her till he drew up before the house. Then he condescended, "Better jump out here and I'll take the boat around back. Say, see if the back door is unlocked, will you?" She unlatched the door for him. She realized that she still carried the damp glove she had stripped off for Erik. She drew it on. She stood in the center of the living-room, unmoving, in damp coat and muddy rubbers. Kennicott was as opaque as ever. Her task wouldn't be anything so lively as having to endure a scolding, but only an exasperating effort to command his attention so that he would understand the nebulous things she had to tell him, instead of interrupting her by yawning, winding the clock, and going up to bed. She heard him shoveling coal into the furnace. He came through the kitchen energetically, but before he spoke to her he did stop in the hall, did wind the clock.

He sauntered into the living-room and his glance passed from her drenched hat to her smeared rubbers. She could hear—she could hear, see, taste, smell, touch—his "Better take your coat off, Carrie; looks kind of wet." Yes, there it was:

"Well, Carrie, you better——" He chucked his own coat on a chair, stalked to her, went on with a rising tingling voice, "——you better cut it out now. I'm not going to do the outraged husband stunt. I like you and I respect you, and I'd probably look like a boob if I tried to be dramatic. But I think it's about time for you and Valborg to call a halt before you get in Dutch, like Fern Mullins did."

"Do you——"

"Course. I know all about it. What d' you expect in a town that's as filled with busybodies, that have plenty of time to stick their noses into other folks' business, as this is? Not that they've had the nerve to do much tattling to *me*, but they've hinted around a lot, and anyway, I could see for myself that you liked him. But of course I knew how cold you were, I knew you wouldn't stand it even if Valborg did try to hold your hand or kiss you, so I didn't worry. But same time, I hope you don't suppose this husky young Swede farmer is as innocent and Platonic and all that stuff as you are! Wait now, don't get sore! I'm not knocking him. He isn't a bad sort. And he's young and likes to gas about books. Course you like him. That isn't the real rub. But haven't you just seen what this town can do, once it goes and gets moral on you, like it did with Fern? You probably think that two young folks making love are alone if anybody ever is, but there's nothing in this town that you don't do in company with a whole lot of uninvited but awful interested guests. Don't you realize that if Ma Westlake and a few others got started they'd drive you up a tree, and you'd find yourself so well advertised as being in love with this Valborg fellow that you'd *have* to be, just to spite 'em!"

"Let me sit down," was all Carol could say. She drooped on the couch, wearily, without elasticity.

He yawned, "Gimme your coat and rubbers," and while she stripped them off he twiddled his watch-chain, felt the radiator, peered at the thermometer. He shook out her wraps in the hall, hung them up with exactly his usual care. He pushed a chair near to her and sat bolt up. He looked like a physician about to give sound and undesired advice.

Before he could launch into his heavy discourse she desperately got in, "Please! I want you to know that I was going to tell you everything, tonight."

"Well, I don't suppose there's really much to tell."

"But there is. I'm fond of Erik. He appeals to something in here." She touched her breast. "And I admire him. He isn't just a 'young Swede farmer.' He's an artist——"

"Wait now! He's had a chance all evening to tell you what a whale of a fine fellow he is. Now it's my turn. I can't talk artistic, but—— Carrie, do you understand my work?" He leaned forward, thick capable hands on thick sturdy thighs, mature and slow, yet beseeching. "No matter even if you are cold, I like you better than anybody in the world. One time I said that you were my soul. And that still goes. You're all the things that I see in a sunset when I'm driving in from the country, the things that I like but can't make poetry of. Do you realize what my job is? I go round twenty-four hours a day, in mud and blizzard, trying my damnedest to heal everybody, rich or poor. You—that 're always spieling about how scientists ought to rule the world, instead of a bunch of spread-eagle politicians—can't you see that I'm all the science there is here? And I can stand the cold and the bumpy roads and the lonely rides at night. All I need is to have you here at home to welcome me. I don't expect you to be passionate—not any more I don't—but I do expect you to appreciate my work. I bring babies into the world, and save lives, and make cranky husbands quit being mean to their wives. And then you go and moon over a Swede tailor because he can talk about how to put ruchings on a skirt! Hell of a thing for a man to fuss over!"

She flew out at him: "You make your side clear. Let me give mine. I admit all you say—except about Erik. But is it only you, and the baby, that want me to back you up, that demand things from me? They're all on me, the whole town! I can feel their hot breaths on my neck! Aunt Bessie and that horrible slavering old Uncle Whittier and Juanita and Mrs. Westlake and Mrs. Bogart and all of them. And you welcome them, you encourage them to drag me down into their cave! I won't stand it! Do you hear? Now, right now, I'm done. And it's Erik who gives me the courage. You say he just thinks about ruches (which do not usually go on

skirts, by the way!). I tell you he thinks about God, the
God that Mrs. Bogart covers up with greasy gingham
wrappers! Erik will be a great man some day, and if I
could contribute one tiny bit to his success——"

"Wait, wait, wait now! Hold up! You're assuming that
your Erik will make good. As a matter of fact, at my age
he'll be running a one-man tailor shop in some burg about
the size of Schoenstrom."

"He will not!"

"That's what he's headed for now all right, and he's twenty-
five or -six and—— What's he done to make you think he'll
ever be anything but a pants-presser?"

"He has sensitiveness and talent——"

"Wait now! What has he actually done in the art line?
Has he done one first-class picture or—sketch, d' you call
it? Or one poem, or played the piano, or anything except gas
about what he's going to do?"

She looked thoughtful.

"Then it's a hundred to one shot that he never will. Way
I understand it, even these fellows that do something pretty
good at home and get to go to art school, there ain't more
than one out of ten of 'em, maybe one out of a hundred, that
ever get above grinding out a bum living—about as artistic
as plumbing. And when it comes down to this tailor, why,
can't you see—you that take on so about psychology—can't
you see that it's just by contrast with folks like Doc Mc-
Ganum or Lym Cass that this fellow seems artistic? Suppose
you'd met up with him first in one of these reg'lar New York
studios! You wouldn't notice him any more 'n a rabbit!"

She huddled over folded hands like a temple virgin shiv-
ering on her knees before the thin warmth of a brazier. She
could not answer.

Kennicott rose quickly, sat on the couch, took both her
hands. "Suppose he fails—as he will! Suppose he goes back
to tailoring, and you're his wife. Is that going to be this
artistic life you've been thinking about? He's in some bum
shack, pressing pants all day, or stooped over sewing, and
having to be polite to any grouch that blows in and jams a
dirty stinking old suit in his face and says, 'Here you, fix
this, and be blame quick about it.' He won't even have
enough savvy to get him a big shop. He'll pike along doing his
own work—unless you, his wife, go help him, go help him in
the shop, and stand over a table all day, pushing a big heavy
iron. Your complexion will look fine after about fifteen years

of baking that way, won't it! And you'll be humped over like an old hag. And probably you'll live in one room back of the shop. And then at night—oh, you'll have your artist—sure! He'll come in stinking of gasoline, and cranky from hard work, and hinting around that if it hadn't been for you, he'd of gone East and been a great artist. Sure! And you'll be entertaining his relatives—— Talk about Uncle Whit! You'll be having some old Axel Axelberg coming in with manure on his boots and sitting down to supper in his socks and yelling at you, 'Hurry up now, you vimmin make me sick!' Yes, and you'll have a squalling brat every year, tugging at you while you press clothes, and you won't love 'em like you do Hugh up-stairs, all downy and asleep——"

"Please! Not any more!"

Her face was on his knee.

He bent to kiss her neck. "I don't want to be unfair. I guess love is a great thing, all right. But think it would stand much of that kind of stuff? Oh, honey, am I so bad? Can't you like me at all? I've—I've been so fond of you!"

She snatched up his hand, she kissed it. Presently she sobbed, "I won't ever see him again. I can't, now. The hot living-room behind the tailor shop—— I don't love him enough for that. And you are—— Even if I were sure of him, sure he was the real thing, I don't think I could actually leave you. This marriage, it weaves people together. It's not easy to break, even when it ought to be broken."

"And do you want to break it?"

"No!"

He lifted her, carried her up-stairs, laid her on her bed, turned to the door.

"Come kiss me," she whimpered.

He kissed her lightly and slipped away. For an hour she heard him moving about his room, lighting a cigar, drumming with his knuckles on a chair. She felt that he was a bulwark between her and the darkness that grew thicker as the delayed storm came down in sleet.

II

He was cheery and more casual than ever at breakfast. All day she tried to devise a way of giving Erik up. Telephone? The village central would unquestionably "listen in." A letter? It might be found. Go to see him? Impossible. That evening Kennicott gave her, without comment, an envelope. The letter was signed "E. V."

> I know I can't do anything but make trouble for you, I think. I am going to Minneapolis tonight and from there as soon as I can either to New York or Chicago. I will do as big things as I can. I   I can't write I love you too much God keep you.

Until she heard the whistle which told her that the Minneapolis train was leaving town, she kept herself from thinking, from moving. Then it was all over. She had no plan nor desire for anything.

When she caught Kennicott looking at her over his newspaper she fled to his arms, thrusting the paper aside, and for the first time in years they were lovers. But she knew that she still had no plan in life, save always to go along the same streets, past the same people, to the same shops.

III

A week after Erik's going the maid startled her by announcing, "There's a Mr. Valborg down-stairs say he vant to see you."

She was conscious of the maid's interested stare, angry at this shattering of the calm in which she had hidden. She crept down, peeped into the living-room. It was not Erik Valborg who stood there; it was a small, gray-bearded, yellow-faced man in mucky boots, canvas jacket, and red mittens. He glowered at her with shrewd red eyes.

"You de doc's wife?"

"Yes."

"I'm Adolph Valborg, from up by Jefferson. I'm Erik's father."

"Oh!" he was a monkey-faced little man, and not gentle.

"What you done wit' my son?"

"I don't think I understand you."

"I t'ink you're going to understand before I get t'rough! Where is he?"

"Why, really—— I presume that he's in Minneapolis."

"You presume!" he looked through her with a contemptuousness such as she could not have imagined. Only an insane contortion of spelling could portray his lyric whine, his mangled consonants. He clamored, "Presume! Dot's a fine word! I don't want no fine words and I don't want no more lies! I want to know what you *know!*"

"See here, Mr. Valborg, you may stop this bullying right now. I'm not one of your farmwomen. I don't know where your son is, and there's no reason why I should know." Her defiance ran out in face of his immense flaxen stolidity. He raised his fist, worked up his anger with the gesture, and sneered:

"You dirty city women wit' your fine ways and fine dresses! A father come here trying to save his boy from wickedness, and you call him a bully! By God, I don't have to take nothin' off you nor your husband! I ain't one of your hired men. For one time a woman like you is going to hear de trut' about what you are, and no fine city words to it, needer."

"Really, Mr. Valborg——"

"What you done wit' him? Heh? I'll yoost tell you what you done! He was a good boy, even if he was a damn fool. I want him back on de farm. He don't make enough money tailoring. And I can't get me no hired man! I want to take him back on de farm. And you butt in and fool wit' him and make love wit' him, and get him to run away!"

"You are lying! It's not true that—— It's not true, and if it were, you would have no right to speak like this."

"Don't talk foolish. I know. Ain't I heard from a fellow dot live right here in town how you been acting wit' de boy? I know what you done! Walking wit' him in de country! Hiding in de woods wit' him! Yes and I guess you talk about religion in de woods! Sure! Women like you—you're worse dan street-walkers! Rich women like you, wit' fine husbands and no decent work to do—and me, look at my hands, look how I work, look at those hands! But you, oh God no, you mustn't work, you're too fine to do decent work. You got to play wit' young fellows, younger as you are, laughing and rolling around and acting like de animals! You let my son alone, d' you hear?" He was shaking his fist in her face. She could smell the manure and sweat. "It ain't no use talkin' to women like you. Get no trut' out of you. But next time I go by your husband!"

He was marching into the hall. Carol flung herself on him, her clenching hand on his hayseed-dusty shoulder. "You horrible old man, you've always tried to turn Erik into a slave, to fatten your pocketbook! You've sneered at him, and overworked him, and probably you've succeeded in preventing his ever rising above your muck-heap! And now because you can't drag him back, you come here to vent—— Go tell my husband, go tell him, and don't blame me when he kills you, when my husband kills you—he will kill you——"

The man grunted, looked at her impassively, said one word, and walked out.

She heard the word very plainly.

She did not quite reach the couch. Her knees gave way, she pitched forward. She heard her mind saying, "You haven't fainted. This is ridiculous. You're simply dramatizing yourself. Get up." But she could not move. When Kennicott arrived she was lying on the couch. His step quickened. "What's happened, Carrie? You haven't got a bit of blood in your face."

She clutched his arm. "You've got to be sweet to me, and kind! I'm going to California—mountains, sea. Please don't argue about it, because I'm going."

Quietly, "All right. We'll go. You and I. Leave the kid here with Aunt Bessie."

"Now!"

"Well yes, just as soon as we can get away. Now don't talk any more. Just imagine you've already started." He smoothed her hair, and not till after supper did he continue: "I meant it about California. But I think we better wait three weeks or so, till I get hold of some young fellow released from the medical corps to take my practice. And if people are gossiping, you don't want to give them a chance by running away. Can you stand it and face 'em for three weeks or so?"

"Yes," she said emptily.

IV

People covertly stared at her on the street. Aunt Bessie tried to catechize her about Erik's disappearance, and it was Kennicott who silenced the woman with a savage, "Say, are you hinting that Carrie had anything to do with that fellow's beating it? Then let me tell you, and you can go right out and tell the whole bloomin' town, that Carrie and I took Val—took Erik riding, and he asked me about getting a better job in Minneapolis, and I advised him to go to it. . . . Getting much sugar in at the store now?"

Guy Pollock crossed the street to be pleasant apropos of California and new novels. Vida Sherwin dragged her to the Jolly Seventeen. There, with every one rigidly listening, Maud Dyer shot at Carol, "I hear Erik has left town."

Carol was amiable. "Yes, so I hear. In fact, he called me

up—told me he had been offered a lovely job in the city. So sorry he's gone. He would have been valuable if we'd tried to start the dramatic association again. Still, I wouldn't be here for the association myself, because Will is all in from work, and I'm thinking of taking him to California. Juanita—you know the Coast so well—tell me: would you start in at Los Angeles or San Francisco, and what are the best hotels?"

The Jolly Seventeen looked disappointed, but the Jolly Seventeen liked to give advice, the Jolly Seventeen liked to mention the expensive hotels at which they had stayed. (A meal counted as a stay.) Before they could question her again Carol escorted in with drum and fife the topic of Raymie Wutherspoon. Vida had news from her husband. He had been gassed in the trenches, had been in a hospital for two weeks, had been promoted to major, was learning French.

V

She left Hugh with Aunt Bessie.

But for Kennicott she would have taken him. She hoped that in some miraculous way yet unrevealed she might find it possible to remain in California. She did not want to see Gopher Prairie again.

The Smails were to occupy the Kennicott house, and quite the hardest thing to endure in the month of waiting was the series of conferences between Kennicott and Uncle Whittier in regard to heating the garage and having the furnace flues cleaned.

Did Carol, Kennicott inquired, wish to stop in Minneapolis to buy new clothes?

"No! I want to get as far away as I can as soon as I can. Let's wait till Los Angeles."

"Sure, sure! Just as you like. Cheer up! We're going to have a large wide time, and everything'll be different when we come back."

VI

Dusk on a snowy December afternoon. The sleeper which would connect at Kansas City with the California train rolled out of St. Paul with a chick-a-chick, chick-a-chick, chick-a-chick as it crossed the other tracks. It bumped through the factory belt, gained speed. Carol could see nothing but gray

fields, which had closed in on her all the way from Gopher
Prairie. Ahead was darkness.

"For an hour, in Minneapolis, I must have been near Erik.
He's still there, somewhere. He'll be gone when I come back.
I'll never know where he has gone."

As Kennicott switched on the seat-light she turned drearily
to the illustrations in a motion-picture magazine.

chapter 34

THEY journeyed for three and a half months. They saw the
Grand Canyon, the adobe walls of Sante Fe and, in a
drive from El Paso into Mexico, their first foreign land. They
jogged from San Diego and La Jolla to Los Angeles, Pasadena, Riverside, through towns with bell-towered missions
and orange-groves; they viewed Monterey and San Francisco
and a forest of sequoias. They bathed in the surf and climbed
foothills and danced, they saw a polo game and the making
of motion-pictures, they sent one hundred and seventeen
souvenir post-cards to Gopher Prairie, and once, on a dune
by a foggy sea when she was walking alone, Carol found an
artist, and he looked up at her and said, "Too damned wet to
paint; sit down and talk," and so for ten minutes she lived in
a romantic novel.

Her only struggle was in coaxing Kennicott not to spend
all his time with the tourists from the ten thousand other
Gopher Prairies. In winter, California is full of people from
Iowa and Nebraska, Ohio and Oklahoma, who, having traveled thousands of miles from their familiar villages, has-
ten to secure an illusion of not having left them. They hunt
for people from their own states to stand between them and
the shame of naked mountains; they talk steadily, in Pull-
mans, on hotel porches, at cafeterias and motion-picture
shows, about the motors and crops and county politics back
home. Kennicott discussed land-prices with them, he went
into the merits of the several sorts of motor cars with
them, he was intimate with train porters, and he insisted
on seeing the Luke Dawsons at their flimsy bungalow in

Pasadena, where Luke sat and yearned to go back and make some more money. But Kennicott gave promise of learning to play. He shouted in the pool at the Coronado, and he spoke of (though he did nothing more radical than speak of) buying evening-clothes. Carol was touched by his efforts to enjoy picture galleries, and the dogged way in which he accumulated dates and dimensions when they followed monkish guides through missions.

She felt strong. Whenever she was restless she dodged her thoughts by the familiar vagabond fallacy of running away from them, of moving on to a new place, and thus she persuaded herself that she was tranquil. In March she willingly agreed with Kennicott that it was time to go home. She was longing for Hugh.

They left Monterey on April first, on a day of high blue skies and poppies and a summer sea.

As the train struck in among the hills she resolved, "I'm going to love the fine Will Kennicott quality that there is in Gopher Prairie. The nobility of good sense. It will be sweet to see Vida and Guy and the Clarks. And I'm going to see my baby! All the words he'll be able to say now! It's a new start. Everything will be different!"

Thus on April first, among dappled hills and the bronze of scrub oaks, while Kennicott seesawed on his toes and chuckled, "Wonder what Hugh'll say when he sees us?"

Three days later they reached Gopher Prairie in a sleet storm.

II

No one knew that they were coming, no one met them; and because of the icy roads, the only conveyance at the station was the hotel 'bus, which they missed while Kennicott was giving his trunk-check to the station agent—the only person to welcome them. Carol waited for him in the station, among huddled German women with shawls and umbrellas, and ragged-bearded farmers in corduroy coats; peasants mute as oxen, in a room thick with the steam of wet coats, the reek of the red-hot stove, the stench of sawdust boxes which served as cuspidors. The afternoon light was as reluctant as a winter dawn.

"This is a useful market-center, an interesting pioneer post, but it is not a home for me," meditated the stranger Carol.

Kennicott suggested, "I'd 'phone for a flivver but it'd take quite a while for it to get here. Let's walk."

They stepped uncomfortably from the safety of the plank platform and, balancing on their toes, taking cautious strides, ventured along the road. The sleety rain was turning to snow. The air was stealthily cold. Beneath an inch of water was a layer of ice, so that as they wavered with their suit-cases they slid and almost fell. The wet snow drenched their gloves; the water underfoot splashed their itching ankles. They scuffled inch by inch for three blocks. In front of Harry Haydock's Kennicott sighed:

"We better stop in here and 'phone for a machine."

She followed him like a wet kitten.

The Haydocks saw them laboring up the slippery concrete walk, up the perilous front steps, and came to the door chanting:

"Well, well, well, back again, eh? Say, this is fine! Have a fine trip? My, you look like a rose, Carol. How did you like the coast, doc? Well, well, well! Where-all did you go?"

But as Kennicott began to proclaim the list of places achieved, Harry interrupted with an account of how much he himself had seen, two years ago. When Kennicott boasted, "We went through the mission at Santa Barbara," Harry broke in, "Yeh, that's an interesting old mission. Say, I'll never forget that hotel there, doc. It was swell. Why, the rooms were made just like these old monasteries. Juanita and I went from Santa Barbara to San Luis Obispo. You folks go to San Luis Obispo?"

"No, but——"

"Well you ought to gone to San Luis Obispo. And then we went from there to a ranch, least they called it a ranch——"

Kennicott got in only one considerable narrative, which began:

"Say, I never knew—did you, Harry?—that in the Chicago district the Kutz Kar sells as well as the Overland? I never thought much of the Kutz. But I met a gentleman on the train—it was when we were pulling out of Albuquerque, and I was sitting on the back platform of the observation car, and this man was next to me and he asked me for a light, and we got to talking, and come to find out, he came from Aurora, and when he found out I came from Minnesota he asked me if I knew Dr. Clemworth of Red Wing, and of course, while I've never met him, I've heard of Clemworth lots of times, and seems he's this man's brother! Quite a coincidence! Well, we got to talking, and we called the porter—that was a pretty good porter on that car—and we had a couple bottles of ginger ale, and I happened to mention the Kutz Kar, and this man—seems he's driven a lot of different kinds of cars—he's got a Franklin now—and he said that he'd tried the Kutz and liked it first-rate. Well, when we got into a station—I don't remember the name of it—Carrie, what the deuce was the name of that first stop we made the other side of Albuquerque?—well, anyway, I guess we must have stopped there to take on water, and this man and I got out to stretch our legs, and darned if there wasn't a Kutz drawn right up at the depot platform, and he pointed out something I'd never noticed, and I was glad to learn about it: seems that the gear lever in the Kutz is an inch longer——"

Even this chronicle of voyages Harry interrupted, with remarks on the advantages of the ball-gear-shift.

Kennicott gave up hope of adequate credit for being a traveled man, and telephoned to a garage for a Ford taxicab, while Juanita kissed Carol and made sure of being the first to tell the latest, which included seven distinct and proven scandals about Mrs. Swiftwaite, and one considerable doubt as to the chastity of Cy Bogart.

They saw the Ford sedan making its way over the water-lined ice, through the snow-storm, like a tug-boat in a fog. The driver stopped at a corner. The car skidded, it turned about with comic reluctance, crashed into a tree, and stood tilted on a broken wheel.

The Kennicotts refused Harry Haydock's not too urgent offer to take them home in his car "if I can manage to get it out of the garage—terrible day—stayed home from the store—but if you say so, I'll take a shot at it." Carol gurgled, "No, I think we'd better walk; probably make better time, and I'm just crazy to see my baby." With their suit-cases they waddled on. Their coats were soaked through.

Carol had forgotten her facile hopes. She looked about with impersonal eyes. But Kennicott, through rain-blurred lashes, caught the glory that was Back Home.

She noted bare tree-trunks, black branches, the spongy brown earth between patches of decayed snow on the lawns. The vacant lots were full of tall dead weeds. Stripped of summer leaves the houses were hopeless—temporary shelters.

Kennicott chuckled, "By golly, look down there! Jack Elder must have painted his garage. And look! Martin Mahoney has put up a new fence around his chicken yard. Say, that's a good fence, eh? Chicken-tight and dog-tight. That's certainly a dandy fence. Wonder how much it cost a yard? Yes, sir, they been building right along, even in winter. Got more enterprise than these Californians. Pretty good to be home, eh?"

She noted that all winter long the citizens had been throwing garbage into their back yards, to be cleaned up in spring. The recent thaw had disclosed heaps of ashes, dog-bones, torn bedding, clotted paint-cans, all half covered by the icy pools which filled the hollows of the yards. The refuse had stained the water to vile colors of waste: thin red, sour yellow, streaky brown.

Kennicott chuckled, "Look over there on Main Street! They got the feed store all fixed up, and a new sign on it, black and gold. That'll improve the appearance of the block a lot."

She noted that the few people whom they passed wore their raggedest coats for the evil day. They were scarecrows in a shanty town. . . . "To think," she marveled, "of coming two thousand miles, past mountains and cities, to get off here, and to plan to stay here! What conceivable reason for choosing this particular place?"

She noted a figure in a rusty coat and a cloth cap.

Kennicott chuckled, "Look who's coming! It's Sam Clark! Gosh, all rigged out for the weather."

The two men shook hands a dozen times and, in the Western fashion, bumbled, "Well, well, well, well, you old hell-hound, you old devil, how are you, anyway? You old horse-thief, maybe it ain't good to see you again!" While Sam nodded at her over Kennicott's shoulder, she was embarrassed.

"Perhaps I should never have gone away. I'm out of practise in lying. I wish they would get it over! Just a block more and—my baby!"

They were home. She brushed past the welcoming Aunt Bessie and knelt by Hugh. As he stammered, "O mummy, mummy, don't go away! Stay with me, mummy!" she cried, "No, I'll never leave you again!"

He volunteered, "That's daddy."

"By golly, he knows us just as if we'd never been away!" said Kennicott. "You don't find any of these California kids as bright as he is, at his age!"

When the trunk came they piled about Hugh the bewhiskered little wooden men fitting one inside another, the miniature junk, and the Oriental drum, from San Francisco

Chinatown; the blocks carved by the old Frenchman in San Diego; the lariat from San Antonio.

"Will you forgive mummy for going away? Will you?" she whispered.

Absorbed in Hugh, asking a hundred questions about him—had he had any colds? did he still dawdle over his oatmeal? what about unfortunate morning incidents?—she viewed Aunt Bessie only as a source of information, and was able to ignore her hint, pointed by a coyly shaken finger, "Now that you've had such a fine long trip and spent so much money and all, I hope you're going to settle down and be satisfied and not——"

"Does he like carrots yet?" replied Carol.

She was cheerful as the snow began to conceal the slatternly yards. She assured herself that the streets of New York and Chicago were as ugly as Gopher Prairie in such weather; she dismissed the thought, "But they do have charming interiors for refuge." She sang as she energetically looked over Hugh's clothes.

The afternnon grew old and dark. Aunt Bessie went home. Carol took the baby into her own room. The maid came in complaining, "I can't get no extra milk to make chipped beef for supper." Hugh was sleepy, and he had been spoiled by Aunt Bessie. Even to a returned mother, his whining and his trick of seven times snatching her silver brush were fatiguing. As a background, behind the noises of Hugh and the kitchen, the house reeked with a colorless stillness.

From the window she heard Kennicott greeting the Widow Bogart as he had always done, always, every snowy evening: "Guess this 'll keep up all night." She waited. There they were, the furnace sounds, unalterable, eternal: removing ashes, shoveling coal.

Yes. She was back home! Nothing had changed. She had never been away. California? Had she seen it? Had she for one minute left this scraping sound of the small shovel in the ash-pit of the furnace? But Kennicott preposterously supposed that she had. Never had she been quite so far from going away as now when he believed she had just come back. She felt oozing through the walls the spirit of small houses and righteous people. At that instant she knew that in running away she had merely hidden her doubts behind the officious stir of travel.

"Dear God, don't let me begin agonizing again!" she sobbed. Hugh wept with her.

"Wait for mummy a second!" She hastened down to the cellar, to Kennicott.

He was standing before the furnace. However inadequate the rest of the house, he had seen to it that the fundamental cellar should be large and clean, the square pillars white-washed, and the bins for coal and potatoes and trunks convenient. A glow from the drafts fell on the smooth gray cement floor at his feet. He was whistling tenderly, staring at the furnace with eyes which saw the black-domed monster as a symbol of home and of the beloved routine to which he had returned—his gipsying decently accomplished, his duty of viewing "sights" and "curios" performed with thoroughness. Unconscious of her, he stooped and peered in at the blue flames among the coals. He closed the door briskly, and made a whirling gesture with his right hand, out of pure bliss.

He saw her. "Why, hello, old lady! Pretty darn good to be back, eh?"

"Yes," she lied, while she quaked, "Not now. I can't face the job of explaining now. He's been so good. He trusts me. And I'm going to break his heart!"

She smiled at him. She tidied his sacred cellar by throwing an empty bluing bottle into the trash bin. She mourned, "It's only the baby that holds me. If Hugh died——" She fled upstairs in panic and made sure that nothing had happened to Hugh in these four minutes.

She saw a pencil-mark on a window-sill. She had made it on a September day when she had been planning a picnic for Fern Mullins and Erik. Fern and she had been hysterical with nonsense, had invented mad parties for all the coming winter. She glanced across the alley at the room which Fern had occupied. A rag of a gray curtain masked the still window.

She tried to think of some one to whom she wanted to telephone. There was no one.

The Sam Clarks called that evening and encouraged her to described the missions. A dozen times they told her how glad they were to have her back.

"It is good to be wanted," she thought. "It will drug me. But—— Oh, is all life, always, an unresolved But?"

chapter 35

SHE tried to be content which was a contradiction in terms. She fanatically cleaned house all April. She knitted a sweater for Hugh. She was diligent at Red Cross work. She was silent when Vida raved that though America hated war as much as ever, we must invade Germany and wipe out every man, because it was now proven that there was no soldier in the German army who was not crucifying prisoners and cutting off babies' hands.

Carol was a volunteer nurse when Mrs. Champ Perry suddenly died of pneumonia.

In her funeral procession were the eleven people left out of the Grand Army and the Territorial Pioneers, old men and women, very old and weak, who a few decades ago had been boys and girls of the frontier, riding broncos through the rank windy grass of this prairie. They hobbled behind a band made up of business men and high-school boys, who straggled along without uniforms or ranks or leader, trying to play Chopin's Funeral March—a shabby group of neighbors with grave eyes, stumbling through the slush under a solemnity of faltering music.

Champ was broken. His rheumatism was worse. The rooms over the store were silent. He could not do his work as buyer at the elevator. Farmers coming in with sled-loads of wheat complained that Champ could not read the scale, that he seemed always to be watching some one back in the darkness of the bins. He was seen slipping through alleys, talking to himself, trying to avoid observation, creeping at last to the cemetery. Once Carol followed him and found the coarse, tobacco-stained, unimaginative old man lying on the snow of the grave, his thick arms spread out across the raw mound as if to protect her from the cold, her whom he had carefully covered up every night for sixty years, who was alone there now, uncared for.

The elevator company, Ezra Stowbody president, let him go. The company, Ezra explained to Carol, had no funds for giving pensions.

She tried to have him appointed to the postmastership, which, since all the work was done by assistants, was the one sinecure in town, the one reward for political purity. But it proved that Mr. Bert Tybee, the former bartender, desired the postmastership.

At her solicitation Lyman Cass gave Champ a warm berth as night watchman. Small boys played a good many tricks on Champ when he fell asleep at the mill.

II

She had vicarious happiness in the return of Major Raymond Wutherspoon. He was well, but still weak from having been gassed; he had been discharged and he came home as the first of the war veterans. It was rumored that he surprised Vida by coming unannounced, that Vida fainted when she saw him, and for a night and day would not share him with the town. When Carol saw them Vida was hazy about everything except Raymie, and never went so far from him that she could not slip her hand under his. Without understanding why, Carol was troubled by this intensity. And Raymie— surely this was not Raymie, but a sterner brother of his, this man with the tight blouse, the shoulder emblems, the trim legs in boots. His face seemed different, his lips more tight. He was not Raymie; he was Major Wutherspoon, and Kennicott and Carol were grateful when he divulged that Paris wasn't half as pretty as Minneapolis, that all of the American soldiers had been distinguished by their morality when on leave. Kennicott was respectful as he inquired whether the Germans had good aeroplanes, and what a salient was, and a cootie, and Going West.

In a week Major Wutherspoon was made full manager of the Bon Ton. Harry Haydock was going to devote himself to the half-dozen branch stores which he was establishing at cross-roads hamlets. Harry would be the town's rich man in the coming generation, and Major Wutherspoon would rise with him, and Vida was jubilant, though she was regretful at having to give up most of her Red Cross work. Ray still needed nursing, she explained.

When Carol saw him with his uniform off, in a pepper-and-salt suit and a new gray felt hat, she was disappointed. He was not Major Wutherspoon; he was Raymie.

For a month small boys followed him down the street, and everybody called him Major, but that was presently shortened to Maje, and the small boys did not look up from their marbles as he went by.

III

The town was booming, as a result of the war price of wheat. The wheat money did not remain in the pockets of the farmers; the towns existed to take care of all that. Iowa farmers were selling their land at four hundred dollars an acre and coming into Minnesota. But whoever bought or sold or mortgaged, the townsmen invited themselves to the feast—millers, real-estate men, lawyers, merchants, and Dr. Will Kennicott. They bought land at a hundred and fifty, sold it next day at a hundred and seventy, and bought again. In three months Kennicott made seven thousand dollars, which was rather more than four times as much as society paid him for healing the sick.

In early summer began a "campaign of boosting." The Commercial Club decided that Gopher Prairie was not only a wheat-center but also the perfect site for factories, summer cottages, and state institutions. In charge of the campaign was Mr. James Blausser, who had recently come to town to speculate in land. Mr. Blausser was known as a Hustler. He liked to be called Honest Jim. He was a bulky, gauche, noisy, humorous man, with narrow eyes, a rustic complexion, large red hands, and brilliant clothes. He was attentive to all women. He was the first man in town who had not been sensitive enough to feel Carol's aloofness. He put his arm about her shoulder while he condescended to Kennicott, "Nice lil wifey, I'll say, doc," and when she answered, not warmly, "Thank you very much for the *imprimatur*," he blew on her neck, and did not know that he had been insulted.

He was a layer-on of hands. He never came to the house without trying to paw her. He touched her arm, let his fist brush her side. She hated the man, and she was afraid of him. She wondered if he had heard of Erik, and was taking advantage. She spoke ill of him at home and in public places, but Kennicott and the other powers insisted, "Maybe he is kind of a roughneck, but you got to hand it to him; he's got more git-up-and-git than any fellow that ever hit this burg. And he's pretty cute, too. Hear what he said to old Ezra? Chucked him in the ribs and said, 'Say, boy, what do you want to go to Denver for? Wait 'll I get time and I'll move the mountains here. Any mountain will be tickled to death to locate here once we get the White Way in!' "

The town welcomed Mr. Blausser as fully as Carol snubbed him. He was the guest of honor at the Commercial Club Banquet at the Minniemashie House, an occasion for menus printed in gold (but injudiciously proof-read), for free cigars, soft damp slabs of Lake Superior whitefish served as fillet of sole, drenched cigar-ashes gradually filling the saucers of coffee cups, and oratorical references to Pep, Punch, Go, Vigor, Enterprise, Red Blood, He-Men, Fair Women, God's Country, James J. Hill, the Blue Sky, the Green Fields, the Bountiful Harvest, Increasing Population, Fair Return on Investments, Alien Agitators Who Threaten the Security of Our Institutions, the Hearthstone the Foundation of the State, Senator Knute Nelson, One Hundred Per Cent. Americanism, and Pointing with Pride.

Harry Haydock, as chairman, introduced Honest Jim Blausser. "And I am proud to say, my fellow citizens, that in his brief stay here Mr. Blausser has become my warm personal friend as well as my fellow booster, and I advise you all to very carefully attend to the hints of a man who knows how to achieve."

Mr. Blausser reared up like an elephant with a camel's neck —red faced, red eyed, heavy fisted, slightly belching—a born leader, divinely intended to be a congressman but deflected to the more lucrative honors of real-estate. He smiled on his warm personal friends and fellow boosters, and boomed:

"I certainly was astonished in the streets of our lovely little city, the other day. I met the meanest kind of critter that God ever made—meaner than the horned toad or the Texas lallapaluza! (Laughter.) And do you know what the animile was? He was a knocker! (Laughter and applause.)

"I want to tell you good people, and it's just as sure as God made little apples, the thing that distinguishes our American commonwealth from the pikers and tin-horns in other countries is our Punch. You take a genuwine, honest-to-God homo Americanibus and there ain't anything he's afraid to tackle. Snap and speed are his middle name! He'll put her across if he has to ride from hell to breakfast, and believe me, I'm mighty good and sorry for the boob that's so unlucky as to get in his way, because that poor slob is going to wonder where he was at when Old Mr. Cyclone hit town! (Laughter.)

"Now, frien's, there's some folks so yellow and small and so few in the pod that they go to work and claim that those

of us that have the big vision are off our trolleys. They say
we can't make Gopher Prairie, God bless her! just as big as
Minneapolis or St. Paul or Duluth. But lemme tell you right
here and now that there ain't a town under the blue canopy of
heaven that's got a better chance to take a running jump and
go scooting right up into the two-hundred-thousand class than
little old G. P.! And if there's anybody that's got such cold
kismets that he's afraid to tag after Jim Blausser on the
Big Going Up, then we don't want him here! Way I figger it,
you folks are just patriotic enough so that you ain't going to
stand for any guy sneering and knocking his own town, no
matter how much of a smart Aleck he is—and just on the
side I want to add that this Farmers' Nonpartisan League and
the whole bunch of socialists are right in the same category,
or, as the fellow says, in the same scategory, meaning This
Way Out, Exit, Beat It While the Going's Good, This
Means You, for all knockers of prosperity and the rights of
property!

"Fellow citizens, there's a lot of folks, even right here in
this fair state, fairest and richest of all the glorious union,
that stand up on their hind legs and claim that the East and
Europe put it all over the golden Northwestland. Now let me
nail that lie right here and now. 'Ah-ha,' says they, 'so Jim
Blausser is claiming that Gopher Prairie is as good a place
to live in as London and Rome and—and all the rest of the
Big Burgs, is he? How does the poor fish know?' says they.
Well, I'll tell you how I know! I've seen 'em! I've done
Europe from soup to nuts! They can't spring that stuff on Jim
Blausser and get away with it! And let me tell you that the
only live thing in Europe is our boys that are fighting there
now! London—I spent three days, sixteen straight hours a
day, giving London the once-over, and let me tell you that
it's nothing but a bunch of fog and out-of-date buildings that
no live American burg would stand for one minute. You may
not believe it, but there ain't one first-class skyscraper in the
whole works. And the same thing goes for that crowd of
crabs and snobs Down East, and next time you hear some zob
from Yahooville-on-the-Hudson chewing the rag and bulling
and trying to get your goat, you tell him that no two-fisted
enterprising Westerner would have New York for a gift!

"Now the point of this is: I'm not only insisting that Gopher
Prairie is going to be Minnesota's pride, the brightest ray in the
glory of the North Star State, but also and furthermore that
it is right now, and still more shall be, as good a place to live

in, and love in, and bring up the Little Ones in, and it's got
as much refinement and culture, as any burg on the whole
bloomin' expanse of God's Green Footstool, and that goes, get
me, that goes!"

Half an hour later Chairman Haydock moved a vote of
thanks to Mr. Blausser.

The boosters' campaign was on.

The town sought that efficient and modern variety of
fame which is known as "publicity." The band was reorgan-
ized, and provided by the Commercial Club with uniforms
of purple and gold. The amateur baseball-team hired a semi-
professional pitcher from Des Moines, and made a schedule
of games with every town for fifty miles about. The citizens
accompanied it as "rooters," in a special car, with banners
lettered "Watch Gopher Prairie Grow," and with the band
playing "Smile, Smile, Smile." Whether the team won or lost
the *Dauntless* loyally shrieked, "Boost, Boys, and Boost
Together—Put Gopher Prairie on the Map—Brilliant Record of Our Matchless Team."

Then, glory of glories, the town put in a White Way. White
Ways were in fashion in the Middlewest. They were com-
posed of ornamented posts with clusters of high-powered
electric lights along two or three blocks on Main Street.
The *Dauntless* confessed: "White Way Is Installed—Town
Lit Up Like Broadway—Speech by Hon. James Blausser—
Come On You Twin Cities—Our Hat Is In the Ring."

The Commercial Club issued a booklet prepared by a great
and expensive literary person from a Minneapolis advertising
agency, a red-headed young man who smoked cigarettes in a
long amber holder. Carol read the booklet with a certain
wonder. She learned that Plover and Minniemashie Lakes were
world-famed for their beauteous wooded shores and gamey
pike and bass not to be equalled elsewhere in the entire country; that the residences of Gopher Prairie were models of
dignity, comfort, and culture, with lawns and gardens known
far and wide; that the Gopher Prairie schools and public
library, in its neat and commodious building, were celebrated
throughout the state; that the Gopher Prairie mills made the
best flour in the country; that the surrounding farm lands were
renowned, where'er men ate bread and butter, for their incomparable No. 1 Hard Wheat and Holstein-Friesian cattle; and that the stores in Gopher Prairie compared favorably
with Minneapolis and Chicago in their abundance of
luxuries and necessities and the ever-courteous attention

of the skilled clerks. She learned, in brief, that this was the one Logical Location for factories and wholesale houses. "*There's* where I want to go; to that model town Gopher Prairie," said Carol.

Kennicott was triumphant when the Commercial Club did capture one small shy factory which planned to make wooden automobile-wheels, but when Carol saw the promoter she could not feel that his coming much mattered—and a year after, when he failed, she could not be very sorrowful.

Retired farmers were moving into town. The price of lots had increased a third. But Carol could discover no more pictures nor interesting food nor gracious voices nor amusing conversation nor questing minds. She could, she asserted, endure a shabby but modest town; the town shabby and ego-maniac she could not endure. She could nurse Champ Perry, and warm to the neighborliness of Sam Clark, but she could not sit applauding Honest Jim Blausser. Kennicott had begged her, in courtship days, to convert the town to beauty. If it was now as beautiful as Mr. Blausser and the *Dauntless* said, then her work was over, and she could go.

$$\overline{chapter}\ 36$$

K ENNICOTT was not so inhumanly patient that he could continue to forgive Carol's heresies, to woo her as he had on the venture to California. She tried to be inconspicuous, but she was betrayed by her failure to glow over the boosting. Kennicott believed in it; demanded that she say patriotic things about the White Way and the new factory. He snorted, "By golly, I've done all I could, and now I expect you to play the game. Here you been complaining for years about us being so poky, and now when Blausser comes along and does stir up excitement and beautify the town like you've always wanted somebody to, why, you say he's a roughneck, and you won't jump on the band-wagon."

Once, when Kennicott announced at noon-dinner, "What do you know about this! They say there's a chance we may get another factory—cream-separator works!" he added, "You might try to look interested, even if you ain't!" The baby was frightened by the Jovian roar; ran wailing to hide his face in Carol's lap; and Kennicott had to make himself humble and court both mother and child. The dim injustice of not being understood even by his son left him irritable. He felt injured.

An event which did not directly touch them brought down his wrath.

In the early autumn, news came from Wakamin that the sheriff had forbidden an organizer for the National Nonpartisan League to speak anywhere in the county. The organizer had defied the sheriff, and announced that in a few days he would address a farmers' political meeting. That night, the news ran, a mob of a hundred business men led by the sheriff—the tame village street and the smug village faces ruddled by the light of bobbing lanterns, the mob flowing between the squatty rows of shops—had taken the organizer from his hotel, ridden him on a fence-rail, put him on a freight train, and warned him not to return.

The story was threshed out in Dave Dyer's drug store, with Sam Clark, Kennicott, and Carol present.

"That's the way to treat those fellows—only they ought to have lynched him!" declared Sam, and Kennicott and Dave Dyer joined in a proud "You bet!"

Carol walked out hastily, Kennicott observing her.

Through supper-time she knew that he was bubbling and would soon boil over. When the baby was abed, and they sat composedly in canvas chairs on the porch, he experimented, "I had a hunch you thought Sam was kind of hard on that fellow they kicked out of Wakamin."

"Wasn't Sam rather needlessly heroic?"

"All these organizers, yes, and a whole lot of the German and Squarehead farmers themselves, they're seditious as the devil—disloyal, non-patriotic, pro-German pacifists, that's what they are!"

"Did this organizer say anything pro-German?"

"Not on your life! They didn't give him a chance!" His laugh was stagey.

"So the whole thing was illegal—and led by the sheriff! Precisely how do you expect these aliens to obey your law if the officer of the law teaches them to break it? Is it a new kind of logic?"

"Maybe it wasn't exactly regular, but what's the odds? They knew this fellow would try to stir up trouble. Whenever it

comes right down to a question of defending Americanism and
our constitutional rights, it's justifiable to set aside ordinary
procedure."

"What editorial did he get that from?" she wondered, as
she protested, "See here, my beloved, why can't you Tories
declare war honestly? You don't oppose this organizer because
you think he's seditious but because you're afraid that the
farmers he is organizing will deprive you townsmen of the
money you make out of mortgages and wheat and shops.
Of course, since we're at war with Germany, anything that
any one of us doesn't like is 'pro-German,' whether it's business competition or bad music. If we were fighting England,
you'd call the radicals 'pro-English.' When this war is over,
I suppose you'll be calling them 'red anarchists.' What an
eternal art it is—such a glittery delightful art—finding hard
names for our opponents! How we do sanctify our efforts to
keep them from getting the holy dollars we want for ourselves!
The churches have always done it, and the political orators
—and I suppose I do it when I call Mrs. Bogart a 'Puritan' and
Mr. Stowbody a 'capitalist.' But you business men are going
to beat all the rest of us at it, with your simple-hearted, energetic, pompous——"

She got so far only because Kennicott was slow in shaking
off respect for her. Now he bayed:

"That'll be about all from you! I've stood for your sneering at this town, and saying how ugly and dull it is. I've stood
for your refusing to appreciate good fellows like Sam. I've
even stood for your ridiculing our Watch Gopher Prairie
Grow campaign. But one thing I'm not going to stand: I'm not
going to stand my own wife being seditious. You can cam-
ouflage all you want to, but you know darn well that these
radicals, as you call 'em, are opposed to the war, and let me
tell you right here and now, and you and all these long-haired
men and short-haired women can beef all you want to,
but we're going to take these fellows, and if they ain't patriotic, we're going to make them be patriotic. And—Lord knows
I never thought I'd have to say this to my own wife—but if
you go defending these fellows, then the same thing applies
to you! Next thing, I suppose you'll be yapping about free
speech. Free speech! There's too much free speech and free
gas and free beer and free love and all the rest of your
damned mouthy freedom, and if I had my way I'd make you
folks live up to the established rules of decency even if I
had to take you——"

"Will!" She was not timorous now. "Am I pro-German
if I fail to throb to Honest Jim Blausser, too? Let's have my
whole duty as a wife!"

He was grumbling, "The whole thing's right in line with
the criticism you've always been making. Might have known
you'd oppose any decent constructive work for the town or
for——"

"You're right. All I've done has been in line. I don't belong
to Gopher Prairie. That isn't meant as a condemnation of
Gopher Prairie, and it may be a condemnation of me. All
right! I don't care! I don't belong here, and I'm going. I'm
not asking permission any more. I'm simply going."

He grunted. "Do you mind telling me, if it isn't too much
trouble, how long you're going for?"

"I don't know. Perhaps for a year. Perhaps for a life-
time."

"I see. Well, of course, I'll be tickled to death to sell out
my practise and go anywhere you say. Would you like to
have me go with you to Paris and study art, maybe, and
wear velveteen pants and a woman's bonnet, and live on
spaghetti?"

"No, I think we can save you that trouble. You don't quite
understand. I am going—I really am—and alone! I've got
to find out what my work is——"

"Work? Work? Sure! That's the whole trouble with you!
You haven't got enough work to do. If you had five kids and
no hired girl, and had to help with the chores and separate
the cream, like these farmers' wives, then you wouldn't be
so discontented."

"I know. That's what most men—and women—like you
would say. That's how they would explain all I am and all
I want. And I shouldn't argue with them. These business
men, from their crushing labors of sitting in an office seven
hours a day, would calmly recommend that I have a dozen
children. As it happens, I've done that sort of thing. There've
been a good many times when we hadn't a maid, and I
did all the housework, and cared for Hugh, and went to Red
Cross, and did it all very efficiently. I'm a good cook and a
good sweeper, and you don't dare say I'm not!"

"No-no, you're——"

"But was I more happy when I was drudging? I was not.
I was just bedraggled and unhappy. It's work—but not my
work. I could run an office or a library, or nurse and teach
children. But solitary dish-washing isn't enough to satisfy me

—or many other women. We're going to chuck it. We're going to wash 'em by machinery, and come out and play with you men in the offices and clubs and politics you've cleverly kept for yourselves! Oh, we're hopeless, we dissatisfied women! Then why do you want to have us about the place, to fret you? So it's for your sake that I'm going!"

"Of course a little thing like Hugh makes no difference!"

"Yes, all the difference. That's why I'm going to take him with me."

"Suppose I refuse?"

"You won't!"

Forlornly, "Uh—— Carrie, what the devil is it you want, anyway?"

"Oh, conversation! No, it's much more than that. I think it's a greatness of life—a refusal to be content with even the healthiest mud."

"Don't you know that nobody ever solved a problem by running away from it?"

"Perhaps. Only I choose to make my own definition of 'running away.' I don't call—— Do you realize how big a world there is beyond this Gopher Prairie where you'd keep me all my life? It may be that some day I'll come back, but not till I can bring something more than I have now. And even if I am cowardly and run away—all right, call it cowardly, call me anything you want to! I've been ruled too long by fear of being called things. I'm going away to be quiet and think. I'm—I'm going! I have a right to my own life."

"So have I to mine!"

"Well?"

"I have a right to my life—and you're it, you're my life! You've made yourself so. I'm damned if I'll agree to all your freak notions, but I will say I've got to depend on you. Never thought of that complication, did you, in this 'off to Bohemia, and express yourself, and free love, and live your own life' stuff!"

"You have a right to me if you can keep me. Can you?"

He moved uneasily.

II

For a month they discussed it. They hurt each other very much, and sometimes they were close to weeping, and invariably he used banal phrases about her duties and she used phrases quite as banal about freedom, and through it all, her discovery that she really could get away from Main Street was as sweet as the discovery of love. Kennicott never consented definitely. At most he agreed to a public theory that she was "going to take a short trip and see what the East was like in war-time."

She set out for Washington in October—just before the war ended.

She had determined on Washington because it was less intimidating than the obvious New York, because she hoped to find streets in which Hugh could play, and because in the stress of war-work, with its demand for thousands of temporary clerks, she could be initiated into the world of offices.

Hugh was to go with her, despite the wails and rather extensive comments of Aunt Bessie.

She wondered if she might not encounter Erik in the East, but it was a chance thought, soon forgotten.

III

The last thing she saw on the station platform was Kennicott, faithfully waving his hand, his face so full of uncomprehending loneliness that he could not smile but only twitch up his lips. She waved to him as long as she could, and when he was lost she wanted to leap from the vestibule and run back to him. She thought of a hundred tendernesses she had neglected.

She had her freedom, and it was empty. The moment was not the highest of her life, but the lowest and most desolate, which was altogether excellent, for instead of slipping downward she began to climb.

She sighed, "I couldn't do this if it weren't for Will's kindness, his giving me money." But a second after: "I wonder how many women would always stay home if they had the money?"

Hugh complained, "Notice me, mummy!" He was beside her on the red plush seat of the day-coach; a boy of three and a half. "I'm tired of playing train. Let's play something else. Let's go see Auntie Bogart."

"Oh, no! Do you really like Mrs. Bogart?"

"Yes. She gives me cookies and she tells me about the Dear Lord. You never tell me about the Dear Lord. Why don't you tell me about the Dear Lord? Auntie Bogart says I'm going to be a preacher. Can I be a preacher? Can I preach about the Dear Lord?"

"Oh, please wait till my generation has stopped rebelling before yours starts in!"

"What's a generation?"

"It's a ray in the illumination of the spirit."

"That's foolish." He was a serious and literal person, and rather humorless. She kissed his frown, and marveled:

"I am running away from my husband, after liking a Swedish ne'er-do-well and expressing immoral opinions, just as in a romantic story. And my own son reproves me because I haven't given him religious instruction. But the story doesn't go right. I'm neither groaning nor being dramatically saved. I keep on running away, and I enjoy it. I'm mad with joy over it. Gopher Prairie is lost back there in the dust and stubble, and I look forward——"

She continued it to Hugh: "Darling, do you know what mother and you are going to find beyond the blue horizon rim?"

"What?" flatly.

"We're going to find elephants with golden howdahs from which peep young maharanees with necklaces of rubies, and a dawn sea colored like the breast of a dove, and a white and green house filled with books and silver tea-sets."

"And cookies?"

"Cookies? Oh, most decidedly cookies. We've had enough of bread and porridge. We'd get sick on too many cookies, but ever so much sicker on no cookies at all."

"That's foolish."

"It is, O male Kennicott!"

"Huh!" said Kennicott II, and went to sleep on her shoulder.

IV

The theory of the *Dauntless* regarding Carol's absence:

Mrs. Will Kennicott and son Hugh left on No. 24 on Saturday last for a stay of some months in Minneapolis, Chicago, New York, and Washington. Mrs. Kennicott confided to Ye Scribe that she will be connected with one of the multifarious war activities now centering in the Nation's Capital for a brief period before returning. Her countless friends who appreciate her splendid labors with the local Red Cross realize how valuable she will be to any war board with which she chooses to become connected. Gopher Prairie thus adds another shining star to its service flag, and without wishing to knock any neighboring communities, we would like to know any town of anywheres near our size in the state that has such a sterling war record. Another reason why you'd better Watch Gopher Prairie Grow.

* * *

Mr. and Mrs. David Dyer, Mrs. Dyer's sister, Mrs. Jennie Dayborn of Jackrabbit, and Dr. Will Kennicott drove to Minniemashie on Tuesday for a delightful picnic.

chapter 37

SHE found employment in the Bureau of War Risk Insurance. Though the armistice with Germany was signed a few weeks after her coming to Washington, the work of the bureau continued. She filed correspondence all day; then she dictated answers to letters of inquiry. It was an endurance of monotonous details, yet she asserted that she had found "real work."

Disillusions she did have. She discovered that in the afternoon, office routine stretches to the grave. She discovered that an office is as full of cliques and scandals as a Gopher Prairie. She discovered that most of the women in the government bureaus lived unhealthfully, dining on snatches in their crammed apartments. But she also discovered that business women may have friendships and enmities as frankly as men, and may revel in a bliss which no housewife attains —a free Sunday. It did not appear that the Great World needed her inspiration, but she felt that her letters, her contact with the anxieties of men and women all over the country, were a part of vast affairs, not confined to Main Street and a kitchen but linked with Paris, Bangkok, Madrid.

She perceived that she could do office work without losing any of the putative feminine virtue of domesticity; that cooking and cleaning, when divested of the fussing of an Aunt Bessie, take but a tenth of the time which, in a Gopher Prairie, it is but decent to devote to them.

Not to have to apologize for her thoughts to the Jolly Seventeen, not to have to report to Kennicott at the end of the day all that she had done or might do, was a relief which made up for the office weariness. She felt that she was no longer one-half of a marriage but the whole of a human being.

II

Washington gave her all the graciousness in which she had
had faith: white columns seen across leafy parks, spacious
avenues, twisty alleys. Daily she passed a dark square
house with a hint of magnolias and a courtyard behind it,
and a tall curtained second-story window through which a
woman was always peering. The woman was mystery,
romance, a story which told itself differently every day; now
she was a murderess, now the neglected wife of an ambassa-
dor. It was mystery which Carol had most lacked in Gopher
Prairie, where every house was open to view, where every
person was but too easy to meet, where there were no secret gates opening upon moors over which one might walk
by moss-deadened paths to strange high adventures in an
ancient garden.

As she flitted up Sixteenth Street after a Kreisler recital,
given late in the afternoon for the government clerks, as the
lamps kindled in spheres of soft fire, as the breeze flowed into
the street, fresh as prairie winds and kindlier, as she glanced
up the elm alley of Massachusetts Avenue, as she was rested
by the integrity of the Scottish Rite Temple, she loved the
city as she loved no one save Hugh. She encountered Negro
shanties turned into studios, with orange curtains and pots of
mignonette; marble houses on New Hampshire Avenue, with
butlers and limousines; and men who looked like fictional
explorers and aviators. Her days were swift, and she knew
that in her folly of running away she had found the courage
to be wise.

She had a dispiriting first month of hunting lodgings in the
crowded city. She had to roost in a hall-room in a moldy
mansion conducted by an indignant decayed gentlewoman,
and leave Hugh to the care of a doubtful nurse. But later she
made a home.

III

Her first acquaintances were the members of the Tincomb
Methodist Church, a vast red-brick tabernacle. Vida Sherwin
had given her a letter to an earnest woman with eye-glasses,
plaid silk waist, and a belief in Bible Classes, who introduced
her to the Pastor and the Nicer Members of Tincomb. Carol
recognized in Washington as she had in California a trans-
planted and guarded Main Street. Two-thirds of the church-
members had come from Gopher Prairies. The church was

their society and their standard; they went to Sunday service, Sunday School, Christian Endeavor, missionary lectures, church suppers, precisely as they had at home; they agreed that ambassadors and flippant newspapermen and infidel scientists of the bureaus were equally wicked and to be avoided; and by cleaving to Tincomb Church they kept their ideals from all contamination.

They welcomed Carol, asked about her husband, gave her advice regarding colic in babies, passed her the gingerbread and scalloped potatoes at church suppers, and in general made her very unhappy and lonely, so that she wondered if she might not enlist in the militant suffrage organization and be allowed to go to jail.

Always she was to perceive in Washington (as doubtless she would have perceived in New York or London) a thick streak of Main Street. The cautious dullness of a Gopher Prairie appeared in boarding-houses where ladylike bureau-clerks gossiped to polite young army officers about the movies; a thousand Sam Clarks and a few Widow Bogarts were to be identified in the Sunday motor procession, in theater parties, and at the dinners of State Societies, to which the emigrés from Texas or Michigan surged that they might confirm themselves in the faith that their several Gopher Prairies were notoriously "a whole lot peppier and chummier than this stuck-up East."

But she found a Washington which did not cleave to Main Street.

Guy Pollock wrote to a cousin, a temporary army captain, a confiding and buoyant lad who took Carol to tea-dances, and laughed, as she had always wanted some one to laugh, about nothing in particular. The captain introduced her to the secretary of a congressman, a cynical young widow with many acquaintances in the navy. Through her Carol met commanders and majors, newspapermen, chemists and geographers and fiscal experts from the bureaus, and a teacher who was a familiar of the militant suffrage headquarters. The teacher took her to headquarters. Carol never became a prominent suffragist. Indeed her only recognized position was as an able addresser of envelopes. But she was casually adopted by this family of friendly women who, when they were not being mobbed or arrested, took dancing lessons or went picnicking up the Chesapeake Canal or talked about the politics of the American Federation of Labor.

With the congressman's secretary and the teacher Carol leased a small flat. Here she found home, her own place and her own people. She had, though it absorbed most of her salary, an excellent nurse for Hugh. She herself put him to bed and played with him on holidays. There were walks with him, there were motionless evenings of reading, but chiefly Washington was associated with people, scores of them, sitting about the flat, talking, talking, talking, not always wisely but always excitedly. It was not at all the "artist's studio" of which, because of its persistence in fiction, she had dreamed. Most of them were in offices all day, and thought more in card-catalogues or statistics than in mass and color. But they played, very simply, and they saw no reason why anything which exists cannot also be acknowledged.

She was sometimes shocked quite as she had shocked Gopher Prairie by these girls with their cigarettes and elfish knowledge. When they were most eager about soviets or canoeing, she listened, longed to have some special learning which would distinguish her, and sighed that her adventure had come so late. Kennicott and Main Street had drained her self-reliance; the presence of Hugh made her feel temporary. Some day—oh, she'd have to take him back to open fields and the right to climb about hay-lofts.

But the fact that she could never be eminent among these scoffing enthusiasts did not keep her from being proud of them, from defending them in imaginary conversations with Kennicott, who grunted (she could hear his voice), "They're simply a bunch of wild impractical theorists sittin' round chewing the rag," and "I haven't got the time to chase after a lot of these fool fads; I'm too busy putting aside a stake for our old age."

Most of the men who came to the flat, whether they were army officers or radicals who hated the army, had the easy gentleness, the acceptance of women without embarrassed banter, for which she had longed in Gopher Prairie. Yet they seemed to be as efficient as the Sam Clarks. She concluded that it was because they were of secure reputation, not hemmed in by the fire of provincial jealousies. Kennicott had asserted that the villager's lack of courtesy is due to his poverty. "We're no millionaire dudes," he boasted. Yet these army and navy men, these bureau experts, and organizers of multitudinous leagues, were cheerful on three or four thou-

sand a year, while Kennicott had, outside of his land specu-
lations, six thousand or more, and Sam had eight.

Nor could she upon inquiry learn that many of this reckless race died in the poorhouse. That institution is reserved
for men like Kennicott who, after devoting fifty years to
"putting aside a stake," incontinently invest the stake in
spurious oilstocks.

IV

She was encouraged to believe that she had not been abnormal in viewing Gopher Prairie as unduly tedious and slatternly. She found the same faith not only in girls escaped
from domesticity but also in demure old ladies who, tragical-
ly deprived of esteemed husbands and huge old houses, yet
managed to make a very comfortable thing of it by living in
small flats and having time to read.

But she also learned that by comparison Gopher Prairie
was a model of daring color, clever planning, and frenzied
intellectuality. From her teacher-housemate she had a sar-
donic description of a Middlewestern railroad-division town,
of the same size as Gopher Prairie but devoid of lawns and
trees, a town where the tracks sprawled along the cinder-
scabbed Main Street, and the railroad shops, dripping soot
from eaves and doorway, rolled out smoke in greasy coils.

Other towns she came to know by anecdote: a prairie village where the wind blew all day long, and the mud was two
feet thick in spring, and in summer the flying sand scarred
new-painted houses and dust covered the few flowers set out
in pots. New England mill-towns with the hands living in
rows of cottages like blocks of lava. A rich farming-center in
New Jersey, off the railroad, furiously pious, ruled by old
men, unbelievably ignorant old men, sitting about the grocery
talking of James G. Blaine. A Southern town, full of the magnolias and white columns which Carol had accepted as proof
of romance, but hating the Negroes, obsequious to the Old
Families. A Western mining-settlement like a tumor. A booming semi-city with parks and clever architects, visited by
famous pianists and unctuous lecturers, but irritable from a
struggle between union labor and the manufacturers' association, so that in even the gayest of the new houses there was a
ceaseless and intimidating heresy-hunt.

V

The chart which plots Carol's progress is not easy to read.

The lines are broken and uncertain of direction; often instead of rising they sink in wavering scrawls; and the colors are watery blue and pink and the dim gray of rubbed pencil marks. A few lines are traceable.

Unhappy women are given to protecting their sensitiveness by cynical gossip, by whining, by high-church and new-thought religions, or by a fog of vagueness. Carol had hidden in none of these refuges from reality, but she, who was tender and merry, had been made timorous by Gopher Prairie. Even her flight had been but the temporary courage of panic. The thing she gained in Washington was not information about office-systems and labor unions but renewed courage, that amiable contempt called poise. Her glimpse of tasks involving millions of people and a score of nations reduced Main Street from bloated importance to its actual pettiness. She could never again be quite so awed by the power with which she herself had endowed the Vidas and Blaussers and Bogarts.

From her work and from her association with women who had organized suffrage associations in hostile cities, or had defended political prisoners, she caught something of an impersonal attitude; saw that she had been as touchily personal as Maud Dyer.

And why, she began to ask, did she rage at individuals? Not individuals but institutions are the enemies, and they most afflict the disciples who the most generously serve them. They insinuate their tyranny under a hundred guises and pompous names, such as Polite Society, the Family, the Church, Sound Business, the Party, the Country, the Superior White Race; and the only defense against them, Carol beheld, is unembittered laughter.

chapter 38

SHE had lived in Washington for a year. She was tired of the office. It was tolerable, far more tolerable than housework, but it was not adventurous.

She was having tea and cinnamon toast, alone at a small

round table on the balcony of Rauscher's Confiserie. Four débutantes clattered in. She had felt young and dissipated, had thought rather well of her black and leaf-green suit, but as she watched them, thin of ankle, soft under the chin, seventeen or eighteen at most, smoking cigarettes with the correct ennui and talking of "bedroom farces" and their desire to "run up to New York and see something racy," she became old and rustic and plain, and desirous of retreating from these hard brilliant children to a life easier and more sympathetic. When they flickered out and one child gave orders to a chauffeur, Carol was not a defiant philosopher but a faded government clerk from Gopher Prairie, Minnesota.

She started dejectedly up Connecticut Avenue. She stopped, her heart stopped. Coming toward her were Harry and Juanita Haydock. She ran to them, she kissed Juanita, while Harry confided, "Hadn't expected to come to Washington—had to go to New York for some buying—didn't have your address along—just got in this morning—wondered how in the world we could get hold of you."

She was definitely sorry to hear that they were to leave at nine that evening, and she clung to them as long as she could. She took them to St. Mark's for dinner. Stooped, her elbows on the table, she heard with excitement that "Cy Bogart had the 'flu, but of course he was too gol-darn mean to die of it."

"Will wrote me that Mr. Blausser has gone away. How did he get on?"

"Fine! Fine! Great loss to the town. There was a real public-spirited fellow, all right!"

She discovered that she now had no opinions whatever about Mr. Blausser, and she said sympathetically, "Will you keep up the town-boosting campaign?"

Harry fumbled, "Well, we've dropped it just temporarily, but—sure you bet! Say, did the doc write you about the luck B. J. Gougerling had hunting ducks down in Texas?"

When the news had been told and their enthusiasm had slackened she looked about and was proud to be able to point out a senator, to explain the cleverness of the canopied garden. She fancied that a man with dinner-coat and waxed mustache glanced superciliously at Harry's highly form-fitting bright-brown suit and Juanita's tan silk frock, which was doubtful at the seams. She glared back, defending her own, daring the world not to appreciate them.

Then, waving to them, she lost them down the long train shed. She stood reading the list of stations: Harrisburg, Pittsburg, Chicago. Beyond Chicago——? She saw the lakes and stubble fields, heard the rhythm of insects and the creak of a buggy, was greeted by Sam Clark's "Well, well, how's the little lady?"

Nobody in Washington cared enough for her to fret about her sins as Sam did.

But that night they had at the flat a man just back from Finland.

II

She was on the Powhatan roof with the captain. At a table, somewhat vociferously buying improbable "soft drinks" for two fluffy girls, was a man with a large familiar back.

"Oh! I think I know him," she murmured.

"Who? There? Oh, Bresnahan, Percy Bresnahan."

"Yes. You've met him? What sort of a man is he?"

"He's a good-hearted idiot. I rather like him, and I believe that as a salesman of motors he's a wonder. But he's a nuisance in the aeronautic section. Tries so hard to be useful but he doesn't know anything—he doesn't know anything. Rather pathetic: rich man poking around and trying to be useful. Do you want to speak to him?"

"No—no—I don't think so."

III

She was at a motion-picture show. The film was a highly advertised and abysmal thing smacking of simpering hairdressers, cheap perfume, red-plush suites on the back streets of tenderloins, and complacent fat women chewing gum. It pretended to deal with the life of studios. The leading man did a portrait which was a masterpiece. He also saw visions in pipe-smoke, and was very brave and poor and pure. He had ringlets, and his masterpiece was strangely like an enlarged photograph.

Carol prepared to leave.

On the screen, in the rôle of a composer, appeared an actor called Eric Valour.

She was startled, incredulous, then wretched. Looking straight out at her, wearing a beret and a velvet jacket, was Erik Valborg.

He had a pale part, which he played neither well nor badly. She speculated, "I could have made so much of him——" She did not finish her speculation.

She went home and read Kennicott's letters. They had seemed stiff and undetailed, but now there strode from them a personality, a personality unlike that of the languishing young man in the velvet jacket playing a dummy piano in a canvas room.

IV

Kennicott first came to see her in November, thirteen months after her arrival in Washington. When he announced that he was coming she was not at all sure that she wished to see him. She was glad that he had made the decision himself.

She had leave from the office for two days.

She watched him marching from the train, solid, assured, carrying his heavy suit-case, and she was diffident—he was such a bulky person to handle. They kissed each other questioningly, and said at the same time, "You're looking fine; how's the baby?" and "You're looking awfully well, dear; how is everything?"

He grumbled, "I don't want to butt in on any plans you've made or your friends or anything, but if you've got time for it, I'd like to chase around Washington, and take in some restaurants and shows and stuff, and forget work for a while."

She realized, in the taxicab, that he was wearing a soft gray suit, a soft easy hat, a flippant tie.

"Like the new outfit? Got 'em in Chicago. Gosh, I hope they're the kind you like."

They spent half an hour at the flat, with Hugh. She was flustered, but he gave no sign of kissing her again.

As he moved about the small rooms she realized that he had had his new tan shoes polished to a brassy luster. There was a recent cut on his chin. He must have shaved on the train just before coming into Washington.

It was pleasant to feel how important she was, how many people she recognized, as she took him to the Capitol, as she told him (he asked and she obligingly guessed) how many feet it was to the top of the dome, as she pointed out Senator La-Follette and the vice-president, and at lunch-time showed herself an habitué by leading him through the catacombs to the senate restaurant.

She realized that he was slightly more bald. The familiar

way in which his hair was parted on the left side agitated her. She looked down at his hands, and the fact that his nails were as ill-treated as ever touched her more than his pleading shoe-shine.

"You'd like to motor down to Mount Vernon this afternoon, wouldn't you?" she said.

It was the one thing he had planned. He was delighted that it seemed to be a perfectly well bred and Washingtonian thing to do.

He shyly held her hand on the way, and told her the news: they were excavating the basement for the new schoolbuilding, Vida "made him tired the way she always looked at the Maje," poor Chet Dashaway had been killed in a motor accident out on the Coast. He did not coax her to like him. At Mount Vernon he admired the paneled library and Washington's dental tools.

She knew that he would want oysters, that he would have heard of Harvey's apropos of Grant and Blaine, and she took him there. At dinner his hearty voice, his holiday enjoyment of everything, turned into nervousness in his desire to know a number of interesting matters, such as whether they still were married. But he did not ask questions, and he said nothing about her returning. He cleared his throat and observed, "Oh say, been trying out the old camera. Don't you think these are pretty good?"

He tossed over to her thirty prints of Gopher Prairie and the country about. Without defense, she was thrown into it. She remembered that he had lured her with photographs in courtship days; she made a note of his sameness, his satisfaction with the tactics which had proved good before; but she forgot it in the familiar places. She was seeing the sun-speckled ferns among birches on the shore of Minniemashie, wind-rippled miles of wheat, the porch of their own house where Hugh had played, Main Street where she knew every window and every face.

She handed them back, with praise for his photography, and he talked of lenses and time-exposures.

Dinner was over and they were gossiping of her friends at the flat, but an intruder was with them, sitting back, persistent, inescapable. She could not endure it. She stammered:

"I had you check your bag at the station because I wasn't quite sure where you'd stay. I'm dreadfully sorry we haven't

room to put you up at the flat. We ought to have seen about
a room for you before. Don't you think you better call up
the Willard or the Washington now?"

He peered at her cloudily. Without words he asked,
without speech she answered, whether she was also going to
the Willard or the Washington. But she tried to look as
though she did not know that they were debating anything
of the sort. She would have hated him had he been meek
about it. But he was neither meek nor angry. However impatient he may have been with her blandness he said readily:

"Yes, guess I better do that. Excuse me a second. Then
how about grabbing a taxi (Gosh, isn't it the limit the way
these taxi shuffers skin around a corner? Got more nerve
driving than I have!) and going up to your flat for a while?
Like to meet your friends—must be fine women—and I
might take a look and see how Hugh sleeps. Like to know how
he breathes. Don't think he has adenoids, but I better make
sure, eh?" He patted her shoulder.

At the flat they found her two housemates and a girl who
had been to jail for suffrage. Kennicott fitted in surprisingly.
He laughed at the girl's story of the humors of a hunger-
strike; he told the secretary what to do when her eyes were
tired from typing; and the teacher asked him—not as the
husband of a friend but as a physician—whether there was
"anything to this inoculation for colds."

His colloquialisms seemed to Carol no more lax than their
habitual slang.

Like an older brother he kissed her good-night in the midst
of the company.

"He's terribly nice," said her housemates, and waited for
confidences. They got none, nor did her own heart. She could
find nothing definite to agonize about. She felt that she was
no longer analyzing and controlling forces, but swept on by
them.

He came to the flat for breakfast, and washed the dishes.
That was her only occasion for spite. Back home he never
thought of washing dishes!

She took him to the obvious "sights"—the Treasury, the
Monument, the Corcoran Gallery, the Pan-American Building, the Lincoln Memorial, with the Potomac beyond it and
the Arlington hills and the columns of the Lee Mansion. For
all his willingness to play there was over him a melancholy
which piqued her. His normally expressionless eyes had
depths to them now, and strangeness. As they walked through

Lafayette Square, looking past the Jackson statue at the lovely tranquil façade of the White House, he sighed, "I wish I'd had a shot at places like this. When I was in the U., I had to earn part of my way, and when I wasn't doing that or studying, I guess I was roughhousing. My gang were a great bunch for bumming around and raising Cain. Maybe if I'd been caught early and sent to concerts and all that—— Would I have been what you call intelligent?"

"Oh, my dear, don't be humble! You are intelligent! For instance, you're the most thorough doctor——"

He was edging about something he wished to say. He pounced on it:

"You did like those pictures of G. P. pretty well, after all, didn't you!"

"Yes, of course."

"Wouldn't be so bad to have a glimpse of the old town, would it!"

"No, it wouldn't. Just as I was terribly glad to see the Haydocks. But please understand me! That doesn't mean that I withdraw all my criticisms. The fact that I might like a glimpse of old friends hasn't any particular relation to the question of whether Gopher Prairie oughtn't to have festivals and lamp chops."

Hastily, "No, no! Sure not. I und'stand."

"But I know it must have been pretty tiresome to have to live with anybody as perfect as I was."

He grinned. She liked his grin.

V

He was thrilled by old Negro coachmen, admirals, aeroplanes, the building to which his income tax would eventually go, a Rolls-Royce, Lynnhaven oysters, the Supreme Court Room, a New York theatrical manager down for the try-out of a play, the house where Lincoln died, the cloaks of Italian officers, the barrows at which clerks buy their box-lunches at noon, the barges on the Chesapeake Canal, and the fact that District of Columbia cars had both District and Maryland licenses.

She resolutely took him to her favorite white and green cottages and Georgian houses. He admitted that fanlights, and white shutters against rosy brick, were more homelike than a painty wooden box. He volunteered, "I see how you mean. They make me think of these pictures of an old-fashioned

Christmas. Oh, if you keep at it long enough you'll have Sam
and me reading poetry and everything. Oh say, d' I tell you
about this fierce green Jack Elder's had his machine painted?"

VI

They were at dinner.

He hinted, "Before you showed me those places today,
I'd already made up my mind that when I built the new
house we used to talk about, I'd fix it the way you wanted
it. I'm pretty practical about foundations and radiation and
stuff like that, but I guess I don't know a whole lot about
architecture."

"My dear, it occurs to me with a sudden shock that I
don't either!"

"Well—anyway—you let me plan the garage and the
plumbing, and you do the rest, if you ever—I mean—if you
ever want to."

Doubtfully, "That's sweet of you."

"Look here, Carrie; you think I'm going to ask you to love
me, I'm not. And I'm not going to ask you to come back to
Gopher Prairie!"

She gaped.

"It's been a whale of a fight. But I guess I've got myself
to see that you won't ever stand G P. unless you *want* to
come back to it. I needn't say I'm crazy to have you. But
I won't ask you. I just want you to know how I wait for you.
Every mail I look for a letter, and when I get one I'm kind
of scared to open it, I'm hoping so much that you're coming
back. Evenings—— You know I didn't open the cottage down
at the lake at all, this past summer. Simply couldn't stand all
the others laughing and swimming, and you not there. I used
to sit on the porch in town, and I—I couldn't get over the
feeling that you'd simply run up to the drug store and would
be right back, and till after it got dark I'd catch myself
watching, looking up the street, and you never came, and the
house was so empty and still that I didn't like to go in.
And sometimes I fell asleep there, in my chair, and didn't
wake up till after midnight, and the house—— Oh, the devil!
Please get me, Carrie. I just want you to know how welcome
you'll be if you ever do come. But I'm not asking you to."

"You're—— It's awfully——"

" 'Nother thing. I'm going to be frank. I haven't always
been absolutely, uh, absolutely, proper. I've always loved you

more than anything else in the world, you and the kid. But sometimes when you were chilly to me I'd get lonely and sore, and pike out and—— Never intended——"

She rescued him with a pitying, "It's all right. Let's forget it."

"But before we were married you said if your husband ever did anything wrong, you'd want him to tell you."

"Did I? I can't remember. And I can't seem to think. Oh, my dear, I do know how generously you're trying to make me happy. The only thing is—— I can't think. I don't know what I think."

"Then listen! Don't think! Here's what I want you to do! Get a two-weeks leave from your office. Weather's beginning to get chilly here. Let's run down to Charleston and Savannah and maybe Florida."

"A second honeymoon?" indecisively.

"No. Don't even call it that. Call it a second wooing. I won't ask anything. I just want the chance to chase around with you. I guess I never appreciated how lucky I was to have a girl with imagination and lively feet to play with. So—— Could you maybe run away and see the South with me? If you wanted to, you could just—you could just pretend you were my sister and—— I'll get an extra nurse for Hugh! I'll get the best dog-gone nurse in Washington!"

VII

It was in the Villa Margherita, by the palms of the Charleston Battery and the metallic harbor, that her aloofness melted.

When they sat on the upper balcony, enchanted by the moon glitter, she cried, "Shall I go back to Gopher Prairie with you? Decide for me. I'm tired of deciding and undeciding."

"No. You've got to do your own deciding. As a matter of fact, in spite of the honeymoon, I don't think I want you to come home. Not yet."

She could only stare.

"I want you to be satisfied when you get there. I'll do everything I can to keep you happy, but I'll make lots of breaks, so I want you to take time and think it over."

She was relieved. She still had a chance to seize splendid indefinite freedoms. She might go—oh, she'd see Europe, somehow, before she was recaptured. But she also had a

firmer respect for Kennicott. She had fancied that her life
might make a story. She knew that there was nothing heroic
or obviously dramatic in it, no magic of rare hours, nor valiant challenge, but it seemed to her that she was of some significance because she was commonplaceness, the ordinary
life of the age, made articulate and protesting. It had not
occurred to her that there was also a story of Will Kennicott,
into which she entered only so much as he entered into hers;
that he had bewilderments and concealments as intricate
as her own, and soft treacherous desires for sympathy.

Thus she brooded, looking at the amazing sea, holding his
hand.

VIII

She was in Washington; Kennicott was in Gopher Prairie,
writing as dryly as ever about water-pipes and goose-hunting
and Mrs. Fageros's mastoid.

She was talking at dinner to a generalissima of suffrage.
Should she return?

The leader spoke wearily:

"My dear, I'm perfectly selfish. I can't quite visualize the
needs of your husband, and it seems to me that your baby
will do quite as well in the schools here as in your barracks at
home."

"Then you think I'd better not go back?" Carol sounded
disappointed.

"It's more difficult than that. When I say that I'm selfish
I mean that the only thing I consider about women is whether
they're likely to prove useful in building up real political
power for women. And you? Shall I be frank? Remember
when I say 'you' I don't mean you alone. I'm thinking of
thousands of women who come to Washington and New
York and Chicago every year, dissatisfied at home and seeking a sign in the heavens—women of all sorts, from timid
mothers of fifty in cotton gloves, to girls just out of Vassar
who organize strikes in their own fathers' factories! All of
you are more or less useful to me, but only a few of you can
take my place, because I have one virtue (only one): I have
given up father and mother and children for the love of God.

"Here's the test for you: Do you come to 'conquer the
East,' as people say, or do you come to conquer yourself?

"It's so much more complicated than any of you know—so
much more complicated than I knew when I put on Ground

Grippers and started out to reform the world. The final complication in 'conquering Washington' or 'conquering New York' is that the conquerors must beyond all things not conquer! It must have been so easy in the good old' days when authors dreamed only of selling a hundred thousand volumes, and sculptors of being fêted in big houses, and even the Uplifters like me had a simple-hearted ambition to be elected to important offices and invited to go round lecturing. But we meddlers have upset everything. Now the one thing that is disgraceful to any of us is obvious success. The Uplifter who is very popular with wealthy patrons can be pretty sure that he has softened his philosophy to please them, and the author who is making lots of money—poor things, I've heard 'em apologizing for it to the shabby bitter-enders; I've seen 'em ashamed of the sleek luggage they got from movie rights.

"Do you want to sacrifice yourself in such a topsy-turvy world, where popularity makes you unpopular with the people you love, and the only failure is cheap success, and the only individualist is the person who gives up all his individualism to serve a jolly ungrateful proletariat which thumbs its nose at him?"

Carol smiled ingratiatingly, to indicate that she was indeed one who desired to sacrifice, but she sighed, "I don't know; I'm afraid I'm not heroic. I certainly wasn't out home. Why didn't I do big effective——"

"Not a matter of heroism. Matter of endurance. Your Middlewest is double-Puritan—prairie Puritan on top of New England Puritan; bluff fontiersman on the surface, but in its heart it still has the ideal of Plymouth Rock in a sleet-storm. There's one attack you can make on it, perhaps the only kind that accomplishes much anywhere: you can keep on looking at one thing after another in your home and church and bank, and ask why it is, and who first laid down the law that it had to be that way. If enough of us do this impolitely enough, then we'll become civilized in merely twenty thousand years or so, instead of having to wait the two hundred thousand years that my cynical anthropologist friends allow. . . . Easy, pleasant, lucrative home-work for wives: asking people to define their jobs. That's the most dangerous doctrine I know!"

Carol was meditating, "I will go back! I will go on asking questions. I've always done it, and always failed at it, and it's all I can do. I'm going to ask Ezra Stowbody why he's opposed to the nationalization of railroads, and ask Dave

Dyer why a druggist always is pleased when he's called 'doctor,' and maybe ask Mrs. Bogart why she wears a widow's veil that looks like a dead crow."

The woman leader straightened. "And you have one thing. You have a baby to hug. That's my temptation. I dream of babies—or a baby—and I sneak around parks to see them playing. (The children in Dupont Circle are like a poppy-garden.) And the antis call me 'unsexed'!"

Carol was thinking, in panic, "Oughtn't Hugh to have country air? I won't let him become a yokel. I can guide him away from street-corner loafing. . . . I think I can."

On her way home: "Now that I've made a precedent, joined the union and gone out on one strike and learned personal solidarity, I won't be so afraid. Will won't always be resisting my running away. Some day I really will go to Europe with him . . . or without him.

"I've lived with people who are not afraid to go to jail. I could invite a Miles Bjornstam to dinner without being afraid of the Haydocks. . . . I think I could.

"I'll take back the sound of Yvette Guilbert's songs and Elman's violin. They'll be only the lovelier against the thrumming of crickets in the stubble on an autumn day.

"I can laugh now and be serene . . . I think I can."

Though she should return, she said, she would not be utterly defeated. She was glad of her rebellion. The prairie was no longer empty land in the sun-glare; it was the living tawny beast which she had fought and made beautiful by fighting; and in the village streets were shadows of her desires and the sound of her marching and the seeds of mystery and greatness.

IX

Her active hatred of Gopher Prairie had run out. She saw it now as a toiling new settlement. With sympathy she remembered Kennicott's defense of its citizens as "a lot of pretty good folks, working hard and trying to bring up their families the best they can." She recalled tenderly the young awkwardness of Main Street and the makeshifts of the little brown cottages; she pitied their shabbiness and isolation; had compassion for their assertion of culture, even as expressed in Thanatopsis papers, for their pretense of greatness, even as trumpeted in "boosting." She saw Main Street in the dusty prairie sunset, a line of frontier shanties with solemn lonely

people waiting for her, solemn and lonely as an old man who
has outlived his friends. She remembered that Kennicott and
Sam Clark had listened to her songs, and she wanted to run
to them and sing.

"At last," she rejoiced, "I've come to a fairer attitude
toward the town. I can love it, now."

She was, perhaps, rather proud of herself for having acquired so much tolerance.

She awoke at three in the morning, after a dream of being
tortured by Ella Stowbody and the Widow Bogart.

"I've been making the town a myth. This is how people
keep up the tradition of the perfect home-town, the happy
boyhood, the brilliant college friends. We forget so. I've
been forgetting that Main Street doesn't think it's in the least
lonely and pitiful. It thinks it's God's Own Country. It isn't
waiting for me. It doesn't care."

But the next evening she again saw Gopher Prairie as her
home, waiting for her in the sunset, rimmed round with
splendor.

x

She did not return for five months more; five months
crammed with greedy accumulation of sounds and colors to
take back for the long still days.

She had spent nearly two years in Washington.

When she departed for Gopher Prairie, in June, her second
baby was stirring within her.

chapter 39

SHE wondered all the way home what her sensations would
be. She wondered about it so much that she had every
sensation she had imagined. She was excited by each familiar
porch, each hearty "Well, well!" and flattered to be, for a day,
the most important news of the community. She bustled
about, making calls. Juanita Haydock bubbled over their
Washington encounter, and took Carol to her social bosom.

This ancient opponent seemed likely to be her most intimate friend, for Vida Sherwin, though she was cordial, stood back and watched for imported heresies.

In the evening Carol went to the mill. The mystical Om-Om-Om of the dynamos in the electric-light plant behind the mill was louder in the darkness. Outside sat the night watchman, Champ Perry. He held up his stringy hands and squeaked, "We've all missed you terrible."

Who in Washington would miss her?

Who in Washington could be depended upon like Guy Pollock? When she saw him on the street, smiling as always, he seemed an eternal thing, a part of her own self.

After a week she decided that she was neither glad nor sorry to be back. She entered each day with the matter-of-fact attitude with which she had gone to her office in Washington. It was her task; there would be mechanical details and meaningless talk; what of it?

The only problem which she had approached with emotion proved insignificant. She had, on the train, worked herself up to such devotion that she was willing to give up her own room, to try to share all of her life with Kennicott.

He mumbled, ten minutes after she had entered the house, "Say, I've kept your room for you like it was. I've kind of come round to your way of thinking. Don't see why folks need to get on each other's nerves just because they're friendly. Darned if I haven't got so I like a little privacy and mulling things over by myself."

II

She had left a city which sat up nights to talk of universal transition; of European revolution, guild socialism, free verse. She had fancied that all the world was changing.

She found that it was not.

In Gopher Prairie the only ardent new topics were prohibition, the place in Minneapolis where you could get whisky at thriteen dollars a quart, recipes for home-made beer, the "high cost of living," the presidential election, Clark's new car, and not very novel foibles of Cy Bogart. Their problems were exactly what they had been two years ago, what they had been twenty years ago, and what they would be for twenty years to come. With the world a possible volcano, the husbandmen were plowing at the base of the mountain. A volcano does occasionally drop a river of lava on even the best of agriculturists, to their astonishment and considerable injury, but their cousins inherit the farms and a year or two later go back to the plowing.

She was unable to rhapsodize much over the seven new bungalows and the two garages which Kennicott had made to seem so important. Her intensest thought about them was, "Oh yes, they're all right I suppose." The change which she did heed was the erection of the schoolbuilding, with its cheerful brick walls, broad windows, gymnasium, classrooms for agriculture and cooking. It indicated Vida's triumph, and it stirred her to activity—any activity. She went to Vida with a jaunty, "I think I shall work for you. And I'll begin at the bottom."

She did. She relieved the attendant at the rest-room for an hour a day. Her only innovation was painting the pine table a black and orange rather shocking to the Thanatopsis. She talked to the farmwives and soothed their babies and was happy. Thinking of them she did not think of the ugliness of Main Street as she hurried along it to the chatter of the Jolly Seventeen.

She wore her eye-glasses on the street now. She was beginning to ask Kennicott and Juanita if she didn't look young, much younger than thirty-three. The eye-glasses pinched her nose. She considered spectacles. They would make her seem older, and hopelessly settled. No! She would not wear spectacles yet. But she tried on a pair at Kennicott's office. They really were much more comfortable.

III

Dr. Westlake, Sam Clark, Nat Hicks, and Del Snafflin were talking in Del's barber shop.

"Well, I see Kennicott's wife is taking a whirl at the rest-room, now," said Dr. Westlake. He emphasized the "now."

Del interrupted the shaving of Sam and, with his brush dripping lather, he observed jocularly:

"What'll she be up to next? They say she used to claim this burg wasn't swell enough for a city girl like her, and would we please tax ourselves about thirty-seven point nine and fix it all up pretty, with tidies on the hydrants and statoos on the lawns——"

Sam irritably blew the lather from his lips, with milky small bubbles, and snorted, "Be a good thing for most of us roughnecks if we did have a smart woman to tell us how to fix up the town. Just as much to her kicking as there was to Jim Blausser's gassing about factories. And you can bet Mrs. Kennicott is smart, even if she is skittish. Glad to see her back."

Dr. Westlake hastened to play safe. "So was I! So was I! She's got a nice way about her, and she knows a good deal about books—or fiction anyway. Of course she's like all the rest of these women—not solidly founded—not scholarly— doesn't know anything about political economy—falls for every new idea that some windjamming crank puts out. But she's a nice woman. She'll probably fix up the rest-room, and the rest-room is a fine thing, brings a lot of business to town. And now that Mrs. Kennicott's been away, maybe she's got over some of her fool ideas. Maybe she realizes that folks simply laugh at her when she tries to tell us how to run everything."

"Sure. She'll take a tumble to herself," said Nat Hicks, sucking in his lips judicially. "As far as I'm concerned, I'll say she's as nice a-looking skirt as there is in town. But yow!" His tone electrified them. "Guess she'll miss that Swede Valborg that used to work for me! They was a pair! Talking poetry and moonshine! If they could of got away with it, they'd of been so darn lovey-dovey—"

Sam Clark interrupted, "Rats, they never even thought about making love. Just talking books and all that junk. I tell you, Carrie Kennicott's a smart woman, and these smart educated women all get funny ideas, but they get over 'em after they've had three or four kids. You'll see her settled down one of these days, and teaching Sunday School and helping at sociables and behaving herself, and not trying to butt into business and politics. Sure!"

After only fifteen minutes of conference on her stockings, her son, her separate bedroom, her music, her ancient interest in Guy Pollock, her probable salary in Washington, and every remark which she was known to have made since her return, the supreme council decided that they would permit Carol Kennicott to live, and they passed on to a consideration of Nat Hicks's New One about the traveling salesman and the old maid.

IV

For some reason which was totally mysterious to Carol, Maud Dyer seemed to resent her return. At the Jolly Seven-

teen Maud giggled nervously, "Well, I suppose you found
war-work a good excuse to stay away and have a swell time.
Juanita! Don't you think we ought to make Carrie tell us
about the officers she met in Washington?"

They rustled and stared. Carol looked at them. Their curiosity seemed natural and unimportant.

"Oh yes, yes indeed, have to do that some day," she yawned.

She no longer took Aunt Bessie Smail seriously enough to
struggle for independence. She saw that Aunt Bessie did not
mean to intrude; that she wanted to do things for all the
Kennicotts. Thus Carol hit upon the tragedy of old age, which
is not that it is less vigorous than youth, but that it is not
needed by youth; that its love and prosy sageness, so important a few years ago, so gladly offered now, are rejected with laughter. She divined that when Aunt Bessie came
in with a jar of wild-grape jelly she was waiting in hope of
being asked for the recipe. After that she could be irritated but she could not be depressed by Aunt Bessie's simoom
of questioning.

She wasn't depressed even when she heard Mrs. Bogart
observe, "Now we've got prohibition it seems to me that the
next problem of the country ain't so much abolishing cigarettes as it is to make folks observe the Sabbath and arrest
these law-breakers that play baseball and go to the movies
and all on the Lord's Day."

Only one thing bruised Carol's vanity. Few people asked
her about Washington. They who had most admiringly
begged Percy Bresnahan for his opinions were least interested
in her facts. She laughed at herself when she saw that she had
expected to be at once a heretic and a returned hero; she
was very reasonable and merry about it; and it hurt just as
much as ever.

v

Her baby, born in August, was a girl. Carol could not
decide whether she was to become a feminist leader or marry
a scientist or both, but did settle on Vassar and a tricolette
suit with a small black hat for her Freshman year.

vi

Hugh was loquacious at breakfast. He desired to give his
impressions of owls and F Street.

"Don't make so much noise. You talk too much," growled Kennicott.

Carol flared. "Don't speak to him that way! Why don't you listen to him? He has some very interesting things to tell."

"What's the idea? Mean to say you expect me to spend all my time listening to his chatter?"

"Why not?"

"For one thing, he's got to learn a little discipline. Time for him to start getting educated."

"I've learned much more discipline, I've had much more education, from him than he has from me."

"What's this? Some new-fangled idea of raising kids you got in Washington?"

"Perhaps. Did you ever realize that children are people?"

"That's all right. I'm not going to have him monopolizing the conversation."

"No, of course. We have our rights, too. But I'm going to bring him up as a human being. He has just as many thoughts as we have, and I want him to develop them, not take Gopher Prairie's version of them. That's my biggest work now—keeping myself, keeping you, from 'educating' him."

"Well, let's not scrap about it. But I'm not going to have him spoiled."

Kennicott had forgotten it in ten minutes; and she forgot it—this time.

VII

The Kennicotts and the Sam Clarks had driven north to a duck-pass between two lakes, on an autumn day of blue and copper.

Kennicott had given her a light twenty-gauge shotgun. She had a first lesson in shooting, in keeping her eyes open, not wincing, understanding that the bead at the end of the barrel really had something to do with pointing the gun. She was radiant; she almost believed Sam when he insisted that it was she who had shot the mallard at which they had fired together.

She sat on the bank of the reedy lake and found rest in Mrs. Clark's drawling comments on nothing. The brown dusk was still. Behind them were dark marshes. The plowed acres smelled fresh. The lake was garnet and silver. The voices of the men, waiting for the last flight, were clear in the cool air.

"Mark left!" sang Kennicott, in a long-drawn call.

Three ducks were swooping down in a swift line. The guns banged, and a duck fluttered. The men pushed their light boat out on the burnished lake, disappeared beyond the reeds. Their cheerful voices and the slow splash and clank of oars came back to Carol from the dimness. In the sky a fiery plain sloped down to a serene harbor. It dissolved; the lake was white marble; and Kennicott was crying, "Well, old lady, how about hiking out for home? Supper taste pretty good, eh?"

"I'll sit back with Ethel," she said, at the car.

It was the first time she had called Mrs. Clark by her given name; the first time she had willingly sat back, a woman of Main Street.

"I'm hungry. It's good to be hungry," she reflected, as they drove away.

She looked across the silent fields to the west. She was conscious of an unbroken sweep of land to the Rockies, to Alaska; a dominion which will rise to unexampled greatness when other empires have grown senile. Before that time, she knew, a hundred generations of Carols will aspire and go down in tragedy devoid of palls and solemn chanting, the humdrum inevitable tragedy of struggle against inertia.

"Let's all go to the movies tomorrow night. Awfully exciting film," said Ethel Clark.

"Well, I was going to read a new book but—— All right, let's go," said Carol.

VIII

"They're too much for me," Carol sighed to Kennicott. "I've been thinking about getting up an annual Community Day, when the whole town would forget feuds and go out and have sports and a picnic and a dance. But Bert Tybee (why did you ever elect him mayor?)—he's kidnapped my idea. He wants the Community Day, but he wants to have some politician 'give an address.' That's just the stilted sort of thing I've tried to avoid. He asked Vida, and of course she agreed with him."

Kennicott considered the matter while he wound the clock and they tramped up-stairs.

"Yes, it would jar you to have Bert butting in," he said amiably. "Are you going to do much fussing over this Community stunt? Don't you ever get tired of fretting and stewing and experimenting?"

"I haven't even started. Look!" She led him to the nursery
door, pointed at the fuzzy brown head of her daughter.
"Do you see that object on the pillow? Do you know what
it is? It's a bomb to blow up smugness. If you Tories were
wise, you wouldn't arrest anarchists; you'd arrest all these
children while they're asleep in their cribs. Think what that
baby will see and meddle with before she dies in the year
2000! She may see an industrial union of the whole world,
she may see aeroplanes going to Mars."

"Yump, probably be changes all right," yawned Kennicott.

She sat on the edge of his bed while he hunted through his
bureau for a collar which ought to be there and persistently
wasn't.

"I'll go on, always. And I am happy. But this Community
Day makes me see how thoroughly I'm beaten."

"That darn collar certainly is gone for keeps," muttered
Kennicott and, louder, "Yes, I guess you—— I didn't quite
catch what you said, dear."

She patted his pillows, turned down his sheets, as she reflected:

"But I have won in this: I've never excused my failures by
sneering at my aspirations, by pretending to have gone beyond them. I do not admit that Main Street is as beautiful
as it should be! I do not admit that Gopher Prairie is
greater or more generous than Europe! I do not admit that
dish-washing is enough to satisfy all women! I may not have
fought the good fight, but I have kept the faith."

"Sure. You bet you have," said Kennicott. "Well, good
night. Sort of feels to me like it might snow tomorrow. Have
to be thinking about putting up the storm-windows pretty
soon. Say, did you notice whether the girl put that screw-
driver back?"